CW00471659

Mathias Spahlinger

Critical Guides to Contemporary Composers

Series Editor: Martin Iddon

Intellect's Critical Guides to Contemporary Composers are accessible but rigorous introductions to key figures in the world of contemporary music. Neither simply biographies, nor exclusively analytical discussions, the focus is on critical issues highlighted by historical and biographical context and the musical content of the work. Particularly, the series seeks to engage with composers whose place within contemporary musical cultures is prominent and secure, but who have been overlooked within the Anglo-American sphere. Designed for scholars and students alike, this series presents insights into vital figures in contemporary music, previously unavailable within English-language musicology

Published previously:

Lois Fitch, *Brian Ferneyhough* (2014)

Mathias Spahlinger

Neil Thomas Smith

 intellect

Bristol, UK / Chicago, USA

First published in the UK in 2021 by
Intellect, The Mill, Parnall Road, Fishponds, Bristol, BS16 3JG, UK

First published in the USA in 2021 by
Intellect, The University of Chicago Press, 1427 E. 60th Street,
Chicago, IL 60637, USA

Copyright © 2021 Intellect Ltd

All rights reserved. No part of this publication may be reproduced, stored in a
retrieval system, or transmitted, in any form or by any means, electronic,
mechanical, photocopying, recording, orotherwise, without written permission.

A catalogue record for this book is available from the British Library.

Copy editor: Newgen Knowledge Works
Cover designer: Aleksandra Szumlas
Cover image: Photo from the personal archive of Mathias Spahlinger
Production managers: Emma Berrill and Sophia Munyengeterwa
Typesetter: Newgen Knowledge Works

Print ISBN 978-1-78938-334 8
ePDF ISBN 978-1-78938-335-5
ePUB ISBN 978-1-78938-336-2

Part of the Critical Guides to Contemporary Composers series
ISSN 2043-9288 | Online ISSN 2043-9296

Printed and bound by Hobbs.

To find out about all our publications, please visit our website.
There you can subscribe to our e-newsletter, browse or download our current
catalogue, and buy any titles that are in print.

www.intellectbooks.com

This is a peer-reviewed publication.

Contents

List of Figures   vii
Preface   ix

Introduction   1

PART 1   11

1. Modernism Underestimated   12
2. Biography and Context: Spahlinger and Twentieth-Century Germany   29

PART 2   53

3. Musique Concrète Instrumentale   54
4. Order   82
5. Open Form   108
6. Perception   141

Conclusion   177

Mathias Spahlinger: List of Works   187
Index   197

Figures

Chapter 2

2.1   *RoaiuGHFF (strange?)* title.   33

Chapter 3

3.1   *Pression* by Helmut Lachenmann, page 4.   58

3.2   *entlöschend*, sketch.   60

3.3   *éphémère*, bars 80–92.   64

3.4A *adieu m'amour*, bars 12–20.   75

3.4B *Adieu m'amour, adieu mon joye* by Guillaume Dufay, bars 10–18.   76

Chapter 4

4.1   *akt, eine treppe herabsteigend*, bars 566–573, bass clarinet and trombone.   88

4.2   *akt, eine treppe herabsteigend*, bars 92–106, string reduction.   89

4.3   *akt, eine treppe herabsteigend*, bars 74–79, violins 1 and 2.   89

4.4   *akt, eine treppe herabsteigend*, rising ostinato.   89

4.5   *akt, eine treppe herabsteigend*, bars 279–286, second violins.   90

4.6   *farben der frühe*, bars 63–106, shows number of notes per bar and dynamic.   92

4.7   *farben der frühe*, fourth movement, scale.   93

4.8   *farben der frühe*, bars 201–209, fourth movement.   94

4.9   *farben der frühe*, fourth movement, listening diagram.   95

Chapter 5

5.1A *128 erfüllte augenblicke*, Augenblick .232.   112

5.1B *128 erfüllte augenblicke*, Augenblick .432.   112

5.2   *128 erfüllte augenblicke*, orthographic cuboid.   113

5.3   *passage/paysage* opening, Spahlinger sketch.   115

5.4   *passage/paysage*, Spahlinger sketch.   119

5.5   *doppelt bejaht*, '04. "punktefeld"' extract.   123

5.6   *doppelt bejaht*, 04. "punktefeld" extract.   125
5.7   *doppelt bejaht*, 04. "punktefeld" transition.   126
5.8   *verlorener weg*, Spahlinger explanatory sketch.   128
5.9   *extension* programme note, page 5.   136

Chapter 6

6.1   *und als wir ...*, seating layout.   144
6.2   *gegen unendlich*, bars 51–60.   148
6.3   *gegen unendlich*, page 19, top stave.   149
6.4   *off*, bars 335–339.   150
6.5   *off*, rhythmic patterns.   151
6.6   *off*, bars 253–256.   152
6.7   *ocean*, partial reduction from 6′53″.   157
6.8   *ocean*, first layer of material.   158
6.9   *ocean*, first and second layers of material.   159
6.10 *ocean*, three layers of material.   161

Preface

I first encountered Mathias Spahlinger in 2011 at a rehearsal of his epic work for seven pianos, *farben der frühe*, at the Frankfurt Hochschule für Musik und Darstellende Kunst. After benefiting from a (Northern) British musical education, I was still acclimatizing to a rather different artistic environment after one year of studying composition at the Hochschule in Stuttgart on a life-changing Leverhulme Study Abroad Studentship. Spahlinger's music, and the talk he gave afterwards, struck me forcefully. The palpable sense of challenge to the players and listeners, one that immediately struck me as worth grappling with, and the wide-ranging, sometimes timetable-bustingly lengthy, explications of the composer were something that I had never encountered before.

That I experienced the music and discussion together, almost simultaneously, has shaped the course of this research. Spahlinger, whose presentation invoked the French Revolution, Adorno, Hegel and Aristotelian logic in a dense cluster that brought me to the limit, and beyond, of my German comprehension at the time, showed me a composer most wonderfully un-British. Before leaving home, one of the last composer talks I had attended had been a rather pedestrian affair in which the speaker had had little to say save that they 'like[d] hexachordal rotation'. Familiarity with this specific technique is not necessary to understand the different scales of ambition and reference that these two approaches hold. British 'modesty' in intellectualizing musical experience is a position for which I now have more patience than then, and the perils of Spahlinger's own intellectual position are a vital theme running through this book, but the combined music and thought of this composer were the spark that ignited my interest.

This research began as a PhD project, undertaken on my return to the United Kingdom at the University of Nottingham, one that was made possible by a studentship from the Arts and Humanities Research Council for which I am very grateful. It has benefited from the help and support of a great many people, too many, alas, to list here in full. My early interest in the composer was encouraged in Stuttgart by Caspar Johannes Walter and Christoph Löser, as well as by Philipp Blume, the latter two in particular being enthusiastic advocates for Spahlinger's music. At Nottingham, I also benefited from two study grants from the Music Department, as well as two AHRC Research Training Grants from the University, to attend the International Summer Courses at Darmstadt and to present my research at a symposium on the composer in Dresden. Thanks must go, too, to Caspar Johannes and Carola Bauckholt, who were very generous hosts on a research trip to the Freiburg Musik Hochschule.

I would like to thank my PhD co-supervisor Jeremy Lane for his great help assessing the thought of Rancière, while particular thanks must go to my primary supervisor, Robert Adlington, whose generosity of time, encouragement and superb critical faculties I have benefited from so very much. I was also very lucky to be part of a friendly and supportive research team at the University of Nottingham, including Drs Anne Macgregor, Alexander Kolassa, Sarah Doxat-Pratt, James Cook and Adam and Angela Whittaker – as well as further colleagues at the University of York: Martin Scheuregger, Christopher Leedham and Patrick John Jones. In making the gradual transition from thesis to critical companion, I have been most fortunate to have had Martin Iddon's editorial assistance and knowledge of the German music scene, from which this volume has benefited greatly. Thanks also to the team at Intellect, particularly Tim Mitchell, Emma Berrill and Sophia Munyengeterwa.

Only two further people remain to be recognized for their contribution. First, Mathias Spahlinger himself. It is hard to imagine a more willing, helpful and encouraging subject of study, a fact that made the research all the more enjoyable and effective. His generous spirit, and *Marzipantorte*, will live long in my memory. Finally, I would like to thank my partner Rachel, for all her love, friendship and support.

Introduction

Mathias Spahlinger's rise to prominence was a gradual affair. Even in his native Germany he was long considered an 'outsider' or even 'a stubborn maverick' within the contemporary music scene.[1] Yet his position as one of the most venerable exponents of post-Second World War modernist music in his homeland is now undeniable: for Kerstin Holm, writing in the *Frankfurter Allgemeine Zeitung* with perhaps a little journalistic embellishment, he is even an 'old master'.[2] Spahlinger has received commissions from many of the major orchestras and new music groups in Germany, and in 2014 he received the Großen Berliner Kunstpreis from the city's Akademie der Künste. Despite this, performance of his music in his homeland is far from frequent, hinting at the challenges his pieces pose.

With Helmut Lachenmann and Nicolaus A. Huber, Spahlinger forms a trio that has had an immense influence on the course of German contemporary music. All three share a profound debt to modernist influences and to the political upheaval caused by the student protests of 1968, the context of which shaped their common leftist political consciousness.[3] Of this group of composers, it is Spahlinger who has most extensively described a political and aesthetic stance in his many articles, programme notes and interviews, as well as his musical works, which comprise solo, chamber, orchestral and choral pieces. His reputation rests both on the rich, multifarious experience of his music and his regularly provocative writings. Deep, intellectual meditation upon the issues his pieces address, and on new music in general, accompany his compositional practice, with his thought and music creating a sometimes intimidating edifice that makes practice and discourse extremely difficult to separate. They combine to form a political and aesthetic stance, one which, it will be argued here, perpetuates vital tenets of previous instances of modernist music and modernist thought.

Despite now receiving widespread recognition in Germany, Spahlinger has remained little known in the Anglophone world, with performances and commissions coming almost exclusively from within the Central European context. This lack of knowledge is particularly telling in comparison with the widespread international fame that Lachenmann has achieved in recent years through performances, newspaper articles and invited talks. Lachenmann's own rise to prominence was, however, preceded by musicological work that first brought his ideas to an

1

international audience, and he too was initially an established figure in Central Europe alone.[4] Spahlinger is going through a similar, if more sedate, process to the elder composer, with increased musicological interest in Germany, particularly since the new millennium, and subsequent translation – both cultural and linguistic – by Anglophone scholars preceding a wider recognition of his music. As so often with translations of important international figures, the English editions of Spahlinger's writings present a chronological mirror image, with the most recent the first to appear in translation. Indeed, until recently, with Alistair Zaldua's translation of 'political implications of the material of new music',[5] 'this is the time of conceptive ideologues no longer' was the only essay of the composer's to have appeared in English, translated by Philipp Blume.[6]

Recent events also show that scholarship on the composer, as well as performances of his music, are picking up pace, with his attendance at days with a focus on his music in Graz (2013), Chicago (2015), Goldsmiths (London, 2015) and Dresden (2016) showing a lively interest both in Germany and abroad. That a complete festival, 'there is no repetition: Mathias Spahlinger at 70', was dedicated to his music in Chicago is particularly significant as it comprised the most extensive opportunity to hear his music outside of Germany to date. Two consecutive weekends were given over to performances of, and talks on, the composer's work, including *furioso* (1991), *doppelt bejaht* (2009) and the world premiere of a piece for drum-kit, *ausnahmslos ausnahmen* (2013). Nevertheless, there is still a divide between knowledge of his music within his homeland and in the rest of the world, as well as significant barriers for those who wish to engage in detail with his texts and pieces. Few libraries outside of Germany hold his works, the production of which is shared among various publishers including the composer himself, while the pieces require intense engagement on the part of the performers. In addressing Spahlinger's music and thought in English, while also giving equal weight to German scholarship, this volume is currently the most extensive effort to bridge this gap.[7]

Spahlinger and Modernism

At the core of this project is the belief that both Spahlinger's thought and practice rely fundamentally on an individual response to, and continuation of, modernist ideas, meaning that assessing his relationship with modernism is crucial in understanding his artistic project and the new perspectives it offers. Assessing the composer's work in this manner allows for both the recognition of his individual approach, as well as a better understanding of the broader milieu of which he is part. It is also a potential mode of criticism, the chief objection levelled against the composer being that he is the spokesperson for an outdated, Adornian negativism. Though he does not mention Spahlinger or any other composer specifically, this is the tenor of composer James MacMillan's critique when he states that 'the once powerfully cocksure analysis of the '68ers has been proved wrong [...] They are perplexed at how the world has gone. Their view has not prevailed, even in modern music.' He goes on to say that 'the case for modernism has been undermined by the flow and permanence of traditions, and many other things that they didn't see either as important or effective in the making of the modern world'.[8] More specific criticisms are voiced by composer and theorist Claus-Steffen Mahnkopf, who states that Spahlinger is the 'representative of a neurotically exaggerated negativity principle', which in its rigidity begins to take on the form of a 'positive', that is fixed, musical approach.[9] Mahnkopf calls for an approach that moves more with the times in its negation. The threads of this modernist legacy are present in many of the themes explored in this volume and will be unpicked throughout.

Hitherto, Spahlinger's music has generally received analytical and aesthetic examinations that focus on isolated pieces or aspects of his thought.[10] Yet, even these attempts are the result of intense engagement with the composer himself, continuing to give Spahlinger an outsized influence on the reception of his own music. Historical and cultural factors that inform his practice have, rather ironically for a Marx-inspired composer, fallen by the wayside. Outside of his favoured Frankfurt School models, there is little discussion of how his thought intersects with other sources of critical theory and philosophy, while critical perspectives on *his* music are too seldom voiced. The hermeticism of scholarship on the composer, and the sense that writers are sometimes advocating for him rather than investigating his work dispassionately, points to the fact that the body of literature is still youthful: it is regularly written by friends, supporters and former pupils in an attempt to elucidate his ideas and illuminate his music. Through the inclusion of a number of critical commentaries, a biography with significant cultural context and sustained reference to the thought of French philosopher Jacques Rancière, this study begins the work of connecting Spahlinger to a wider frame of reference in musicology and aesthetics, bringing his thought and music into contact with discourses from which it has all too often remained aloof.

Naturally, in a project focusing on the persistence of modernism, it is vital to define what kind of modernism is under discussion. The term has famously resisted comprehensive definition, resulting in its identification in a wide variety of places and times. Recent work has broadened the field of modernism studies even further, expanding its geographical and temporal reach and showing suspicion of the hierarchies and assumptions deemed part of the modernist project, whether postcolonial, gendered or anti-democratic. There is something of a democratization of the definition of modernism at play, as scholars, artists and critics wrestle control of its history and meaning from the Western, primarily male figures who had dominated its discourse. Modernism has, therefore, been identified in the art of 1960s Nigeria,[11] in a queer reading of the aesthetics of Walter Pater,[12] in the work of Filipino author Carlos Bulosan[13] and in the development of feminism in the twentieth century.[14] In music, even composers such as Elgar have been discussed in relation to modernist ideas as part of a wider argument that there was a developing British modernism concurrent with its continental counterpart.[15] The result is an understanding of modernism as a plural phenomenon, a set of modernisms rather than one unified narrative.

Any study involving itself with modernism must, therefore, seek solid ground in a sea of definitions, with two such areas having particular relevance here. The first is the fact that this volume does not attempt the comprehensive definition that has eluded so many others. Such a search would be fruitless and unhelpful in assessing the work of this composer. Rather, the purpose is to illuminate the challenges, achievements and contradictions of Spahlinger's own modernist project in order to contribute to the picture of modernism as a multifaceted and critical approach. This study concerns itself with Spahlinger's modernism and no other. The second piece of solid ground is the fact that Spahlinger's project shows a vital continuity with ideas widely recognized as fundamentally modernist, often by detractors and supporters alike. His debt to Schoenberg, Webern and Adorno is all part of this reliance on ideas long considered modernist touchstones. It will be argued, therefore, that Spahlinger is certainly a modernist composer, but, in light of the aforementioned difficulties in forming any kind of general definition, this is by no means synonymous with advancing the opinion that he is the only, and certainly not the 'right', kind of modernist composer. The crucial point is that Spahlinger has used a certain reading of modernist ideas to forge a distinct artistic and aesthetic identity, a reading that is rather narrower and more circumscribed than the recontextualizing studies of modernism mentioned above. Focusing on the composer's ideas in this study is no attempt to deny the possibility of other ideas of modernism, but it is to remain faithful to the context in which Spahlinger works. On the other hand, the approach here does not preclude criticism of the composer's position and his reliance on certain well-established modernist tropes means that there are established critical positions that must be considered alongside his work: both the modernist hero and modernist villain will be explored in what follows.

This reading of modernism also serves to align the present study with a series of contributions to discussions of modernism that maintain it is still a vital creative force. To Björn Heile's edited collection on *The Modernist Legacy* might be added Arved Ashby's *The Pleasure of Modernist Music*; Karol Berger and Anthony Newcomb's collection, *Music and the Aesthetics of Modernity*; Erling E. Gulbrandsen and Julian Johnson's edited collection, *The Transformations of Musical Modernism*; David Metzer's *Musical Modernism at the Turn of the Twenty-First Century*;[16] as well as many volumes that have looked at the social interactions and contexts that formed modernist aesthetics in many locations and historical situations.[17] Heile talks of a younger generation that is tired of the 'binary oppositions' of the past, which include 'those between modernism and postmodernism, between conceptions of musical autonomy and of cultural contingency and between formalist-analytical and cultural-historical approaches'.[18] All are keen to show modernism as a complex, multifaceted phenomenon, with critical thought at its centre, not the conservative, oppressive monolith its critics claim. It is this critical potential, these authors assert, that is the basis of its constant renewal and continued relevance rather than any belief in any specific technical innovations. As in the case of serialism in the view of both Spahlinger and Adorno, there is always the threat that these innovations, once achieved, themselves become an uncritical status quo: the same criticism that Mahnkopf makes of Spahlinger above. Modernism's critical potential, however, can run and run, leading to Heile using the term 'critical modernism',[19] which connects strongly with Spahlinger's ideas.

Outline

This study is divided into two primary sections. Part 1 serves as an introduction to the composer and his thought, beginning with instant immersion in his aesthetic world through a discussion of one of his most important essays, 'this is the time of conceptive ideologues no longer' (2006). From this essay, many of the vital concerns that define Spahlinger's artistic project will be drawn out, including his belief in the radical achievements of new music and his thoughts on music and politics. Following this swift dip into the primary concerns of the composer is a contextual biography, which describes the composer's life while also providing a cultural appraisal of the Germany in which he grew up. This context here is important as many of the composer's concerns can be traced to particular aspects of German cultural life, while the modernism he evinces is of a particular national character. This is not to say that he is parochial or to argue that modernism is essentially German, but it is contended that certain aspects of his rhetoric and worldview are best explained by referring to national trends of 'coming to terms with the past' and, particularly, the course of German sociology after the Second World War. It is important to consider such connections to counteract the impression that Spahlinger's concerns arose in a social vacuum.

In Part 2, the discussion of Spahlinger's thought continues but with greater reference to his musical works. Four concerns are isolated, all of which are crucial to understanding the aims of much of the composer's oeuvre. The intention is to cover a good deal of ground to give the reader both an understanding of these important themes, as well as exposure to many of his most significant pieces. The first topic covered is the composer's relationship with Helmut Lachenmann's *musique concrète instrumentale*, a term that is often related solely to the work of Spahlinger's composer colleague. Spahlinger's conception is rather more general, however, while the works from the 1960s and 1970s, with their noisy techniques and extrovert expression, have had a significant impact on his approach. The latter part of this chapter also discusses some of the early justifications for *musique concrète instrumentale*, which share a number of the composer's concerns and are expressed within a similar musico-political discourse.

The second theme, explored in Chapter 4, is the idea of musical order, which is a wide-ranging term that covers the intricacies of compositional system, as well as large-scale form and genre relationships. 'Ordered' musical ideas, such as single pitches or regular pulses, appear in Spahlinger's music, often with the intention of having them dissolve before listeners' ears. In particular, the large work for pianos *farben der frühe* (*colours of morning*, 2005) and the orchestral work *akt, eine treppe herabsteigend* (*nude descending a staircase*, 1997) are investigated. The chapter ends with a critical commentary that discusses the implications of some of the composer's more political intentions, with particular reference to the idea of 'aesthetic contingency' in the philosophy of Jacques Rancière, an idea that creates a bridge between the musical and the political. Before this, there is a brief note on Spahlinger and his potential relationship to postmodern theory, a connection that is perhaps implied by his use of the term 'deconstruction'.

This leads on to the third topic, that of open form. Chapter 5 investigates the composer's formal experimentations, as well as his belief that all new music is in some kind of open form. Previous modernist approaches to this idea are first discussed, before Spahlinger's most important open form pieces are examined, including a group of works that investigate transition and formal arbitrariness. The conclusion of this chapter comprises the second critical commentary, which reflects on the difficulties of presenting a truly 'open' form with fixed materials and within a fixed score, while once again investigating the political implications of his approach, this time in relation to his use of the Marxian 'means of production' in relation to music.

The final topic is that of perception, which in many ways is vital to understanding the other three. Perception for the composer is related to informing the consciousness of listeners, which may sound rather abstract, yet it manifests itself in very tangible musical ideas and materials. Pieces are discussed that show this interest most overtly, such as the work for strings *und als wir ...* ('and when we ...', 1993) as well as the less obvious example of *in dem ganzen ocean von empfindungen eine welle absondern, sie anhalten* (1985). In the final critical commentary, the modes of listening presumed by the composer will be critiqued and the philosophy of Rancière will be called on for a second time to give a new perspective on the aesthetic and the political.

While far from all of Spahlinger's pieces will be covered in this study, the discussion of these vital elements in his approach will mean that the touchstones of his oeuvre will be covered, while illuminating in some depth the concerns that will also inform other pieces. Chief among these is a reflexive relationship with the legacy of modernism, which is examined throughout and pulled together in the conclusion. The nature of this relationship, and the framework of the composer's thought, will be established in the next chapter, with the discussion of one of his most important essays.

NOTES

1. Markus Hechtle describes Spahlinger as an 'outsider': *198 Fenster zu einer imaginierten Welt* (Saarbrücken: Pfau-Verlag, 2005), 98. Gerh-Wolfgang Baruch states the composer has been seen as a 'Querkopf', a by no means overwhelmingly positive epithet, which can be translated in various ways including 'awkward customer' and 'pigheaded': 'Mit Chorsängern gegen den Welthunger: Zur Uraufführung von Mathias Spahlinger in der Alten Reithalle'. *Stuttgarter Zeitung*, 13 November 1987.

2. Kerstin Holm, 'Die Tränen des alten Meisters', *Frankfurter Allgemeine*, March 2015, http://fazarchiv.faz.net/fazSearch/index/searchForm?q=Mathias+Spahlinger&search_in=q&tim%20ePeriod=timeFilter&timeFilter=&DT_from=&DT_to=&KO=&crxdefs=&NN=&CO=&CN=&BC=&submitSearch=Suchen&sext=0&maxHits=&sorting=&toggleFilter=&dosearch=new#hitlist (accessed 29 March 2016).

3. Philipp Blume stresses that these three composers should not be taken as some kind of compositional 'school', yet certain common attitudes to musical material, their geographical proximity, and the fact all three are well acquainted with each other, nevertheless, make it advantageous to consider them together. Philipp Blume, 'Preface: Music of Nicolaus A. Huber and Mathias Spahlinger', *Contemporary Music Review* 27, no. 6 (2008): 561–63.

4. It is only in the 1990s that Lachenmann began to receive critical attention in English language literature with the following articles: John Warnaby, 'A New Left-Wing Radicalism in Contemporary German Music?', *TEMPO* 193 (1995): 18–26; Elke Hockings, 'Helmut Lachenmann's Concept or Rejection', *TEMPO* 193 (1995): 4–14; Ian Pace, 'Positive or Negative 1', *Musical Times* 139, no. 1859 (1998): 9–17.

5. Mathias Spahlinger, 'political implications of the material of new music', *Contemporary Music Review* 34, nos. 2–3 (2015b): 127–66.

6.   Mathias Spahlinger, 'this is the time of conceptive ideologues no longer', trans. Philipp Blume, *Contemporary Music Review* 27, no. 6 (2008): 579–94.

7.   Major contributions to English scholarship on the composer come from Blume ('Preface: Music of Nicolaus A. Huber and Mathias Spahlinger', and 'Mathias Spahlinger's *128 erfüllte augenblicke* and the Parameters of Listening', *Contemporary Music Review* 27, no. 6 [2008]: 625–42) and Alistair Zaldua's translation of a recent essay (Mathias Spahlinger, 'political implications of the material of new music', *Contemporary Music Review* 34, nos. 2–3: 127–66). The extensive use of German literature here has also raised the question of translation. In this study, English translations of German sources have been used where available. All other German sources have been translated by the author, unless otherwise indicated.

8.   James MacMillan, 'Music and Modernity', *Standpoint Magazine*, November 2009, http://www.standpointmag.co.uk/text-november-09-music-and-modernity-james-macmillan?page=0%2C0%2C0%2C0%2C0%2C0%2C0%2C0%2C0%2C0%2C4 (accessed 16 September 2016).

9.   Claus-Steffen Mahnkopf, 'What Does "Critical Composition" Mean?', in *Critical Composition Today*, eds. Claus-Steffen Mahnkopf, Frank Cox and Wolfram Schurig (Hofheim: Wolke Verlag, 2006), 81.

10. Tobias Schick and Dorothea Ruthemeier's more comprehensive studies being the exceptions: Tobias Eduard Schick, *Weltbezüge in der Musik Mathias Spahlingers* (Stuttgart: Franz Steiner Verlag, 2018); Dorothea Ruthemeier, *Antagonismus oder Konkurrenz? Zu zentralen Werkgruppen der 1980er Jahre von Wolfgang Rihm und Mathias Spahlinger* (Schliengen: Edition Argus, 2012).

11. Chika Okeke-Agulu, *Postcolonial Modernism: Art and Decolonization in Twentieth-Century Nigeria* (Durham, NC: Duke University Press, 2015).

12. Heather K. Love, 'Forced Exile: Walter Pater's Queer Modernism', in *Bad Modernisms*, ed. Douglas Mao and Rebecca L. Walkowitz (Durham, NC: Duke University Press, 2006), 19–43.

13. Joshua L. Miller, 'The Gorgeous Laughter of Filipino Modernity: Carlos Bulosan's *The Laughter of My Father*', in *Bad Modernisms*, ed. Douglas Mao and Rebecca L. Walkowitz (Durham, NC: Duke University Press, 2006), 238–68.

14. Rita Felski, *The Gender of Modernity* (Cambridge, MA: Harvard University Press, 1995).

15. See Jenny Doctor, 'The Parataxis of "Musical Modernism"', *Musical Quarterly* 91, nos. 1–2 (2008): 89–115; and J. P. E. Harper-Scott, *Edward Elgar, Modernist* (Cambridge: Cambridge University Press, 2006).

16. Björn Heile, ed., *The Modernist Legacy* (Farnham: Ashgate, 2009); Arved Ashby, ed., *The Pleasure of Modernist Music* (Rochester: University of Rochester Press, 2004); Karol Berger and Anthony Newcomb, eds., *Music and the Aesthetics of Modernity* (Cambridge, MA: Harvard University Press, 2005); Erling E. Gulbrandsen and Julian Johnson, *Transformations of Musical Modernism* (Cambridge: Cambridge University Press, 2015); David

Metzer, *Musical Modernism at the Turn of the Twenty-First Century* (Cambridge: Cambridge University Press, 2009).

17. See, for example, Amy C. Beal, *New Music, New Allies: American Experimental Music in West Germany, from Zero Hour to Reunification* (Berkeley: University of California Press, 2006); Beate Kutschke, *Neue Linke/Neue Musik: Kulturtheorien und künstlerischen Avantgarde in den 1960er und 70er Jahren* (Cologne: Böhlau Verlag, 2007); and Robert Adlington, ed., *Sound Commitments* (Oxford: Oxford University Press, 2009).

18. Björn Heile, 'Introduction', in *The Modernist Legacy*, ed. Björn Heile (Farnham: Ashgate, 2009), 3.

19. Heile, 'Introduction', 5.

PART 1

1

Modernism Underestimated

'this is the time of conceptive ideologues no longer'

By way of introduction to the composer's compositional project, this chapter engages with one of Spahlinger's most important essays. Once this immediate impression of his aesthetic project has been established, a lengthier biography follows in the next chapter, showing how certain traits of German culture are manifest in the composer's practice. The essay, 'this is the time of conceptive ideologues no longer',[1] despite its rather opaque title, contains many of the ideas that drive Spahlinger, while also introducing the general rhetorical flavour of his writing. First given as a talk in Dresden in 2006, it discusses what it means to be progressive today, both in music and politics. In it, Spahlinger accuses composers of propagating the regressive ideology of the ruling classes: they are said to have blunted the revolutionary potential of the achievements of new music because of a fear of losing their relatively privileged position in society. Issues of politics and aesthetics are seen to have similar challenges and, perhaps, similar solutions. Spahlinger does not put his faith in one shining, positive answer. Rather, progress is to be made by a true reflection of an older revolutionary impulse. Immediately, Spahlinger's essay presents a composer greatly concerned with the place of music and composers in society. Though he does not mention it by name, the debates around modernism are a vital backdrop to these concerns, an idea explored more fully at the end of this chapter where potential criticisms of the composer are related to pre-existing critiques of modernist positions.

The Potential of New Music and the Composer in Society

Two things immediately strike the reader about this essay, both of which are perhaps surprising for such a recent contribution to debates in new music. The first is Spahlinger's undaunted belief in the unprecedented nature of the new music revolution: he states that 'new music is or reflects the very revolution of revolutions' because it 'has discarded the conventions, without [...] having replaced them with new conventions'.[2] No other music in the world, he contends, has achieved what music, or rather *new* music, has achieved since 1910. This thesis, that the revolutionary character of new music has gone unnoticed and is at present 'underestimated',[3] is more systematically expounded in an earlier essay, 'against the post-modern fashion',[4] which lists various achievements of new music such as 'rigorous organisation', 'the alien or unintegratable in the work of art' and 'composition with time rather than in it'.[5] The fact that these might appear like a list of new anti-convention conventions to replace the old will be returned to, but for Spahlinger it is important that they should be seen as open-ended rather than restrictive, nor does he consider his list exhaustive.

The second arresting feature of 'this is the time' is the continued use of unapologetic Marxian terminology to situate the position of the composer in society, a trait usually associated with engaged musicians of the 1960s and 1970s and, therefore, a sign of the legacy of 1968 in Spahlinger's thought. He claims to know 'not a single representative of the bourgeoisie who is truly interested in radical art', while composers 'look upward in search of funding' as a 'kind of competitive bicyclist of culture [...] unified only by the name of a mutual sponsor'.[6] Composers are said to inhabit a middle layer of society, the petit (or petty) bourgeoisie, who do not own the means of production but do have a major impact on the ideology, or dominant worldview, of any particular time. For Spahlinger, this position constitutes a certain kind of power to change society, if composers truly wished it.[7] There is a utopian strain to this conception of political potential, which again is reminiscent of debates from previous decades.

The class-based analysis offered by Spahlinger, as well as his firm belief in the potential of new music, are employed to explore two theses: first, that the revolutionary potential of new music has still to be fully, or even partially, exploited; and second, in a challenge to composers, or indeed anyone involved in making new music, that 'the dominant culture-bearer, the petty bourgeoisie, comes up with all kinds of "innovations" which resemble and stand in the way of new music to render her harmless, to rescind her promise'. He argues that 'out of a poorly understood self-interest', the petit bourgeoisie carry on the 'ideological business of the real ruling class, the bourgeoisie'.[8] So, political and aesthetic regression are combined, as members of this liminal class attempt to soften new music's radical edge. Spahlinger believes that the way forward is to step outside this ideological cycle, and to embrace what was most radical about the advent of new music, both in aesthetics and politics. He states that 'petit bourgeois composers want to know which direction is forward; but they don't want to go there – out of fear of losing their privileges, even if these are not yet fully attained'.[9]

The view of society articulated here depicts the composer as potentially influential in defining the direction that culture takes, yet reliant on those 'above' to continue to practise their art. Fear of losing position blunts the radical potential of new music. In this, Spahlinger appears keenly aware of the paradoxes of holding the permanent revolutionary ideal of modernism within fixed institutions: he rejects the idea that composers are part of some monolithic modernist establishment together with arts institutions and the academy, arguing instead that they are creative figures within a financial ecosystem with particular pressures and expectations. Moreover, the composer in his view is not a free autonomous artistic agent making creative decisions as they please, this essay making no appeal to the idea of autonomous art that would excuse artistic collaboration with institutions on any terms.

Autonomy

Debates around musical autonomy have been a mainstay of critiques of modernism. Critics pick up on its supposed belief that there is a sphere of music divorced from society in which the innovation of musical language takes precedence over all else. Fodder for these commentaries is more than forthcoming in Milton Babbitt's infamous 'Who Cares If You Listen?',[10] from which it is not difficult to extract lengthy passages that talk of the 'elimination of the public and social aspects of musical composition',[11] with the void to be replaced by composers writing for a connoisseurship cloistered in universities. For the version of European modernism explored here, however, the figure of Babbitt is fairly peripheral.[12] More significant are the views of Schoenberg, which Susan McClary argues are afflicted by 'Terminal Prestige'.[13] She contends that in Schoenberg's autonomous world, music must advance, must *progress*, regardless of whether the public is in any way interested. That Schoenberg, according to McClary, took pride in his music being difficult, and worried about any kind of popular success, is a sign of an 'economy of prestige' at work that will result in a musical death spiral.[14]

Spahlinger in fact makes a similar criticism when he accuses composers, and the petit bourgeoisie in general, of denying their position in society and attempting to neutralize the revolutionary potential of art through insisting on an autonomous artistic sphere. The petit bourgeoisie are said to encourage the idea that art is a 'dispassionate pleasantry' without purpose, 'thus its conception of ideology remains ideological. freedom from ideology becomes itself a kind of ideology'.[15] The idea of autonomous music, according to the composer, is widely accepted even though music that has a function (such as a text) is much more common than that without. The assumption of art's autonomy is seen as ideology now bereft of its progressive power: it defends the status quo. What was once an emancipatory impulse – the belief that music could stand alone without programme, patron, text or devotional occasion – now serves only to mask music's social and political implications: 'the function of autonomous music today is to disguise and deny its function'.[16] This manifests itself in the widespread belief in the 'transcendental', that is, other-worldly, power of music. Spahlinger believes music is firmly of this world with potentially powerful real-world effects, a position that has come to some prominence in the *Diesseitigkeit* or 'New Discipline' composers in the twenty-first century.[17]

In his faith that the break between the music of pre- and post-1910 is the most important rupture in the history of Western art music (one that cannot even be paralleled in any other tradition), Spahlinger is quite in keeping with certain modernist ideas of teleological progress, including, for example, Adorno's continued belief in the historical importance of early atonal works.[18] For composers not wishing to follow Spahlinger in accepting the radicality of this break, and the necessity of this new understanding, there is the sense that their failings are not only musical but also political in his eyes. This presents a potentially troubling portrait of occidental superiority, one that would give quite a different perspective to the composer's engagements with, for example, African drumming or South American Marxism. In this light, Spahlinger remains within the tradition of a politicized modernist discourse, one that was also in evidence in previous manifestations of European modernism such as Dadaism and the Futurists, in the more recent writings of Italian composer Luigi Nono and in the writings of the '68-inspired German composers. With this he courts the same dangers as these figures, who have been critiqued for significant overestimation of the power of music to engage in political discourse and hostility towards opposing opinions on political, as much as aesthetic, grounds.

New Music and Self-Determination

The title of 'this is the time of conceptive ideologues no longer' is a 'portmanteau'[19] of two quotations, one from Friedrich Hölderlin, the other from Marx and Engels. Hölderlin's contribution is taken from his unfinished drama *The Death of Empedocles* and it introduces the search for apparently outmoded hierarchies. The following quotation is taken from a different translation of the Hölderlin text, which would have rendered the title of the essay the less cumbersome (but less accurate) 'the time of conceptive ideologues is passed forever':

> The time of kings has passed forever [...]
> [...] Shame on you, that you should still want kings.

15

You are too old; your fathers' times
Were different. You can't be helped,
If you won't help yourselves.[20]

The sentiments expressed here are very much a pre-echo of Spahlinger's belief that new music, in breaking down the tonal system, requires musicians to become aware of their freedom and potential for self-determination. The second half of the title, taken from *The German Ideology* by Marx and Engels, relates strongly to the position of the composer in society explained above. It puts the composer '(as well as musicologist)' in the position of the 'conceptive ideologue' that perpetuates the ideals of the ruling class and its ideology, in this case the bourgeoisie.[21] Spahlinger says that composers – as members of the petit bourgeoisie – should struggle to avoid the position of the 'active, conceptive ideologue, who makes the perpetuation of the illusions of this class about itself into their principal source of sustenance'.[22] In other words, Spahlinger seeks a way in which composers can write politically progressive music rather than propping up any ruling ideology.

The lack of new rules implied by the title is a fundamental aspect of new music for Spahlinger, as it shows a more conscious knowledge of humanity's active role in rule creation: 'our laws will all be identified as man-made, even the divine ones. it's about time!!'[23] When speaking with musicologist Hans Heinrich Eggebrecht, he compares the advent of new music as akin to the revelation of the French Revolution, in which 'every law and moral rule was suddenly understood as an agreement among people and was changeable'.[24] Thus, new music encourages a level of self-determination not previously present, as every convention can be brought into question. The composer often uses the formulation that new music has forced a fundamental reconsideration of 'the relation of the parts to the whole'.[25] The whole here refers to the hierarchical structures of tonal music, such as antecedent and consequent phrases, harmonic rhythm, beginning and ending in the same key, the necessary relation between melody and accompaniment, and so on. The dissolution of tonality means the seeming necessity of the connections between part and whole is exploded: with the advent of non-tonal harmony, harmonic rhythm no longer holds its normative function, melody can exist separately from its harmonic context, and rhythm can repeat mechanically without recourse to any kind of function. The parameters that Spahlinger describes as unified in the tonal system are now free to be explored or controlled in isolation. This provides opportunities for less hierarchical structures in both the composition and organization of musical works.

The new reality of rule creation in new music is related to the role of tonality in perception for Spahlinger, as well as its more recent problematization:

'what is sounding in reality?' is the question that new music asks; asks again in a new, material-oriented way.

in the time of tonality, this question was synonymous with the question 'what is sounding in reference to the system?' because the system was the human reality of perception. sounds that didn't act within the system were not music.[26]

The composer's example of how this idea functions is the clash of cymbals, which was apparently always appreciated in a kind of tonal manner as it stressed the tonic.[27] Only with new music is the sound of cymbals, or of a tam-tam in his own piece, *entlöschend* (1974), heard as a noisy sonic event. Isolation and appreciation of the cymbals within the context of new music has changed how this instrument can be heard. In discussion with Eggebrecht, Spahlinger also points to an 'anticipation' of Cage in Webern's more equal weighting between sound and silence, which allows 'coincidental' sounds to be considered music.[28] Cage's radical approach to everyday sounds is an important predecessor in attempting to break down systematized modes of listening, though it led to rather different results. That Spahlinger prefers to talk of Webern in relation to this topic will not be the first time that Cage appears conspicuous by his absence, despite his significant influence on German new music.

Spahlinger states that the ability to hear these sounds outside of tonal perception has led to an increase in the reflexive knowledge of consciousness – that is, that consciousness better understands itself – and increased self-awareness of the nature of perception: what is usually described as self-reflexion. Listeners to new music come closer to sound 'in itself' but in so doing realize the hugely significant role of their own perception in defining what sound 'is'.[29] Increasing listeners' awareness of the work of their own perception is a crucial and contested aim of much of the composer's music. Exploring the nature of perception often manifests itself in the use of compositional processes and systems that transform a material into another form. The intention is to explore the nature of transition and how listeners' categorization of musical events can be challenged. When listening to Spahlinger's music there is regularly an urge to 'pin the music down', though it remains elusive. That this is Spahlinger's stated aim can be an important realization when listening to his pieces.

This connects with the thorny issue of tradition, as a vital aspect of Spahlinger's approach is to challenge and provoke listening habits. Like his compatriot Lachenmann,[30] Spahlinger describes a constant battle with traditional listening and reception. In discussion with Eggebrecht, he states that he tries to show that tradition 'functions because of agreement' rather than any ultimate truth, and that the meaning of tradition rests on actively 'making sense, which is a contingent reflex rehearsed through particular conventions'.[31] The influence of the Frankfurt

School makes itself manifest in this critical attitude. Adornian negativity is vital to this approach, though this is not meant to act as an excuse to voice blanket distaste for the contemporary world. Rather, it is intended as a constant questioning of perceived wisdom and established positions, one that is suspicious of a positive, all-too-simple solution to the world's problems. This relationship with tradition is further complicated, however, by the way in which both Spahlinger and Lachenmann have relied on, arguably bourgeois, establishments such as orchestras and broadcasters to sustain their careers.

Blunting the Potential of New Music

To put some meat on the bones of his contention that new music has been underestimated, Spahlinger discusses at some length examples of progressive material brought into being by new music that are now 'stood still in mid-path'.[32] He cites dodecaphony, mechanical repetition, open form and chance procedures, each of which are influential in his own composition. On the first, *dodecaphony*, he explains that tonal music constituted a 'collective subjectivity', that is, not a natural system of order (otherwise all tonal systems would be the same) but an arbitrary agreement within a collective, that is, society. Dodecaphony replaces the 'collective subjectivity' with the arbitrary rules of an individual, thus making this arbitrariness clear: this is its revolutionary aspect. Spahlinger argues, against whom it is not entirely clear, that twelve-tone music reveals that tonality was never a natural musical system and that to continue to treat it as such is to cling to outmoded thought. However, as Adorno also noted,[33] the revolutionary tendency of Schoenberg's technique transformed into a search for unity (a classical idea) in which 'everything must relate to everything else'. Memorably, Spahlinger describes the worst examples of serial composition as a 'knitting pattern'.[34] Here, he would save twelve-tone technique from the claims of its most famous exponent, Schoenberg, who saw it as a replacement for certain structural features of the tonal system.[35] Such arbitrary systems of order, brought to music by primarily serial constructions, and in particular their employment and disintegration, are hugely important in Spahlinger's practice and have, for him, a certain degree of political resonance. On the one hand, this shows a modernist constructivist preoccupation but at the same time it always goes hand in hand with a view of systems' limitations and contradictions. These are often not positive systems employed to generate material, rather they are contraptions that in their progress fundamentally alter, or even destroy, themselves.[36]

The second material Spahlinger identifies as 'stood still' is *mechanical repetition*, the exploration of which 'can be found nowhere in tradition'.[37] He contrasts it with traditional, 'figurative' repetition, saying that the latter has 'a qualitative beginning and end', whereas mechanical repetition 'is practically endless: one cannot identify the beginning of a loop or of a wheel'.[38] Rather than the Futurists, or Honegger's *Pacific 231*, he cites Berg's *Lyric Suite* in as an example of a piece that shows an awareness of mechanical repetition's potential. Here, the twelve pitches of the tone row are split into cells of five, four and three notes, which are then permutated 'so that each tone comes into contact with all the others'. This process ends 'when all permutations are over' yet 'it is clear that this is no qualitative end, nothing that has the same effect as a v-i cadence'. This ending has occurred simply because 'all possibilities have been heard', which is a very different feeling from the 'qualitative ending' of tonal music.[39] Endings in new music are, for the composer, cuts of the musical fabric that could occur at many different places.[40]

This idea contrasts strongly with the 'exclusive' concepts of harmony and musical material that were in play in earlier music, that is, that only very particular pitches defined the 'permitted' chords and only certain (primarily pitched) materials were considered musical. The harmony of the *Lyric Suite* is the result of an exhaustive system, bringing with it an element of arbitrariness, one that is also present in his ideas about 'qualitative' conclusions. Spahlinger's belief in the radical potential of mechanical repetition does not, however, lead to an appreciation of minimal music, which he criticizes forcibly as 'often nothing more than wallpaper'.[41] That there are certain ironies in this criticism will be explored in Chapter 6.

Spahlinger then moves on to the implications of *chance procedures* which, like another of his favourite topics, open form, are said to encourage the listener to realize the nature of the manner in which they listen. Chance, indeterminacy and open form are easily confused and it is important to note Spahlinger's emphasis on the former, which involves the use of chance procedures in the composition of a piece, usually resulting in a relatively fixed score. Indeterminacy, on the other hand, leaves certain aspects of a piece open for the performer. Spahlinger states that, in chance music, 'the nonfigurative is exposed to the figure-making consciousness, which thereby comes to a consciousness of its self'.[42] This relies to a degree on an exaggeration of the role of chance in Cage's compositional process, which is rather more tightly controlled and ordered than the composer's own statements would suggest. Take, as one example, Cage's exhortation to wake up to the 'very life we're living, which is so excellent once one gets one's mind and one's desires out of its way'.[43] Spahlinger appears to take on some of this myth-making when he argues that when a listener makes sense of chance music they should become aware that it is not the music that creates any narrative, logical connections or figures, but rather it is their own perception that forms these: 'nonintentional composing refers the listener to the intentionality of perception itself.'[44] Listeners seek, and to a significant extent *create*, order and familiar patterns and new music should, for the composer, make them more aware of this search. This 'central idea of new music'[45] is one that Spahlinger believes is not sufficiently taken into account. He writes, primarily from the very particular perspective of the German reception of the American's music, that 'few performances of cage's music take this radicality seriously! how many compositions supposedly in the tradition of cage are half-hearted and wishy-washy'.[46]

The final and most recent example of material that Spahlinger believes has foundered is *musique concrète instrumentale*, described succinctly by Blume as 'a notion and a set of techniques that regard sound not as an abstract vehicle for musical ideas in the traditional sense of motivic development, but as the by-product of physical work, of the tension and release of human effort'.[47] The term was invented by Lachenmann, and Spahlinger is one of the few to attempt to generalize it, in part because he employs many of its significant elements in his own music. After briefly mentioning the 'anarchic' qualities of noise,[48] Spahlinger states that *musique concrète instrumentale* introduced a sense of tension and release that was not tonal, while also reintroducing 'the causal relation'[49] that Cage's chance music necessarily denies. This causal relation is presumably that between the act of production or playing technique and the sounding result. The radical spirit of this compositional approach has, according to Spahlinger, subsequently been tempered as 'with salt and pepper shakers these playing techniques, which have become harmless, are sprinkled over the score to convey the impression of yesterday's radicality': composers merely create the 'illusion' of new music.[50] Just like twelve-tone technique, then, *musique concrète instrumentale* has been mis-used by composers who, to continue Spahlinger's metaphor, flavour their music with its exciting techniques, while not realizing its radical implications regarding noise as musical material.

All these aspects – dodecaphony, chance procedures, mechanical repetition and *musique concrète instrumentale* – have in Spahlinger's opinion been manipulated to obscure their revolutionary potential. It is not wholly clear whether, or in what manner, he believes this potential can be resuscitated. Clearly, these are some of the vital areas in which modernist composers have sought to innovate: Boulez and Stockhausen attempted to explore open or mobile form during the 1950s, while Cage (over whom there is some argument in the modernism/postmodernism debate[51]) is the innovator par excellence in the realm of chance music. The history of mechanical repetition in music is less widely acknowledged, yet Spahlinger's own favoured example is Berg. Finally, *musique concrète instrumentale* was a term invented by Lachenmann who, for all his interest in deconstruction, has much in common with Spahlinger when it comes to perpetuating a modernist agenda.

Despite Spahlinger's advocacy for these achievements, they appear here as elements unexploited by contemporary composers: this is no parade of triumphal compositional techniques. There appears to be a group of composers 'misusing' these techniques, unaware of their potential, with no mention of any composers who continue to use these materials in full awareness of their radical natures. Modernists of the past would perhaps insist that fresh innovations must take the place of those that have apparently become stale and lifeless. The fact that he demands no such thing – rather he implores composers to revisit what made these achievements radical in the first place – is an indication of his faith in the achievements of modernism, and also his scepticism toward any belief that innovations can be found to advance musical material. In this he both perpetuates modernist convictions – having confidence in the importance of their achievements – while also renouncing any, arguably modernist, faith in unambiguous teleological progress. What he appears to regard as unconscionable, however, is the possibility of finding musical progress in the materials and practices of popular music, or even music of the common practice era. This betrays a quite classic modernist suspicion of tonality, as well as an absence of dialectical consideration when it comes to such materials.[52]

Possible Progress

What progress means in a world so described by the composer is a difficult question, the answer to which rests on composers not becoming the 'conceptive ideologue' of the essay's title. Spahlinger appears to admit this difficulty, though he argues there may be some wilful blindness obscuring a way out: 'composers (i.e. we) do not know what forward progress means aesthetically, because we do not know, or don't want to know, what it means politically.'[53] Again, fear of losing certain privileges prevents composers gaining 'friends' and 'an audience, too, as far as i'm concerned'.[54] Here, Spahlinger returns to the idea of self-reflexivity. He states – after Frankfurt philosopher Bruno Liebrucks – that encouraging thought that 'fathoms the conditions of its own genesis and takes these as its central theme' is the only means by which thought can be 'non-ideological or even an ideology critique'.[55] Once more he appeals to a sceptical position regarding positive, unreflexive solutions. For Spahlinger, the only way to achieve non-ideological thought is to reflect on the nature of thought itself. This is regularly translated into reflexion on musical parameters, categories of perception and, tacitly, the legacy of modernism.

Spahlinger believes music has an important role in reflecting and encouraging a more reflexive consciousness for modern times and, therefore, spurring progress in thought to match modern technological progress. He contrasts social progress, supported by the radical proletariat, with this technological progress, which is backed by the bourgeoisie whose 'history is the history of the industrial revolution'.[56] The presence of technological progress is 'undeniable'[57] but evidence for social progress is less easy to detect, even in the artistic avant-garde, which had previously claimed to be on the right side of historical progression.[58] Despite this scepticism, he states that 'a corresponding progress of freedom, an adequately equipped consciousness'[59] must develop to match this technological progress, and it is here composers have a contribution to make.

New music has a role to play in developing this consciousness, a point argued more fully in the essay 'against the postmodern fashion'. One of Spahlinger's favourite phrases comes from Kurt Tucholsky, who said in 1930 that 'on account of bad weather, the German revolution took place in music'.[60] Though rather flippant sounding, it represents a serious truth for the composer: that within new music there is a radical reconfiguration of fundamental aspects of understanding and perception. Even though its potential for encouraging revolutionary thought has gone unexploited, this capacity for engendering a more self-reflexive consciousness remains. Self-reflexion is the means by which progress can be made, not through any exclusive support of one particular technique or style.

Potential Criticisms

This brief introduction has already revealed some of the tensions that Spahlinger's project contains, some of which have gone unrecognized and undiscussed in Spahlinger scholarship. These include questions of elitism, hierarchies in new music and how constant reflexion nevertheless appears to result in a characteristic style. For example, for all his talk of music and society, he does not make any attempt to engage 'the people'.[61] He believes strongly in music's political potential and its social basis, yet many of his works appear to affirm an autonomous musical sphere that demands only the most radical material, and he is unwilling to touch on anything remotely akin to popular taste. Such sentiments are a common source of complaint for modernism's critics who question the validity of a sphere of music divorced from societal influence in which musical innovation must be propagated, as well as the allegedly elitist assumptions of those within this sphere. This final section will engage with some of the more prominent critics of modernism to show their potential relevance.

The composer's quest for constant self-reflexion implies music that is forever changeable, yet listeners to his pieces will certainly be able to identify certain quasi-stylistic traits. These go unremarked upon in his writings but are surely some of the most significant elements of his music for its devotees and detractors alike: they are what binds his musical output as much as his critical attitude. In this, his list of anti-conventions described in 'against the postmodern fashion' can be seen to have the opposite effect from that intended: for example, his desire to avoid established means of expression results in an almost complete absence of tonal material, which he achieves by a consistently dissonant musical language. A 'positive' harmonic language can be seen to rise from this negation, though he would likely argue that consonance comprises only a tiny portion of harmonic possibilities, while tonal syntax he considers dominant and, therefore, regressive.

Such criticisms connect with wider debates around hierarchies that modernism allegedly sets up and the institutions it uses to enforce them. McClary identifies a siege mentality among the members of circles pushing for radical, autonomous music: the forces of capitalist society and their alleged musical representatives in the world of popular music are 'barbarians' at the gates of culture.[62] In this formation, modernist music becomes the *only* music that is serious and authentic; it is the sole genre to truly meet the demands of a vision of art that requires constant innovation to progress. Modernism is seen to encourage an 'aesthetic denial of popular music'[63] and more widely to reflect a contempt for ordinary tastes and practices:

> It would undoubtedly come as a surprise to that whistling barbarian that music is an endangered species, the last remnants of which are being carefully protected in university laboratories. Because to anyone who has not been trained in terms of the modernist partyline, it is quite obvious that the twentieth century has witnessed an unparalleled explosion in musical creativity.[64]

Either by omission, or by specific singling out, such as in the case of Adorno's well-known views on 'jazz',[65] modernism appears to create a hierarchy of genres, naturally placing itself very much at the top. Its blindness to the rich tapestry of musics that make up most people's experiences is seen as complete ignorance of, or disregard for, how audiences listen and how music functions within people's lives.

Such hierarchies, according to McClary, are sustained by institutions and particularly Higher Education curricula that enforce a modernist understanding of musical life,[66] while modernism is seen not as the revolutionary force but as 'the conservative stronghold of the current music scene'.[67] A perhaps more nuanced take on the relationship between modernism and institutionalization is provided by Georgina Born, who states that this institutionalization of the modernist project is a central contradiction in the foundation of IRCAM (Institut de Recherche et Coordination Acoustique/Musique), a French state-funded organization for supporting the interface between new music and technology based at the Centre

Pompidou in Paris. Two impulses that stand in complete contradiction are seen to be at play here: first, a discourse with a 'utopian stress on innovation and progress' and an 'orientation to the future'; second, the creation of structures that imply the 'historical continuity of modernism and so the cumulative authority and legitimacy that it has accrued'. These two together are said to create a 'formidable legitimacy, satisfying the desire for both rupture, newness, change, and for historical continuity and consolidation'.[68] There is a criticism here that IRCAM, and modernism in general, cannot have it both ways: it cannot be radical while being enshrined in powerful institutions; it is not revolutionary when it has become the status quo. This unresolved tension between institutions and innovation can also be viewed more positively as the spur in modernism's flank, keeping it running well into its second century. Yet, Born's point is one on which many critics would agree, for, despite trenchant criticism, many are not attempting to suppress completely the music of Schoenberg, Stockhausen or even Babbitt, they are simply highly critical of modernism's institutional policing of musical material and, above all, its claims to be the only music of significance.[69]

Finally, there is the sense that by engaging with 'perception', Spahlinger is creating a rather monolithic totality through which he engages with wider society, something that should set off alarm bells for any Adornian-inspired critique. His engagement with perception also requires a specific, analytical and philosophically engaged mode of listening, one that is unlikely to be reflected in the majority of listeners and which appears to exclude the free-flowing, subjective association of ideas that the listening experience entails. Questions of the mode of listening he presumes in his listener will be taken up at various points throughout this study, but the tension between perception as an individual site of almost chaotic possibility and perception as an arena in which to engage a more homogeneous society is already apparent.

Autonomy, the relationship between politics and music, the political potential of perception and the nature of progress in music are all crucial topics that cut to the heart of Spahlinger's thought and continuing debates in studies of modernism. Yet, it remains to be seen how his professed self-reflexivity actually functions in practice rather than solely taking his writings as evidence. Part 2 will explore just these issues with extended reference to his works to show their manifestations in practice. Now that the fundaments of his aesthetic project have been established, it will be valuable to take a step back and assess these concerns within the composer's biography and the societal currents that flowed through post-Second World War Germany. Outside of his debt to '68, this topic has been left largely untouched in Spahlinger literature. It is argued in the next chapter that considering the composer through such a lens gives important insight to his compositional project as, in part, a product of his times.

NOTES

1. Mathias Spahlinger, 'this is the time of conceptive ideologues no longer', trans. Philipp Blume, *Contemporary Music Review* 27, no. 6 (2008): 579–94.
2. Ibid., 580.
3. Ibid., 579.
4. Mathias Spahlinger, 'gegen die postmoderne mode', *MusikTexte* 27 (1989): 2–7.
5. Ibid., 6.
6. Spahlinger, 'this is the time of conceptive ideologues no longer', 582.
7. Bridget Fowler identifies a similar idea in the thought of Bourdieu – another theorist heavily influenced by Marx – as here the 'major emphasis is […] on the "contradictory class location" of the artist, a space which is simultaneously dominant and dominated'. Bridget Fowler, *Pierre Bourdieu and Cultural Theory: Critical Investigations* (London: Sage, 1997).
8. Spahlinger, 'this is the time of conceptive ideologues no longer', 580.
9. Ibid., 583.
10. Originally named 'The Composer as Specialist' by the author, it first appeared as 'Who Cares If You Listen?'. Milton Babbitt, 'Who Cares If You Listen?' (1958), in *Source Readings in Music History*, vol. 7: *The Twentieth Century*, rev. ed., ed. Robert P. Morgan (New York: Norton, 1998), 35–41.
11. Ibid., 40.
12. Beal comments that Babbitt 'had little interest in cultivating a career in Europe' and his work 'remained less known there than that of some of his peers' (Amy C. Beal, *New Music, New Allies: American Experimental Music in West Germany, from Zero Hour to Reunification* [Berkeley: University of California Press, 2006]). When the composer finally did accept an invitation to the courses at Darmstadt in 1964, he was not particularly well received and found the experience quite unpleasant (ibid., 140).
13. Susan McClary, 'Terminal Prestige: The Case of Avant-Garde Music Composition', *Cultural Critique* 12 (1989): 57–81. According to a much later chapter by McClary, a 'careful reading' of 'Terminal Prestige' reveals that it is no attack on 'modernist music per-se but only the ideologies that had upheld its hegemony' (McClary, 'The Lure of the Sublime: Revisiting the Modernist Project', in *Transformations of Musical Modernism*, ed. Erling E. Gulbrandsen and Julian Johnson [Cambridge: Cambridge University Press, 2015], 21–35).
14. McClary, 'Terminal Prestige: The Case of Avant-Garde Music Composition', 58.
15. Spahlinger, 'this is the time of conceptive ideologues no longer', 583.
16. Ibid., 585.
17. See the *Diesseitigkeit* issue of *Positionen* 93 (2012).
18. Theodor W. Adorno, 'The Aging of the New Music (1955)', in *Essays on Music*, ed. Richard Leppert (London: University of California Press, 2002), 181–202.
19. Spahlinger, 'this is the time of conceptive ideologues no longer', 579.

20. Friedrich Hölderlin, *The Death of Empedocles: A Mourning Play*, trans. David Farrell Krell (New York: State University of New York Press, 2008), 87.

21. Spahlinger, 'this is the time of conceptive ideologues no longer', 580.

22. Marx and Engels in Spahlinger, 'this is the time of conceptive ideologues no longer', 579.

23. Spahlinger, 'this is the time of conceptive ideologues no longer', 581.

24. Hans Heinrich Eggebrecht and Mathias Spahlinger, *Geschichte der Musik als Gegenwart*, Musikkonzepte Special Edition, ed. Heinz-Klaus Metzger and Rainer Riehn (Munich: Richard Boorberg Verlag, 2000), 22. Spahlinger's enthusiasm for the French Revolution led to him often wearing the *tricolore* colours of red, white and blue (though not necessarily all at once). It is a move somewhat reminiscent of Karlheinz Stockhausen's fashion choices being associated with the days of the week.

25. Spahlinger, 'this is the time of conceptive ideologues no longer', 580.

26. Ibid. It will not have escaped the reader's attention that Spahlinger is an implementer of *Kleinschreibung*, that is, he never uses capital letters. All Spahlinger's articles are written solely in lower case and this approach has also been extended to remarks made in interview with the author. This form of writing was fairly common among post-war leftist intellectuals in German-speaking lands. Hans Magnus Enzensberger began his career by writing only in lower case but changed as early as 1970, which Clayton gives as one reason for his increased readability (Alan J. Clayton, *Writing with the Words of Others: Essays on the Poetry of Hans Magnus Enzensberger* [Würzburg: Königshausen & Neumann, 2010], 254). The history of opposing the traditional *Großschreibung* goes much further back, however. Jacob Grimm was an early opponent, though he did not advocate dispensing with capital letters altogether. Perhaps more influential is the Bauhaus's implementation of *Kleinschreibung* in 1925, ostensibly, and aptly for a movement concerned with craft, on practical grounds. This will have had an effect on artistic movements in the mid-twentieth century, particularly considering Spahlinger's training as a typesetter. This writing style is another realm in which the composer appears to be holding to conventions that many others have dispensed with.

27. Spahlinger, 'gegen die postmoderne mode', 6.

28. Eggebrecht and Spahlinger, *Geschichte der Musik als Gegenwart*, 108.

29. This is a pivotal argument of another of the composer's essays, 'actuality of the consciousness and actuality for the consciousness' (Mathias Spahlinger, 'wirklichkeit des bewußtseins und wirklichkeit für das bewußtsein: politische aspekte der music', *MusikTexte* 39 [1991]: 39–41), which is also his most concentrated discussion of the ways in which music can be political.

30. Helmut Lachenmann, 'The "Beautiful" in Music Today', *TEMPO* 135 (1980): 20–24, 23.

31. Eggebrecht and Spahlinger, *Geschichte der Musik als Gegenwart*, 110.

32. Spahlinger, 'this is the time of conceptive ideologues no longer', 588.

33. Adorno, 'The Aging of the New Music (1955)'.

34. Spahlinger, 'this is the time of conceptive ideologues no longer', 588. Though perhaps the composer underestimates the potential of radical craft movements and modernist textiles when casting this aspersion.

35. Arnold Schoenberg, 'Composition with Twelve Tones (1)', in *Style and Idea*, ed. Leonard Stein (Berkeley: University of California Press, 1975), 214–15.

36. For further details see: Tobias Eduard Schick, *Weltbezüge in der Musik Mathias Spahlingers* (Stuttgart: Franz Steiner Verlag, 2018).

37. Eggebrecht and Spahlinger, *Geschichte der Musik als Gegenwart*, 62.

38. Spahlinger, 'this is the time of conceptive ideologues no longer', 589.

39. Eggebrecht and Spahlinger, *Geschichte der Musik als Gegenwart*, 62.

40. This does not, however, appear to translate into an acceptance of ending his own pieces at any point during their performance.

41. Spahlinger, 'this is the time of conceptive ideologues no longer', 590.

42. Ibid.

43. John Cage, 'Experimental Music', in *Silence* (Middletown, CT: Wesleyan University Press), 12.

44. Spahlinger, 'this is the time of conceptive ideologues no longer', 591.

45. Ibid., 590.

46. Ibid., 591.

47. Philipp Blume, 'Preface: Music of Nicolaus A. Huber and Mathias Spahlinger', *Contemporary Music Review* 27, no. 6 (2008): 561–63, 561.

48. Eggebrecht and Spahlinger, *Geschichte der Musik als Gegenwart*, 58.

49. Spahlinger, 'this is the time of conceptive ideologues no longer', 591.

50. Ibid.

51. See Benjamin Piekut, ed., *Tomorrow Is the Question: New Directions in Experimental Music* (Michigan: University of Michigan Press, 2014).

52. This is despite his own piece *adieu m'amour* (*hommage à guillaume dufay*, (1982–83), which is based on a piece by Dufay. This is an area in which theory and practice diverge somewhat, though it must be said the majority of his pieces carefully avoid tonal materials to avoid what he sees as a dominant mode of listening.

53. Spahlinger, 'this is the time of conceptive ideologues no longer', 591.

54. Ibid., 592.

55. Ibid., 582.

56. Ibid., 592.

57. Ibid.

58. Spahlinger, 'gegen die postmoderne mode', 2.

59. Spahlinger, 'this is the time of conceptive ideologues no longer', 592.

60. Kurt Tucholsky, *Gesammelte Werke*, vol. 8 (Reinbek bei Hamburg: Rowohlt, 1975), 346.

61. Robert Adlington explores this tension between modernism *for* the people and modernism *in spite of* the people in 'Modernism: The People's Music', in *The Routledge*

Research Companion to Modernism in Music, ed. Björn Heile and Charles Wilson (London: Routledge, 2019), 216–38.

62. McClary, 'Terminal Prestige', 62.

63. Georgina Born, *Rationalizing Culture: IRCAM, Boulez, and the Institutionalization of the Musical Avant-Garde* (London: University of California Press, 1995), 325.

64. McClary, 'Terminal Prestige', 63.

65. See Robert W. Witkin, 'Why Did Adorno "Hate" Jazz?', *Sociological Theory* 18, no. 1 (2000): 145–70.

66. McClary, 'Terminal Prestige', 66.

67. Ibid., 67.

68. Born, *Rationalizing Culture*, 327.

69. Björn Heile argues that the position of Born, in common with a number of anti-modernist critiques, is based on a reductive conception of the European avant-garde: 'Darmstadt as Other: British and American Responses to Musical Modernism', *Twentieth-Century Music* 1, no. 2 (2004): 161–78.

2

Biography and Context: Spahlinger and Twentieth-Century Germany

A lack of awareness of Spahlinger in Anglophone territories, and indeed a dearth of extensive biographical information elsewhere, mean that a brief sketch of the composer's life is a useful addition to Spahlinger scholarship. That such a biographical focus is lacking is perhaps not unusual for a contemporary composer as early studies tend to preference the 'work' side of the standard 'work and life' format. Yet, this deficit is also part of a tendency to assess the composer within the hermetic sphere of his work and the thinkers with whom he engages while ignoring wider factors that might be influential. His own intellectual engagement can also obscure such contextual factors. Where some composers might relate pieces to collaborators, episodes in their lives or other arts such as poetry and painting, Spahlinger is more likely to talk of his pieces in terms of musico-philosophic and political issues.

There has been little consideration, for example, of the cultural currents in which the composer is situated, excepting new music, 'critical composition' and 1968. There has been even less discussion of how biographical events have shaped his practice, which is in no small part due to the composer himself very rarely mentioning his personal life. Even the modernism that is so palpable throughout Spahlinger's practice is assumed rather than probed. In exploring the details of the composer's life, then, the effects of his generational and geographical location will also be discussed alongside his formative musical experiences. The scope of the following chapter will, therefore, range widely from the specifics of Spahlinger's experiences to cultural currents that swept through the entire nation's artistic practice.

'what's with this kid?': Post-War Frankfurt

Spahlinger was born on 15 October 1944, in Frankfurt am Main, immediately entering one of the darkest years in the city's history. On 22 March, a British air raid had destroyed the Altstadt, killing 1,001 people and destroying many of the city's most significant buildings, including the Opera House at which his father was employed. This year places him in a very specific generational context: essentially, he is one of the *Nachgeborenen*, those born after the war who had no direct experience of its horrors. This was a generation with new political concerns that would later manifest themselves in the youth movements around 1968.

The effects of life among the rubble of national socialist dreams manifested themselves very quickly in German arts. In literature, this is seen in the relatively short-lived *Trümmerliteratur* ('rubble literature') written directly after the war, the characters of which often return to stare into the destruction of homes and ideals. This movement is also called *Kahlschlagliteratur* ('clear-cutting literature'), indicating that its economical language was in part an attempt to cut through the rhetoric of the National Socialist time and return to a more objective, and often extremely grim, reality. Within two years of the cessation of hostilities, Victor Klemperer published his *Lingua Tertii Imperii*, which explores the manipulation of the German language during the time of National Socialism.[1] Giles Radice identifies and describes this 'manipulation and distortion': '[w]ords like "*Volk*" and "*Heimat*", so important in the past, were "out". Patriotism was a dirty word.'[2] Even the word 'Kultur' was contested due to its lingering association with German militarism.[3]

In music, this suspicion of traditional forms of expression could not take on quite the same specificity as in literature: there are few musical gestures that have the resonance and specificity of words like 'Volk', though the music favoured by the Nazis such as Carl Orff and, famously, Wagner, comes close as a substitute.[4] Any kind of romantic pathos after the Second World War was considered with some suspicion, which is one reason why Hans Werner Henze was, for modernist composers at least, a problematic figure later in the century.[5] Instead, the talk of the 1950s is far more of creating an international, modern aesthetic, best demonstrated by those composers active at Darmstadt during this period, though the festival itself still offered performances of mid-century composers such as Hindemith and Bartók. For Stockhausen, for example, the festival represented a 'new freedom' in which 'universal experience' rather than the 'prejudices of history' was the priority.[6] This unique historical situation may seem curiously unrecognized by rhetoric from this time, with talk of a complete reinvention of artistic language and a clean slate from which to begin culture anew. Yet, such an attitude, in seeking to distance itself from a particularly unpleasant recent past, is paradoxically a clear product of its time.

While German artists tried to come to terms with this unique historical situation, Spahlinger's early life was in fact filled with as much early music as it was new. He took lessons in viola da gamba, vielle [*Fidel*] and later violoncello with his father, who was an early advocate of *alte Musik*. This exposure to period instruments created a perhaps surprising lifelong passion for music of the Baroque and the Renaissance in the composer: the duo *adieu m'amour hommage à guillaume dufay* (1982–83), which uses the original Dufay work as a scaffold for the entire piece, is its most obvious expression. In 1952, Spahlinger began piano lessons, allowing him his most immediate contact with the history and tradition of Germanic music – and particularly Beethoven – which is so key to his understanding of music today. Spahlinger's interest in composition first became evident during these lessons, in which he would 'show off' with 'a new piece only he could play'.[7]

In correspondence with the current author, Spahlinger himself also stresses the importance of the household tape recorder in his musical development, with which he recorded all manner of musics from different times and cultures:

> i was always interested in music […] early on (i was perhaps 8 or 10) we had a tape recorder and we got tape scraps from a colleague of my father, that as children we glued together, wound on spools and used. from then on i *always*, up to this very day, recorded from the radio, and later also from borrowed records: old music, new music, jazz and non-european music. up until around 15 years ago (it is different now with satellite and internet radio) i could have said: there is no music in this world (if it exists on a recording medium) that i do not know through listening.[8]

This exposure to a wide variety of music also led to an early interest in more contemporary works, as demonstrated by his first recording:

> as a six-year-old i loved webern […] op. 5, op. 7, op. 9 and op. 11 ('what's with this kid?' the musician colleagues of my father asked). [i] listened to varèse *ionisation* the whole day ('turn that din down or off!'), i listened to stravinsky, symphony in three movements and schönberg op. 45 (these three pieces were on my first tape).[9]

From an early stage, therefore, Spahlinger was familiar with various traditions of classical music making, including the nascent historically informed performance movement, canonical piano works and pre-Second World War European modernism. This reference to mass-produced technology having such an early effect places the young composer firmly within the Germany of the 1950s and the *Wirtschaftswunder* ('Economic Miracle'), a time in which the swift rise of consumerism gave a new perspective on questions of material versus social progress that Spahlinger later addresses. These questions had long been established, however, by the industrialized murder that took place in mid-century Europe, as is explored further below.

An Education

The school career of the young composer did not always run smoothly. His father 'mistrusted the academic practices of the *Gymansien* [grammar schools]'[10] so Spahlinger left his *Gymnasium* in 1959 for the more practically orientated *Realschule*, from which he graduated in 1962. He then undertook a three-year apprenticeship in typesetting on the wishes of his father, who wanted his son to learn a trade due to the difficulties he himself had experienced in gaining work as a musician. Reihnhard Oehlschlägel relates how Spahlinger felt like an 'outsider' in his youth: too bookish for his apprenticeship but with a humbler background than most of his *Gymnasium* fellows.[11] His extracurricular composition lessons, which he began with Konrad Lechner in 1964, would have made him a somewhat unusual apprentice. Spahlinger relates the noisy, mechanical repetition of his first orchestral piece, *morendo* (1975), to these unhappy years 'at the typeface'.[12] He states, too, that it was during this time that he began to engage intensively with Marxism, first by reading poet, essayist and editor Hans Magnus Enzensberger. It was this that led him down the intellectual path that has had such an influence on his work:

> out of concrete sadness i occupied myself with marx, through marx i came to enzensberger, who played a big role for me at that time as a crucial literary experience, because that was ultimately political poetry; and then of course the theoretical things, *die einzelheiten* [*The Particulars*, by Enzensberger, 1962]. through this i came around to reading adorno; therein lie the whole aesthetic approaches. and then it became clear to me that i really have to know hegel precisely, and i sank my teeth into that. and there somewhere the circle is complete.[13]

It is clear that this experience as an apprentice was crucial in the formation of Spahlinger's political consciousness, one that, importantly, occurred pre-1968. The composer states that he was a '68-er before 68' though his political consciousness will have been heightened all the more by the events and experiences of solidarity from this time.[14]

The year 1959 also saw Spahlinger begin saxophone lessons, reflecting his increasingly intense engagement with jazz music. This led him to consider a career as a jazz musician: 'charles parker, thelonious monk, billie holiday and then ornette coleman were my people!'[15] In an email to Nonnenmann, he relates how, like his older sister before him, he frequented the Frankfurt Jazzkeller at an age 'relevant' to the authorities.[16] When inspections were carried out the musicians helped him hide, at one point in a double bass case. This establishment benefited from the continued presence of American soldiers as both audience and performers due to Frankfurt having been in the American Zone of Occupation. It also gave the young Spahlinger a first-hand encounter with American racial politics of the time.[17] Passive listening soon led to active participation as a 'wild and unconventional' improviser,[18] though, according to the composer, he enjoyed on occasion imitating the rather more mainstream Louis Armstrong.[19] This interest in jazz is notable, considering some modernists' dismissal of the genre, most significantly Adorno's famous critique.[20]

Though he never realized his early ambition to become a professional jazz musician, it remains an important part of his musical experience: he believes his three musical 'mother tongues' are the opera repertoire, the piano literature and jazz.[21] In the development of free jazz, Spahlinger sees a movement comparable to the radical atonality of the Second Viennese School, one worthy of corresponding levels of respect.[22] Jazz and improvisation both heavily influenced his compositional work, most obviously in *RoaiuGHFF (strange?)* (1981, see Figure 2.1 for the title format) for orchestra and improvising jazz soloists and the more recent, *doppelt bejaht* (*doubly affirmed*, 2009) which is defined by improvisation within certain limits. The former was written for jazz musicians personally known to the composer from his time in Frankfurt. Something of the cross-genre approach can be gleaned from the title, which references 'rough', 'riff' and 'rag'.

In 1965, Spahlinger began his formal musical education, studying piano with Werner Hoppstock and continuing his composition studies with Konrad Lechner at the Städtische Akademie für Tonkunst, Darmstadt. He vowed, however, not to attend the famous International Summer Courses – a highly significant centre of modernist music – until they invited him to speak on his own music there, an invitation for which he had to wait until 1986. This is a small sign that, even in relation to the modernist music that is his primary influence, Spahlinger wanted to forge his own musical path. Martin Iddon also notes that 'Darmstadt's significance appeared to have declined in the 1960s' from its influential zenith in the previous

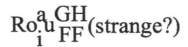

FIGURE 2.1: *RoaiuGHFF (strange?)* title.

decade,[23] though for a young German composer this is still a significant refusal. In 1968, after his studies in Darmstadt, Spahlinger took the exam to become a music teacher and, once qualified, he moved to Stuttgart where he worked at the Stuttgarter Musikschule (a specialist high school) as a teacher of piano, music theory, experimental music and early musical education. Perhaps unsurprisingly, making a living from composition or performance appears not have been an option for the composer at this time. The city of Stuttgart is most strongly associated with the composer Helmut Lachenmann, who was born there and spent most of his teaching career at the city's Musikhochschule ('music conservatoire'). The year 1968 saw Lachenmann, nine years Spahlinger's senior, win the composition prize of the city of Stuttgart, and the two composers became close associates during the 1970s and 1980s.

1968 and Vergangenheitsbewältigung

1968 was of course also a year of great unrest across Europe and North America. Though not as extreme as in France for example, the German protests of 1968 (in fact most notable in 1967 and 1969[24]) still had a significant cultural impact as young students stood up to perceived government infringements on freedom and the nation's difficult National Socialist past. This past was far from abstract due to the continued presence of prominent Nazis in such professions as teaching and the judiciary. This revolutionary atmosphere further encouraged Spahlinger's socialist ideals: he describes himself as a 'well-known 68-er' and consistently voices political ideas heavily influenced by Marxism and Frankfurt School philosophy.[25] Despite their widespread cultural impact, the protests of 1968 did not achieve many of their key political aims and, after the revolutionary fervour had faded somewhat, there was a desire to change, rather than dispense with, the structures of government. Spahlinger's subtle understanding of the political in music – and (highly qualified) belief in musical progress – mirror this change from black and white revolutionary politics to a more refined sense of evolution. In common with Adorno, the idea of utopia appears regularly in both his music and writings; it is tempting to see as its foundation this revolution that never was.

For German writers and painters of the 1960s and 1970s, the utopian dreams of doing away with the old and creating an entirely new creative language did not seem possible, indeed symbolized an evasion of difficult questions. Themes of history and national identity emerge as a major theme in German art from this point, whether in the novels of Heinrich Böll or the canvases of Anselm Kiefer. These artists reacted against the repressive silence of the country under its post-war chancellor Konrad Adenauer, in which 'very little was said about Nazism', 'next to nothing was taught about it in the schools' and 'critical enquiry into the German past was discouraged'.[26] Reactions against this 'wall of silence',[27] and the unchallenged status of many former Nazis in German society, were important elements of the cultural change that '68-ers' wanted to achieve. Another perspective is given by studies of the period that foreground the widespread view in Germany at the time that the country was a *victim* of the war and that, rather than collective amnesia, there was a feeling it had suffered enough. This led to significant antipathy towards the denazification process. Robert G. Moeller describes the view of Germany as 'doubly victimized, first by a Nazi regime run amok, then by Communists' with a view of history in which 'perpetrators and victims were never the same people'.[28]

The manifestation of artists' reactions to this cultural backdrop is usually understood as *Vergangenheitsbewältigung*, a 'coming to terms with the past'. This has been widely discussed, particularly in literature, with Vicki Lawrence describing it as an 'ongoing literary and social phenomenon'.[29] Peter Arnds finds the same theme in the work of Günter Grass and Edgar Hilsenrath,[30] while Lawrence also explores these concerns in works by Bernhard Schlink, Christoph Ransmayr and Peter Schneider.[31] Nor, as the century progresses, is this phenomenon limited solely to the traditional fields of high art, with Andreas Huyssen describing how the late 1970s – and admittedly American – TV programme *Holocaust* was a major success in Germany,[32] while the German 1980s series *Heimat* also explores themes around cultural inheritance. This process was crucial, as the German people directly after the war were by no means unanimously ready to consider culpability for Nazi crimes, believing 'party leaders and fanatical members' were responsible, while avoiding more difficult questions that called into question 'hallowed traditions' and 'ingrained habits of thinking'.[33] Artists wanted to raise important questions of culpability that many would have preferred to leave dormant. Kiefer's early *Occupations* (1969, not displayed until 1975), in which he posed throughout Europe wearing his father's military coat, were, therefore, a deliberate provocation. Yet, this was no homogeneous process with serious debates as to the 'appropriateness' of certain approaches or media in engaging with these issues: disrespect for the victims, commodification of their suffering or an 'easy' means of assuming artistic gravity are all potential failings.

The appropriation of the icons of German culture by the National Socialists, whether it was Hölderlin, Wagner or Caspar David Friedrich, presented potential problems both for parodic recycling, as well as for an uncritical continuation of the German artistic tradition. Writing or painting had an air of assumed complicity in the actions of artists' forebears, even if they themselves had no direct experience of these times, while appropriation of tradition could be seen as, at best, an inappropriately jocular approach to a sensitive issue and, at worst, as an imitation of the techniques of fascism. The former complicity is part of the meaning of Adorno's statement, that 'to write poetry after Auschwitz is barbaric', which also refers to the impossibility of representing such an issue in art.[34] The effect of the seemingly unavoidable historical situation is seen in the examples of pop art from the 1960s. While Warhol and others created the flat, colourful advertising-board canvases that explored issues of consumerism, German pop artists appeared more overtly socially and historically aware. One particularly explicit example is Thomas Bayrle's *Nürnberger Orgie* (1966) in which a crowd of swastika-wielding figures are dwarfed by a vast arm performing a Hitler salute. The issues involved appeared too grave to take lightly.

The relevance of tradition and history, and the corresponding seriousness with which German artists sought to engage such issues, is also a factor in the particularly German reaction to, and understanding of, what were labelled 'postmodern' ideas in other countries.[35] This understanding is very much manifest in Spahlinger's own essay 'against the postmodern fashion' (1989). Such a conception of postmodernism will be discussed below, but a more general sense of 'belatedness' in German arts is important to grasp. This description comes from Lisa Saltzman's analysis of the work of Kiefer, in which she argues it is as if he is working in an era that is conceived of coming 'after' rather than 'before'.[36] Such belatedness has already been seen in Spahlinger, with his loyalty to the achievements of new music and philosophical outlook heavily influenced by Adorno, though it is argued in the present study that such a position is best characterized as being a continuation of modernism rather than occurring solely 'after' it. Saltzman's observations, however, offer the perspective that this is a specifically German feature, one heavily influenced by a strong philosophical and artistic tradition that it simultaneously struggles against and is constituted by, as well as the specific historical situation after the Second World War.

The phenomenon of *Vergangenheitsbewältigung* has not, on the surface at least, been identified in the practice of a great many home-grown composers.[37] Few of the composers that dominate post-Second World War histories explicitly expressed a desire to overcome the history of their nation through musical means, while directly after the war the main stylistic novelty was 'late objectivity'.[38] The most prominent exception is the work of Argentinian-born Mauricio Kagel, whose playful engagements with German tradition, notably Beethoven, very much took history and its construction as themes. Mention might also be made of Bernd Alois Zimmerman, Wilhelm Killmayer and Hans Werner Henze in their various distinct ways of appropriating and filtering canonical German composers.[39] While figures such as Stockhausen focused on technical and compositional issues, there was also a layer of discourse and debate in Germany in which music was heavily politicized, with the spectre of fascism always lurking under the surface, even if the content of the works – as described by the composers – did not deal explicitly with such themes.[40] This politicization becomes particularly notable in the student movements around 1968. Political engagement after this was far from unusual, yet this often took Marxist positions that were orientated towards the international working classes rather than specifically German situations. Yet, elements of *Vergangenheitsbewältigung* can be discerned in the manner Spahlinger engages with society; his critical attitude and his continued belief in modernism's potential can themselves be seen as reactions to these historical trends. He employs 'serious' modernist models to critically reflect their practice and society at large, while maintaining, for the most part, the belief that art can in some way make a societal contribution. This is by no means the only reaction to this particular set of issues, however. For example, composer Gerhard Stäbler, born five years after Spahlinger, stopped composing altogether during the late 1970s, preferring direct political action through distributing a left-wing magazine.[41] He returned to composing after this, engaging with a diverse range of social groups in an attempt to more directly intervene in social situations.

Artist and Intellectual

Spahlinger began the final episode of his formal education in 1973 when he enrolled at the Musikhochschule in Stuttgart, studying with his most influential teacher, Erhard Karkoschka (1923–2009). Karkoschka was a keen analyst as well as composer and will have encouraged the analytical bent of the younger man, particularly in relation to Webern. Spahlinger himself highlights the great debt he owes to Karkoschka's thoughts on musical time and the ways in which it can be articulated.[42] An impression of the material Karkoschka used in his lessons is given by his book *Notation in New Music*, first published in 1966, which contains examples from, among others, Messiaen, Boulez, Penderecki, Cage, Ligeti, Stockhausen, Kagel, Pousseur, Lachenmann and Nono: a wide diet of modernist music to which the composer will have been exposed, if he was not already familiar with it. The works from Spahlinger's years as a student in Stuttgart are the first he considers mature: the earliest piece inserted into many work lists is his *entlöschend* for large tam-tam, which was written in 1974, one year after starting under Karkoschka, though the first in his archive is the *fünf sätze* for two pianos (1969). Stuttgart was also the scene of some early experiments with electronic music and radio *Hörspiele*, but it is the instrumental works from this period that really stand out. The mechanistic *morendo* dates from this time, as well as two of his most performed works: *128 erfüllte augenblicke* (*128 fulfilled instants*,

1976) for voice, clarinet and cello; and the percussion-heavy *éphémère* (1977). In 1977, Spahlinger graduated from Stuttgart and in June of that year took his final, *großes Kompositionsexamen*.

The composer's work in the 1980s is bookended by the substantial duo *extension* (1979–80) for violin and piano and the 'gleaming treasure-trove'[43] of *passage/paysage* for large orchestra (1989–90). Together with *inter-mezzo* for piano and orchestra (1986), these works comprise the major milestones of this decade and form a rather unconventional cycle, part of which Spahlinger presented in his first lecture at the Darmstädter Ferienkurse in 1986. The pieces are linked musically by their 'decomposition of principles of order',[44] an idea that will be discussed further in Chapter 4. During the 1990s, the composer's focus shifts from these principles of order to an emphasis on perception, making *passage/paysage* a pivotal work.[45] Oehlschlägel comments that he 'knows of no other orchestral music of comparably forceful musical stringency composed after 1970',[46] while Hechtle considers it 'one of the most outstanding and significant works' of the second half of the twentieth century.[47]

In 1990, Spahlinger succeeded Klaus Huber as professor of composition at the Musikhochschule in Freiburg where he remained until his retirement in 2009. He was 'one of the leading professors of composition in Germany'[48] and an extremely committed pedagogue, influencing many of the young composers now active on the German music scene. One of these is Kranichstein Musikpreis winner Johannes Kreidler. He describes the intense engagement his teacher had with his students: 'teaching was not just a job for Spahlinger, but a cause [*Anliegen*].'[49] Each student received a one-to-one lesson of two hours every week, including on public holidays if they desired, and Spahlinger himself gave two seminars each week of term, which were apparently continued in the pubs of Freiburg once the allotted time was over.[50] Kreidler paints an idyllic picture of Spahlinger's seminars, yet the composer's intense political and intellectual engagement is likely to have repelled as many as it attracted.

The relationship between Spahlinger and the academy is notable as it is part of a wider conception of the artist as intellectual that was highly influential in Germany. There was a particularly exalted place for artists within German society post-1918, as they were seen as 'mediators between German culture and the external world [...] very much on the level of culture what a chief of state or an ambassador is at the political level: *representatives* of their country'.[51] Jochen Vogt, in an Adornian vein, characterizes the post-Second World War situation as one in which intellectuals are 'outsiders and *at the same time* representatives of society itself',[52] referencing both their critical and representative functions. As Spahlinger was establishing himself, however, the importance of intellectuals in public debate was waning. The absence of such titanic figures as Adorno was noted, and there appeared not to be such intellectually and politically engaged figures as Heinrich Böll or Günter Grass among the younger generation. The phenomenon was even given a name, the 'Twilight of the Intellectuals' [*die Intellektuellendämmerung*], in an important collection of essays published in 1992.[53] This was in part due to circumstances around reunification: Andreas Huyssen, in an article that proclaims the 'failure' of the German intellectual, accuses them of 'repeated misreadings of events during the year of *Wende* ['turning point', i.e. unification]' and an 'inability to keep up with the pace of events, to provide cogent analysis, to function as a seismograph for the changes underway'.[54]

The conflation of artistic and intellectual circles provides some useful insights as criticisms of one can often usefully be applied to the other. Writing in 2003, Eric D. Weitz describes how German historiography favours class critique over other approaches, stating that 'the huge role of *Vergangenheitsbewältigung* has made it inordinately difficult to move out of the intellectual confines of Germany, to pose comparative issues seriously, to raise new perspectives', meaning that 'not only gender but all sorts of other categories and approaches disappear from the intellectual and political horizon'.[55] The sense that there is a correct, serious, and potentially modernist, tone in which to deal with the past has, for Weitz, become a constricting influence on thought that has led to a widespread conservatism. To the pressure of history might be added the fact that the Soviet bloc was on the doorstep of West German intellectuals, encouraging a protectionist rather than experimental outlook in these fields.

The relevance of tradition and history, and the corresponding seriousness with which German artists sought to engage such issues, can be seen as a factor in the particularly German reaction to, and understanding of, what were labelled 'postmodern' ideas in other countries. Joakim Tillman points to the significance of Habermas's views on postmodernity to this debate within music,[56] an important point considering that Habermas identifies the postmodern artistic viewpoint with neoconservative tendencies, stating that modernity is an 'incomplete project'.[57] A rejection of postmodern ideas in favour of a continuing modernism is, therefore, a key aspect of this German debate. Judith Ryan also describes how postmodernism within literature, as characterized by 'eclecticism, multiple intertextuality, and pastiche', arrived late in Germany and was approached only 'gingerly' in the decades after the Second World War.[58] This means that 'later modernist forms, with their emphasis on difficulty and their manifest challenges to the reader's intellect, became the accepted medium for serious literary reflection on the past', while the 'superficial ease and evident fun of the international postmodern movement seemed ill suited to this serious task'.[59] German novels of the 1950s and 1960s, categorized as postmodern by certain critics outside of Germany are, according to Ryan, understood within the German context as 'merely [...] moderner modern'.[60] The story of the reception of these postmodern ideas is important in understanding why the climate was so positive for continued modernist approaches. Spahlinger's rather dismissive description of the postmodern 'fashion' should be understood within this context.

In many ways, Spahlinger embodies the classic figure of the male German artist: an intellectual struggling against the weight of his own tradition. Saltzman, discussing Kiefer, provides a psychoanalytically influenced reading of such relationships with tradition and the 'fathers' of German culture: not for nothing is Peter Schneider's important novel in literary *Vergangenheitsbewältigung* called *Vati*, or 'Daddy' (1987). She goes further by linking this to 'the loss of ego ideals, those tainted and disavowed paternal signifiers, and with that, the loss of an ability to unselfconsciously articulate and embody a German identity'.[61] This was not made any easier by the post-war period in which the nation was literally split in two, giving a further, and rather literal, representation of psychic rupture. In a less psychoanalytical vein, Jarausch also observes that 'mounting self-criticism' among intellectuals created an 'emphatically negative conception of German identity'[62] as '"the nation" remained a rather traumatic point of reference'.[63]

The conclusions of these readings can be usefully applied to Spahlinger: in his continued interest in dialectical thinking, and the way he defines his music against motivic, teleological development, there are few composers more self-consciously steeped in the intellectual, philosophical and musical traditions of their country yet who so systematically attempt to negate its features: stifling 'tradition' is one of his key aims, thereby hinting at the 'loss' of an unselfconscious German identity that Saltzman and Jarausch describe. His continuity with past models is forced to be critical, a constant questioning, and self-questioning, as regards his cultural heritage. The opening of *passage/paysage* is a sort of smeared quotation from the Eroica Symphony, which the composer hopes brings to mind the – ultimately retracted – dedication to Napoleon Beethoven set on the opening page. Napoleon, as militaristic dictator, might well be read as a precursor to Hitler, while this reference is also symbolic of Spahlinger's engagement with, and deconstruction of, the Germanic tradition on a more abstract level of motives and 'modes of production': he eschews motivic development, triumphal climactic arrivals and looks to problematize the set-up of the orchestra. In critically re-evaluating the Germanic motivic tradition, puncturing its climactic moments and reconfiguring one of the main vehicles for its dissemination, Spahlinger's work also has something of the *Vergangenheitsbewältigung* about it, though the medium of music forces us to look past the surface subject matter, as well as the statements of the composer regarding the content of his pieces.

Mid- to Late Career

In 1992, Spahlinger completed his *vorschläge: konzepte zur ver(über)flüssigung der funktion des komponisten* (*suggestions: concepts for making the role of the composer superfluous*, 1993, trans. Blume), a short collection of musical situations primarily described in text and with no prescribed instrumentation and performable by groups of mixed ability. The concepts often describe how individual players should relate to the group in the creation of the music. For example, in 'own tempo' and 'own dynamic' each player must find an individual playing technique to express their own tempo and dynamic respectively, though this individuality is defined in its relation to the collective. The flexibility of the *suggestions* connects both to Spahlinger's work in music education, as well as to earlier socialist pieces that do not necessarily require performance by professional musicians. There is a sense that even in the writing of his fixed scores Spahlinger is composing only one possible outcome of his own conceptual directives, and it is this framework of concepts that he often connects to political and philosophical discourse. Though a small book, Kreidler describes it as a 'major work' which illuminates Spahlinger's wider compositional practice: it finds its orchestral expression in the much more recent *doppelt bejaht*.[64] Such pieces are not just about finding new ways of generating materials or exploring different methods of notation, they are part of a wider project of exploring the 'way music is made' as a realm of political critique. It also creates a perhaps surprising link between the composer and the experimental text scores that were popular among American Fluxus artists: Christian Wolff's *Burdocks* (1971) and Yoko Ono's *Grapefruit* (1964) are two well-known examples. As with the *suggestions*, many of these can also be performed by non-musicians, though their free-wheeling fantasy, in contrast to Spahlinger's carefully calculated musical and political ramifications, is telling in pointing to two quite distinct artistic directions.

The steady stream of pieces from Spahlinger's pen slows somewhat at the end of the 1990s, due in part to his work on the titanic *farben der frühe* (*morning colours*) for seven pianos, an extremely complex and, by all accounts, exceptionally demanding score. Work began in 1997 but the piece was not completed until 2005, though the not insignificant *akt, eine treppe herabsteigend* (*nude descending a staircase*, 1998) for bass clarinet, trombone and orchestra, and *verlorener weg* (*lost way/path*, both I and II from 2000) for ensemble were written in the intervening years. The late 1990s did, however, see the production of one of the most significant sources of the composer's thought, albeit one created in collaboration with another. *Geschichte der Musik als Gegenwart* (*Music History as a Facet of the Present*, trans. Blume) is the written transcript of 'historic' conversations between the composer and musicologist Hans Heinrich Eggebrecht,[65] the forerunners of which were seminars given by the two men at the Musikhochschule in Freiburg.[66] The resulting publication is the most comprehensive source of Spahlinger's thought, which has remained remarkably consistent throughout his development. Highlighted topics include Spahlinger's conception of musical history, the particular features of new music, musical time and, finally, his ideas of music as potentially utopian.[67]

In 2009, the 'orchestral environment' *doppelt bejaht – études für orchester* was premiered at the Donaueschinger Musiktage by the SWR Symphony Orchestra Baden Baden and Freiburg. The performance lasted four hours with the orchestral musicians working in shifts to occupy the performance stations, which were distributed around the space. The public were allowed to come and go as they pleased: the idea of the listener's perception forming the piece is key. The elimination of the conductor from the work is not only a musical but also a political statement, linking with a tradition of conductorless orchestral works, as well as Cage's negation of the interpretative role of the conductor in pieces like his Concert for Piano and Orchestra (1957). Spahlinger seeks to create conditions in which the orchestral musicians have increased control over decision-making processes, which – like human laws – are completed by finding agreement within the collective.[68] The practical challenges of this approach are severe and the success of these attempts will be discussed further in Chapter 5.

Recent years have seen premieres of *ausnahmslos ausnahmen* (*except without exception*, 2013) for solo drum kit, the guitar work *entfernte ergänzung* (*distant addition* or alternatively *remote extension*, 2012), the cello concerto *lamento, protokoll* (2008), and chamber works *still/moving* (2014), *nachtstück mit sonne* (*nocturne with sun*, 2015) and *faux faux bourdon* (2016), all pieces that show significant continuity with his previous artistic practice. In this project, however, the emphasis has been laid on his more established works, due to the fact that they are still under-represented in Anglophone scholarship and are widely recognized as significant parts of Spahlinger's artistic efforts. These milestones will provide a framework in which listeners can place his more recent musical offerings.

Before moving on to a more in-depth investigation of the composer's music, there is one further thread in twentieth-century German culture that gives an important insight into the nature of Spahlinger's aesthetic and political project: the particular nature of German sociology. Attempting to inform or challenge 'society', as described above, is a vital part of the engaged, intellectually active German artistic ideal. Discussing upon what assumptions this understanding is based, therefore, is a vital perspective on the artistic practice of this period.

Spahlinger and German Sociology

According to Alasdair King, the politically engaged Enzensberger believed that writing 'effectively' requires a 'sociological overview of the dynamics at work in German cultural practices at any given historical moment'.[69] King describes this understanding as being based 'largely on a traditional class analysis', which does not address 'potential and actual conflicts in German society deriving from the continuing inequalities in the Federal Republic based either on gender or ethnicity'.[70] These comments, it is argued here, can in fact be applied to a much wider range of German artists, with the consequences of this tendency felt right up to the present day. Not only are these artists likely to engage with societal issues, but this engagement is based on the contemporary German understanding of the subject of sociology. This is influenced heavily by sociological theory – as opposed to empiricism – that seeks to describe the structure and direction of society as a whole rather than particular cultural practices. Any political art is based upon a specific understanding of how society functions and the examination of sociology here is particularly helpful in coming to terms with the views of Spahlinger's modernist position. In particular, the composer's interest in a generalized 'perception' stems from this kind of analysis, while the Marxian, class-based view of society observed in 'this is the time of conceptive ideologues no longer' is directly linked.

German sociology post-Second World War, while very much part of an international conversation, retained certain unique characteristics. One of these features is a different conception of what constitutes social theory than, for example, their counterparts in the United States or the United Kingdom, with a greater freedom to speculate on empirical data than the latter would usually allow. This leads to Germany's most highly regarded sociologists being perceived abroad 'as philosophers or social and political theorists' concerned with the 'ethical, philosophical, and methodological foundations of social science'.[71] They are not, in other words, necessarily seen as sociologists. In their work questioning the 'methodological foundations of social science', Meja et al. identify a self-reflexive and self-questioning foundation at the base of German sociology that leads to regular fundamental evaluations of the entire field: a constant self-assessment that is influenced by the fact some sociologists carried out work that ultimately supported fascism.[72] A similar reflexive impulse has already been discussed in relation to culture. As with the modernist inheritance for Spahlinger and others, a critical, reflexive attitude is in evidence when sociologists negotiate their own sociological inheritance.

Receptivity to the critical theory of the Frankfurt School, many of whose major figures inhabit this area between political and social theorists and sociologists, is a crucial link between artistic practice and the sociological field. Critical theory's influence on sociology again promotes a more global understanding of society, regarded by some as a 'mixed blessing' due to its strong political overtones and theoretical component.[73] The role of empirical analysis in Adorno, for example, is to explore theoretical questions, as opposed to theory arising out of empirical studies. Frankfurt School thought places more emphasis on the 'system of society', forming a 'concept of the society and of the objectivity of social process and structure' leading to 'the development of rationalization in terms of a dialectical theory still inspired by Marx'.[74] Social Theory and societal totality are strongly linked in this viewpoint. Continuity also appears in discussions of rationalization – a concept made famous by the 'classical' German sociologist Max Weber – using a methodology that owes much to Marx, and indeed, by extension, Hegel. Marx, Hegel and Adorno, it should be noted, are also the thinkers at the heart of Spahlinger's aesthetic project.

The types of debates occurring in sociology should not be taken as completely separate from those in wider German society, or at least those occurring in the spheres of the *Intellektuellen*. As with modernist music, the audience for sociological debate in contemporary Germany, as well as the West Germany of the 1970s and 1980s, is significant, and sociologists were influential in shaping national debates: Meja et al. identify how 'widespread participation of sociologists in public debates and disputes' indicates a 'receptivity to and an audience for sociological ideas and sociologically informed opinion which is considerably broader than in many English-speaking countries'.[75] These are debates of which the artists discussed here will have been very much aware. Enzensberger, in his political and more theoretical writings, contributes to this particularly German union of sociology and political theory through an engagement with a politicized societal totality.

The consideration of society on such a global level is one reason why the questions of gender and ethnicity identified by King do not figure as much as those of class and power in post-Second World War German art. It is clear that even well-established currents in society, such as feminism – in which the personal is often brought into the realm of the political – might struggle to make an impression on this understanding, while personal, more lyrical expression might be excluded for similar reasons. Beate Kutschke, while discussing depictions of women in the work of Luigi Nono, describes an 'old leftist' viewpoint in which '[t]he emancipation of women would be achieved [...] within the frame of the workers' movement, as a by-product as it were of the *general* emancipatory means of a radical societal revolution'.[76] Though she describes a newer viewpoint emerging, a residue of these idea remains in modernist art in the period under discussion. The connection between the arts and sociology is crucial in understanding how German artists interacted with society and how their oppositional role as intellectuals was articulated. Such a global, class-based analysis informs the particular kind of social debate with which Spahlinger engages, one that confidently asserts class divides while also positing a shared musical experience in which there is homogeneity of composer and listener subjectivity.

Spahlinger's outlook, or *Weltbild*, is heavily influenced by these debates, which encourage a collective and theoretical, rather than individualized and empirical, understanding. In describing the persistence of a particular modernist perspective, therefore, the sociological influence is crucial. There is a parallel, too, in that German sociologists were mainly concerned with German society during this time, and from this created many of their theoretical ideas.[77] This resonates strongly with Spahlinger's musical theoretical writings, which are very much a product of a modernist, German new music scene, while at times appearing to speak for music in general.

Continuity and Reinvention in German Modernism

This chapter has traced various interconnected themes that run through Spahlinger's practice and post-Second World War German culture, with reactions to history, non-teleological views of progress, tradition and a global view of society all contributing to a continued modernist strain within his work. While reflections on the ambivalence of cultural heritage and the importance of tradition to contemporary debates will have been made all the more urgent by the historical situation, it is vital to understand the continuity of many of these concerns with those from earlier in the twentieth century. In critical theory, as in German sociology described above, strong elements of their previous traditions remain, though the critical edge – the need to constantly reassess the foundations upon which they stand – is strengthened all the more by the advent of fascism. In fact, there was already an established line of thought that doggedly questioned linear ideas of progress with Walter Benjamin's *Theses on the Philosophy of History*, written in 1940, and Adorno and Horkheimer's *Dialectic of Enlightenment* (first published 1944) challenging an unwavering belief in the enlightenment ideals and scientific thinking, while similar criticisms can be found in the work of Bauman, Foucault and Nietzsche.[78] Enzensberger, too, sought to 'discredit the myth of the holocaust as malignant excrescence on an otherwise healthy history', examining instead the '"hiccups of barbarism" within the framework of modernity, rejecting the notion that civilization is a linear process'.[79] Questions of Germany's historical progression were also central in the *Historikerstreit*, which arose from attempts by right-wing historians to frame the Holocaust as an event not qualitatively different from other historical mass murders, including the Allies' actions towards the end of the Second World War. This was intended to relieve to some extent the burden of guilt. A popular response to this argument was that of the *Sonderweg* ('special path'), which saw Germany as transitioning into democracy and modernity in a very particular way that made the advent of Nazism more likely.[80]

The suspicion of progress and an intense scepticism regarding shining solutions to humanity's problems is, therefore, firmly embedded in late twentieth-century culture, with the horrors of the holocaust giving particular relevance to these ideas in Spahlinger's Germany. Crucially, however, the critical standpoint from which these works are written did not spring out of thin air after the rise of Hitler. The continuity displayed by highly influential sociologists and social theorists goes some way to contextualizing the work of Spahlinger.

Many of the aspects of Spahlinger's approach that have been observed – a perhaps surprising continued reliance on aspects of critical theory; a keen engagement with society and politics through a class-based model; a self-confessed continuity with early twentieth-century models; a belief in a modernist musical language to express such political and philosophical ideas – can all be seen in wider currents in German arts. It is worth stressing that exceptions will certainly exist and that similar trends might be observed in other countries; yet, in the discussions of *Vergangenheitsbewältigung*, sociology and issues around Marxian class-based analysis, a particular German situation in artistic practice can be identified. It is this situation that has nurtured a continuing interest in modernism. In identifying such general trends, however, it is by no means the intention that Spahlinger should be labelled somehow a wholly typical or unoriginal figure. On the contrary, it is the individuality of his music, and of the situation of new music in general, that led to this discussion of how it might relate to wider German society and wider modernist ideas. In particular, it remains to be seen how his engagement with society functions in his pieces, rather than referring to the social analysis he delivers in 'this is the time'.

The discussion of sociology also raises an important question as to whether the critical thought that Spahlinger encourages masks a larger underlying continuity and whether the 'critical' attitude is in fact a contributing factor in creating a consistent artistic approach rather than facilitating an aesthetic sphere of continual reinvention. Critical thought is idealized in its attempt to perpetually interrogate its basis: like any attitude, its real-world manifestations are based upon particular assumptions. Yet, unlike some more positivist positions, it sees its duty as continually attempting to renew itself. This paradoxical relationship between reinvention and continuity has been observed throughout this chapter in artists' relationship with history and tradition, and the need for moving on despite a scepticism regarding progress. It is also a fundamental contradiction at the heart of Spahlinger's practice: critics see his attitude as an old-fashioned instantiation of critical thought, yet there are significant areas in which this approach yields important new understandings. For Spahlinger, faith in a now venerable modernist view of society is a source of continued renewal.

NOTES

1. Victor Klemperer, *Lingua Tertii Imperii: A Philologist's Notebook*, trans. Martin Brady (London: Athlone, 1999).

2. Giles Radice, *The New Germans* (London: Michael Joseph, 1995), 158.

3. Wolf Lepenies, *The Seduction of Culture in German History* (Oxford: Princeton University Press, 2006), 17.

4. The Allied Powers made concerted efforts to broaden the diet of concert and broadcast music in the post-war period, with each particularly keen to show the German people the musical achievements of their respective composers. See Toby Thacker, *Music after Hitler 1945–1955* (Aldershot: Ashgate, 2007), 23–29; and David Monod, *Settling Scores: German Music, Denazification, and the Americans, 1945–1953* (Chapel Hill: University of North Carolina Press, 2005).

5. See Martin Iddon, *New Music at Darmstadt* (Cambridge: Cambridge University Press, 2013), 126.

6. Robin Maconie, *Other Planets: The Music of Karlheinz Stockhausen* (Lanham, MD: Scarecrow Press, 2005), 39.

7. Reinhard Oehlschlägel, 'Radicality and Contradiction: Variations on Mathias Spahlinger', *Contemporary Music Review* 12 (1995): 85–91, 86.

8. Mathias Spahlinger, private correspondence with Neil Thomas Smith, 31 August 2016.

9. Ibid.

10. Oehlschlägel, 'Radicality and Contradiction', 86.

11. Ibid.

12. Mathias Spahlinger, 'Maßstäbe außer Kraft Setzen. Mathias Spahlinger im Gespräch mit Reinhard Oehlschlägel', *Musik Texte* 95 (2002): 73–79, 77.

13. Ibid., 79.

14. Mathias Spahlinger, interview with Neil Thomas Smith, 11 August 2014, Groß Glienicke. Recording: unarchived.

15. Mathias Spahlinger, private correspondence with Neil Thomas Smith, 31 August 2016.

16. Rainer Nonnenmann, '"dass etwas anders im Anzug ist"; Mathias Spahlingers individualisierte Orchesterkollektive', *Musik-Konzepte* 155 (2012): 47–74, 57–58; for further discussion of the early jazz movement within Germany, see Andrew Wright Hurley, *The Return of Jazz: Joachim-Ernst berendt and West German Cultural Change* (Oxford: Berghahn Books, 2009), 15–34.

17. Spahlinger, interview with Neil Thomas Smith, 11 August 2014.

18. Nonnenmann, 'dass etwas anders im Anzug ist', 58.

19. Spahlinger, interview with Neil Thomas Smith, 11 August 2014.

20. See Robert W. Witkin, 'Why Did Adorno "Hate" Jazz?', *Sociological Theory* 18, no. 1 (2000): 145–70.

21. Spahlinger in Nonnenmann, 'dass etwas anders im Anzug ist', 58.

22. Mathias Spahlinger, '"Ich sehe im Free Jazz … die fortgeschrittenste Entwicklung" Mathias Spahlinger im Gespräch', *MusikTexte*, 86, no. 87 (2000): 62–65.

23. Martin Iddon, 'The Haus That Karlheinz Built: Composition, Authority, and Control at the 1968 Darmstadt Ferienkurse', *Musical Quarterly* 87, no. 1 (2004): 87–118, 89.

24. Beate Kutschke, 'Anti-Authoritarian Revolt by Musical Means on Both Sides of the Berlin Wall', in *Music and Protest in 1968*, ed. Beate Kutschke and Barley Norton (Cambridge: Cambridge University Press, 2013), 188–204, 188.

25. Spahlinger, interview with Neil Thomas Smith, 11 August 2014.

26. Richard J. Evans, *In Hitler's Shadow: West German Historians and the Attempt to Escape from the Nazi Past* (London: Tauris, 1989), 11.

27. David Art, *The Politics of the Nazi Past in Germany and Austria* (Cambridge: Cambridge University Press, 2006), 9.

28. Robert G. Moeller, *War Stories: The Search for a Usable Past in the Federal Republic of Germany* (London: University of California Press, 2003), 173. See also Norbert Frei, *Adenauer's Germany and the Nazi Past: The Politics of Amnesty and Integration* (New York: Columbia University Press, 2002).

29. Vicki Lawrence, '*Vergangenheitsbewältigung*: Coming to Terms with the Nazi Past', *Agni* 48 (1998): 100–14, 100. See also Peter Arnds, 'On the Awful German Fairy Tale: Breaking Taboos in Representations of Nazi Euthanasia and the Holocaust in Günter Grass's "Die Blechtrommel", Edgar Hilsenrath's "Der Nazi & der Friseur", and Anselm Kiefer's Visual Art', *German Quarterly* 75, no. 4 (2002): 422–39; Judith Ryan, 'Postmodernism as "Vergangenheitsbewältigung,"' *German Politics & Society* 27 (1992): 12–24; Stephanie D'Alessandro, 'History by Degrees: The Place of the Past in Contemporary German Art', *Art Institute of Chicago Museum Studies* 28, no. 1 (2002): 66–81 and 110–11; and Susan G. Figge and Jennifer K. Ward (eds.), *Reworking the German Past: Adaptations in Film, the Arts, and Popular Culture* (Rochester: Camden House, 2013).

30. Arnds, 'On the Awful German Fairy Tale', 422–39.

31. Lawrence, '*Vergangenheitsbewältigung*: Coming to Terms with the Nazi Past', 100–14.

32. Andreas Huyssen, *After the Great Divide: Modernism, Mass Culture, Postmodernism* (Basingstoke: Macmillan, 1988), 95–114.

33. Konrad H. Jarausch, *After Hitler: Recivilizing the Germans, 1945–1995*, trans. Brandon Hunziker (Oxford: Oxford University Press, 2006), 96.

34. See Mary Cosgrove, *Born under Auschwitz: Melancholy Traditions in Postwar German Literature* (Rochester: Camden House, 2014), 1.

35. See Ryan, 'Postmodernism as "Vergangenheitsbewältigung"', 12–24; Joakim Tillman, 'Postmodernism and Art Music in the German Debate', in *Postmodern Music/Postmodern Thought*, eds. Judy Lochhead and Joseph Auner (London: Routledge, 2002), 75–91; and Jürgen Habermas, 'Modernity – An Incomplete Project', in *Postmodern Culture*, ed. Hal Foster (London: Pluto Press, 1985): 3–15.

36. Lisa Saltzman, *Anselm Kiefer and Art after Auschwitz* (Cambridge: Cambridge University Press, 1999), 5.

37. In the post-war German context, the most significant examples are the collaborative cantata *Jüdische Chronik* (1960) organized by East German composer Paul Dessau that includes contributions from Karl Amadeus Hartmann, Boris Blacher and Hans Werner Henze; and, among other works by this composer, Luigi Nono's *Ricorda cosa ti hanno fatto ad Auschwitz* (*Remember what they did to you at Auschwitz*, 1966), which began as incidental music to Peter Weiss's holocaust drama *Die Ermittlung* ('The Investigation', 1965). This play is also the basis for Frederic Rzewski's *Triumph of Death* (see Beate Kutschke, '"Holocaust Heroizations" in Avant-Garde Music' [paper presented at the International Conference on Music since 1900 at the University of Glasgow, UK, September 2015]).

38. See Ian Pace, 'The Reconsturction of Post-War West German New Music during the Early Allied Occupation (1945–46), and Its Roots in the Weimar Republic and Third Reich (1918–45)' (PhD thesis, Cardiff University, unpublished), 360.

39. See Alastair Williams, *Music in Germany since 1968* (Cambridge: Cambridge University Press, 2013).

40. See Heinz-Klaus Metzger, *Musik wozu Literatur zu Noten*, ed. Rainer Riehn (Frankfurt am Main: Suhrkamp, 1980), in particular 'Es bleibt beim Musikalischen Fascismus'; and Hans G. Helms, *Fetisch Revolution: Marxismus und Bundesrepublik* (Darmstadt: Luchterhand, 1973).

41. Werner M. Grimmel, 'ausbrechen: Der Komponist Gerhard Stäbler', *Neue Zeitschrift für Musik* 160, no. 1 (1999): 45–47.

42. Eggebrecht and Spahlinger, *Geschichte der Musik als Gegenwart*, 86.

43. Häusler in Dorothea Ruthemeier, *Antagonismus oder Konkurrenz? Zu zentralen Werkgruppen der 1980er Jahre von Wolfgang Rihm und Mathias Spahlinger* (Schliengen: Edition Argus, 2012), 384.

44. Spahlinger in Ruthemeier, *Antagonismus oder Konkurrenz?*, 103.

45. See Neil Thomas Smith, 'Mathias Spahlinger's *passage/paysage* and the "Barbarity of Continuity"', *Contemporary Music Review* 34, nos. 2–3 (2015): 176–86.

46. Oehlschlägel, 'Radicality and Contradiction', 89.

47. Markus Hechtle, *198 Fenster zu einer imaginierten Welt* (Saarbrücken: Pfau-Verlag, 2005), 96.

48. Oehlschlägel, 'Radicality and Contradiction', 86.

49. Johannes Kreidler, 'Mathias Spahlingers Zumutungen; Gegen Unendlich und gegen Krieg', *Musik-Konzepte* 155 (2012): 23–30, 27.

50. Ibid.

51. Emphasis in original. Louis Dumont, *Essays on Individualism* (Chicago: University of Chicago Press, 1986), 152.

52. Emphases in original. Jochen Vogt, 'Have the Intellectuals Failed? On the Sociopolitical Claims and the Influence of Literary Intellectuals in West Germany', trans. Stephen Brockmann, *New German Critique* 58 (1993): 3–23, 4.

53. Martin Meyer (ed.), *Intellektuellendämmerung* (Munich: Hanser, 1992).

54. Andreas Huyssen, 'After the Wall: The Failure of German Intellectuals', *New German Critique* 52 (1991): 109–43, 110.

55. Eric D. Weitz, 'Still Two Trains Passing in the Night? Labor and Gender in German Historiography', *International Labor and Working-Class History* 63 (2003): 32–36, 35.

56. Joakim Tillman, 'Postmodernism and Art Music in the German Debate', in *Postmodern Music/Postmodern Thourght*, eds. Judy Lochhead and Joseph Auner (London: Routledge, 2001), 75.

57. Jürgen Habermas, 'Modernity – An Incomplete Project', in *Postmodern Culture*, ed. Hal Foster (London: Pluto Press, 1985), 7.

58. Judith Ryan, 'Postmodernism as "Vergangenheitsbewältigung"', *German Politics & Society* 27 (1992): 12–24, 12–14.

59. Ibid., 14.

60. Christine Brooke-Rose in ibid., 13.

61. Saltzman, *Anselm Kiefer and Art after Auschwitz*, 94.

62. Jarausch, *After Hitler*, 65.

63. Ibid., 69.

64. Kreidler, 'Mathias Spahlingers Zumutungen', 27.

65. Philipp Blume, 'Preface: Music of Nicolaus A. Huber and Mathias Spahlinger', *Contemporary Music Review* 27, no. 6 (2008): 561–63, 563.

66. That history is a contemporary issue in Germany is further indicated by the debate around Eggebrecht's own activities during the Second World War. See Anne C. Schreffler, Boris von Haken and Christopher Browning, 'Musicology, Biography, and National Socialism: The Case of Hans Heinrich Eggebrecht', *German Studies Review* 35, no. 2 (2012): 289–318.

67. For an English summary, see Petra Musik, 'The Rest Is History – Mathias Spahlinger and Hans Heinrich Eggebrecht on Utopia in New Music', *Contemporary Music Review* 27, no. 6 (2008): 665–72.

68. Eggebrecht and Spahlinger, *Geschichte der Musik als Gegenwart*, 22.

69. Alasdair King, *Hans Magnus Enzensberger: Writing, Media, Democracy* (Bern: Peter Lang, 2007), 321.

70. Ibid., 331.

71. Volker Meja, Dieter Misgeld and Nico Stehr, 'Introduction', in *Modern German Sociology*, ed. Misgeld Stehr Meja (New York: Columbia University Press, 1987), 6.

72. Ibid., 21.

73. Ibid., 14.
74. Ibid., 17.
75. Ibid., 4.
76. Emphasis in original. Beate Kutschke, 'Le Donne in Rivolta o La Rivolta Femminile?', in *Musikkulturen in der Revolte*, ed. Beate Kutschke (Stuttgart: Franz Steiner, 2008): 141–52, 147.
77. Meja et al., 'Introduction', ix.
78. King, *Hans Magnus Enzensberger*, 202.
79. Catherine Nichols, 'Looking Back at the End of the World: Hans Magnus Enzensberger on 1989 and the Millenium', *Monatshefte* 92, no. 4 (2000): 412–44, 423.
80. For a more detailed discussion of these issues, see Richard J. Evans, *In Hitler's Shadow*; and Jarausch, *After Hitler*, 74–77.

PART 2

3

Musique Concrète Instrumentale

One of the most recognizable tendencies in German music of the late 1960s is that of *musique concrète instrumentale*, a term strongly associated with – but, according to Spahlinger, not exclusive to – its inventor, Helmut Lachenmann. It is a renewal of modernist ambitions, though one quite different from the high tide of serial thinking in the 1950s. As such, it is a vital component of the German music scene into which Spahlinger entered and to which he contributed, while its influence is still part of new music today. The relevance of *musique concrète instrumetale* to the composer will be investigated here from two different angles. The first relates to the direct influence of this music, which is evident in his works from the 1970s and 1980s. The second focuses on what the composer considers its primary revolutionary achievement, that is, the introduction of noise as viable musical material, which has a wide-ranging impact on his entire oeuvre. The composer has never stated that he *is a musique concrète instrumentale* composer as such, yet in his writings he does state that it is a significant achievement of new music, while his pieces display its importance in forming his musical language. If, as Spahlinger contends, *musique concrète instrumentale* has a more general meaning than simply referring to Lachenmann's music, his early work would be a prime contender for inclusion. Kreidler appears to agree, as he describes Spahlinger's 'turn away' from *musique concrète instrumentale* during the 1990s, thereby implying his teacher's former adherence.[1] In discussing the composer's relationship to this phenomenon, the term itself comes under scrutiny: is it simply a placeholder for the work of Lachenmann or does a more general compositional strategy emerge from its concerns? The traces of this approach will be discussed with reference to a number of important chamber works from across Spahlinger's career, as well as a discussion of the related concept of mechanical repetition. Finally, an examination of the rhetorical justifications for *musique concrète instrumentale* will point to some similarities with the composer's own position. First, however, a more detailed consideration of the term and its notational manifestations is required with reference to its originator Lachenmann.

1. Defining the Term

Musique concrète instrumentale is a term that resists any definitive definition, but it is perhaps best described as a compositional and philosophical attitude, one with results too diverse to fit into an overarching musical style or compositional technique. Blume, in a succinct attempt at definition mentioned in Chapter 1, states that it is 'a notion and a set of techniques that regard sound not as an abstract vehicle for musical ideas in the traditional sense of motivic development, but as the by-product of physical work, of the tension and release of human effort'.[2] In the programme note to *Pression*, which is considered a 'locus classicus' of the genre,[3] Lachenmann states that what is meant by '"instrumental *musique concrète*" [...] is music in which the acoustic events are chosen and organised so that one includes the way in which the sounds are created, as much as the resulting acoustic characteristics themselves, in the musical experience'. This means that 'timbre, volume etc. do not sound for their own sake, rather they indicate or signal the concrete situation: one listens to them, and hears with which energies and against which resistances a sound is brought into being'.[4] The most immediate consequence of this approach is a huge expansion in permissible playing techniques, which often require players to use instruments in ways their makers would never have foreseen. Less immediate, yet still noteworthy, is its philosophical and political justification: since its inception in the 1960s, these works have been framed by aesthetic thought that owes much to Frankfurt School philosophy in its attempted critical position in relation to society. According to Frank Sielecki, 'for Lachenmann the politicization of his compositions seems to coincide with the beginning of *musique concrète instrumentale*'.[5]

Most obviously, the term is an appropriation of Pierre Schaeffer's *musique concrète*, which was used as a label for a school of, primarily French, electroacoustic composition that employed real-world sounds as compositional material. Lachenmann states that Schaeffer 'uses life's everyday noises or sounds, recorded and put together by collage' and that he 'tried to apply this way of thinking, not with the sounds of daily life, but with our instrumental potentialities'.[6] Early pieces by Lachenmann clearly present such a collage of non-traditional playing techniques, a noteworthy aspect of his compositional technique when comparing him with Spahlinger. The 'instrumental potentialities' here are not those of typical, beautiful instrumental tone, nor are they a collage of differing musical styles which sometimes characterize *musique concrète* pieces. Often, they are sounds that are ignored in traditional musical discourse: the brushing of the left hand over the strings as it makes a large leap, or the initial bite of the bow on the string. These are then taken as the essential material of a work.

The idea of 'defamiliarizing' sounds from their sources is a particularly powerful parallel between Lachenmann and Schaeffer's music. The latter's idea of 'acousmatic' listening, in which sounds are to be listened to not in terms of their source but solely through their aural properties, is transferred onto the realm of instrumental music. Defamiliarization in Lachenmann should in fact be achieved almost by an inversion of Schaeffer's idea: the source – the musical instrument – is the centre of attention but the sounds produced go against all expectations. Were they heard without the visual confirmation of their origin they would often be difficult to attribute to any particular instrument. However, Schaeffer's intended concentration on the aural plane should also be present in Lachenmann as the listener is invited to explore an unfamiliar sonic landscape, without traditional instrumental tone as a means of orientation. Both composers can be seen to problematize the sound/source relationship.

Frank Hillberg, in his study of noise in Lachenmann's music, in fact, argues that 'the "concrète" refers to the starting point of the composition and is not an attribute of the material'.[7] He describes Schaeffer's view that the traditional compositional process – an expression of the mind; its trace in a score; and its performance by another person – is 'abstract'. By contrast, the *concrète* method comprises 'appropriation of the material – experiments or sketches – material composition'.[8] Schaeffer's definition of *concrète* is then a 'hands-on', sculptural attitude to material, which eventually leads to the finished object of the piece. In this light, there is in fact quite a fundamental difference between Lachenmann's conception of *musique concrète instrumentale* and its electronic predecessor: in Schaeffer's terms, he is still often composing in the abstract as he never renounces precompositional, post-serial calculation.[9] Yet, the 'hands-on' method does translate to the physical, exploratory nature of Lachenmann's music, which is an often overlooked aspect of its expressive power.[10] Later, Lachenmann questioned the adequacy of the compositional techniques employed by *musique concrète* composers,[11] indicating that he does not fully endorse their musical results. Yet, the influence during this period is undeniable, fossilized as it is in his own musical term. Despite their differences, Schaeffer's influence on Lachenmann is still a significant example of the way electronic music has influenced the realm of the 'purely' acoustic in the twentieth century.

Finally, it is important to note that many of the ideas of *musique concrète instrumentale*, such as noisy sounds and unconventional playing techniques, did not spring out of thin air into Lachenmann's pen. A number of composers were experimenting with extended string techniques in particular: Michael von Biel's String Quartet no. 2 (1963) includes a good deal of gritty over-bowing and is a work that Lachenmann apparently admired;[12] while the more theatrically orientated music of Mauricio Kagel also strayed into this territory. Somewhat more peripheral to the German context but also significant are composers such as Iannis Xenakis, György Ligeti, Sylvano Bussotti (who again displays a more overt theatricality[13]) and the sonoristic work of Krzysztof Penderecki. The features explored here are, therefore, present in a large number of works of the period, some of which are now overlooked,[14] yet it is undeniable that the extent to which Lachenmann integrates these techniques into his musical approach, and his ability to exploit their nuances, is unparalleled. Part of this achievement rests on his notational ingenuity, which is a response to the challenges of representing noisier timbres.

Noise and Notation

Technique and sounding result are bound together by particular expressive 'energies' in Lachenmann's approach, leading to many sounds that contain a high noise component. This presents some pressing issues regarding notation, as traditional stave notation can capture neither the complex timbres of the composer's music, nor give instructions for the new movement parameters many techniques contain. These are the issues that lead to the detailed unconventional notation of Lachenmann's scores, which are a striking visual expression of the composer's approach. His solution is to employ an elaborate system of 'action notation', in which the *technique* is described rather than its intended sounding result.[15] This is in itself nothing new: Spahlinger points out that the sustain pedal in piano literature is but one historically grounded example,[16] guitar tablature being another. These two conventional examples are notational shortcuts that define only traditional aspects of instrumental technique; the novelty of Lachenmann's approach is to break out of these traditional idioms. The result in this instance is idiomatic writing taken to the extreme as playing this piece on a different instrument would be at worst impossible and at best produce a complete change in its character.

How Lachenmann's notational approach functions is best expressed by a short example (see Figure 3.1). Perhaps the greatest difference between this and traditional notation is its complication of the conventional relationship between pitch and the vertical plane. Since its earliest forms, Western notation has connected the y-axis of the stave with pitch, yet here the cello clef refers not to a general tessitura but to the physical properties of the cello: the four strings, which, as the dotted lines indicate, are displayed horizontally; the fingerboard and – in the second stave – the bridge are also depicted so that the actions of the performer, rather than the resulting changes in sound, can be described. The relationship between the vertical plane and pitch is not dispensed with entirely, however, as the parts of the instrument that produce higher pitches remain at the top. Additional directions are given in the lower half of the stave, instructing the performer to rub the

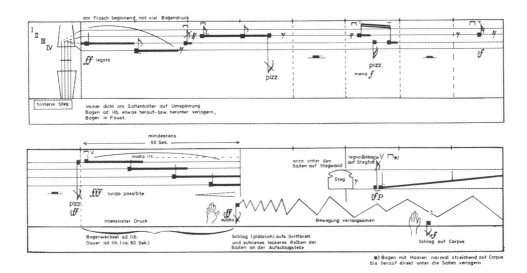

FIGURE 3.1: *Pression* by Helmut Lachenmann, page 4.

These examples are taken from the older edition of *Pression*, which the publisher says has now been superseded. As the emphasis here is on the period around its composition, however, the older edition has been used.

strings of the instrument with the left hand and hit the wooden body. The physicality of the performance is manifest in the notation. A *scordatura* is also in place
so that the gently affirmative sound of open fifths is avoided:[17] the conventional
sound of the instrument is circumvented through a change of its 'default settings'
in addition to unconventional techniques.

The notational ingenuity displayed here is a far from trivial element in *musique
concrète instrumentale*'s influence, it is a vital part of Lachenmann's approach
alongside extended techniques and its relationship with noise. It is also an
important aspect of the composer's international reception, powerfully presenting
his aesthetic approach, even as he himself uses increasingly conventional notation as his career progresses. From the above discussion, the defining features of
Lachenmann's *musique concrète instrumentale* can be condensed into three particular aspects: (1) a new-found focus on *techniques* of producing sound and their
inherent physicality or 'resistance' and – to communicate these techniques – an
increasingly refined use of notation; (2) an emphasis on *Klang* (sound) and particularly upon controlling noise to create musical material; and (3) a provocative attitude towards the listener and traditional categories of listening.[18] The third point
will be taken up in more detail at the end of this chapter. While all three remain
important, it will be shown that the emphasis shifts over time in Spahlinger's music,
as indeed it does in the work of Lachenmann.

Musique Concrète Instrumentale *and Spahlinger*

The direct musical influence of *musique concrète instrumentale* on Spahlinger is displayed most readily by his *entlöschend* for large tam-tam (literally: 'un-erasing', trans. Philipp Blume, 1974). The piece is a particularly good fit as Stockhausen's *Mikrophonie I* (also for tam-tam, as well as microphones and filters, 1964) can be seen as an important forerunner of Lachenmann's approach. All three of the fundamental features of *musique concrète instrumentale* described above are evident in *entlöschend*'s score. First, it uses a wide range of techniques and implements to produce sound, showing an emphasis on different techniques similar to early Lachenmann. Second, it is a prolonged timbral exploration of the possibilities of the instrument that formally consists of a collage-like succession of different sounds and soundworlds. Finally, the fact that it is an entire piece for the still rather unusual solo tam-tam, which is scraped and struck with the everday implements indicated in Figure 3.2, can be seen as maintaining a provocative attitude towards traditional practices of the concert hall with its focus on clarity and, arguably, beauty. Such responses were very much *en vogue* during the time, as borne out by Lachenmann's writings.[19]

Unlike Lachenmann's early works, however, no definitive score exists for this piece, which was first performed by the composer from rough notes that served to jog the memory rather than fully explicate the intricacies of the techniques. These notes still make for a rather evocative document. In Figure 3.2, there appear to be two sections IV and V, with the first consisting of a list of ways in which the tam-tam can be brought to sound, including brushes, a comb, various uses of the hand and a bow. As with classic *musique concrète instrumentale* pieces, technique is paramount.

The form of the piece is defined heavily by these different means of bringing the instrument into vibration. An astonishing range of timbres is coaxed, or sometimes forced, from the metal surface of the tam-tam. Particularly noteworthy are the various sonic spaces the piece creates, from huge resonant chasms out of which individual partials arise to closely brittle noises that are scraped from the metal surface. These different timbral territories occur one after the other without any strong sense of narrative or repetition. From the middle of the piece, more sustained sounds are created by continual grating or rubbing against the metal, building to the conclusion, at which point colossal attacks are partially damped to give concentrated and varied resonances. There is a curious air of domesticity around the collection of objects used to excite the instrument, one that contrasts markedly with the soundworld. Aside from those already mentioned, a hammer, pliers and a nail, a kitchen plate, a knitting needle, an iron file and a handheld window cleaner are all employed. Again, this leads to the impression that the

FIGURE 3.2: *entlöschend*, sketch.

instrument is being thoroughly examined, here with whatever materials the composer had to hand.

A second version of the piece was prepared with Christian Dierstein of Ensemble Recherche for their 1998 disc, which, while a little tidier, is still not an attempt to make the piece playable without instruction from the composer. Spahlinger states that in this latter attempt to create a score he realized that the boundary between composition and improvisation had been 'overstepped',[20] suggesting that he felt the amount of instruction required to exactly define all the actions in this piece would be too great and that it is best left with certain quasi-improvisatory elements. This decision on Spahlinger's part marks an important departure from Lachenmann, in whose work there is a contrasting attempt to define his repertoire of 'sounds and actions' with as much precision as possible.

The score of *entlöschend*, which could conceivably have been subject to the kind of detailed instructions of a score like Lachenmann's *Pression*, is left as a high point of *musique concrète instrumentale* in Spahlinger's practice as relates to the first point above, the focus on technique and its notation. None of his major pieces return to this kind of narrative and later quasi-improvisatory works take a very different approach. While he certainly uses extended techniques throughout much of his later music, it is rare for him to focus on these with quite the same energy as displayed here. However, even when technique is not explored in such depth, the soundworld of *musique concrète instrumentale* pieces is still very much in evidence in Spahlinger's works from the late 1970s and 1980s, even if he has left elements of its musical logic behind. This is most obvious in the works including voice, such as *vier stücke* for voice and chamber ensemble (1975), *128 erfüllte augenblicke* (1976) and *música impura* for voice, guitar and percussion (1983). In all these, unconventional, often noisy and brash instrumental techniques are very much in evidence.

That vocal pieces are a cornerstone of the *musique concrète instrumentale* repertoire relates at least as far back as one of Lachenmann's pivotal early works: *temA* for flute, cello and voice (1968). The voice parts of this period appear to have been fundamental in moulding Spahlinger's rather expressionistic approach to vocal writing, one characterized by wide leaps, breath noises, spoken text, cries and atomized text setting. In this, both Spahlinger and Lachenmann were significantly influenced by Luigi Nono.[21]

For Spahlinger in particular, the earliest *musique concrète instrumentale* pieces mark the zenith of a focus on technique, while the second and third aspects of the approach retain their importance. For example, point three – the provocative attitude towards the listener – can be seen in Spahlinger's interest in perception. Of all three aspects, however, it is the emphasis on *Klang*, and particularly the introduction of noisy material, that is for him of primary importance, and it is this that Spahlinger focuses on in his own descriptions of *musique concrète instrumentale*'s revolutionary potential.[22]

Noise and Mechanical Repetition

Mechanical repetition is a distinct area of interest from *musique concrète instrumentale* for Spahlinger, yet it finds its beginnings around the same time and in the same pieces. Both were made possible by the employment of noise as musical material and the exploration of *Klang* in pieces of the late 1960s. This, Spahlinger argues, opens up any kind of sound from the world for use as music. The composer's definition of noise is material that is 'not defined as musical from the outset',[23] thereby setting up a noise/music binary of which Lachenmann too is aware.[24] He also explains that noise is 'n-dimensional' by which he means its parameters cannot be brought into a hierarchical order in the manner of pitch or rhythm, which can be arranged on spectra of high versus low, or short versus long. Noise, he maintains, is an 'anarchic' force in music.[25] This latter description of course provides a frisson of rule-breaking attractive to a radical composer but it is useful in overcoming the often pejorative connotations that noise implies: considering noise as inherently anti-musical is one of the very preconceptions Lachenmann and others set out to dispel. Although Spahlinger in some ways sets out to musicalize noise, that is, to bring it into his musical discourse, it is clear that this anarchic quality can never be fully 'domesticated'. In a similar vein, Lachenmann states that if he hears a car crash, he will 'hear maybe some rhythms or some frequencies' but does not say 'Oh, what interesting sounds!' but rather 'What happened?' Listening from this perspective is what he calls *musique concréte instrumentale*.[26] At the same time, however, Lachenmann does set out to create a syntax of noises, most significantly in his 'Klangtypen der neuen Musik' (1966), with no attempt made by Spahlinger to do the same.[27]

At the opening of the latter's piano concerto *inter-mezzo* (1986), for example, the percussionist knocks a whole stand of cymbals onto the floor: a dramatic gesture certainly, and also one in which 'real-world' sounds and actions intrude on the musical. The same sense of interruption is present in *el sonido silencioso* (1973–80) in which a pre-recorded scream punctures the hermeticism of the concert hall, while *in dem ganzen ocean von empfindungen eine welle absondern, sie anhalten* (1985) contains a continued dialogue between musical and non-musical sounds and gestures.[28] Noisy material for Spahlinger often resists its immediate musical context.

The introduction of noise into the musical sphere is of course not without precedent. Peter Niklas Wilson cites both the Futurists and Edgard Varèse as important figures in the 'emancipation of noise',[29] while Spahlinger also mentions the industrial sounds of Alexander Mosolov's *Iron Foundry* (1927),[30] which is a triumphant paean to technological progress complete with blaring horns and piercing anvils. To this should be added Cage's rather different aestheticization of noise, which was very much part of the conversation at this time. The Futurists' zealous belief in technical progress and a new art based purely on noise was a striking development, though Spahlinger argues that this innovation did not transfer to the sphere of compositional technique, an area in which Varèse is said to be rather more nuanced.[31] Spahlinger's early orchestral work *morendo* (1975) stands as a critical counterbalance to Mosolov's factory soundscape. The experience of his typesetting apprenticeship did not leave him with an unequivocally positive view of technological development, and machines in particular, and this piece attempts to express a more dialectical viewpoint than his Russian Futurist counterpart. The composer himself makes no mention of this backstory in his programme note, though, as mentioned in Chapter 2, this is far from unusual.

morendo begins like a great clanking machine in motion with whistles and rattles, seemingly articulating the various sounds emitted by the constituent parts of an imaginary contraption. The mechanism attempts to repeat, but is not running smoothly, as the rhythmic displacements and unexpected silences show. Over the work's duration sounds are removed, or 'die out', as this aural machine comes to a less-than-peaceful rest. The extinction implied in the title, *morendo* ('dying away'), relates not only to the dispersion of energy in the work but is, according to Rainer Nonnenmann, an industrial swansong for the position of typesetter, which was gradually made redundant by advances in computer technology.[32] Considering the composer's father encouraged the apprenticeship on the grounds of long-term employability, it is a rather cruel irony that the job of composer and teacher has proved more secure.

As well as displaying the importance of noisy techniques to Spahlinger's music, *morendo* introduces at a very early stage the importance of mechanical repetition. This does not just appear in this work but is present in the majority of his pieces, though usually not as the central idea and not in the illustrative manner Nonnenmann identifies here. *éphémère* for piano and three percussionists (1977), for example, contains a long section of altered repetitions in a similar vein to *morendo* (see Figure 3.3). This is what Brian Kane identifies in his phenomenological analysis as 'a cyclic pattern that repeats again and again, without allowing me to form a clear *gestalt*. I can't quite grasp its beginning or its ending, I don't know how to parse it into a unity'.[33] This is an example of the search for order or unity explored in the next chapter.

That each cycle is slightly altered is important in that it shows how Spahlinger's interest in mechanical repetition rarely includes exact reproductions of the same musical figure, an important point in his critical view of minimalism. *éphémère* also continues the composer's exploration of 'real-world' sounds, with the percussionists described in the score as playing *veritable instrumente*. In a similar vein to the objects used in *entlöschend*, these include a cooking timer, alarm clock, kettle, wooden, plastic and steel rulers, and various nails and screws. Yet, importantly here, these are brought into dialogue with more traditional 'musical' sounds from the percussion and piano, at times to comic effect rather rare in the composer's music.

Another important contrast the piece explores is between regular repetitive, almost groove-like, rhythms and short bursts of rhythmic activity that cannot fit within any rhythmic scaffold, the latter including ping-pong balls coming to rest, rulers vibrating against tables or, rather more conservatively, trills. At first, these are explored in tentative phrases interspersed with long silences, with different instruments looping asynchronous materials. Some more sustained resonances are provided by soft piano chords, while the ensuing 'piano solo' is an introverted passage, using primarily harmonics. This precedes the repetitive cycles discussed above, which are then interrupted from two very different perspectives. First, certain 'fluxus' elements are introduced, such as hitting the floor with a large rope,

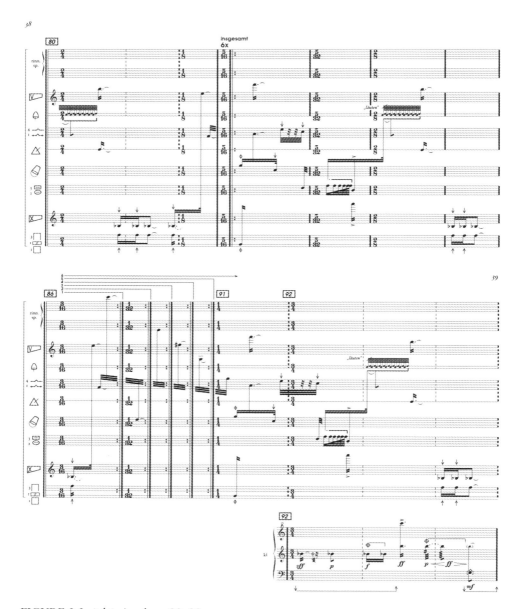

FIGURE 3.3: *éphémère*, bars 80–92.

throwing sweets into the audience, taking a photograph and holding aloft large signs on which 'PENG' and 'Aaaaa' are written.[34] Second, there is what in performance can be over five minutes of repeated rimshots on a snare drum, an intentionally provocative gesture that completely overhauls the formal proportions of the piece experienced thus far. The provocation of a piece like *éphémère* is, therefore, not only present in the sounds employed but in its form and theatrical elements.

This piece is typical of Spahlinger's works, however, in that it regularly contains moments in which mechanical repetition surfaces for a period before disappearing. Indeed, when it appears in larger pieces such as *passage/paysage* or his choral works, such material can be of quite secondary importance. The widespread recurrence of these mechanical repetitions is notable, considering what Spahlinger identifies as the revolutionary aspect of this material: that it is 'practically endless' as 'one cannot identify the beginning of a loop or of a wheel'.[35] This suggests that short references to it are intended to point towards infinity, to an impossible concept. Yet, the recurrence of these moments also speaks of a more positive relation for the composer, a simple penchant for this material to which he returns so often. As seen regarding Spahlinger's negative, critical attitude, there is little room in his artistic vision of new music for such whims of preference, indicating this is a significant area in which theory and practice might be seen to diverge. This theme will be taken up again in relation to the materials that repeatedly appear when he explores open form. Certainly, the appearance of mechanically repeating musical moments is a characteristic of many of the composer's works, one that first came to prominence with the 'emancipation of noise' brought about by *musique concrète instrumentale*.

The Musique Concrète Instrumentale Surface

It was argued above that *entlöschend* was a high point of *musique concrète instrumentale*'s collage-like structure in Spahlinger's music. It remains to be seen, therefore, how his continued use of these techniques works within his later pieces. Three will be briefly considered here to give an account of his approach: the string quartet *apo do* (1982); *música impura* for soprano, guitar and percussion; and *furioso* for large ensemble (1991). First, however, it is worth noting the most obvious influence is far less remarked upon in comparison to Spahlinger's self-identified interest in mechanical repetition and the anarchic potential of noise. This lies in the surface characteristics of almost all his pieces. His music rarely has a smooth exterior, either in the sense of a classical transparency, or in the sometimes disembodied sounds of certain examples of 1950s modernism. Rather, his instrumental and vocal writing presents a porous, impure – one might almost say *ramshackle* – musical edifice. Chords will begin with staggered rhythms or with conflicting dynamics rather than in unison; extended techniques often do not allow instruments to speak easily for clean entries, with players attempting less usual harmonics, or playing with extreme bow pressure. Nor are the techniques given much room to breathe. In a very different way to early Lachenmann – who himself develops significantly from these pieces – these sounds are placed strictly within Spahlinger's compositional systems: their individual characteristics are often subordinate to his processes that have wider formal implications. This creates a tension the composer himself notes regarding the position of sound within a system and their own life, one also noted in relation to noise's 'anarchic' qualities:

> one of my artistic ideals is that, when notes sound, one should hear what they
> are within the context within which they are composed, and what they are inde-
> pendent of the context in which the composer put them: that they are part there-
> fore of a particular order but, at the same time, also possess their own being.[36]

After *entlöschend*, Spahlinger's interest in construction tends to trump his interest in a musical narrative created from a Schaeffer-like collage of sounds. Yet, the surface features of *musique concrète instrumentale* are still present in the majority of his works.

apo do, música impura *and* furioso

The string quartet ἀπὸ δῶ ('*apo do*', '*from here*') has one central formal idea. The fragments that make up the surface of the two main sections are, according to the composer, composed in parallel so that the same series of ideas occurs in each.[37] A third repetition of this series begins but is cut short by the piece ending, according to the score, 'as if interrupted'. The composer references the Chopin direction '*da capo senza fine*', which is found in some editions of the last Mazurka. From this, he says, he has created a '*quasi da capo senza fine*'.[38] There are obstacles, however, to perceiving this formal idea that is so central to descriptions of the piece. The first is that there is six minutes of music in between the start points of the two iterations. With the density of material involved, this repetition is not immediately apparent. The second obstacle is that the material itself is transformed signifi-cantly from one version to the next. Putting the two versions side by side, similar gestures and pitches appear but the porous nature of the material does not make for easy recognition of these repeats. The effect is that there are familiar elements that return but in surprising configurations, while the narrative is a characteristic mixture of extremes of density: sometimes lingering on single pitches or types of articulation, at other times rushing through explosive textures that contain a panoply of timbres and gestures.

The techniques of *musique concrète instrumentale* are essential to *apo do*'s makeup, particularly in relation to the breath sounds that are usually found in its vocal music. Airy hisses are created by bowing the body of the instruments rather than the strings while the players themselves contribute with their own breathy vocalizations. The performing instructions indicate a level of detail that approaches that of Lachenmann, though never quite lets go of traditional notation to the level of a piece like *Pression*. Nevertheless, there are indications of where on the bow to hit the strings, when to dampen strings with the finger, various types of extreme pressure and use of a bow as a clef similar to the cello clef found in Lachenmann. Importantly, however, these sounds are juxtaposed with more traditionally musical, 'pure' timbres. There are, for example, unison Abs that appear almost out of nowhere to give a clean and concentrated moment of focus. These appear as exotica within the texture, though their relationship to traditional modes of playing gives such moments particular emphasis for listeners. Such sudden shifts between noise and musical tones are a regular event in Spahlinger's music.

The title for *apo do* is taken from 'The Last Century before Humanity' by poet Yannis Ritsos, which was written in 1942 while under German occupation. In the middle of the starvation, death and suffering described in the poem a mysterious wooden sign – 'incongruous, bewildering/almost intolerable' – appears at a crossing that reads 'from here to the Sun'.[39] As part of this influence, according to the composer, Greek rhythms are employed in the piece, as well as 'carefully hidden' references to a German work song 'Brother, to the sun, to freedom', out of which 'to the Sun' is isolated. Both these influences are buried rather deep within the musical fabric and Spahlinger would not be the first composer to be open to criticism in the way that much of the extra musical meaning is communicated on a level that is far from audible. That he considers it a feature important enough to tell potential listeners is revealing regarding the kind of listening experience the composer encourages, or perhaps even expects: a search for something that will not easily reveal itself. Perhaps more readily apparent is his reaction to the structure of the poem, which proceeds through a series of images, of moments, from which the reader constructs an impression of the whole. Spahlinger looks to reflect in his music the fragments of the poem that are 'isolated from each other' yet feel like they are from a common source, though the poem's overt subject matter unifies it more than does the composer's choice of material.[40] Though the influence of *musique concrète instrumentale* is evident in this piece, it is put to expressive and structural ends that are by no means specifically aimed at furthering musical timbres or exploring unconventional techniques.

Johannes Menke makes the same observation in relation to a piece written one year after this string quartet, *música impura*, stating that 'for him it is not about the mere extension of the repertoire of new playing techniques'.[41] This piece covers similar ground in its porous surface, isolated fragments and interest in the limits of musical expression. Even though Spahlinger tries to engage with some intimidatingly substantial themes in his pieces, such as war in *apo do* or world hunger in *in dem ganzen ocean von empfindungen eine welle absondern, sie anhalten*, in his texts he is keen to emphasize music's limitations when approaching them. In *música impura*, this manifests itself in the sentence 'pobre por culpa de los ricos' ('poor by the guilt of the rich') from Pablo Neruda's *España en el Corazón* (*Spain in our Hearts*, 1936), a text also set by Nono in his *Epitaffio per Federico García Lorca* (1953). According to the composer's programme note, this phrase is 'orchestrated' by using sounds that have similarities to speech, with the intention to show the 'inability of music to speak directly'. This technique of repeated 'settings' accounts for the fragmentary nature of the expression that is particularly prevalent at the opening, though as the preceding piece, and earlier example *128 erfüllte augenblicke*, demonstrate this is a happy match with the composer's usual narrative flow. The hope is then to express the 'inadequacy and impotence of musical expression as permitted by european art music when faced with concrete suffering'.[42] After the fragmentary opening, a sense of continuity does increase through the use of extended sections that have a simple pulse, the first of which on guiro. This serves to focus listening on the variations of timbre within this simplest of materials, and relates not only the timbral but also the rhythmic field to instrumental technique. The back and forth of the guiro defines the rhythm, the colour and the intensity of this moment, just as in *apo do* the violinist's bow is allowed to bounce and come to rest on the string. Technique, then, does make an important contribution to a sense of form, yet there is an equally strong effort towards fragmentation that comes from *outside* of the material and its physical performance.

Such external force is also in evidence in *furioso* for ensemble, in which there is an unconventional attitude to the instrumental group. The players come and go, meaning there is no real fixed instrumentation for the piece, which begins with piano, harp and string quartet (with double bass rather than second violin) and ends as a wind quartet of oboe, Eb clarinet, soprano saxophone and piccolo trumpet. Players move around the space, and some are heard behind a curtain or offstage. There are important differences between this and traditional distinction of sections through instrumental colour; intended here is a destabilization of the instrumentation as a fixed element that can be used to categorize the musical experience, an idea fundamental to so much chamber music: string quartets, piano trios, wind quintets and so forth. Directions in the score paint a diverting picture by stating that 'the ideal situation would be to have the musicians pulled across the stage on podiums with wheels' as they make their contributions then depart. During this process, the cellist moves to what appears to be a solo stand in front of the ensemble, raising expectations of a conventional concerto. These are disappointed somewhat by the lack of openly virtuosic material and the cellist's complete inactivity during the last section, a 'lack' of material emphasized by the player's conspicuous location.[43]

What distinguishes *furioso* in terms of the approach to instrumental technique is both the range of colours employed and the fact that, even more than the pieces discussed above, conventional instrumental colour is included as 'one sound among many'. Carsten Häcker talks of an attempt on the part of the composer to create a table of 120 playing techniques, within which there are various instrumental variations. The 'classical "beautiful"' sound appears as only a small part of this collection, yet it is present. The piece begins with the quiet sounds of strings choked and damped in various ways, at first apparently disordered. Nonnenmann describes how at the opening the composer seeks each new sound to be the opposite of what has come before, with the option as to whether it should contrast with a sound that has directly preceded it or with a collection of sounds that came before it. So, a soft, high sound might be followed by something that is loud and high, both of which could then be contrasted with a sound that is low. As this simple example already demonstrates, there are a great number of ways in which one sound might be said to be the 'opposite' of another and it is this that allows the music to move on from a binary alternation of opposing entities. The composer describes how he set out in this piece to work in a manner that he could not predetermine, after realizing he had developed a means of justifying his work even before writing the piece.[44]

Nonnenmann argues that 'the emergence of larger structural units is avoided by this oppositional placement and instead a punctual surface is created'. In front of this background, more ordered ideas such as 'regular pulsations, symmetrical and parallel formations, regular metres, repetitions, motivic cells, unisons and other tonal allusions' are heard as exceptions.[45] Yet, there are times in this piece when perceivable ostinatos, or even grooves, are formed. One of the meanings of the title, according to the composer, is a reference to the Bohemian 'furiant' – a dance in triple metre with prominent hemiolas – and some of this rhythmic stability can be attributed to this influence.

By *furioso*'s conclusion, the remaining wind players perform only regular pitches, albeit in a register that is piercing to say the least. Though the 'classical' sound is one of many options, it encroaches on the piece, until the final moments contain no noise at all. Häcker describes this process, which begins with the introduction of instrumentalists playing wine glasses, as a 'return from the "factual world" of concrete sound into the *Innerlichkeit* of listening itself';[46]

while Nonnenmann understands the final section as an attempted negation of traditional ideas of melody, which implies smooth contour, repeated notes and stepwise movement.[47] What seems particularly important about this moment, however, is the contradiction it contains. There is a process moving from 'noisy' techniques to 'clean' tone, yet the concurrent move to stratospheric registers in the wind negates a sense that this a move towards traditional *Klang*. One process negates the other, revealing the false binary between noise and music that is so pivotal to his conception of *musique concrète instrumentale*.

While Spahlinger has far from abandoned the techniques that were developed during the earlier period of *musique concrète instrumentale*, it is clear that discovering new instrumental sounds is less of a priority, while the sounds themselves are not paramount in defining the formal processes or compositional systems that are involved. There is a general tendency for the gamut of playing techniques used by the composer to congeal somewhat while its importance to his compositional technique wanes. Nevertheless, the techniques developed during the 1960s and 1970s remain an important part of his musical language throughout his career. This goes hand in hand with the continuation of a strident political tone in Spahlinger's writings, which matches Lachenmann's early writings to a significant degree. The latter will be the focus of the next section, though importantly this should not be seen purely as a story of direct influence of Lachenmann on Spahlinger, but a sign of common origins and concerns.

2. Politics and Noisy Philosophy

Today, Lachenmann distances himself from quite a number of concepts that were common currency in the early reception of his music: rejection, critical composition and the battle with bourgeois social consciousness.[48] His position as a cornerstone of German (new) music culture, his commissions from many of its most prestigious institutions, and the various major prizes he has received also suggest a rather more comfortable relationship with bourgeois musical, and social, culture. Yet, it is undeniable that hand in hand with the musical elements of *musique concrète instrumentale* came a good deal of explication in Lachenmann's texts and printed interviews. These expound the tenets of a music philosophy that has proven as influential – and contested – as much of the music written during this time. However, as Eberhard Hüppe notes, codifying the details of Lachenmann's philosophy is complicated,[49] Elke Hockings stating that his essays are best taken as the 'fascinating and even at times paradoxical expressions of a creative mind'.[50] The intricacies of these contradictions can in the main be left to lie in the present study, however, as it is Lachenmann's early, most uncompromising and apparently political writings that are of primary interest, due to their immediate effect on Spahlinger and his contemporaries.

A key concept here is Lachenmann's idea of the 'aesthetic apparatus', which he describes as the 'sum total of categories of musical perception as they have evolved throughout history to the present day', embodying 'the ruling aesthetic needs and norms'.[51] He believes it is the duty of the composer to work against these prevailing listening habits, but not in the sense of a *tabula rasa* or wholesale expulsion of tradition. Instead, the relationship between the 'aesthetic apparatus' and the avant-garde composer is dialectical as they are 'at once fascinated by, and highly suspicious of, this aesthetic apparatus', for they 'must master it, technically and spiritually' rather than simply 'using it'.[52] This suspicion is present in his work *Accanto* (1976), in which the Mozart Clarinet Concerto is used as a distant aural backdrop. The composer describes the piece as the 'destructive manipulation of that which one loves, in order to preserve its truth'.[53] Truth and beauty are both to be achieved by radical engagement with tradition.

Thus, self-expression – contrary to the romantic, subjective ideal – is defined in relation to this rich yet restrictive sum of listening habits. Listener and composer both have important places in Lachenmann's thought: the 'aesthetic-apparatus' is external to the composer and internalized by her inculcation into society – simultaneously, the source of her creativity and the gatekeeper of her imagination. In this manner, it is akin to an aesthetic manifestation of ideology, which for Marx and Engels represents the 'production of ideas, of conceptions, of consciousness', controlling all that people 'say, imagine, conceive'.[54] For Marx, ideology serves the interests of those in power, while the 'aesthetic apparatus' for Lachenmann is similarly abused by the desires of bourgeois musical consumption. The 'aesthetic apparatus' contains within it an expression of the essential dialectic between new and old, tradition and innovation. Adorno expressed similar sentiments to Lachenmann in his pursuit of a renewal of philosophy, stating it was foolish to believe that 'the old problems [of philosophy] could simply be removed by forgetting them and starting afresh from the beginning'.[55]

The composer's struggle with the 'aesthetic apparatus' is the basis for Lachenmann's contested use of the term 'rejection', which he has himself rejected since 1982. According to Hockings, 'Lachenmann's concept of rejection is most audibly an attitude of general provocation.'[56] The musical instrument as a quasi-sacred symbol of musical refinement, technology and perhaps even progress, is scraped, hit and scrubbed in a subversion of the norms of instrumental technique. Meanwhile, tonality – which was used as a 'euphemism [...] for habitual reception, for an ignorant audience and for a musicianship of mere virtuosity'[57] – is eradicated from the musical surface. The dissolution of tonality had of course been underway for decades, yet Lachenmann states that even the post-war serialists 'could never annul the tonal categories of experience and the aesthetic consciousness tied to them, as a potential hiding place for bourgeois consciousness'.[58] The search for new musical structures and models was always 'handicapped by the unavoidable conflict with the tonal listening habits'.[59] By ignoring these listening habits and believing music could be a sphere of logic divorced from social reality, by not engaging with the 'aesthetic apparatus' in other words, Lachenmann believes that serial composers never truly overcame the tonality they professed to have eliminated.

It is through the aesthetic apparatus that music appears to be able to influence society more widely. This connects with the concept of 'critical composition', with which Spahlinger and Huber are also regularly connected. Lachenmann's distaste for bourgeois listening habits, which, according to Jörn Peter Hiekel, are synonymous with the 'pervasive search for comfort that tends to see art as a pretty, harmless accessory',[60] is wrapped up in this critical stance to conventional instrumental technique and the orchestral *Schönklang*. The concepts of rejection and *musica negativa* that have been attached to Lachenmann's work relate to this provocative aspect of this early stance.[61] Spahlinger's engagement with perception runs along similar lines, though its political effect is not seen as immediate as that implied by some of Lachenmann's more extravagant claims.

The renewal of beauty and artistic truth, the rejection of habit, and self-expression constitute an interconnected web of concepts that define early Lachenmann's musical philosophy. These in turn are built upon the philosophical foundations of dialectical, Marxian/Hegelian historical development and the Second Frankfurt School's critique of the culture industry. The polemical character of Lachenmann's early writings should not be underestimated. In this sense, they are political: they set out the composer's individual identity to distinguish him from his fellows, promoting a specific conception of music in universal terms. But it is also very tempting to read these texts as political in a wider sense: rejection and beauty for Lachenmann are key in the development of the individual consciousness. Sielecki states that Lachenmann (and N.A. Huber) both believe that music is part of the 'traffic' (*Verkehrsverhältnis*) between the Marxian superstructure and the base, making it a part of social and political interaction despite any intentions to the contrary.[62]

Lachenmann was, however, quick to limit the political implications of his music. As early as 1971–72, he says that music 'as a deposit of critical thinking will and should provoke critical engagement with itself' and that this is the 'only socio-political contribution of which it is capable'.[63] Yet, the line between reflexively critical art, or music that is 'critical of reality',[64] and criticism of social reality and institutions is far from clearly defined. The contradiction is expressed most succinctly in a later interview, in which the composer was asked about how the social criticism of his work would play out in North America:

> We should not talk too much about social critique. If a piece is authentic, it is automatically a critique of our standardized culture, without even the intention of being so […] A composer is not a missionary. A composer is not a prophet. A composer is not John the Baptist, who made critiques to the people, saying 'You are all sinners.' This political aspect is an illusion […] My teacher was Luigi Nono, a communist. He always had the hope of touching people and changing their consciousness. I think art does such things, but the composer who wants to manipulate the spirit or conscience of another will always fail. It is not possible.[65]

This answer brings some clarity to Lachenmann's position on the political in music. He rejects the potential of music to make specific social and cultural criticisms that can directly change political reality: art is not a medium for the transmission of a composer's unambiguous political message. Yet, he maintains that art can inform consciousness and make the audience more aware of their reality, albeit in a quite unpredictable manner. There is evidence here of the self-reflexion that Spahlinger also seeks, though a less specific attempt to pin down the avenues through which it takes place. Lachenmann's view of works of art is still staunchly materialist, that is, he believes that they are products in and of society, and, while these changes of consciousness may have political consequences, they are neither an inherent part of the artwork nor a necessary element in its appreciation. Spahlinger's own view of music's political potential will be a theme running throughout this volume, with a specific discussion in the next chapter.

Modernism and Musique Concrète Instrumentale

The preceding discussion has shown that *musique concrète instrumentale* inhabits difficult terrain, somewhere between style and compositional technique, but completely satisfying the criteria for neither. Blume, mentioning three of the composers most associated with the term, rightly states that there is no 'unified avant-garde "school" of which [Lachenmann, Spahlinger and N. A. Huber] are the leading lights'.[66] It is difficult to argue that the development of *musique concrète instrumentale* constitutes a movement in the manner of serialism, or any other -ism one cares to mention. The composers themselves have never expressed common allegiance to a particular cause, though this is not in fact unusual among -isms: just look at the disquiet over the term 'minimalism' or 'new complexity' among composers regularly cited as belonging to these camps. In the course of their careers,

Spahlinger et al. have developed in quite different directions and cannot be said to compose in a particular, unified style. According to John Warnaby, Huber is 'one of the very few genuinely "modern" composers who has embraced popular culture' with his emphases on the vernacular, on rhythmic composition and 'forthright' expression distinct from the other two.[67] Yet, all three still owe much to a shared context, of which *musique concrète instrumentale* is the most obvious expression. It is also clear that Spahlinger holds a great deal of respect for the others' music, as demonstrated by his published analyses of both their work, though, perhaps revealingly, neither example is particularly recent.[68] For him at least, this context was a (relatively brief) creative moment in which he was closest to his counterpart Lachenmann and from which he moved away, though forever bearing the marks of this connection. Even for Lachenmann, there is a sense of this *musique concrète instrumentale* 'moment' from which he learns a great deal but does not repeat. As he stated in a talk at Darmstadt: 'I thought I had found my [creative] paradise. But a paradise can also become a prison'.[69]

While the surface of Spahlinger's and Lachenmann's music is quite different from the stereotypical sound of Darmstadt modernism of the 1950s, it can be argued that it becomes an example of the 'new sound' of German modernism during the late 1960s and 1970s, one identified with a particular leftist political outlook after 1968.[70] Several aspects of *musique concrète instrumentale* display this continuity with a modernist stance. These include a problematic relationship with tradition, a critique of social norms and an interest in noise, which has various modernist precursors. Arguably, too, it shows a modernist desire to totalize by bringing the body of the performer under the control of the composer. That this new articulation of the modernist impulse had widespread influence over music from the 1970s onwards is identified by Spahlinger himself when he complains of Lachenmann's techniques being 'sprinkled' on scores in an attempt to sound radical.[71] The implication here is that pieces without anything essentially new or interesting about them would superficially employ these techniques to look the part, or – in a point that fits into critics' views of previous incarnations of modernism – to fit into an oppressive artistic environment. They had essentially become the new status quo. Spahlinger's feelings on this issue may have contributed to the 'turn away' from *musique concrète instrumentale* Kreidler identifies,[72] which provides a good example of flexibility and reflexivity in Spahlinger's artistic approach. The sense that *musique concrète instrumentale* is a continuation rather than a refutation of modernist impulses can also be observed in the term's distance from any other movement of this time that openly brought the achievements of modernism into question such as the 'new simplicity', neo-romanticism or a postmodern aesthetic based on reference and quotation.[73]

FIGURE 3.4A: *adieu m'amour*, bars 12–20.

Spahlinger's piece *adieu m'amour* (*hommage à guillaume dufay*, 1983) for violin and cello is an instructive final example of the relationship between *musique concrète instrumentale* and modernism, based as it is entirely on the structure of *Adieu m'amour, adieu mon joye* by Dufay. This fact may seem to bring it closer to these counter-modernist movements mobilized during the 1980s. In Spahlinger's piece, however, it is as if the original has been put through a process of filtration. Large swathes of it sound scrubbed out, and the original source is by no means always audible: much is transformed through various string techniques, such as harmonics, extreme *sul ponticello*, half-stopping the string, extreme bow pressure and both instruments' scordatura. Due to the latter, the score has two staves per instrument, the upper written at sounding pitch (see Figure 3.4A). The connections with the original Dufay (Figure 3.4B) can most easily be observed in bar 13 of both the original and Spahlinger's reimagination. The falling tenor quavers are here stated in the cello.

This short example displays a number of these techniques that mask the original material, while also showing moments – such as bar 13 – when it shines through. The extract begins with the cellist bowing on the bridge and, in bar 14, playing extreme *sul ponticello*,

FIGURE 3.4B: *Adieu m'amour, adieu mon joye* by Guillaume Dufay, bars 10–18.

bringing out one particular partial of the detuned C string. The violin in bar 14 uses the 'fawsetts' harmonic technique, discovered by R. Fawsetts according to the composer, that allows a quick succession of harmonics to sound.

From this initially noisy and abrasive exterior the original Dufay emerges, usually in performance played in a historically aware manner, which is in itself revealed in this context as one of many types of string timbre. Menke describes how the sound qualities of the piece define its relationship to its historical basis, showing that there is a non-identity between the modern experience of older music and its original reception, presumably even if performed as written. Quoting Spahlinger, he describes a 'timbral veiling and fragmented deconstruction of that which is passed down through history', through which a 'distance to a "beloved tradition that we cannot reach, that deprives the grasp of ownership, that does not let itself be reconstructed" is made audible'.[74] It is partly through the continued use of these techniques favoured in *musique concrète instrumentale* pieces that, even in this piece based on a type of quotation, the modernist impulse remains dominant. There is no feeling here that history, and historical music, are a store of material that can be summoned at will. Rather, the past is a 'foreign country', which cannot be regained.[75] The farewell of the title is a melancholy admission of this very impossibility.

NOTES

1. Johannes Kreidler, 'Mathias Spahlingers Zumutungen; Gegen Unendlich und gegen Krieg', *Musik-Konzepte* 155 (2012): 23–30, 26.
2. Philipp Blume, 'Preface: Music of Nicolaus A. Huber and Mathias Spahlinger', *Contemporary Music Review* 27, no. 6 (2008): 561–63, 561.
3. Ibid.
4. Lachenmann in Hans-Peter Jahn, '*Pression*: Einige Bemerkungen zur Komposition Helmut Lachenmanns und zu den interpretationstechnischen Bedingungen', *Musik-Konzepte* 61/62 (1988): 40–61, 58.
5. Frank Sielecki, *Das Politische in den Kompositionen von Helmut Lachenmann und Nicolaus A. Huber* (Saarbrücken: Pfau, 1993), 129. Lachenmann will be considered here as *musique concrète instrumentale*'s chief protagonist but this is not to underestimate the influence of previous composers, such as Michael von Biel and Sylvano Bussotti, or its subsequent development by younger composers such as Mark Andre, Rebecca Saunders or Pierluigi Billone.
6. Lachenmann in Paul Steenhuisen, 'Interview with Helmut Lachenmann – Toronto 2003', *Contemporary Music Review* 23, nos. 3–4 (2004): 9–14, 9. Further influences are discussed by Williams, who identifies sonorism and 'instrumental theatre' as influential forerunners of *musique concrète instrumentale*. As evidence for the latter influence, he cites Kagel's *Match* (1964) 'in which a percussionist "referees" tennis-like exchanges between two cellists' (Alastair Williams, *Music in Germany Since 1968* [Farnham: Ashgate, 2013], 76). Williams cites Heile's comments on *Match*, which are unwittingly a remarkably apt description of *musique concrète instrumentale* in general: 'the instrumental playing has to be regarded as a fusion of kinetic energy with its acoustic result'. Björn Heile, *The Music of Mauricio Kagel* (Farnham: Ashgate, 2006), 49.
7. Frank Hillberg, 'Geräusche? Über das Problem, dem Klangwelt Lachenmanns gerecht zu werden', *Musik-Konzepte* 146 (2009): 60–75, 69.
8. Ibid.
9. Ibid., 73.
10. Tanja Orning, '*Pression* – a Performance Study', *Music Performance Research* 5 (2012), 12–31.
11. Hillberg, 'Geräusche? Über das Problem, dem Klangwelt Lachenmanns gerecht zu werden', 73.
12. See: https://www.swr.de/swrclassic/donaueschinger-musiktage/michael-von-biel-quartettnr-2,article-swr-258.htm (accessed 21 June 2019).

13. This is illustrated by *La Passion selon Sade* (1966), which requires the flautist to partially undress.

14. Passages from somewhat forgotten figures such as Günther Becker, or Johannes Fritsch, whose *Modulation I* (1966), for example, contain similarly adventurous string techniques.

15. As Tanja Orning states, these can also be understood as prescriptive (action notation) and descriptive (traditional) notation (see Orning, '*Pression* – A Performance Study', 13).

16. Hans Heinrich Eggebrecht and Mathias Spahlinger, *Geschichte der Musik als Gegenwart*, Musikkonzepte Special Edition, ed. Heinz-Klaus Metzger and Rainer Riehn (Munich: Richard Boorberg Verlag, 2000), 8.

17. All but one of the cello strings are retuned: I down to F; II down to Db; and IV down to Ab.

18. Hillberg identifies five: '1. The way in which the sounds are created. 2. Their acoustic properties 3. Compositional technique 4. Listening habits 5. The aesthetic provocation' ('Geräusche? Über das Problem, dem Klangwelt Lachenmanns gerecht zu werden', 67). The three here omit his 'compositional technique' as it relates primarily to Lachenmann, while his fourth and fifth points are described together. The idea of 'resistance' is discussed in Jörn Peter Hiekel, 'Die Freiheit zum Staunen: Wirkungen und Weitungen von Lachenmanns Komponieren', *Musik-Konzepte* 146 (2009): 5–25, 8.

19. See Helmut Lachenmann, 'The "Beautiful" in Music Today', *TEMPO* 135 (1980): 20–24; and, looking back on this time, Steenhuisen, 'Interview with Helmut Lachenmann – Toronto 2003', 9–14.

20. Mathias Spahlinger, private correspondence with Neil Thomas Smith, 11 November 2015.

21. Nono would not have been the only influence but, as Lachenmann's teacher, will have been the most important. Similarly, expressionistic vocal writing can also be found in the works of Giacomo Manzoni and Sylvano Bussotti.

22. Illuminating contributions on the subject of *Klang* in Lachenmann's works can be found in Hillberg, who sees a tendency for the term to be used uncritically in writing on the composer (Hillberg, 'Geräusche? Über das Problem, dem Klangwelt Lachenmanns gerecht zu werden', 60); and in Orning, whose own experiences in a masterclass with Lachenmann introduce an important debate concerning how the sounds he writes are in fact highly specific, despite a faint sense of aleatoricism in his notation ('*Pression* – A Performance Study', 21).

23. Mathias Spahlinger, 'gegen die postmoderne mode', *MusikTexte* 27 (1989): 2–7, 6.

24. Many of Lachenmann's titles include the word 'music' – such as *Accanto*, music for solo clarinet and orchestra (1976), *Salut für Caudwell*, music for two guitarists and *Das Mädchen mit den Schwefelhölzern*, music with images – as if gently reminding the listener of the composer's musical intentions.

25. Eggebrecht and Spahlinger, *Geschichte der Musik als Gegenwart*, 58.

26. Lachenmann in Steenhuisen, 'Interview with Helmut Lachenmann – Toronto 2003', 10.

27. Helmut Lachenmann, 'Klangtypen der neuen Musik', in *Musik als existentielle Erfahrung*, ed. Josef Häusler (Wiesbaden: Breitkopf & Härtel): 1–20. For an English language

discussion, see Abigail Heatlicote, 'Liberating Sounds: Philosophical Perspectives on the Music and Writings of Helmut Lachenmann', master's thesis, Durham University, 2003), http://etheses.dur.ac.uk/4059/. Though Lachenmann mentions him only rarely, the figure of Henri Pousseur appears to have been influential in encouraging a systematization, or ordering, of the timbral plane: see Helmut Lachenmann, 'regards', henripousseur.net, https://www.henripousseur.net/views.php?author=lachenmann (accessed 21 August 2019).

28. See Neil Thomas Smith, 'Presenting the Irreconcilable: Protest and Abstraction in Mathias Spahlinger's "ocean"', *Music&Letters* 99, no. 3 (2018): 1–21.

29. Peter Wilson, 'Geräusche in der Musik – zwischen Illustration und Abstraktion', *Die Musikforschung* 38 (1985): 108–13, 109.

30. Eggebrecht and Spahlinger, *Geschichte der Musik als Gegenwart*, 129.

31. Ibid., 59.

32. Rainer Nonnenmann, '"dass etwas anders im Anzug ist"; Mathias Spahlingers individualisierte Orchesterkollektive', *Musik-Konzepte* 155 (2012): 47–74, 52.

33. Brian Kane, 'Aspect and Ascription in the Music of Mathias Spahlinger', *Contemporary Music Review* 27, no. 6 (2008): 595–609, 599.

34. Ulla Herpers, 'ephemere momente: fluxus-aspekte in werken mathias spahlingers', *Neue Zeitschrift für Musik* 162, no. 4 (1991), 38–39.

35. Mathias Spahlinger, 'this is the time of conceptive ideologues no longer', trans. Philipp Blume, *Contemporary Music Review* 27, no. 6 (2008): 579–94, 589.

36. Spahlinger in Johannes Menke, 'Música impura – Aufklärung über die Aufklärung: Ausgewählte Kammermusik von Mathias Spahlinger', *Musik und Ästhetik* 3, no. 11 (1999): 117–20, 11.

37. Mathias Spahlinger, Programme note to *apo do*.

38. Ibid.

39. Jannis Ritsos, *Das letzte Jahrhundert vor dem Menschen* (Munich: R. Piper, 1988), 38–39.

40. Ibid.

41. Menke, 'Música impura', 119.

42. Mathias Spahlinger, Programme note to *música impura*.

43. Carsten Häcker, '"furioso" für Ensemble (1991) – Zur Kompositionstechnik Mathias Spahlingers', *Positionen* 17 (1993): 46–49, 47.

44. Rainer Nonnenmann, 'Bestimmte Negation: Anspruch und Wirklichkeit einer umstrittenen Strategie anhand von Spahlingers "furioso"', *MusikTexte* 95, (2002): 57–69, 62.

45. Ibid., 63.

46. Häcker, '"furioso" für Ensemble (1991)', 49.

47. One of the quotations with which the work is inscribed is Hegel's famous description of the 'fury of disappearance', which relates to ideas of determinate negation discussed in the next chapter.

48. Elke Hockings, 'Helmut Lachenmann's Concept of Rejection', *TEMPO* 193 (1995): 4–14, 6.

49. Eberhard Hüppe, 'Von einem Mädchen und seiner Dynamik, Sozialgeschichte, Sinnschichtungen, Oberflächen, Tiefenschichten in der Oper *Das Mädchen mit den Schwefelhölzern. Musik mit Bildern*', *Musik-Konzepte* 146 (2009): 26–45, 36.

50. Hockings, 'Helmut Lachenmann's Concept of Rejection', 5.

51. Helmut Lachenmann, 'The "Beautiful" in Music Today', *TEMPO* 135 (1980): 20–24, 23.

52. Ibid.

53. Lachenmann in Clytus Gottwald, 'Vom Schönen im Wahren: Zu einigen Aspekten der Musik Helmut Lachenmanns', *Musik-Konzepte* 61/62 (1988): 3–11, 6.

54. Karl Marx and Friedrich Engels, *The German Ideology*, ed. C. J. Arthur (New York: International, 1970), 47.

55. Theodor Adorno, 'The Actuality of Philosophy', *Telos* 20 (1977): 120–33, 130.

56. Hockings, 'Helmut Lachenmann's Concept of Rejection', 7.

57. Helmut Lachenmann and Jeffrey Stadelman, 'Open Letter to Hans Werner Henze', *Perspectives of New Music* 35, no. 2 (1997): 189– 200, 7.

58. Helmut Lachenmann, 'Werkstatt-Gespräch mit Ursula Stürzbecher', in *Musik als existentielle Erfahrung*, ed. Josef Häusler (Wiesbaden: Breitkopf & Härtel, 1996), 145.

59. Ibid.

60. Hiekel, 'Die Freiheit zum Staunen: Wirkungen und Weitungen von Lachenmanns Komponieren', 6.

61. See Elke Hockings, 'Helmut Lachenmann's Concept of Rejection', 4–14; and Ian Pace, 'Positive or Negative 2', *Musical Times* 139, no. 1860 (1998), 6.

62. Sielecki, *Das Politische in den Komposisionen von Helmut Lachenmann und Nicolaus A. Huber*, 14.

63. Helmut Lachenmann, 'Zum Verhältnis Kompositionstechnik – Gesellschaftlicher Standort', in *Musik als existentielle Erfahrung*, ed. Josef Häusler (Wiesbaden: Breitkopf und Härtel): 93–97, 96.

64. Hiekel, 'Die Freiheit zum Staunen', 6.

65. Lachnemann in Paul Steenhuisen, 'Interview with Helmut Lachenmann – Toronto 2003', 12. For explication of Luigi Nono's own political position and its influence on the compositional process, see Luigi Nono, *Nostalgia for the Future*, eds. Angela Ida de Benedictis and Veniero Rizzardi (Oakland: University of California Press, 2019).

66. Blume, 'Preface: Music of Nicolaus A. Huber and Mathias Spahlinger', 561.

67. John Warnaby, 'The Music of Nicolaus A. Huber', *TEMPO* 57, no. 224 (2003): 22–37, 36–37. Warnaby also points to a different 'lineage' of influence for Huber's work through Josef Anton Riedl and Dieter Schnebel, indicating another context in which *musique concrète instrumentale* arose. The figure of Nono, however, is also vital, with Huber studying with him between 1967 and 1968.

68. Mathias Spahlinger, 'Das starre – erzittert', *MusikTexte* 2 (1983): 15–18; and Mathias Spahlinger, 'eröffnungs-schlußfall: über die ersten vier takte der *kontrakadenz*', *Musik-Konzepte* 61/62 (1988): 19–29.

69. Helmut Lachenmann, 'Got Lost Werkstatt Konzert' (unpublished presentation, Internationale Darmstädter Ferienkurse für neue Musik, Akademie für Tonkunst, Großer Saal, 8 August 2014).

70. See Beate Kutschke, *Neue Linke Neue Musik: Kulturtheorien und künstlerischen Avantgarde in den 1960er und 70er Jahren* (Cologne: Böhlau Verlag, 2007); and John Warnaby, 'A New Left-Wing Radicalism in Contemporary German Music?', *TEMPO* 193 (1995): 18–26.

71. Spahlinger, 'this is the time of conceptive ideologues no longer', 591.

72. Kreidler, 'Mathias Spahlingers Zumutungen; Gegen Unendlich und gegen Krieg', 26.

73. The conflictual relationship between *musique concrète instrumentale* and a certain neo-romantic attitude can be observed in the rather hostile exchange between Hans Werner Henze and Lachenmann (Lachenmann and Stadelman, 'Open Letter to Hans Werner Henze').

74. Menke, 'Música impura – Aufklärung über die Aufklärung', 119.

75. L. P. Hartley, *The Go-Between* (London: Penguin, 2000), 1.

4

Order

1. Conceptions of Order

Spahlinger's exploration of principles of order and their deconstruction appears alongside *musique concrète instrumentale* as a cornerstone of the composer's practice. Indeed, it ultimately outlasts it. Order was recognized early on as an important part of Spahlinger's project: a 1988 article by the composer's friend, musicologist Peter Niklas Wilson, highlights the issue; Werner Klüppelholz's 'Post-Mortem of Order' discusses the duo *extension*; while, in a recent book, Tobias Eduard Schick explores the same theme in works from 1997 to 2009, all of which indicates a significant period of time in which these ideas play a role.[1] This theme defines both Spahlinger's approach to local and formal musical organization and part of his conception of music's relationship with the political, as well as an important area of distinction in relation to the music of Lachenmann, in whose music structure and the sounds employed are on more of an even footing. In the turn away from *musique concrète instrumentale*, this interest in systems of order remains, becoming all the more conspicuous. It denotes a distinctive approach to compositional system and structure, one that is achieved primarily through the use of musical process. However, Spahlinger does not wish to engage process and system as a means of simply generating material with which to fill his compositions, rather he employs them to bring about fundamental changes in the material itself. Systems are often instigated to effect transformation and change rather than the perpetuation of particular musical relations.

Approaches to musical order have been manifest in much modernist music. Interest in compositional system came to the fore as composers sought to organize their music outside of tonality. The attempt to negate the tonal system in the first place displays an, originally antagonistic, relationship with these issues. In 1966, Henri Pousseur, for example, tackles the topic specifically in his article on 'The Question of Order in New Music', in which he argues that serial organization does not result in a regimented listening experience.[2] An important development in the debate had already arrived, however, when, in the 1950s, significant similarities were observed between music created from chance operations and compositions 'rigorously' generated through systematic approaches, an issue Spahlinger discusses with Eggebrecht.[3] The distance between 'logical' order and arbitrariness was not as great as was supposed. The question of organizing music after the advent of atonality remains open, with Spahlinger's formative years seeing a good deal of contention over the subject, not least in these debates surrounding determinacy and chance. These were of course also controversial due to composers being seen as relinquishing their responsibility to create an ordered and fixed musical surface. In the examples of construction and deconstruction of order discussed here, the position of the composer and the relationship between score and performance remain traditional, though a critique of just these responsibilities will be discussed again in relation to his conception of open form in the next chapter, which will also explore in greater depth Spahlinger's understanding of the relationship between forms and materials: the literal 'order-ing' of musical events.

Before stepping into the analysis of the pieces, it is worthwhile considering what is really meant by musical order. The composer points to the difficulties in its definition when he states that to make a Beethoven symphony 'orderly' would be to sort 'all C's together and all D's together and all E's together and so on': that, apparently, 'would be order'.[4] 'Order' in a musical sense, then, follows quite a different logic that involves listeners' expectations and established musical traditions. It is contingent on the social and historical situation in which listeners find themselves: there can be no absolute standard. This is, in part, what interests the composer, whose belief in the contingency of social and historical understandings is part of his Marxian heritage.

Order also appears to be a key means of expressing a political message, which makes this chapter a good opportunity to critically assess some of the meanings that the composer ascribes to his music. The critical commentary focuses on the controversial intersection of these concerns, discussing the composer's political approach with reference to the French philosopher Jacques Rancière, a thinker with whom the composer is not particularly familiar but with whose approach there is marked affinity. The composer, it is argued, is not alone in conceiving political relations as he does, though they are still fraught with dangers of composerly self-indulgence. The chapter begins by exploring major pieces to which issues of order are fundamental, including *akt, eine treppe herabsteigend* for bass clarinet, trombone and orchestra (*nude descending a staircase*, 1997) and the mammoth work for seven pianos, *farben der frühe*. A somewhat different take is provided by the piano concerto *inter-mezzo*, in which genre expectations as a system of order are explored. First, however, a brief note on a body of theory that is conspicuous by its absence in the following discussion, and in Spahlinger's handling of these issues in general.

A Brief Note on Deconstruction

It is surprising that in a discussion of the deconstruction of order, scant reference is made to the most widely known deconstructive project of the late twentieth century, which was that propelled by post-structural theorists such as Jacques Derrida. There are a variety of reasons for this but the most telling is that these commentators – though familiar to the composer[5] – do not fit within the intellectual milieu described in Chapter 2, the majority stemming from Franco-American positions. There is also the fact that much deconstructive criticism has been inimical, or at least disruptive, to Marxist critique, to which the composer has held fast. Spahlinger's relationship to post-structural theory is taken as indicative of his backward-looking, historical character by Claus-Steffen Mahnkopf, in what Ruthemeier describes as a 'generation conflict'.[6] This is part of Mahnkopf's accusation that Spahlinger is the 'last representative' of a type of approach that younger composers struggle to take part in because they are 'shaped by other societal, historical, epistemological, aesthetic and musical experiences'.[7] This despite the fact that Marxism of one sort or another continues to be an important influence on many of the former's interlocutors.

No attempt will be made here to integrate the composer's approach to order and this body of post-structural theory, though this would be a most valuable addition to Spahlinger scholarship. Yet, it would be remiss to make no mention of points of contact between his position and other deconstructive approaches, chiefly that of Derrida, even if there are certain challenges to this comparison. Much of the important work in deconstruction centres around language and radical critical approaches thereto. The works of Western philosophy, which have attempted to lay out their arguments according to a logic and style that is inviolable, are shown to rest on the same vagaries of meaning as literary texts. As Paul de Man states, 'literature turns out to be the main topic of philosophy and the model of the kind of truth to which it aspires.'[8] At the same time, language itself is claimed to be irreducible to specific meanings. Rather, meaning is in a constant state of flux through the prisms of readers and in the contexts of other texts.

The focus on language means that there is often a leap when applying these ideas to music. It is the kind of metaphorical equivalence of language and 'musical language' that is exactly the kind of elision Derrida jumps upon in his readings. There is also an open question in deconstructive criticism of how a literary author can respond to the open field of meanings that are exposed. This leads to what is perhaps the most important area of contact between Spahlinger's project and Derrida's. As Christopher Norris states while comparing Derrida and Heidegger: 'It is a matter of making do with the language bequeathed by that tradition, while maintaining a rigorous scepticism about its ultimate validity or meaning.'[9] The composer shares this scepticisim for the workings of the language within which he is working. It is this that leads to his interest in audible disintegration of organized sounds.

Ruthemeier identifies the composer's approach with 'radical constructivism',[10] a position that sees reality 'as a *product*' of 'highly conditional [*voraussetzungsreiche*] processes' rather than simply a given.[11] This is beneficial in that it steps outside of debates that alternate between apparently entrenched modernist versus postmodernist binaries. Interest in the contingency of meaning can be ascribed to both Spahlinger and Derrida, though the former can stray into didacticism. These questions are particularly important to the subject of the next chapter, open form. Here, Spahlinger's approach is designed to show that there is nothing necessary about formal succession and that the experience of the moment is in a dialectical relationship with the music that has been and the music that is still to come. Rather like with Derrida's neologism *différance*, meaning is constantly deferred, creating an open field of contingency. Let this serve simply as a signpost to future considerations of this musico-theoretical intersection, one that is in line with other writers who have also found a 'hidden affinity' between such apparently oppositional figures as Derrida and Adorno.[12] Certainly, there are tantalizing links between the work of the composer and these theoretical approaches, even if they are yet to enter Spahlinger scholarship in any fundamental manner. What will be picked up on, however, is the accusation of theoretical obsolescence that Mahnkopf identifies. As with Ruthemeier's use of radical constructivism, the work of Rancière explored in the critical commentary provides a compelling, and more modern, theoretical counterpart to the composer's ideas, one that shows the continued relevance of Spahlinger's modernist approach.

Order and Disorder in Spahlinger's Pieces: akt, eine treppe herabsteigend

The concept of order usually functions on a number of levels in Spahlinger's music. Wilson describes how the composer sets out to 'criticise, to undermine' and to expose as 'absurd' the traditional concerns of composition, which are described as 'the creation musical hierarchies, the construction of dominant relationships amongst notes' and the channelling of listeners' attention into the paths defined by the composer.[13] Such an attempt at negation of these supposedly traditional concerns can evidently take place on the musical surface, as well as at deeper levels of musical continuity. Hierarchies can be set up between individual pitches, pulses or harmonic areas, as well as between entire formal units, the latter of which traditional composers are said to arrange in a manner that implies a necessary formal succession. Undermining such hierarchies, therefore, can take place on a local level of note-to-note relationships or the global level of sections, movements or even genres. Unsurprisingly, the tonal system as a whole is ripe for criticism from this viewpoint, containing as it does a well-established and theorized hierarchy of musical relations, which is a major reason for Spahlinger's wariness of tonal material. The discussion here will focus more on the smaller-scale explorations of musical order, with questions of continuity taken up in the next chapter.

Surface representations of order in Spahlinger's pieces are most obviously displayed by musical structures or materials that can be understood as unified under one particular parameter or rule. Examples include materials in which all instruments play one pitch, or are rhythmically synchronized, or play particular scales. The regularity or uniformity of the musical surface provides an aural expression of the music 'obeying' one mode of organization. It is worth noting that in this approach the composer remains committed to a serially inspired separation of parameters, rather than any sense of 'order' being characteristic of particular musical material that, for example, displays 'classical balance'. In most cases, Spahlinger will set up the particular 'rule' of the material before introducing exceptions or 'mistakes'. Often these become so numerous that the original principle of order is completely unrecognizable.

Such ideas are starkly demonstrated by Spahlinger's 30-minute piece, *akt, eine treppe herabsteigend*, which was premiered at Donaueschingen in 1998. It is a work that has received little critical attention, which, though perhaps due to its relatively recent date of composition, is nevertheless surprising as it is one of the composer's most immediately appealing works. The title comes from the 1912 painting by Marcel Duchamp, which attempts to show the motion of the nude descending through a cubist overlaying of perspectives, though the Cubists themselves rejected the work as 'too Futurist'.[14] The idea of motion, and of stepped descent, is a fundamental concern for the composer. Spahlinger states that 'pitches in continuous movement, glissandi then, and their presentation in steps is the real theme of the piece'.[15] For much of the work, these glissandi are present inaudibly as a structural background, articulated only by scattered foreground material. Yet, as it progresses, this backdrop is more explicitly articulated, with first an obsessive insistence on upward movement, then a repeated downward trajectory. A particularly clear example of the manner in which points – individual pitches – are used to articulate various background glissandi is given by the passage shown in Figure 4.1 for the two soloists for the two soloists. These apparently disjunct lines are in fact plotting out three clear glissandi: a soprano, alto and bass glissando.

Comparing the top notes in each instrument's line, which together create the 'soprano glissando', shows the detail with which the composer has indicated microtonal inflections, at times demanding specific partials to achieve particular tunings. This is an unusually clear example of the way in which these background glissandi function. For much of the piece, they are not stated as explicitly but are articulated through more unpredictable pointillistic clouds. Such textures often occur in Spahlinger's music as a kind of 'raw state' from which more defined material emerges. In *doppelt bejaht*, the texture is referred to as a 'field of points', while it also appears in other major works such as *verlorener weg*, *passage/paysage* and *farben der frühe*.

Smoother and more sustained glissandi come to the fore in the middle and end of the piece to replace the punctual expressions of Figure 4.1. Often these move slowly and with slightly different trajectories, as seen in Figure 4.2, which shows the background glissandi that occur over the course of 14 measures from bar 92. The passage, a mixture of *pizzicato* and *col legno battuto*, begins with rocking tritones, which are distorted as the lines move towards their final destination, a chord based on sixth-tones (all deviations indicated by up or down arrows are + or – 33 cents). Each glissando here has a distinct gradient, with the middle voices moving far less than the uppermost voice, while the lowest goes against the grain by gently rising.

The result is a feeling of instability after the clear tritones, one further enhanced by the metric changes over this stretch of music. The metre continually shifts to prevent a feeling of an established downbeat. In Figure 4.3, the rhythmic relationship between the two lines is essentially on and off beats – an oom-pa rhythm – but the changes in metre and accents disturb this, at least for the musicians. Such disturbance is heightened by an increasing number of counter-lines and accents that gradually enter. The tritone regularly appears in this piece, in part as a kind of pivot within the octave: a halfway point in the movements up or down. It is not only this piece that displays such interest in glissandi and division of musical space: the infinite potential to divide a continuum is the primary theme of Spahlinger's chamber work, *gegen unendlich* (1995).

akt is permeated by musical structures, and governed by principles of order, that dissolve almost as soon as they appear, yet there are some that take hold to create identifiable sections: islands of homogeneous material that provide formal orientation. The most significant revolves around a rising ostinato that emerges from seemingly unguided individual impulses and repeats in altered fashion for over 100 bars. The blues-scale pitches for the ostinato, the prominence of the brass in its execution and the irregular rhythms provide a fleeting, and somewhat surprising, big band feel.

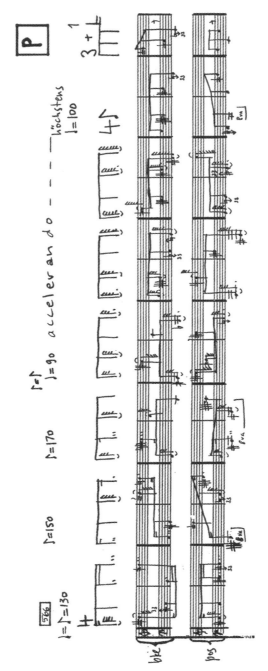

FIGURE 4.1: *akt, eine treppe herabsteigend*, bars 566–573, bass clarinet and trombone.

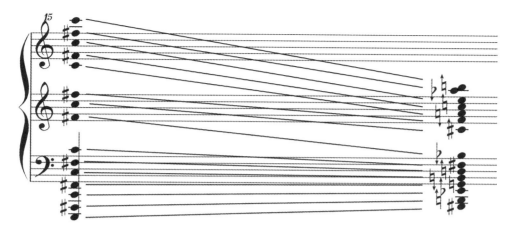

FIGURE 4.2: *akt, eine treppe herabsteigend*, bars 92–106, string reduction.

FIGURE 4.3: *akt, eine treppe herabsteigend*, bars 74–79, violins 1 and 2.

FIGURE 4.4: *akt, eine treppe herabsteigend*, rising ostinato.

This figure is presented in a manner that gives a feeling of constant ascent, which is achieved by blurring the beginnings and endings of phrases. This is the return of Spahlinger's thoughts on mechanical repetition in which it is impossible to identify the beginning of a loop or wheel.

Rather like Shepard tones, instruments join this ostinato low in their range at a quiet dynamic before rising and swelling towards the middle of the phrase. As they reach the top, they fade out so that the ear jumps to another line that is moving towards its dynamic peak. The process then repeats. In Figure 4.5, in which all

FIGURE 4.5: *akt, eine treppe herabsteigend*, bars 279–286, second violins.

strings play *pizzicato*, it can be seen how these dynamics aid this sense of constant movement. The four staves function as two pairs of instruments working
together: the upper two overlapping on G, the lower two overlapping on Eb.
Entries in other voices provide overlap on all other pitches in the sequence, giving,
at least on paper, an equality of emphasis to every note in the figure.

The solo bass clarinet and trombone lines break free from this ostinato, creating an eventually raucous, and rhythmically exciting, disturbance of the order
created. Though there is a good deal of virtuosity displayed by the soloists, particularly in opening up the highest, rather vulnerable sounding ranges of the instruments, this does not mean that there is an overt feeling of a traditional concerto
relationship. Though they have distinct and prominent parts, there is little sense
of the struggle between individual and collective upon which many concertos rely.
In the breakdown of this repetitive section, it is important to note that the supposedly 'ordered' musical moment the composer establishes is itself already partly
disturbed by disordered elements. This can be seen in both the irregularity, and
inexact repetition, of the ostinato in *akt*. This is likely because unadulterated order
does not provide material of sufficient musical interest for the composer: neither
complete order, nor complete disorder, interest him as much as constant movement between these poles.

farben der frühe

This same movement between order and its deconstruction can be regularly
observed in Spahlinger's 45-minute, six-movement behemoth for seven pianos
farben der frühe (*morning colours*, 2005). This piece took the composer eight years

to compose (though other pieces intervened), during which time he missed five deadlines for the work's completion.[16] It is a complex and sometimes austere work in which compositional system plays a vital role, particularly as the soundworld is strictly limited to sounds made by playing the keyboard, an important example of the turn away from *musique concrète instrumentale*. Though there are points when some of the timbres created by the pianos are staggering in their complexity and depth, this timbral restriction, in addition to frequent pointillistic textures, is reminiscent of certain examples of modernist piano music of the 1950s, something that cannot be said for the majority of Spahlinger's music. The title refers in part to the inability to see colours in the dawn light, which is reflected in this restrained palette.

Limitations in instrumental colour channel listeners' attention to other musical parameters, particularly density, dynamic and register, and it is these that are used to establish and deconstruct ideas of musical order. The instrumentation very much brings such explorations to the fore. The end of the first movement contains a typical example of the shifting boundaries of musical order Spahlinger works with and is worth discussing in some depth. Here, the pianos play individual pitches at various divisions of the beat (semiquavers, quintuplets, sextuplets, septuplets), precluding any sense of a regular pulse. There is a general dynamic of pianissimo, which gradually rises to forte throughout the passage, while the texture – thick at first – thins to a few notes per beat. In the score, the composer only notates exceptions to the general dynamic, exceptions that grow in number. The result in the final bar is that the vast majority of the dynamics are 'exceptions' to a rule that no longer holds any sway. In the following table, the height of each moment indicates how many notes per beat are articulated (the density), while the different shades show the different dynamic levels. It can immediately be seen that there is a movement from a dense, dynamically homogeneous texture to a sparser, more dynamically diverse (and louder) surface. By the end, there is no discernible order to the dynamic arrangement. The rough surface of the downward curve also indicates that there is a certain level of unpredictability built into how this process is executed, with occasional spikes (denser moments) or gaps. This moment-to-moment fluctuation gives a more 'natural' feel to the process, rather than plotting out a beautiful curve.

What this table does not express is the fact that the underlying, 'dominant' dynamic is also in a process of change for much of the passage, with a series of gradual crescendi. So, the succession of dominant dynamics (whatever colour is most prevalent) should in fact slowly transition from one to another. What this hammers home is the fact that what were previously dominant dynamics quickly become the exceptions of the next section, that is, that *ppp* begins as dominant but by the middle of the passage is very much an exception.[17]

Schick gives a particularly detailed account of the fourth movement of this piece, in his overview of how the idea of order works throughout. The fourth

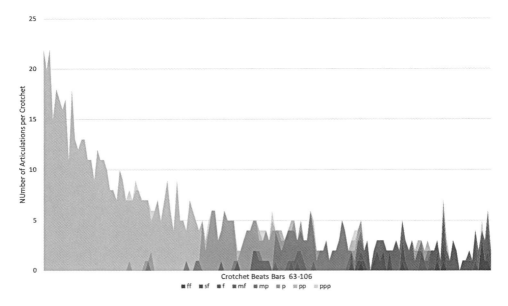

FIGURE 4.6: *farben der frühe*, bars 63–106, shows number of notes per bar and dynamic.

movement's primary principle of order is regular scalic movement from which Schick states there is a 'systematic and almost encyclopaedic variety of possibilities for deviations'.[18] The rather obsessive exploration of scales, disturbed by irregular beats and octave displacements, means this is one of the few times that Spahlinger's music shows certain affinities with that of György Ligeti, an impression naturally heightened by the presence of the piano. The constant descent and feeling of disintegration create a gripping, perhaps even alarming, feeling reminiscent of the Hungarian composer's *L'escalier du diable* (*Devil's Staircase*, from the second book of etudes, 1988–94). It is from this scalic material that the music of the fourth movement deviates in so many different ways. Examples can be as simple as the dominant quaver movement being superseded by dotted rhythms (bar 14) so that the quaver movement that was the norm is now the exception; or more complex examples of descending scalic lines hidden within rising chords with increasingly irregular rhythms. At times the structural principle is almost unrecognizable, with octave and rhythmic displacement obscuring the original idea.

One passage, from bar 201 in the fourth movement, will be taken to show the diversity of experiences that can be achieved by manipulating the dominant scalic movement. It begins with a series of primarily descending pitches, covering the chromatic totality. Each piano only plays one pitch at a time (no chords) as they descend down this row.

FIGURE 4.7: *farben der frühe*, fourth movement, scale.

Rather than performing a unison scale, however, the pianos all begin at a different point in the sequence to create the chords that are seen in the first bar of Figure 4.8. Here, the top line is always taken by piano 1, the second top by piano 2 and so on. These chords are not heard in a synchronized fashion, at first through the use of time/space notation (not indicated in the diagram), then by defined metrical values. The impression at the beginning is of a descending series of asynchronous chords, the makeup of which is not fully obvious to the ear.

Through the constant ritardando, the piano entries drift ever further apart. It is important to note the metric modulation before bar 205 as, essentially, the division of 7 continues right through this passage, though the feeling of an overarching beat encompassing the 7 becomes increasingly difficult to hear as the tempo decreases. The movement of the sound through the pianos, and around the space, displayed here is a typical feature of the piece and is identified by Schick as a third principle of order alongside the descending scales and regular pulse.[19]

As can be seen from Figure 4.8, the pitches of these more spread out articulations in bar 205 are the very same as the chords that opened bar 201. The pitch material remains very static, yet this does not mean the experience of the music is unchanging. Schick, who describes this same passage, states that the 'asynchronous chords of the beginning turn little by little into a successive series of pitches'.[20] There are in fact two transformations in this process. The first is that from chords, the top voice of which is most prominent (I in Figure 4.9), to a collection of individual descending lines played by each piano in which the middle voices are heard more prominently: as the entries drift apart, a mode of listening in which the lines of separate pianos can be heard comes to the fore (II in Figure 4.9). Towards the end of the process, however, the increasingly large gaps prevent the horizontal listening required to join up the pitches of these individual voices in their scalic downward movement, despite the fact each piano is still moving in a stepwise fashion (III in Figure 4.9). From around 205, instead of hearing descending lines, there is a change of emphasis to the large descending gestures that are created by the seven pianos working together. This process flips listeners' attention twice in a short period of time, both times creating changes in the perception of musical gesture or gestalt.

Schick rightly points to the heterogeneity of the structure as different deviations are explored. Often the music moves from one to the other without transition, with

FIGURE 4.8: *farben der frühe*, bars 201–209, fourth movement.

some deviations being explored for only a handful of bars. The deviations themselves can sometimes focus on rhythm, other times on pitch, and have contrasting
approaches for deconstructing these various parameters. The point is important
as such formal discontinuity can also be observed in many of the composer's other
works, even when the theme explored is apparently unified.

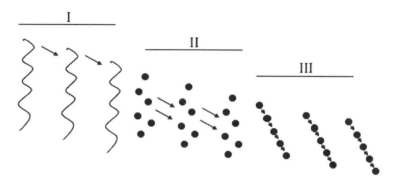

FIGURE 4.9: *farben der frühe*, fourth movement, listening diagram.

The other movements of *farben der frühe* do not display the 'encyclopaedic' exploration of order of the fourth, but there are important moments when its deconstruction is easily perceivable by the listener. Certainly, the most strikingly audible of the principles of order is the third movement, which is almost entirely based on one note. The thinning and thickening of the texture and the Db articulations allow different partials to emerge during the movement while there is a plethora of rhythmic variations. The result is a rather spectral listening experience – again, one unusual for the composer – though this is negated to a degree by a sudden break away from the Db after more than 8 minutes to music that uses harmonic material more familiar from the rest of the piece.

Though forerunners of this work mentioned above, such as 1950s modernism, Ligeti and spectralism, are certainly audible, *farben der frühe* is nevertheless a singular piece and a remarkable compositional achievement. This is true even within Spahlinger's oeuvre, as the work ranges so widely in its reference despite its initial feeling of austerity. It is clear that principles of order lie at the heart of this piece, often as the primary 'motor' of musical exploration; there is a steely focus on this theme, which is approached from various perspectives. Concentration on a particular issue results in a multiplicity of materials and musical experiences, showing that ideas of order have been a rich source of inspiration in Spahlinger's creative practice.

inter-mezzo

That Spahlinger's conception of musical order was from an early stage rather more far reaching than the examples of compositional process discussed thus far is well illustrated by his piano concerto, *inter-mezzo* (1986). There is a temptation here to write 'piano concerto', as part of the negation that occurs here is in the realm of the typical relationship between soloist and tutti. Rather than set up a conflict between the individual and collective, with concomitant virtuosity of the soloist, the intention is to show the same material in a different light as it is transferred from solo to tutti. There should be moments in which 'two individuals say the same thing, but mean something different, or they mean the same thing, but say it in different ways'.[21] This contradictory state of agreement and disagreement is the reason for the hyphen of the title: 'inter' meaning between and 'mezzo' meaning the middle. The implication is either the same thing twice or the contradictory 'between the middle': contradiction and identity exist simultaneously. There is also reference here to what is known of the etymology of the word 'concerto', which appears to stem from roots that imply both cooperation and competition.

The musical means by which these ideas are expressed can be relatively simple on paper. The orchestra is split into two, which for Ruthemeier indicates reference to two types of music making in the concerto: the traditional concerto relationship between soloist and tutti, and the antiphonal works of the sixteenth century.[22] These relationships allow similar or identical material to be passed between the groups, transforming the sound through the differences in instrumental colour, the position of players in the ensemble, or through the interposition of a large variety of playing techniques. Thus, constant semiquaver movement is intended to be transformed by its travelling through different instruments, or, once again, a single pitch is isolated to guide listeners' attention to instrumental colour, what is usually considered a secondary parameter.

The principles of order with which Spahlinger engages, therefore, are not those set up by musical material alone. Rather, he has in mind the whole notion of the concerto as a genre, as well as the hierarchies (pitch relations over instrumental colour, for example) that define tonal, and to some extent serial, music. The result is an extremely disruptive piece, with a hard-edged yet incredibly rich sonic profile. The moment-to-moment discontinuity such negation entails makes *inter-mezzo* one of the composer's more challenging listening experiences, something not helped on disc by the loss of spatial awareness of the antiphony and a lack of visuals for the relationship between solo and tutti.

The example of *inter-mezzo* shows how widely these principles of order can range, presenting a challenge for listeners regarding on what level their negation takes place. For these principles are presumed as present in listeners, in their 'aesthetic apparatus', rather than necessarily established musically, while the multitude of directions in which this negation should take place gives the audience little time to focus. Such criticism connects with an ongoing debate in writing on Spahlinger concerning determinate negation that will be picked up in the following commentary, as well as wider modernist ascriptions of political meaning to matters of musical system. 'Order' is a term that intersects with various notions of listening habits, compositional system and traditional genres. The breadth of this scope makes it difficult to pin down, and is also why the term has become such a fruitful area of exploration in Spahlinger's pieces.

2. Critical Commentary

Determinate Negation

Spahlinger's approach to musical order, often defined by focusing on one or two parameters such as pitch and/or pulse and creating a unity or regularity before introducing the deviations therefrom, is not just fuelled by an interest in particular compositional processes but has definite political overtones. Order, he states, 'in the primitive sense […] means nothing other than that a single principle prevails over all others', which he relates to 'the present destruction of nature: that the interests of the few [*Einzelinteressen*] hold sway over all others'.[23] The influence of Adorno's negative dialectics is also present in Spahlinger's approach to structure and process, both of which are fundamental to the changing sense of order and disorder he attempts to create. The composer paints his attitude to structure as anti-structural, while his approach to narrative is that of anti-narrative. He is fond of employing a quotation from Liebrucks, a philosopher with a similarly Adornian stance, who states that 'truth never appears as itself, rather it appears as a determinate negation of a particular untruth of its time [*einer Zeit*]'.[24] The 'untruths' most relevant here being the hierarchies set up by tonal music.

This idea of determinate negation is closely tied to the principles of order this chapter has explored. The composer states that a primary interest of his is 'determinate negation of pre-established relationships, according to the same principle by which a child takes apart its toys to see how they were put together'.[25] In attempting to create structures and narratives for his time, the composer seeks to negate the examples of these that already exist. Spahlinger wishes to create structures so that they might be disassembled; his compositional systems often have the aim of destroying themselves or rendering their contents unrecognizable; his narratives should appear arbitrary, so that what continuity is heard there is recognized as the work of the listener rather than an inherent property of the music itself.

In assessing this debate around determinate negation, a little background is beneficial. It is a Hegelian term that holds an important place in his conception of the dialectic, occurring in what is popularly known as the 'synthesis' of two determinations ('thesis' and 'antithesis'). Of chief relevance here is the sense that negation is not a destruction of either of the determinates but a specific reaction to the contradictions inherent in their opposition: it is the 'result of that from which it emerges'.[26] An abstract negation would have no such basis in the contradictions of what already exists. Nonnenmann identifies such an accusation of abstract negation in Adorno's critique of early serialism, which is said to suffer from historical amnesia.[27] Schick also provides an example of the distinction between abstract and determinate negation, stating that Spahlinger's approach to continuity has neither a motivically driven, Beethovenian telos, nor the complete rejection thereof, which Schick argues is found in the work of Cage and Feldman. Rather, 'Spahlinger's approach can be described as a determinate negation of a traditional teleological course, since he intentionally sets goal-orientated development in motion as well as undermining it.'[28] This approach is explored further in Chapter 5 in a discussion of *passage/paysage*.

The traces of determinate negation manifest themselves in Spahlinger's writing and music in no minor way, informing his relationship with musical tradition to a significant degree. Rather than rejecting such tradition *tout court*, his intended approach is to engage with the elements that make this tradition effective: negating them in order to make their operations audible. As Nonnenmann states, the idea is not to be 'simply unconventional' but to use no conventions in an unreflexive manner.[29] Spahlinger sees history and convention as unavoidable: there is no potential for a new musical language to emerge unconnected to previous instances.

This interest in determinate negation has been criticized from a number of perspectives. Nonnenmann, for example, is sceptical as to whether the philosophical concept can be applied to music at all, while perhaps more relevant to this discussion, and revealing regarding this composer, are questions regarding what is being negated. For the tonal system, which is a chief object of this negation, is never engaged with to any great extent: as mentioned above, it appears to exist within the listener as a yardstick to which they compare every musical experience. This is the implication of Spahlinger's statement that tonality has 'never gone away'.[30] Questions remain, however, whether primarily atonal works can create their own systems of reference that drive out 'tonal' perception, however briefly.

As mentioned in relation to deconstruction, other critics see this negation as being fixed in time, meaning that Spahlinger continually refers back to a historical moment that does not allow him to develop as a composer. It is within the discussion of Spahlinger as a critical composer that Mahnkopf makes the criticism that he is 'increasingly becoming less the composer of his own works than a representative of a neurotically exaggerated negativity principle',[31] while Andreas Domann also describes certain contradictions in this negative position, particularly when, in his opinion, little is established that can be negated.[32] Mahnkopf also makes the more specific accusation that Spahlinger's negation is one rooted in a particular moment in history,[33] something with which Nonnenmann appears to agree as he finds the composer's mode of criticism is not as 'originary' as that of Wolfgang Rihm, Heiner Goebbels or Helmut Oehring because it 'at times takes on epigonal qualities by directly following Lachenmann and Nicolaus A. Huber'.[34] It is argued here that there are significant differences between Spahlinger's project and those of these two other composers. Yet, the feeling that there is a 'belatedness' to his project is certainly the case. This has already been discussed in the contextual biography as a result of (West) Germany's historical situation. While outwardly stating that he is negating tradition, Nonnenmann would argue that he fails to recognize or negate the new traditions or conventions of contemporary music that have arisen, even if their reach can hardly be compared to that of the tonal system.

In a compositional project that prides itself on self-reflexion and the importance of reacting to material conditions, these criticisms are by no means incidental. Certainly, there are key concerns in Spahligner's work that remain static, while he has done little to reflect the rapid societal changes that have occurred since the spread of digital technologies, to name one example of an important societal trend. Yet, this volume argues, that this relative stasis does not mean the concerns themselves do not offer anything to a contemporary listener, nor do they mean that the compositional approach displayed in his works is without development or variety. While continuing to argue for the relevance of the music, a key part to the argument here is that the composer's political ambitions do relate to more recent aesthetic theory, even theory that was developed in France and, therefore, outside of the 'Germanosphere' of which he is very much part. Before delving into this, it is important to cover the potential criticisms to which his political approach makes him vulnerable.

The Politics of Order

Alongside concerns about the specific applications of determinate negation in Spahlinger's work are wider questions regarding the relationship between compositional technique and the political. For him, the hierarchies that are explored in a musical fashion are seen to rest on the same understanding of the world as those that play out in the political realm. Pulse, rhythm, pitches and dynamics are often employed to create hierarchies of musical ideas in the ears of listeners. In deconstructing these principles of order, Spahlinger is thinking about the dissolution of other more worldly relations. As Schick rightly states, with the critical reflexion of musical hierarchies 'societal ones are also usually vicariously meant too'.[35] In this, he appears to attempt something similar to his close colleague N. A. Huber, who readily associates the political with his compositional techniques. Yet, it is unlikely Spahlinger would go as far as Huber, who in 1983 appears to claim direct political effect and allegiance for his 'conceptual rhythmic composition', stating that the reason for this approach 'is not only solidarity with the Third World countries in world political disputes that lies behind it' but also 'reflects a political, ideological and communicative attitude'.[36] The relationship between elaborate, often abstract, musical system or process and claims of political meaning often suffers from such reductive consideration.

Georgina Born is not alone in identifying such political rhetoric in the aesthetic sphere as a modernist trait, as compositional techniques 'were read as oppositional, as subversive, as politicized critiques of the extant moral and social order' with discussions of '"continuity" and "tradition" versus "change" and "progress"' appearing as 'aesthetic and political, both metaphoric and "real"'.[37] Thus, a description of a compositional system can become a metaphorical criticism of society, despite the fact that its societal effect is negligible. Composers, in Born's description, can be given the sheen of political radicalism while remaining in reality entirely ineffectual, perhaps even regressive. For Susan McClary, too, the modernist avant-garde, characterized by a siege mentality, closes itself off to the 'explosion of musical creativity' in the twentieth century.[38]

Certainly, Spahlinger can very much be considered within the tradition of a politicized modernist discourse, one that was also in evidence in previous manifestations of European modernism such as Dadaism and the Futurists, in the later writings of Luigi Nono, and in the writings of the 1968-inspired German composers, Huber and Lachenmann. He displays the politicized rhetoric that Born identifies. Furthermore, that these kinds of political explorations rest on questions of compositional system and structure provides further continuity with the composer's modernist precursors. Yet, it is easy to forget that Spahlinger never equates his compositional practice with political action in the world: like Adorno, he is critical of art that seeks concrete political outcomes due to the danger of it becoming propaganda. The political effect of this music rests more in the development of the consciousness of each listener than in any unambiguous call to arms. The relationship between the musical exploration of order and political order is described by Schick as one of analogy: this music encourages and challenges certain 'forms of thought',[39] which are the same that are used in understanding society, though Schick is sceptical of any direct relation between the two.

The political meaning of compositional system is much contested. Spahlinger's exploration of musical conceptions of order and politics connects with long-standing debates around 'committed' art and the (im)possibilities of expressing a political message in an aesthetic sphere. For many there is an unassailable gulf that cannot be overreached by even the strongest sentiments on the part of the composer. It will be argued here, however, that there is a way of understanding the political implications of Spahlinger's work as more than empty rhetoric. This makes use of the idea of radical contingency within the work of Rancière.

Political Art and Davis's Aesthetic Contingency

As Rancière puts it, 'an artist can be committed' but 'commitment is not a category of art.'[40] Modernist composers have been criticized for overstating the political significance of their work, particularly when it takes place on the level of notes on the page. As with Spahlinger, the philosopher's exploration of the fundamental question 'how is art political?', is only ever answered 'plurally'.[41] Rancière states that this 'does not mean that art is apolitical. It means that aesthetics has its own politics, or its own meta-politics'.[42] He, too, is wary of any immediate political commitment of an artist transferring to their works.

Yet, Oliver Davis provides a compelling reading of the philosopher's aesthetics as an exploration of what he calls 'radical contingency'. This, he states, is the most consistent way in which Rancière describes the political potential of art. This contingency begins with the philosopher's conception of art in what he calls the 'aesthetic regime', which is open to any object, thought or sound becoming art. Davis states that what is distinctive about art today, in Rancière's aesthetic regime, is what he calls radical contingency as 'anything (any material or conceptual entity whatsoever: any object, person, place, process, vibration, idea, etc.) can, in principle, be art'. Art is contingent on the 'aggregation of individual acts of human meaning-making which collectively constitute the evolving critical-interpretative discourse that allows objects to be recognized, understood and explored as art'.[43]

So far, so unremarkable perhaps. There is a long-held, sometimes begrudging, understanding of contemporary art as open to all sorts of actions and objects; while the 'what is art?' question has for many years related more to social and historical factors than inherent properties of 'the work'. Yet, the crucial point comes in Davis's belief that Rancière's philosophy implies that contemporary art objects accept, and 'educate' the audience in, their own contingency. By exploring how their status as art objects depends on the social discourse surrounding what it means to be a work of art, they can lead the viewer, or listener, to a better understanding of the particular environment in which art is created, as well as providing implications for the world at large. Davis salvages an almost pedagogical edge to the philosopher's thought, which is not the only point in which there is a 'modernist residue' to Rancière's ideas.[44] Here there is a commonality between composer and philosopher as Spahlinger, too, is concerned with 'educating' the listener in their perceptual abilities, as will be explored further in Chapter 6.

It is the education in contingency that allows art to act politically, albeit rarely in the direct manner of action within the world. The aesthetic education offered by works of art in the aesthetic regime prepares the audience for treating other objects in the world – perhaps even institutions – as contingent in the same manner. Davis states that it is through encounters with aesthetic contingency that the 'spectator is not only "emancipated" in the modest sense of being freed to interpret the artwork in question but, by the same token, is emancipated by the experience of aesthetic art, formed for "emancipation" in the properly political sense, by being disposed to recognize contingency in other human artefacts that are not artworks in the strict sense'.[45] Art, therefore, is a lesson in future emancipation, containing something akin to a promise of another world, or at least an invitation to understand that the present world can be changed. Davis suggests that it is a sort of cognitive rehearsal for actions in the real world, an idea that provides a way of interpreting Spahlinger's belief that music can form future consciousness. Neither Rancière nor Davis state this, but it is tempting to infer that the institutional critique will most obviously apply to artistic, in Spahlinger's case musical, institutions first of all, which then themselves can function as a further experience of contingency with which to encounter the outside world.

Spahlinger's Aesthetic Contingency

Working within this realm of radical contingency creates unique problems. Artists are faced with bewildering choice: what materials and subjects should be chosen if all are valid topics for art? Spahlinger and Rancière appear to provide similar answers to these questions. First, they recognize that despite this open field of possibility, all responses from a seeing or hearing audience are shaped by physical and societal factors. What Rancière calls the 'distribution of the sensible' is almost a description of the societal influence on physical perception. Having got this far, both then see these responses as the most important thing to which art can attend. Spahlinger mentions this in relation to the potential of noisy sounds in new music, the introduction of which he says can lead to a false feeling that the composer has achieved complete freedom:

> it would be easy to read into this – and i do not want to do this – that noise music [...] simply developed music further or freed it completely, but the opposite is true. as part of the next highest step of consciousness, one realises that a sound is not heard as it is, rather that a sound is always made sense of by the listener and that the perceived is always changed through the context in which it is perceived.[46]

The context described here is not just one of time and place, but a context of the listener's perceptual apparatus, perceptual apparatus, or as Rancière would put it, the particular 'distribution of the sensible' in play. Spahlinger consciously attempts to bring this work of the listener into the experience of his pieces, thereby engaging with the aesthetic contingency Davis describes.

Key in this regard for the composer is the sense-making potential of the listener: that when presented with disorder the mind is predisposed to seek, and often find, an order of its own. His distaste for what he considers postmodernism's 'anything goes' attitude leads him to advocate engaging with these sense-making faculties. In this he meets the challenge that Jean-Philippe Deranty identifies in the work of Rancière: that the mark of all genuine artistic projects is that they 'have faced and attempted to do something with the overwhelming possibilities opened up by the demise of the constraining representative logic'.[47] Much of Spahlinger's practice can be seen to grapple with this very same problem.

A useful example of Spahlinger's desire to deal directly with these sense-making faculties is felt in what he describes as a refusal to use themes and motives, opting instead to compose 'beneath the level of gestalt perception'.[48] Some illumination on what this means can be found in his essay 'against the post-modern fashion'. Here he plots a development from the motivic writing of Beethoven through Schoenberg's technique of developing variation to more abstracted methods of expanding material used in contemporary music. He sees this as a move from the understanding of motives – gestalts – as solid entities to be manipulated without changing their essential characteristics (as in variation forms), to an apparently deeper comprehension of Gestalt perception:

> all motivic work brings subsidiary motives and spin-offs into being that themselves have a gestalt character and could be perceived by gestalt perception as wholes in themselves, while work beneath the gestalt level, for example with single parameters, reaches a level of abstraction that with luck sensuously facilitates the achievement or implication of a higher level of consciousness of gestalt thinking itself.[49]

Spahlinger, then, refuses motivic development, which creates an important difference between his practice and that of even quite recent serial-inspired composers such as Stockhausen or Nono. He states that he takes no solid musical entity as material but uses abstract processes on a limited number of parameters, allowing listeners to group the results into gestalt 'wholes in themselves'. This is where his ideas of order merge with his explorations of perception, the discussion of which will be reserved for Chapter 6.

For both philosopher and composer, this aesthetic contingency relates in some way to a more general contingency in society at large, which, for Rancière, is ruled by arbitrary laws enforced by various societal institutions. As mentioned in Chapter 2, Spahlinger too is suspicious of moral, natural and religious codes that enforce hierarchies. In 'this is the time of conceptive ideologues no longer', he emphatically states that 'our laws will all be identified as man-made, even the divine ones. it's about time!!'[50] As noted in Chapter 1, the title of this essay refers to the fact that the age of kings has past, replaced by a world in which you must 'help yourselves'.[51] The aesthetic contingency that Davis identifies in Rancière, and that Spahlinger seeks in his compositions, is a rehearsal in the aesthetic realm for realizing the contingency present in the organization of communities. As with Adorno, there is held to be a central and elusive utopian potential in the aesthetic experience. Rancière and Spahlinger, however, provide a counterpoint to Adorno's belief that art 'stands as a reminder of what does not exist'.[52] For them, it is more the case that art 'stands as a reminder that what exists can be altered'.

The work of Rancière provides a theoretical understanding in which the political and the aesthetic can mingle in a manner resembling what Spahlinger wishes to achieve. In this, the composer is seen to engage fruitfully with aesthetic theory of quite a different bent from his preferred Frankfurt School – a theory, moreover, that was developed synchronously with his own compositions. At the same time, it should give pause for thought that the philosopher himself is avowedly anti-modernist. Once again there is far more common ground between the oppositions created for modernism than there might at first appear. Nevertheless, it is important to state that this affinity will by no means guarantee a political experience on the part of the listener, to whom concrete talk of political meaning may feel rather distant. Conscious appreciation of this level requires an intense engagement with the music and reflection upon it, acts that will hitherto have occurred with some knowledge of the composer's intellectual context in the vast majority of cases. Whether this music might have effects on the subconscious can of course not be verified but, if present, are likely to be more circuitous and personal than Spahlinger's statements would allow. The political meaning of any music is contingent on context to a very significant degree and one reading of the composer's texts is as an attempt to create a context for his work so that it can be understood politically. As with so many explorations of the political potential of music, Spahlinger's attempts in this direction remain controversial.

NOTES

1. Peter Niklas Wilson, 'Komponieren als Zersetzen von Ordnung', *Neue Zeitschrift für Musik* 149, no. 4 (1988): 18–22; Werner Klüppelholz, 'Obduktion der Ordnung. Zu Spahlingers

extension', *MusikTexte* 95 (2002): 69–79; Tobias Eduard Schick, *Weltbezüge in der Musik Mathias Spahlingers* (Stuttgart: Franz Steiner Verlag, 2018).

2. Henri Pousseur and David Behrmann, 'The Question of Order in New Music', *Perspectives of New Music* 5, no. 1 (1966): 93–111.

3. An issue that Spahlinger and Eggebrecht discuss: Hans Heinrich Eggebrecht and Mathias Spahlinger, *Geschichte der Musik als Gegenwart*, Musikkonzepte Special Edition, eds. Heinz-Klaus Metzger and Rainer Riehn (Munich: Richard Boorberg Verlag, 2000), 78.

4. Spahlinger in Markus Hechtle, *198 Fenster zu einer imaginierten Welt* (Saarbrücken: Pfau-Verlag, 2005), 106.

5. Mathias Spahlinger, interview with Neil Thomas Smith, 11 August 2014, Groß Glienicke, recording: unarchived.

6. Dorothea Ruthemeier, *Antagonismus oder Konkurrenz? Zu zentralen Werkgruppen der 1980er Jahre von Wolfgang Rihm und Mathias Spahlinger* (Schliengen: Edition Argus, 2012), 243.

7. Claus-Steffen Mahnkopf, *Kritische Theorie der Musik* (Weilerswist: Velbrück Wissenschaft, 2015), 105.

8. Paul de Man in Chrisopher Norris, *Deconstruction: Theory and Practice* (London: Routledge, 1991), 21.

9. Norris, *Deconstruction: Theory and Practice*, 69.

10. Ruthemeier, *Antagonismus oder Konkurrenz?*, 85.

11. Siegfried J. Schmidt, *Der Kopf, die Welt, die Kunst. Konstruktivismus als Theorie und Praxis* (Wien: Böhlau, 1992), 21.

12. Ruthemeier, *Antagonismus oder Konkurrenz?*, 91.

13. Peter Niklas Wilson, 'Mathias Spahlinger', in *Komponisten der Gegenwart*, eds. Hanns-Werner Heister and Walter-Wolfgang Sparrer (Munich: Text+Kritik, 2012), 2.

14. See Michael White, 'Dada Migrations: Definition, Dispersal, and the Case of Schwitters', in *A Companion to Dada and Surrealism*, ed. David Hopkins (Oxford: Wiley-Blackwell, 2016), 54–69, 56.

15. Mathias Spahlinger, programme note to *akt, eine treppe herabsteigend*.

16. Bayerischer Rundfunk, 'Farben der Frühe', Musica Viva, https://www.br-musica-viva.com/cd-dvd/mathias-spahlinger-farben-der-fruehe/ (accessed 28 January 2016).

17. This is presumably the reason behind what at first looks like rather contradictory dynamics. In Piano 4 bar 86, for example, there is a *piano* marking despite this being the dominant dynamic (therefore not requiring notating at all). Yet, due to the underlying crescendo, *piano* is no longer the primary dynamic, rather it should be something in between p and mp. The dominant idea becomes the exception, though the fine gradations of dynamic on which this idea relies would make it very difficult indeed to perceive as a listener.

18. Tobias Eduard Schick, 'Musik, Gesellschaft, Wirklichkeit – Weltbezüge im Werk Mathias Spahlingers' (DPhil diss., Hochschule für Musik Carl Maria von Weber, Dresden, 2016), 200.

19. Schick, *Weltbezüge in der Musik Mathias Spahlingers*, 146.

20. Ibid., 156.

21. Spahlinger in Dorothea Ruthemeier nee Schüle, 'Concertare Means Reaching an Agreement: On Mathias Spahlinger's "Piano Concerto" inter-mezzo (1986)', *Contemporary Music Review* 27, no. 6 (2008): 611–23, 612.

22. Ibid., 614.

23. Spahlinger in Wilson, 'Komponieren als Zersetzen von Ordnung', 20.

24. Bruno Liebrucks in Andreas Domann, '"Wo bleibt das Negativ?" Zur musikalischen Ästhetik Helmut Lachenmanns, Nicolaus A. Hubers und Mathias Spahlingers', *Archiv für Musik Wissenschaft* 62, no. 3 (2005): 177–91, 181.

25. Spahlinger in Ruthemeier nee Schüle, 'Concertare Means Reaching an Agreement', 611.

26. Gottfried Wilhelm Hegel, *Phenomenology of Spirit*, trans. A. V. Miller (Oxford: Oxford University Press, 1977), 79. This is the oft-discussed process of *Aufhebung* or 'sublation', which is discussed by Paddison in an Adornian context highly relevant to Spahlinger: Max Paddison, *Adorno's Aesthetics of Music* (Cambridge: Cambridge University Press, 1993), 112–13.

27. Rainer Nonnenmann, 'Bestimmte Negation: Anspruch und Wirklichkeit einer umstrittenen Strategie anhand von Spahlingers "furioso"', *MusikTexte* 95, (2002): 57–69, 59. Nonnenmann is critical of the application of this term to Spahlinger's music.

28. Schick, *Weltbezüge in der Musik Mathias Spahlingers*, 186.

29. Nonnenmann, 'Bestimmte Negation', 57.

30. Mathias Spahlinger, interview with Neil Thomas Smith, 11 August 2014, Groß Glienicke, recording: unarchived.

31. Claus-Steffen Mahnkopf, 'What Does "Critical Composition" Mean?', in *Critical Composition Today*, ed. Claus-Steffen Mahnkopf, Frank Cox and Wolfram Schurig (Hofheim: Wolke Verlag, 2006), 75–87, 81.

32. Domann, 'Wo bleibt das Negativ?', 190.

33. Mahnkopf, 'What Does "Critical Composition" Mean?', 81.

34. Rainer Nonnenmann, 'A Dead End as a Way Out', in *Critical Composition Today*, eds. Claus-Steffen Mahnkopf, Frank Cox and Wolfram Schurig (Hofheim: Wolke Verlag, 2006), 88–109, 108.

35. Tobias Eduard Schick, 'Aufbau und Zersetzung von Ordnungen: Zu einem zentralen Aspekt im Schaffen Mathias Spahlingers', *MusikKonzepte* 155 (2012): 31–46, 34.

36. Nicolaus A. Huber, 'Translation of Huber's Essay "Konzepetionelle Rhythmuskomposition" on Conceptional Rhythm Composition', trans. Petra Music and Philipp Blume, *Contemporary Music Review* 27, no. 6 (2008): 569–77, 574.

37. Georgina Born, *Rationalizing Culture: IRCAM, Boulez, and the Institutionalization of the Musical Avant-Garde* (London: University of California Press, 1995), 43.

38. Susan McClary, 'Terminal Prestige: The Case of Avant-Garde Music Composition', *Cultural Critique* 12 (1989): 57–81, 62–63.

39. Schick, *Weltbezüge in der Musik Mathias Spahlingers*, 243.

40. Jacques Rancière, *The Politics of Aesthetics*, trans. Gabriel Rockhill (London: Continuum, 2004), 60.

41. Oliver Davis, 'The Politics of Art: Aesthetic Contingency and the Aesthetic Effect', in *Rancière Now: Current Perspectives on Jacques Rancière*, ed. Oliver Davis (Cambridge: Polity, 2013), 155–68, 156.

42. Rancière, *The Politics of Aesthetics*, 60.

43. Davis, 'The Politics of Art', 158.

44. Jakub Stejskal, 'Rancière's Aesthetic Revolution and Its Modernist Residues', trans. Jakub Stejskal, *Filozofski vestnik* 33, no. 3 (2012): 39–51.

45. Davis, 'The Politics of Art', 162.

46. Mathias Spahlinger, 'gegen die postmoderne mode', *MusikTexte* 27 (1989): 2–7, 6.

47. Jean-Philippe Deranty, 'Regimes of the Arts', in *Jacques Rancière: Key Concepts*, ed. Jean-Philippe Deranty (Durham: Acumen, 2010), 116–30, 129.

48. Spahlinger, 'gegen die postmoderne mode', 6.

49. Ibid.

50. Mathias Spahlinger, 'this is the time of conceptive ideologues no longer', trans. Philipp Blume, *Contemporary Music Review* 27, no. 6 (2008): 579–94, 581.

51. Friedrich Hölderlin, *The Death of Empedocles: A Mourning Play*, trans. David Farrell Krell (New York: State University of New York Press, 2008), 87.

52. Theodor Wiesengrund Adorno, *Aesthetic Theory*, trans. R. Hullot-Kentor (London: Continuum, 2004), 313.

5

Open Form[*]

Just as with the explorations of order and the influence of *musique concrète instrumentale*, Spahlinger's interest in open form manifests itself early in the composer's work. Yet, more than in the topics explored in the previous two chapters, there is a sense of creative journey in this field, from early experiments in line with his modernist predecessors to a unique take on the issue in later pieces. Open form is for Spahlinger a significant achievement of new music, one that is tied to the breakdown of formal necessity explored in the previous chapter. The discussion here begins by considering previous instantiations of open form, from which the composer deviates somewhat in his own understanding of what the term denotes. Following this is a discussion of some of Spahlinger's most relevant pieces, beginning with the early chamber work *128 erfüllte augenblicke* and the vitally important orchestral work *passage/paysage*, with the latter's unique approach to repetition discussed in some depth. Open form is shown not just to be a question of the way that composers organize musical material but a fundamental approach to formal progression that manifests itself even in the composer's fully notated scores. A final group of works is then examined, which explore the nature of transition through 'modular' materials, an idea that will be shown as highly relevant, and potentially limiting, to Spahlinger's conception of open form. Finally, the critical commentary will pick up on contradictions relating the composer's political critique supposedly present in these works, exploring the challenges of his performance practice. This gets to the heart of many specific criticisms of his supposedly utopian political standpoint.

[*] Some of the material in this chapter relating to Spahlinger's *passage/paysage* has already appeared in Neil Thomas Smith, 'Mathias Spahlinger's *passage/paysage* and the 'Barbarity of Continuity', *Contemporary Music Review* 24, nos. 2–3 (2015): 176–86.

1. Conceptions of Open Form

Open form has a relatively long history of modernist exploration involving many of the most prominent protagonists of post-Second World War music. For example, in Boulez's *Third Piano Sonata* (1957 with later revisions), the player has a certain amount of choice in deciding which of the composer's materials to play and when, while in Stockhausen's *Zyklus* (1959) the percussionist can begin anywhere in its spiral form and 'travel' in a direction of their choice. Perhaps the most persistent innovator in this area is American composer Earle Brown, much of whose artistic project involved experimenting with open structures. His *Twenty Five Pages* (1953) is a well-known example that comprises a score in which the eponymous pages can be performed either way up and in any order.[1] Open form, then, has primarily referred to pieces with a flexible or 'mobile' structure that can differ from performance to performance. The formal possibilities can be tightly controlled, as in the case of Boulez, or almost boundless, thereby raising similar issues to chance music regarding authorship and work ontology.

Spahlinger's definition of open form, however, includes pieces that do not at first appear to display any open form elements.[2] He explains in 'this is the time of conceptive ideologues no longer' that 'since 1910 form can only be open, or a closed form must reveal itself as arbitrary—which means the same thing'.[3] This implies that his conception of open form is not to be applied solely to those pieces that consciously have formal flexibility. Rather, a sense of formal openness, contingency and incompleteness is a more general achievement of new music. This relates to his Adornian-inspired conception of the fragmentary nature of new music, which supposedly reflects the ravaged surface of atomized contemporary society. As Spahlinger puts it, new music 'begs the question whether the parts indeed still are parts, whether they are the smallest discrete entities that cannot be broken down or if there are only virtual relationships between them'.[4] By this he means that formal units are so unstable their parsing into identifiable entities is extremely difficult, or that identifying formal units has become impossible altogether. Relationships *between* such units trembling on the edge of existence become problematic, with Spahlinger claiming such connections are only imagined, or the work of listeners in projecting meaning. This means that there can be no logical formal progression: no *necessity* for a recapitulation, for example. It appears that for Spahlinger the open form works are just the most extreme examples of a general tendency in new music towards formal ambiguity.

This, for the composer, is a fundamental shift in how music is conceived and perceived, implying that the experience of new music is one quite different from any kind of music that came before it. He describes how form is used in traditional music to refer to a quasi-visual or sculptural presentation of the order of its events.

However, the formal effects of the music – how it functions in time – are not so easily described, for 'music as a whole cannot be referred to, recounted music is like a recounted lunch'.[5] Open form, on the other hand, implies the understanding of form as a process rather than any solid, abstracted and ultimately non-temporal architecture. Spahlinger states that the experience of open form is when 'the parts are recognized as interchangeable, that their formal tendencies become recognizable' and that 'it presents the result of a becoming',[6] even when – as in most of his scores – the order of events *is* fixed in the score. Open form is a complex interaction between the material of the moment, which is interchangeable with any other, and the form that has been built up from previous interchangeable moments, all mediated by the active construction of meaning on the part of the listener.

There are two particularly important contexts to Spahlinger's description of open form: a Hegelian relationship between part and whole, and Adorno's idea of *musique informelle*. Insight into the form is given by Hegel's description of metaphoric organisms, in which part and whole are completely interdependent. In the philosopher's organic conception of the state, for example, the individual depends on the state as the state depends on the individual. Both help realize each other, for if 'individuals find their self-consciousness and self-identity in the community, the ideals of the community are also actualized only through the actions and inner dispositions of specific individuals'.[7] The goal of open form in its constant shifts of connection and meaning is for Spahlinger one of *becoming*, which, again, is a very Hegelian concept. Hegel stresses the importance of process, of becoming, in this dialectical move towards unity, truth and the awareness of freedom. For Peter Singer, Hegel's idea of historical progress 'is none other than the progress of the consciousness of freedom'.[8] History is then the development, the increasing realization, of this consciousness, crucially moving towards a specific goal: the Absolute for Hegel is constantly in a process of becoming as 'only in the *end* is it what it truly is'.[9]

Spahlinger differs from Hegel, however, by following Adorno's scepticism of progress. He does not believe that human development is a case of continuous improvement and that it will someday *become* a manifestation of rationality and freedom. Rather, becoming is a constant, dialectical change of perspective in which something is gained but also lost. In his essay, 'Vers une musique informelle', Adorno offers a vision of music that involves non-identical elements existing in a system that does not seek to dominate them. *Musique informelle* is an attempt at describing a freer compositional practice, stressing that the formal elements of a piece must arise from the material itself rather than contact with rigid, external forms and without the sense that there is progression towards an ultimate revelation. Much of this vision is concerned with what Adorno saw as the deleterious effects of spatial understandings of temporality, overly literal rationality and parameterization in the music of the 1950s, a position that obscures the fact that a number of the pieces from this decade were *informelle* in the manner he advocated.[10]

That parts become interchangeable is for Spahlinger a key feature of the openness of new music in comparison with goal-orientated tonality, while the process of understanding the implications of open form touches on an already noted favourite idea of his: that listeners have an active role in *making sense* of the music.[11] Spahlinger believes open form invites the listener to comprehend the possibilities – perhaps even arbitrariness – of formal progression, while at the same time they should realize they themselves are creating a narrative with what is presented. He attempts to eschew any sense of determinate formal function so that any material has the potential to follow any other. The listener, and their consciousness, should realize there is no such necessity, that it is they that make sense of this music, and, therefore, they that should achieve a more refined knowledge of their capacity for sense-making. There is an Adornian bent to this critique with the philosopher stating that open forms and genres 'free themselves from the lie of being necessary. By the same token, they become more vulnerable to contingency'.[12] This is the aesthetic backdrop to explorations of this theme in Spahlinger's musical works.

Open Form in Spahlinger's Pieces

A number of pieces provide very concrete examples of the composer's interest in these themes. Most obvious is the relatively early *128 erfüllte augenblicke* (*128 fulfilled instants*, 1975), which comprises 128 short pieces of music from which the performers 'curate' a performance.[13] Repetitions are permitted but, to fit within the recommended duration, no performance can include all 128. As Philipp Blume states, there are innumerable possibilities as 'one can design a kind of ritornello form with repetitions of a refrain (consisting of one *Augenblick* or series of *Augenblicke*) at regular or irregular intervals; a long or short version with no repetitions whatsoever; or a randomly generated ordering'. There are perhaps surprising versions permitted in which a 'performance of the work could simply consist of a single *Augenblick* repeated several dozen times'.[14] Figures 5.1A and 5.1B give an impression of what kinds of materials Spahlinger employs and their aphoristic form of expression, with the staves describing the voice, clarinet and cello parts from top to bottom. The first begins with a move to extreme bow pressure, which is then maintained in short scratchy articulations on the cello, punctuated by disjunct pitches from the other two instruments. The second begins with a crescendoing flutter-tongued clarinet cut off by a Bartók pizzicato. The voice

FIGURE 5.1A: *128 erfüllte augenblicke, Augenblick .232.*

FIGURE 5.1B: *128 erfüllte augenblicke, Augenblick .432.*

numbering

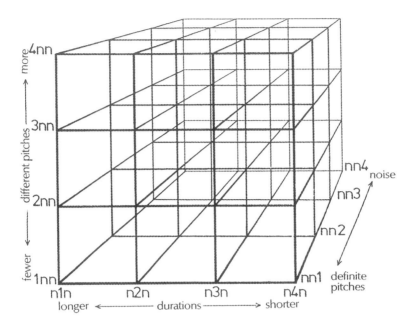

FIGURE 5.2: *128 erfüllte augenblicke*, orthographic cuboid.

begins on a loud in-breath, and the fragment is rounded off by a slap tongue from the clarinet and exclamatory 'a' from the voice: there is no recognizable text here. These materials relate to a precompositional, orthographically projected cuboid which is subdivided into smaller units (Figure 5.2). Each intersection has a three-digit coordinate determining the following musical parameters: whether the 'instant' is long or short, contains more noise or pitch content, and finally whether it contains many or few different pitches. Each *Augenblick* has, therefore, a unique combination of these parameters.[15]

While this compositional design appears constraining, both the composer and performer are afforded a significant degree of freedom. The parameters chosen allow the composer to make many individual decisions within each instant, while the parameters themselves, particularly 'noise content', are somewhat fuzzy. The performers, too, have a good deal of autonomy in choosing and discarding material when deciding upon an order and any repetitions. For Blume, the result of this precompositional process is different from the creation of a collection of fragments. For him, the pieces of material are 'best likened to distillations from some original substance, perhaps one which is too abstract to be translated into sound'.[16]

One consequence of the approach to form in the *Augenblicke* is that the listener should become aware of their own attempts at interpreting the musical events that are unfolding and, eventually, of their interchangeability. This point was hammered home during a rather poor, but extremely instructive, performance of the piece at which I was present. In this, the performers paused after every *Augenblick*, often turning pages, giving the music a rather stilted and stifled surface, with each moment heavily delineated. This is precisely *not* the point of the work, in which the borders of the moments should become blurred: gestures at the end of one moment should at times seamlessly merge with the next, meaning the pauses in longer fragments break up the flow as much as do the moves from one instant to another. Listeners should constantly reassess the boundaries they place around the fragments as they weave the musical fabric. The question of repetition – of hearing the same fragment in a different context – is somewhat sidestepped in this piece by the composer, as the question of how this will function is left up to the performer. However, how repetition can be conceived within the shifting perceptions of new music's open forms is a theme taken up specifically in one of Spahlinger's most significant works.

passage/paysage

passage/paysage, premiered at Donaueschingen in 1990, is one of the composer's most critically acclaimed and important pieces. Enno Poppe, in a speech celebrating Spahlinger as recipient of the Berliner Kunstpreis, goes as far to state that it was 'our *Sacre du Printemps*'.[17] The piece is successful in part because it synthesizes so many of the compositional concerns that commentators, and indeed the composer, have identified in his compositional output. The disruption of order, open form, composition between categories, mechanical repetition and studies of perception are all present in some form in its 45-minute duration.[18] Above all else, however, *passage/paysage* is an in-depth investigation into the nature of continuity and 'meaningful' temporal succession, making it particularly relevant here.

These concerns are hinted at by the two words that make up the title, which provide distinct yet related metaphors for the experience of the piece. To take *passage* first, it is a French term meaning 'passing by'. Spahlinger explains its significance succinctly: '*passage* means transition. everything is transition. truth is only to be had in and as transition, therefore not "to be had" at all'.[19] He also describes this approach as transition 'made absolute':[20] it is not a change from one fixed state to another but continual movement in which no new fixed state is reached. Spahlinger seeks a music of constant flux rather than solid ideas so that the very nature of transition, and the way that it constantly eludes listeners' grasp, comes to the fore.

In seeking to explore transition, he takes the idea to its most extreme by attempting to present what he terms 'all-sided continuous development': a conception of the development of musical material that proceeds in all directions and in all parameters: 'everything should continuously develop out of everything. the theme of the piece is: all-sided continuity [*kontinuität*].'[21] Figure 5.3 shows a diagram Spahlinger uses to illustrate this idea in relation to the opening. Listeners, and musical material, begin in the centre of the sketch and then proceed in all directions at once.

Direct translation of this idea into music is impossible, however, as development in all directions quickly touches upon an infinite number of possibilities, as Spahlinger is well aware. He describes the concept of all-sided continuous development as a 'mode of seeing for the gods'.[22] It serves instead as some kind of ideal towards which the work strives. For him it concerns presenting 'a mode of experience' but we 'never get out of these problems of presentation. you could choose materials that play in a register that you can't hear for the entire piece. it depends on making it compatible with our modes of experience and with our

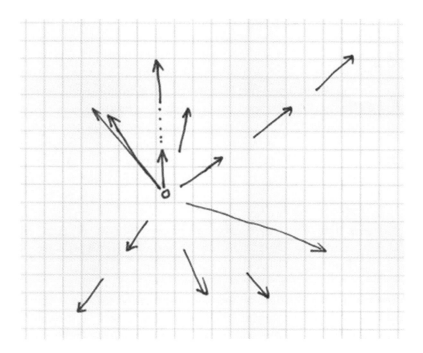

FIGURE 5.3: *passage/paysage* opening, Spahlinger sketch.

aesthetic models [*vorbilder*]'.[23] Spahlinger often selects such impossible conceits for his pieces to explore, probing precisely these 'problems of presentation' and attempting to make them rise to the surface of the music. According to the composer, 22 distinct materials are employed at the opening, which are permutated throughout the section and which develop after their own fashion. These materials correspond to the different trajectories shown in the diagram. That the lines are broken in Figure 5.4 is an indication that the possibilities of 'all-sided continuous development' are explored by shifting between various competing developmental directions, hence the permutation of these materials. Both here and later in the piece, the composer attempts to imply this mode of development by employing a narrative that he describes as 'arbitrary'. Listeners should be aware of the possibility of moving in any direction – of the music developing in any way – even if it eventually has to take just one particular course.

The second half of the title, *paysage*, meaning 'landscape' in French, relates to *passage* in so far as the idea of moving *through* a metaphorical landscape is the most important way Spahlinger conceptualizes the work. He explains this while discussing the arbitrariness of repetition in the piece: recurrence, far from representing some decisive moment of rearrival or return, is an accidental facet of the process of journeying:

> and particularly i have attempted to make the above clear [a particular feeling of arbitrariness of development] by using spirals, which are somewhat different from traditional reprises. firstly, because the sequence that will at some point later be repeated never appears again in the same order, moreover it changes at the very least in tempo or in other more far-reaching features. here the idea of landscape came to my aid. it is similar to when you yourself seek a path [*weg*] and it goes partly in figures of eight or in snaking lines and you either come out at a point at which you already were but you came from somewhere else and go forward elsewhere; or you come to a clearing and see from a distance a point where you already were and it has really taken on a completely different meaning from this perspective and over the course of your journey.[24]

If *passage* is concerned with transience and transition, then *paysage* provides a sense of space, perspective and orientation. The composer does not wish to evoke the spirit of the romantic *Wanderer* here; rather, he uses metaphors of space to describe a topography of time. This includes, most importantly, the experience of arriving at already familiar musical ideas that somehow take on an entirely new meaning.

Markus Hechtle frames the interaction between the two halves of the title within the situation of the perceiver and perceived: 'going, moving, sliding

Bar		Material
386–406	Approach	Very clear A-Eb tritones followed by loud, brassy descending chords. Extreme pressure chords in strings emerge out of texture.
407–419	Idea	Extreme pressure string chords become a series of impulses in which individual instruments drift apart. Move to overlapping entries on F ¾#.
420–447	Withdrawal	Monophonic texture continues with same overlapping entries on a number of different pitches, creating a kind of long melody.
448–455		Brass enter before the music fades out into silence.
456–470		Spacious chords drift in and out of silence.
471–484		Return to one note material which moves to E.
485–526	Approach	E joined by Bb at big bombastic moment with strong rhythmic figure which has more articulations each time it is repeated. Followed immediately by its 'deathly' parody, which moves to an exploration of noisy sounds.
527–540	Idea	Extreme pressure chords that were heard before (though altered in pitch) emerge from white noise. Dispersing chords that become F¾# one note material which moves to Bb.
541–553	Withdrawal	Out of repetitions of Bb an obvious rhythm develops.
554–579		Another loud entry on Bb. Becomes an exploration of different meters before the Bb pitch disappears completely.
580–584		Foreground falls away to reveal background of col legno battuto strings.

TABLE 5.1: *passage/paysage*, musical ideas in bars 386–584.

[*Gleiten*], happening [*Passieren*]; that is the situation of the perceiver', while the perceived is 'ephemeral, disparate, the same, similar, different, but in flux, never stable, always changed'.[25] The music is forever changing, therefore, even when it is 'the same, similar', because of the changing situation of those who perceive it. The composer's idea of spiral repetitions, 'somewhat different from traditional reprises', are central to this experience. Their intention is to create a unique feeling of repetition, one that contrasts with classical forms and with later, primarily nineteenth-century, narrative models.

Spiral Repetitions and Narrative Models in passage/paysage

In attempting to assess what is particularly noteworthy in Spahlinger's spiral repetitions, it is illuminating to explore the relationship between narrative repetition and *passage/paysage*. Byron Almén's defence of narrative's musical applications provides a useful framework here, stating that music that displays narrative features would likely combine:

> 1) a syntax that could group constituent elements into dialogic and/or conflictual relationships; 2) the continued coherence of these groupings over time; 3) teleological directedness (at least one significant change in the relations between elements from the beginning of the piece to the end); and 4) cultural pre-conditions of performance which permit or invite a listener to be attentive to the above features.[26]

Of these, the most relevant points to this discussion are 2 and 3. Point 2 refers to the necessity for material in narrative forms to be grouped together in meaningful units. This is important as Spahlinger's repetitions often appear in radically different contexts, lacking the surrounding material to create a 'coherent' grouping. The arbitrariness of the succession of events creates the impression that there can be no 'coherent', quasi-causal groupings in this music at all as it could always have taken a different path. The relations and hierarchies between musical events, which Almén describes as key to narrative understanding,[27] are in *passage/paysage* made arbitrary. To employ a narrative metaphor: there can be no sense of musical overcoming when protagonist is indistinguishable from setting, and no return when our origin was never defined.

A musical example from the third and longest section of the the piece (see Table 5.1) will give will give an impression of how Spahlinger's spirals interact with Almén's second and third points: coherent groupings and teleological directedness. This section, while containing many different types of music, often provides the listener with very clear and defined musical material, such as repetitions of a single pitch or rhythm. Such graspable musical ideas afford a return to somewhere familiar, making the aptness of Spahlinger's spatial metaphor difficult to ignore: we arrive at the same place and see it with quite different eyes. The passage described here is around 10 minutes in length.

The two most important materials are the 'arrivals' on Bb and the string chords played with extreme bow pressure followed by the F¾# sections. The chords and F¾# are heard twice while various overlapping processes in between provide the constant transition that corresponds to the 'passage' tendency of the work. In particular it should be noted how the approach to and withdrawal from this idea

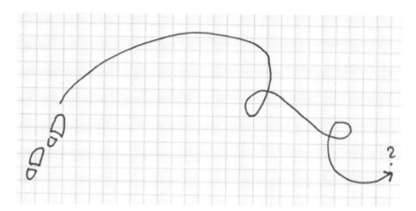

FIGURE 5.4: *passage/paysage*, spahlinger sketch.

are different on each occasion, providing contrasting contexts for its appearance. In this span of music, the repetition of such a short passage is striking but such a durational mismatch adds to the feeling that the return of the chords is not a major event, and that the music is still developing. The prominence of Bb in this section is tantalizing fodder for the analyst but is not obviously part of any long-term pitch architecture. Such pitch relations appear and disappear, crystallize and disintegrate, over the course of the piece, but none hold for long. Two points should be made about the description of this passage before moving on. First, the terms 'approach', 'idea' and 'withdrawal' are only for the purpose of this discussion: many sections here could be considered an 'idea', so relativized is the hierarchy of musical material. Second, it may have already been noted that the 'idea' repeated here is in itself a process or transition. Even in these apparently graspable moments, the *passage* element of the piece is still strong.

Figure 5.4 shows another of Spahlinger's own sketches used to describe the arbitrary path of development in such sections. He attempts to give the sense that the succession of musical events held in the score is but one possible outcome of the course of the piece, even if it is concretely set in the notation. Every development is intended to be arbitrary, the looping path here is not directed towards any end result. At times there can be an idea that sounds like an arrival: for example, the loud brass entries discussed above, but these are quickly shown to be just a passing stage of the journey.

The extreme pressure chords present an obvious moment of repetition, yet their context, provided by the music directly before and after, is quite different. In approaching or leaving the material the experience is always new, while the material itself appears changed by the path we take to it. The chords never return within a 'coherent' group of other musical material that is required by Almén for a sense of narrative to justify the repetition. The constant transition provided by Spahlinger's use of processes creates change without any reference points, corresponding to the absolute transition he seeks to explore. Repetitions, usually moments that provide orientation within traditional forms, here provide no such thing as the form of repetition employed problematizes the very concept of formal orientation. The reappearance of musical ideas, unheralded and unexpected, within a changing context creates a highly complex experience of time as it is in part through a sense of teleology and meaningful repetition that works progress and delineate traditional temporalities.

For all Spahlinger's talk of possibility, it is clear that this path remains within certain limits. The material he employs always stays within the realm of the 'sound' of new music, unlike, for example, *extension* which includes faux-quotations from the classical tradition. This limitation can be seen as a strength in relation to issues of continuity, however, as lack of stylistic upheaval focuses attention on the gradual, continuous changes and creates a greater equality of musical ideas, aiding both the exploration of all-sided continuous development and the effectiveness of the spiral repetitions. A more collage-like surface would detract from the exploration of these concerns: the adherence to a particular type of musical material relates again to the 'problems of presentation'.

There is also an important sense here that the unfolding of the music is unpredictable or unstable and that this becomes a fundamental aim of later works exploring open form. By focusing on the malleability of transition – whether through 'all-sided development' or spiral repetitions – Spahlinger seeks to create the sense that any material can lead to any other and, therefore, that the feeling of ideas *having* to succeed each other is an illusion. These concepts are particularly important for a strand of pieces that focus on collections of basic 'modules' of material that can appear in any order: including the primarily text-based *vorschläge: konzepte zur ver(über)flüssigung der funktion des komponisten* (*suggestions: concepts for making the role of the composer superfluous*, trans. Blume, 1993), which is performable by amateur or school groups; the ensemble piece *verlorener weg* (*lost path*, 2000); and the orchestral piece *doppelt bejaht* (2009), which Kreidler calls an 'orchestral version' of the *vorschläge*.[28] These pieces comprise usually fixed materials – whether it is held chords, pointillistic textures or descriptions of extreme register – and instructions for transitioning between them. In the more defined ensemble and orchestral versions, these transitions are described in some detail, or, as in the case of *verlorener weg*, Spahlinger has prepared two fixed scores. Each piece should give the impression, however, that there is no static or inevitable order of events: the freedom to pursue alternative paths between materials is a vital part of the experience and an obvious reference to more traditional conceptions of open form. Though in *doppelt bejaht*, ostensibly for the sake of performance practicalities, players can choose from a range of options in deciding which material to play next, the impression Spahlinger seeks is that any material can transition to any other. There should be no causal or teleological path that the music follows.

vorschläge: konzepte zur ver(über)flüssigung der funktion des komponisten

suggestions: concepts for making the role of the composer superfluous is a collection of 28 ideas, or concepts, for musical performance. In these, almost entirely text-based, instructions are described various ideas for types of sound and types of relationship between performers that can create musical textures. The instrumentation, number of performers, form and combination of these elements is left open in the main, though some of the concepts by their nature suggest larger or smaller groups, or instruments that are pitched or that can sustain a tone. Others, such as 'irreversibel', suggest the use of non-traditional instruments, as it asks for sounds that 'are the result of an action that in no sense can be undone', such as the popping of a balloon or the splintering of glass. The next concept listed, 'kairos', describes a long sound, pitch or chord, which 'in the right moment' is aborted or interrupted. This process should then be repeated with different lengths of time in between the interruptions. Another, 'meditation I (permutation)' suggests woodblocks, a maximum of seven players, an approximate tempo, dynamic, and a continually varying distribution of who is playing. The 'rules' defined in each concept differ depending on the type of skill or effect Spahlinger wishes to explore, with some containing just a few sentences while others take two pages of explanation.

Spahlinger states that these materials 'can be played in any selection, order or combination, also simultaneously' while 'every form of variation and further development is desired.' The 'preliminary considerations' (*vorüberlegungen*) offered by way of introduction are a fascinating insight into the composer's thoughts on form, musical participation and their relationship with the political. Here, he is first concerned with countering the impression that these suggestions are merely the results of his musical will packaged in another form: they are *suggestions* that can be 'further developed' as noted in the descriptions, albeit most likely in the direction the composer imagines. The rules themselves that are laid out 'should not be orientated towards a result', rather they should be open to influence, change and abolition: breach of the rules is also allowed as 'it will become apparent, that focused breaching of the rules brings more truth to light than a rule can ever have'.

The openness of some of the concepts is not only on practical grounds. Spahlinger states that 'decisions require expertise' and that here an 'artistic competence' rather than the craft of instrumental learning, which is 'always bound to a relatively fixed set of rules', is the goal. The easy bridge between some of the concepts as musical entities and their social meaning – take, for example, 'emphatie' or 'flüsterpropaganda' ('empathy' and 'whispering propaganda') – is not unequivocally encouraged by the composer, stating that 'it is about music. 'only where social processes are almost direct sounding processes are they allowed to come to the fore.' Nevertheless, the political applications of the relationships and processes performed here are far from distant. There is didacticism here certainly, but it is a far cry from many attempts at introducing musical concepts through reference to the canon or the orchestra, such as can be found in the paternal voice of Britten's *Young Person's Guide to the Orchestra*. The composer wants to encourage 'a self-observing, also critical, relationship to one's own will, to existence and to the existences to come, without imposing oneself'. The 'non-intentionality' required in the performance of these concepts 'should not be confused with passivity or fatalism; it was always an artistic and intellectual virtue and should be a social virtue.'

This collection is a condensed expression of much of what is important to Spahlinger's compositional project. The social, the political and the musical are intended to approach one another. It reveals a conceptual edge to the composer's work in general, one that includes the forming of relationships between performers that point outwards from the purely musical. Whether the composer's apparent desire to make his own function superfluous is achieved in this collection is of course another matter. He is clear that rules can be abolished if there is a strong artistic reason for doing so and it is just such artistic reasoning that he wishes to encourage. Yet rules there are, ones that reflect the aesthetic proclivities of the composer to a significant degree, if not entirely. There is a tension between these pieces providing a special insight into this composer's work and his desire to get rid of the composer altogether: there is after all no ego more ripe for criticism than one that claims it is egoless.

Transitions in doppelt bejaht *and* verlorener weg

Spahlinger's 'orchestral environment' *doppelt bejaht – étuden für orchester* was premiered in 2009 at the Donaueschinger Musiktage by the SWR Symphony Orchestra Baden-Baden and Freiburg. The conductorless performance lasted four hours with the orchestral musicians working in shifts to occupy the performance stations, which were distributed around the around the space. As mentioned in Chapter 1, the public public were allowed to come and go as they pleased: another level on which the idea of listeners' perception forming the piece makes itself felt. The piece is made up of 24 contrasting materials, which the musicians move between in what should be a quasi-democratic process of transition. Figure 5.5 isolates one of these materials to give an idea of how they are defined, both practically and sonically. The fourth material, *punktefeld* or 'field of points', is represented in the score by a sketch indicating a cloud of short and timbrally varied sounds. Following this is over a page of text, which describes possible evolutions of the material, and, in the 'overview' (which acts as a kind of score), the instructions given to each instrument are listed, explaining from what pitches and techniques they can choose.

The 'field' is at first defined by incredibly quiet individual impulses from all instruments (except tuba) played in a damped or stifled manner. The effect will

04. "punktefeld"
besetzung: alle ad lib. (ohne nebeninstrumente), keine tuba

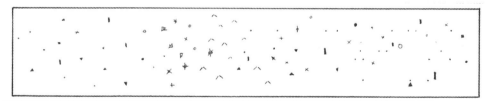

nur kurze oder gedämpfte oder kurz nach dem einschwingvorgang abgedämpfte oder erstickte klänge.
sempre pianissimo oder leiser. die lautstärke richtet sich nach dem geräuschpegel am aufführungsort. alles soll an der grenze des hörbaren sein und den zuhörern stille suggerieren. nur bei absoluter ruhe muss nicht noch leiser als ppp gepielt werden. bitte immer nur einzelne ereignisse spielen, die gut durchhörbar sind. keine punkteschwärme oder –wolken.
alle klänge, die nur paarweise produziert werden können (z. b. holzbläser: klappe schlagen und öffnen, streicher: griff-finger hörbar auf die saite aufsetzen und loslassen) bitte deutlich durch längere pause voneinander trennen, damit kein zusammenhang zwischen beiden gehört werden kann.

FIGURE 5.5: *doppelt bejaht*, '04. "punktefeld"' extract.
English translation: only short, dampened or smothered sounds, or sounds dampened shortly after sounding. always pianissimo or quieter. the volume depends on the noise level of the particular performance location. everything should be on the border of the audible to suggest silence to the audience. only play more quietly than *ppp* in absolute silence. please always play single sounds that are easily audible. no swarms or clouds of points.
all sounds, that can only be produced in pairs (e.g. woodwinds: keys close and open, strings: placing the left hand audibly on the finger board before letting go) please clearly separate from each other through a long pause, so that no connection between the two can be heard.

depend on the performance, but is likely to begin as a hushed, tinkling texture. That Spahlinger has a detailed idea of the material he wishes to hear is shown by the indication that 'all sounds, that can only be produced in pairs' (such as the two sounds caused by depressing and raising the keys of a wind instrument, or placing and releasing the finger on the fingerboard of a string instrument) should be clearly separated from each other by a long pause. These, after all, are specific directions that show he has considered how his instructions will be interpreted. This contrasts somewhat with the *vorschläge* which are far more flexible in instrumentation and, therefore, far less defined in terms of instrumental technique. It is tempting to infer here that Spahlinger is aware of the preferences of modern-day orchestral institutions, in which clear instructions are very much encouraged when branching out from traditional performance practice.

Two further examples from *punktefeld* show how individual instruments are handled in this more detailed context. The bassoon should use key clicks and pitches, while the horns can hit the mouthpiece with the palm or use tongue rams and play the pitches indicated, albeit only once. For both bassoon and horn, pitches and techniques are given with the intention that they should fit into the material characteristics already described.

These are the ways in which Spahlinger defines the sounds of the individual modules but, almost more important, is how to move from one module to another. After the character of the material is established, or conceivably even before it is established, there are options as to where it will transition, the intention being that the players themselves decide, or even argue over, where to go. For *punktefeld* there are three transition options: number 11 '*hommage à scelsi*', 15 '*ritardando moltissimo*' or 16 '*flageolette 5 und 7*'.

Each transition employs a process indicated by one of Spahlinger's diagrams and a textual description. In the first, for example, the pitches of the *punktefeld* should gradually match themselves to the pitch area that will become the focus of *hommage à scelsi*, while also increasing in length. In the third, any player with the facility should begin to play an E natural harmonic, again increasing in duration, before moving to number 16 'harmonics 5 and 7'. The type of transition is dependent on which number the players wish to go to next but is almost always a gradual move away from the previous material. In all transitions shown above, the pitches of the new material emerge from the field of points already established until it dominates the texture. Each of the 24 types of material are similarly organized, with instructions for their performance as well as the transition the players can effect. Three also contain possible, and, according to the score, only 'apparent' conclusions as the piece should feel like it has no qualitative end, relating once again to Spahlinger's conception that new music can provide no genuine sense of conclusion.

fagotte:
klappenschlag und tonhöhen. wird auf dem instrument das rohr belassen aber nicht im mund geschlossen, erbringt der klappenschlag einen klang, der in dieser lage etwa eine kleine terz höher als der griff ist.

hörner:
sehr kurzes anblasgeräusch mit zungenstoß oder (vorsichtiger) schlag auf das mundstück bei vorgeschriebener ventilstellung. tonhöhen.

FIGURE 5.6: *doppelt bejaht*, 04. "punktefeld'" extract.
English translation: bassoon:
key clicks and pitches. if the reed is left on the instrument but not enclosed in the mouth, the key click produces a sound that is approximately a minor third higher than the fingered pitch in this range.
horns:
very short breath sound with tongue slap or (carefully) hit the mouth piece with the prescribed valve positions. pitches.

The processes of transition in *doppelt bejaht* are very reminiscent of Spahlinger's explanatory sketches for *verlorener weg*, which he uses in his essay 'political implications of the material of new music' (2015).[29] This piece is built from similar modules of material – thirteen in all – that are then connected in an apparently arbitrary order: arbitrary as it is quite different in the two versions that currently exist, while other possible versions would have yet another order. More than in *doppelt bejaht*, however, Spahlinger wishes to express the idea that *any* material can transition to *any* other, usually through some kind of process. This he demonstrates by using the same 'field of points' from Figure 5.6 to show how a material can transform itself in any direction. The diagrams here are not intended to be comprehensive but only show some of the paths these transitions can take.

verzweigung
besetzung wie vorher

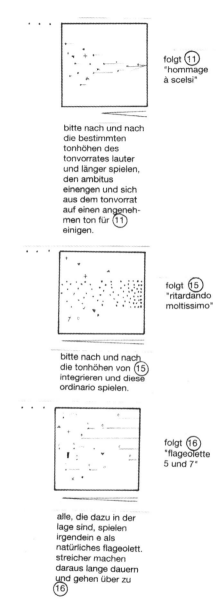

folgt ⑪
"hommage
à scelsi"

bitte nach und nach
die bestimmten
tonhöhen des
tonvorrates lauter
und länger spielen,
den ambitus
einengen und sich
aus dem tonvorrat
auf einen angeneh-
men ton für ⑪
einigen.

folgt ⑮
"ritardando
moltissimo"

bitte nach und nach
die tonhöhen von ⑮
integrieren und diese
ordinario spielen.

folgt ⑯
"flageolette
5 und 7"

alle, die dazu in der
lage sind, spielen
irgendein e als
natürliches flageolett.
streicher machen
daraus lange dauern
und gehen über zu
⑯

FIGURE 5.7: *doppelt bejaht*, '04. "punktefeld"' transition.
Under box 1: please play the prescribed pitches of the prescribed pitches louder and longer little by little,
reduce the ambitus and agree upon one comfortable pitch from the prescribed pitches.
Under box 2: please integrate the pitches from 15 little by little and play these *ordinario*.
Under box 3: all that are able play an E natural harmonic. strings increase the duration and transition to 16.

Figure 5.8 shows how a field of points can transform into – from top to bottom – a held cluster or chord, a rising scale, a sustained melody, a regular repeating chord, Shepard-tone-like rising lines and repeated articulations of a single note. The potential for all-sided development and transition makes the musical material of the present potentially interchangeable with all others in the piece, rather than there being a logical or necessary musical narrative. This is the fundamental theme of *verlorener weg*, which, as a collection of materials that each can transform into any other, could conceivably exist in an infinite number of versions.

It is worth noting that such transformations rely on a particular conception of musical material, one in which the music is dominated by a specific 'rule' of order, such as the field of points which comprises short notes throughout the range of the instruments. This material is, therefore, extremely static when heard divorced from the transitions that are so important to these pieces. In comparison to an organic, developmental approach which might consider a particular material to encompass conflicting elements, such as a smooth melody with a staccato accompaniment, Spahlinger's materials are rather one-sided in order to best demonstrate his compositional concerns. Behind the composer's apparently objective descriptions of 'material', there in fact lies one of the chief elements that links the musical surface of his pieces.

Ruthemeier, whose article on *verlorener weg* explains Spahlinger's intentions relating to open form, states that the 'general interchangeability of individual parts is not all that should be shown, rather Spahlinger lets the material appear as a sequence of different situations, so that constantly different, but in themselves coherent, form-paths are presented'.[30] Each form the music assumes will in itself be 'coherent', even though the succession of modules of material is unpredictable. Ruthemeier goes on to state that this formal approach allows 'the particular capacity of the listener to interpret' to appear, once again referring to the idea of the listeners' sense-making faculties.[31] This approach can be seen to provide a challenge to an audience versed in more traditional modes of listening, in which recapitulation – whether heroic and affirmatory or fatalistic and tragic – is a necessary part of music's continuity. Spahlinger seeks to challenge this mode of listening through his individual approach to musical continuity and repetition.

Considerations of politics are rarely distant from Spahlinger's practice and are often made explicit. In the case of *passage/paysage*, a sense of arbitrary development is seen by the composer to inform and challenge a belief in historical necessity. He seeks to expose a 'barbarity of continuity', which always leaves those unlucky enough not to be part of the main trend at a disadvantage:

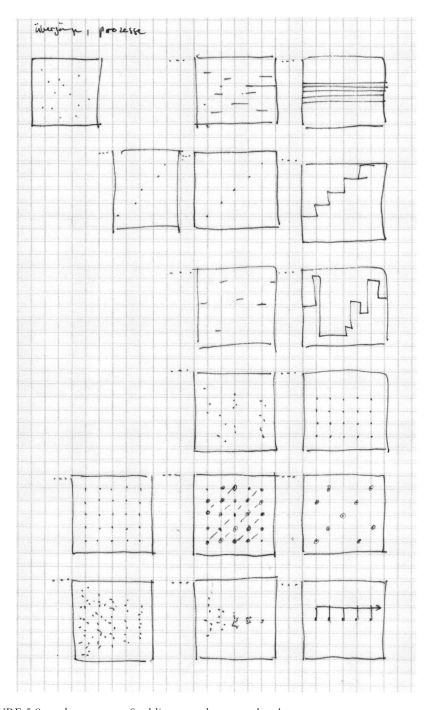

FIGURE 5.8: *verlorener weg*, Spahlinger explanatory sketch.

always then, when one sees where the development has gone one can comfort – or also not comfort – those that fell by the wayside, that were not in the main trend, with the great end result. one can excuse the path of the development, that the masses of victims were not essentially part of the development. if the development had gone elsewhere, then others would have fallen by the wayside. and this contradiction in itself, this barbarity of continuity led me to attempt to make perceptible that every development out of which something qualitatively different arises, has a certain degree of arbitrariness.[32]

The composer's exploration of temporality is intimately tied to this conception of continuity. Listeners are predisposed to treat any musical sequence as a goal-directed path, even if there is no necessary or logical connection between successive events. This is what he calls the *Ergänzungsleistung* or 'ability to complete' that listeners possess.[33] Listeners will make sense of almost any narrative in relation to the revelation of the 'great end result' and to work against this on the level of continuity, it is argued, is in some way related to questioning the necessity of the narrative of history, or the accidental nature of what appears logical. Taken in this way, it raises the injustice of those that 'fell by the wayside' whose suffering we can easily overlook: is where we stand historically simply the result of the blind staggering of history? And do we too easily take 'things as they are' as justification for the crimes of the past? The narrative of these pieces is an education in seemingly arbitrary development, from which these striking and disturbing parallels with history can be made.

Spahlinger's exploration of continuity seeks to bring the temporal order, perhaps even musical time itself, into the realm of the political. He not only 'rebels against the conventional temporal order' as Adorno puts it,[34] but also conducts a nuanced and diverse exploration that engages with listeners' expectations in order to confound them and in so doing demonstrates the inadequacy of verbal temporal categorization. It is the engagement with the listener that makes Spahlinger's exploration so successful: our own faculties are at the centre of his practice as he presents us with something solid and seemingly knowable, before showing its transience and apparent arbitrariness. This engagement is found not only in his experimentation with continuity but is also key to his wider compositional project, leading to his keen interest in perception. The way temporal exploration, achieved through examining transition and formal succession, is very much part of this wider compositional project shows the extent to which it is integrated in Spahlinger's practice. For him at least it is as Adorno predicted: the temporal has very much become 'an element of composition'.[35]

2. Critical Commentary

The Means of Production: Spahlinger's Performance Practice

Before discussing the implications of Spahlinger's open form approach, it is worth detailing how it relates to one of the ways in which the composer believes music can be political. This is his conception, based on Marx, of the 'means of production' in musical dissemination and performance. He considers it to encompass the 'institutions, traditional instruments and their technique, notation etc.' that allow music to be produced.[36] Presumably, we might add to that list the various forms of technology and organizations that are responsible for the dissemination of music in modern society. Much like Marx in his assertion that forces of production create certain relations between people, Spahlinger believes the means of production that reinforce arrangements of production and consumption 'produce [...] and reproduce social circumstances together with their attempts at interpretation and justification'.[37]

The composer states that the musical thought of European new music is determined by the 'hierarchical division of labour between composer, performer (conductor/musicians) and listeners'.[38] The system of notation used today and developed over centuries, for example, seems predicated on the idea of the hierarchical relationship of a single composer to one or many performers. He states that in collective composition groups, in which Spahlinger has himself often participated, musicians must often work 'against the implicit sense [*sinn*] of notation',[39] that is, struggle against the implicit hierarchical relationships it contains. This division of labour has certain negative effects: the third trombone part of a romantic symphony, from which it is impossible to reconstruct the whole, is provided as an example of the assertion of 'structural violence'.[40] The means of production designate that certain members of the orchestra have a less fulfilling musical experience. Like Marx's proletariat suffering under the division of labour, the orchestral musician is apparently alienated from the commodity that they help to produce.

This distaste for the hierarchies thrown up by the traditional means of production in music is part of Spahlinger's justification for organizing his semi-improvisatory pieces in the way he does and for his continued improvisation. *doppelt bejaht*, for example, dispenses with the conductor, linking it with his interest in other improvisatory musics as well as traditions of modernist experimental music that sought new performance processes, such as Cardew's Scratch Orchestra and the conductorless pieces of Cage and Hans Wüthrich.[41] That the piece is dedicated to the latter shows an awareness of this tradition, one heavily influenced by the socio-political movements around 1968 that also made such a deep impression on the composer.

More than simply organizing the performers in a different manner, however, the transitions of *doppelt bejaht* should also be brought about by a sort of musical democratic process. This means that players can have small musical debates concerning to which material they wish to transition. So, in the transitions from *punktefeld* above, one player may start to introduce material in order to transition to 15, 'ritardando moltissimo', while another may disagree and begin to play the harmonics that are fundamental to 16, 'harmonics 5 and 7'. Whether either is successful will depend on the musical choices of their colleagues. Nonnenmann describes how it was these transitions that provided the greatest challenge of their careers for some of the orchestral musicians, as, dispersed around the large performance space, they could not always hear their colleagues in order to make informed musical decisions.[42] A compromise was reached in which screens told the players to which number they were moving, something that hardly corresponds to the composer's intention behind these moments and which, according to Nonnenmann, had a significant effect on the listening experience.[43] These challenges are in part a result of Spahlinger's attempt to disrupt the ordinary working process of the orchestra, which he takes as potentially representative of hierarchies within society, a leap that is much disputed. It may be remembered from the previous chapter that Rancière's aesthetic rehearsals for the political may well apply first to musical institutions, as is the case here. Before considering these debates further, it is important to point out that the composer's efforts in this direction are not without artistic risk: his search for an elusive musical experience has courted the danger of the performed works not functioning at all.

Such an approach is an attempt to avoid what Spahlinger sees as standard classical, and contemporary classical, performance practice: 'the reproduction of music is, like material production, organised in a way that what the elites have concocted can be performed by "them down there" without it having been understood and without the need for a consensus.'[44] The extent to which these pieces are successful is of course up for debate, especially considering the quite restricted parameters in which these so-called freedoms exist: performers are, after all, only allowed to move between materials strictly delineated by the composer, and the idea of gradual transition is imposed.

There is a tension here – one that is part of a wider pressure on performers' abilities in modernist music – in that this institutional critique, and its intended hint at more enlightened work, could be seen to make the work of the orchestral musicians far more difficult. As Kreidler states: 'for the orchestral musician today self-determination is more painful than scraping behind the bridge'.[45] This is to say that in attempting to point towards freedom Spahlinger is in fact imposing his will on the only people he has under his control and who have little say in the matter despite the allegedly increased democratic elements of the performance situation, a debate connecting with the idea of consent within contemporary music that has only recently come to the fore.[46] There is little room in this set-up for ideas of freedom that contradict the composer's. It is clear, therefore, that certain hierarchies between composer and performer are necessary in staging this piece and that the psychology of the orchestral musicians themselves becomes grist to the mill of Spahlinger's critique. Critics of Marxism in practice might see a parallel here between the way states have demanded full totalitarian power in order to bring about the freedom of the people.

In Spahlinger's defence, he appears far from unaware of these contradictions. He discusses similar problems in an interview with Oehlschlägel – carried out prior to the composition of *doppelt bejaht* – regarding more improvisatory versus fixed notational practices, stating that the two approaches are 'not mutually exclusive' and that it is not 'reactionary and dictatorial to write notes that others have to play. The situation is complex and particularly worthy of thought in orchestral music'.[47] He continues,

> 'orchestral musicians are indeed immensely experienced and capable of playing the most complicated texts without great difficulty and it would be a waste of available productive power if one does not want to use that at all. The absent freedom of choice, the opportunity to intervene [*eingriffsmöglichkeit*], also only in the choice of pieces, remains a huge problem.'[48]

Imagining a critique of the orchestra without in some way challenging these musicians is also rather difficult, as they are the most obvious embodiment of this tradition. In interview Spahlinger was keen to point out that this was not an attempt to 'free' the musician from the bonds of their oppressors but to perform or represent these kinds of relations for the audience.[49] In the programme note to *doppelt bejaht*, he states that 'artistic work can at times give an inkling of what non-alienated work would be'.[50] Artistic labour is to act as some kind of representation, yet it is much more than simply feigning the activities of the outside world in the concert hall. Critics might also question why the composer identifies these relations as problematic only to continue to propagate them in his more traditionally organized orchestral and chamber works.

Spahlinger's approach to the means of production is, in a similar way to the construction and deconstruction of order, a way of rehearsing the political in the aesthetic sphere, in this case by presenting the listener with a changed performance environment. This theme of the relationship between the political and the aesthetic is vital for the composer: as he himself states, 'it is of course one of my favourite ideas [*lieblingsvorstellungen*] that an aesthetic attitude become conscious also simultaneously is a political one.'[51] This does not result in contradiction-free political action, any attempt at such would likely be seen as propaganda. In fact, in his large-scale choral work *in dem ganzen ocean von empfindungen eine welle absondern, sie anhalten* contradiction is harnessed to the piece's lasting advantage.[52] In the instrumental open form works discussed here, there is no necessity to view them as political entities, but as often compelling and unusual explorations of musical continuity. Yet, it is the power of the listening experience and the search for meaning it contains that encourages a search for meaning outside of the musical work.

Open Form; Closed Material?

With many pieces that claim an allegiance to open form, there is the potential for criticism from a listener's perspective: that the 'open' element is an abstract, unheard feature that has no bearing on the experience of a piece. Such critique was voiced, for example, by Boulez in 1957 and by Bill Hopkins.[53] This is a criticism that is levelled at many modernist attempts at creating such a formal experience. Eggebrecht, for example, argues in this vein when he states that the 'possibilities' of Cage's music are not audible, only the 'results', though this ignores the important point that if listeners *know* Cage's pieces contain significant openness then their perception is fundamentally altered.[54] Nevertheless, the common thread of these criticisms is that open form is something that composers become terribly interested in, while listeners are left out in the cold, unable to hear how the form is – sometimes only marginally – different in this or that performance. Blume argues, however, that the parameters with which the *128 erfüllte augenblicke* are composed become the 'parameters of listening' rather than any purely abstract construction. The stark presentation of individual instants, seemingly hermetically sealed from one another, is, according to him, not only audible but the most important and unique aspect of the listening experience. Even in this example, then, which is probably Spahlinger's most conventional open form piece, Blume finds a novel formal approach.

The composer, of course, would also answer these criticisms by stating that he believes open form is present in all new music, therefore, it is always fundamental to listeners' experiences. Two issues arise from this position, however. First, if all pieces of new music are in open form, there is a question as to why Spahlinger has gone to such elaborate lengths to compose formal indeterminacy in such pieces as *doppelt bejaht*. This is explained to some extent by the political implications of the means of production, but there is also the sense that with these works the composer is attempting to bring such issues as far as possible into the consciousness of the listener, making them not just an attribute of the music but their fundamental theme. The second issue concerns Spahlinger's insistence that open form is characteristic of all new music. This rather implies that pieces that attempt to come to a satisfying conclusion, and insist on the necessity of their formal progression, are in a kind of denial. This despite the fact that he does not believe that the materials of *passage/paysage*, for example, can be rearranged at will. Despite his belief in formal interchangeability, then, he still holds on to certain traditional composerly rights. Whether this is a selfless act depends on the extent to which Spahlinger really has given over 'control' in these pieces.

The various materials in the quasi-improvisatory open form pieces comprise an attempt by the composer to describe what he sees as the 'typical' materials of new music, whether it be the now familiar 'field of points', 'one tone, many colours', the 'infinite number of tempi' or 'hommage à scelsi'. They shed light not only on the construction of the pieces in which they are present, but also provide concrete evidence of what Spahlinger considers as the fundamentally new materials new music employs, though again, they tend to create relatively static musical textures and situations. That these materials point *outside* of the composer's own practice is shown by the '*hommage à scelsi*', which can be seen to indicate a general store of contemporary material from which he takes the music for the modules of *doppelt bejaht*. This is backed up by the title of the *vorschläge* mentioned above: *suggestions: concepts for making the role of the composer superfluous*. Spahlinger appears to be attempting to compose himself out of this music, allowing an unpredictable formation of the 'typical' materials of new music to take the place of compositional determination.

Yet, the collection of these materials arguably shows a more positivistic, less self-critical and anti-structural attitude to material than the composer would admit, as was the case in the discussion of mechanical repetition in Chapter 3. After all, these materials appear repeatedly across many of his pieces, suggesting they are in fact a key part of his musical language. They can be seen as presenting a new fixed vocabulary or set of musical norms. Arbitrariness of succession, as implied by this idea of open form does not, it seems, imply arbitrariness of material – otherwise materials would vary from piece to piece to a far greater degree. Selecting material at random, which one might infer would make it truly 'interchangeable', does not interest the composer to the same degree, perhaps as this would subscribe to what Spahlinger negatively describes as a 'postmodern', 'anything goes' attitude.[55] On the other hand, the composer might argue that he is less interested in the material than in its disintegration, as effected by his transitions, so that the chosen materials are not as important as the way in which they function within the form. Certainly, these pieces navigate difficult terrain between the poles of material-based composition and complete interchangeability as well as those of performer freedom and composed determinacy.

Another of Spahlinger's pieces, *extension* for violin and piano (1980), is relevant to this discussion, though it does not belong to the less determined open form works discussed in this section. It has a narrative which, like the later *passage/*

paysage, looks to explore musical development in all directions simultaneously. This then leads to an 'explosion' of material as different strands of development burst out in all directions. The piece is made up of numerous small sections, all given a name that involves the prefix 'ex-'. There are then a number of 'expositions', 'extrapolations' and even 'exhumations'.[56] One of the purposes of this approach is to show how order under one principle – listing words beginning with 'ex-' – can create complete disorder in other ways, that is, creates a piece with a highly discontinuous narrative. The programme note to this piece, which is quite an artistic achievement in itself (see Figure 5.9), also displays this idea of a proliferation of connections. The centre lists some of the 'ex-' words in play with more theoretical discussions spinning out from this interior: the influence of both concrete poetry and political pamphlets make themselves felt here.

This piece is unique among these works in that the restrictions on material are not present in the same manner. It includes tonal material, for example, in 'exhumation II and exacerbation' where the composer asks for 'f minor, molto espressivo, a fictional brahms-quotation, all-too-late-romantic', a rare parodic moment in his work, one that, in my experience of the piece, does not fully come across. Listeners are fighting against the learned habits of assigning heightened significance to certain kinds of material. Quotations of tonal music have great power in this context: they are often read as 'revealing' something fundamental about the entire piece, or at the very least, they stick out from their surrounds. With Spahlinger's established interest in perception, these characteristics of quotation may well be an aspect of the 'consciousness' that the composer encourages listeners to reflect upon. In wishing to explore the interchangeability of different materials, however, the significance attributed to quotations would not necessarily be advantageous. Restrictions on material as demonstrated by the open form pieces above are, therefore, beneficial to presenting the sense of formal interchangeability to which Spahlinger aspires. For Schick, they also constitute a vital difference between the composer and his close associate, Huber, who often uses quotation or faux-folk material to evoke, and criticize, musical culture, and indeed to attempt to criticize society at large.[57] Huber is not alone here, with experimentation with vernacular musics also very much part of the approach of figures such as Walter Zimmerman, Kevin Volans or Clarence Barlow (all with a connection to Cologne). Spahlinger, on the other hand 'does not attempt to reveal the historicity of musical semantics through ironic exaggeration, alienation [*Verfremdung*], or the confrontation of contradictory eclecticism'.[58] To explore transition, the materials employed must be relativized to a certain extent, otherwise attention shifts from the primary compositional concern.

That Spahlinger's pieces at times exist more as relations between materials, or even as situations in which a type of aesthetic experience will appear, betrays the

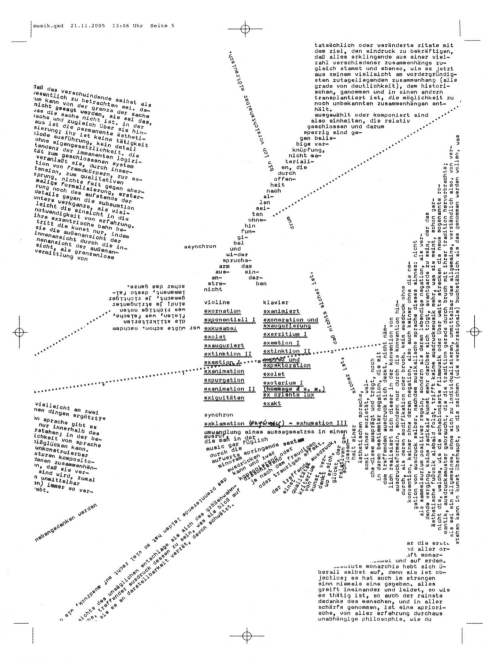

FIGURE 5.9: *extension* programme note, page 5.

conceptual undercurrent to the composer's thought. It is this perhaps more than anything else that connects him with his outwardly rather different pupil, the concept artist Johannes Kreidler, in whose pieces the sounding element often seems very much secondary to its conceptual context.[59] The importance of transporting concepts, often philosophically informed ideas, is also borne out by Spahlinger's sketches which usually begin as written text on his favoured square-ruled notepaper. Quotes from philosophers on the theme of the piece, descriptions of the material, forms and processes to be employed, and even, in the case of *passage/paysage*, a short poem, provide the background before the first chords and rhythms enter the equation.

Some of the tensions indicated in this discussion – between determinacy and indeterminacy, fixed and interchangeable material, anti-structural and structural attitudes – betray areas in which the idealized conceptual thought of Spahlinger meets a reality in which it is challenging to realize such ideas. Again, these tensions are not creative negatives on the side of the composer and his self-professed belief in the importance of contradiction – arguably a modernist trait, certainly when one considers Adorno – may mean he himself will enjoy raising them.[60] Certainly, his interest in contradiction sets him apart from the idea of modernism as a simplifying, rationalizing tendency.[61] The difficulties of presenting impossible concepts in music are a rich seam of inspiration for the composer, as will be seen in his work on perception in the next chapter.

NOTES

1. See John P. Welsh, 'Open Form and Earle Brown's Modules I and II', *Perspectives of New Music* 32, no. 1 (1967): 254–90.

2. This, in fact, matches Umberto Eco's influential description of open form, which discusses a move towards openness over several centuries, including examples from Mallarmé, Kafka and Joyce. Umberto Eco, 'The Poetics of the Open Work', in *The Open Work*, trans. Anna Cancogni (Cambridge, MA: Harvard University Press, 1989). An early version of this essay appeared in Luciano Berio's journal *Incontri musicali* in 1959, meaning it had been part of the musical conversation for some time. For further discussion of the genesis and applications of this idea see: Konrad Boehmer, *Zur Theorie der offenen Form* (Darmstadt: Tonos, 1967); Guy de Mallac, 'The Poetics of the Open Form: (Umberto Eco's Notion of "Opera Aperta")', *Books Abroad* 45, no. 1 (1971): 31–36; and, in relation to 'modular form', James Saunders, 'Modular Music', *Perspectives of New Music* 46, no. 1 (2008): 152–93.

3. Mathias Spahlinger, 'this is the time of conceptive ideologues no longer', trans. Philipp Blume, *Contemporary Music Review* 27, no. 6 (2008): 579–94, 590.

4. Hans Heinrich Eggebrecht and Mathias Spahlinger, *Geschichte der Musik als Gegenwart*, Musikkonzepte Special Edition, eds. Heinz-Klaus Metzger and Rainer Riehn (Munich: Richard Boorberg Verlag, 2000), 18.

5. Mathias Spahlinger, 'gegen die postmoderne mode', *MusikTexte* 27 (1989): 2–7, 5.

6. Ibid.

7. Frederick Beiser, *Hegel* (London: Routledge, 2005), 235.

8. Peter Singer, *Hegel: A Very Short Introduction* (Oxford: Oxford University Press, 2001), 15.

9. Gottfried Wilhelm Hegel, *Phenomenology of Spirit*, trans. A. V. Miller (Oxford: Oxford University Press, 1977), 11. Emphasis in original.

10. Theodor Adorno, 'Vers une musique informelle', in *Quasi una Fantasia: Essays on Modern Music*, trans. Rodney Livingstone (London: Verso, 1992), 269–322.

11. See Spahlinger, 'gegen die postmoderne mode', 6; and Eggebrecht and Spahlinger, *Geschichte der Musik als Gegenwart*, 110.

12. Theodor Wiesengrund Adorno in Max Paddison, *Adorno's Aeshtetics of Music* (Cambridge: Cambridge University Press, 1997), 181.

13. Philipp Blume, 'Mathias Spahlinger's *128 erfüllte augenblicke* and the Parameters of Listening', *Contemporary Music Review* 27, no. 6 (2008): 625–42, 633.

14. Ibid., 625.

15. To each *Augenblick* an inequality symbol (either < or >) is also attached, meaning that there are two versions of each three-figure coordinate. Peter Niklas Wilson, in the liner notes to the 1998 Accord CD recording, states that the moments are not static but either increasing or decreasing, as defined by these symbols.

16. Ibid., 630.

17. Enno Poppe, '*Laudatio an Mathias Spahlinger* anlässlich der Verleihung des Berliner Kunstpreises', in the programme booklet to musica viva Ensemble Modern Orchestra concert, 28 September 2018: 45–50, 46.

18. For further information on composition 'between categories', see Jörg Mainka, 'Mind the Gap; Spahlingers Vorliebe für "die Dinge dazwischen"', *Musik-Konzepte* 155 (2012): 75–94.

19. Mathias Spahlinger with Reinhard Oehlschlägel, '"alles aus allem entwickeln" mathias spahlinger im gespräch über "passage/paysage" für großes orchester', *Musik-Konzepte* 39 (1991): 23–32, 31.

20. Ibid.

21. Ibid., 23.

22. Mathias Spahlinger, interview with Neil Thomas Smith, 11 August 2014, Groß Glienicke, recording: unarchived.

23. Ibid.

24. Spahlinger with Oehlschlägel "alles aus allem entwickeln", 26.

25. Markus Hechtle, *198 Fenster zu einer imaginierten Welt* (Saarbrücken: Pfau-Verlag, 2005), 75.

26. Byron Almén, 'Narrative archetypes: A Critique, Theory, and Method of Narrative Analysis', *Journal of Music Theory* 47 (2003): 1–39, 8.

27. Ibid., 11.

28. Johannes Kreidler, 'Mathias Spahlingers Zumutungen; Gegen Unendlich und gegen Krieg', *Musik-Konzepte* 155 (2012): 23–30, 27.

29. Mathias Spahlinger, 'political implications of the material of new music', *Contemporary Music Review* 34, no. 2–3 (2015): 127–66.

30. Dorothea Ruthemeier nee Schüle, '"…dann wird offenbar, daß alles auf Vereinbarung beruht": Zur Idee der offenen Form in Mathias Spahlingers "verlorener weg" (1999/2000)', *MusikTexte* 95 (2002): 25–49, 37.

31. Ibid.

32. Spahlinger with Oehlschlägel, 'alles aus allem entwickeln', 26.

33. See Spahlinger, 'political implications of the material of new music'.

34. Theodor Wiesengrund Adorno, *Aesthetic Theory*, trans. R. Hullot-Kentor (London: Continuum, 2004), 30.

35. Ibid.

36. Spahlinger, 'political implications of the material of new music', 40.

37. Ibid.

38. Ibid.

39. Ibid.

40. Ibid.

41. See Rainer Nonnemann, 'Wider den Utopieverlust: Mathias Spahlingers "doppelt bejaht" beschreitet neue Bahnen', *MusikTexte* 124 (2010): 57–63, 61.

42. Ibid.

43. Ibid.

44. Spahlinger, 'political implications of the material of new music', 40.

45. Kreidler, 'Mathias Spahlingers Zumutungen', 26.

46. See Tanja Orning, '*Pression* – a Performance Study', *Music Performance Research* 5 (2012): 12–31; and Alex Temple, 'Composers, Performers, and Consent', New Music Box, 24 November 2015, http://www.newmusicbox.org/articles/composers-performers-and-consent/ (accessed 16 June 2016).

47. Spahlinger with Oehlschlägel, 'alles aus allem entwickeln', 75.

48. Ibid., 76.

49. Spahlinger, interview with Neil Thomas Smith, 11 August 2014.

50. Mathias Spahlinger in Kreidler, 'Mathias Spahlingers Zumutungen', 23.

51. Mathias Spahlinger in Peter Niklas Wilson, 'Music as a Play of Language and Society', booklet notes to *Mathias Spahlinger*, CD, Wergo (1993), 22–32, 19.

52. See Neil Thomas Smith, 'Presenting the Irreconcilable: Protest and Abstraction in Mathias Spahlinger's "Ocean"', *Music&Letters* 99, no. 3 (2018): 427–47.

53. Published in Pierre Boulez, 'Alea', in *Stocktakings from an Apprenticeship* (Oxford: Clarendon Press, 1991), 26–38; Bill Hopkins, 'Open form: open question: review of Konrad Boehmer Zur Theorie der offenen Form in der neuen Musik, and Darmstaedter Beitraege zur neuen Musik X: "Form"', *Musical Times* 110, no. 1514 (1969): 380–83.

54. Eggebrecht and Spahlinger, *Geschichte der Musik als Gegenwart*, 78.

55. See Spahlinger, 'gegen die postmoderne mode', 2–7.

56. For a full list of these sections, and further information on this piece, see Dorothea Ruthemeier, *Antagonismus oder Konkurrenz? Zu zentralen Werkgruppen der 1980er Jahre von Wolfgang Rihm und Mathias Spahlinger* (Schliengen: Edition Argus, 2012), 133–40. For a discussion of order in this work, see Werner Klüppelholz, 'Obduktion der Ordnung. Zu Spahlingers *extension*', *MusikTexte* 95 (2002): 69–79.

57. Tobias Eduard Schick, *Weltbezüge in der Musik Mathias Spahlingers* (Stuttgart: Franz Steiner Verlag, 2018), 103.

58. Ibid., 104.

59. For a discussion of the possible aesthetic and political pitfalls of such an approach, see Martin Iddon's discussion of Johannes Kreidler's *Fremdarbeit*: 'Outsourcing Progress: On Conceptual Music', *TEMPO* 70, no. 275 (2016): 36–49.

60. See Eggebrecht and Spahlinger, *Geschichte der Musik als Gegenwart*, 13 and 57. On Adorno see Max Paddison, *Adorno's Aeshtetics of Music* (Cambridge: Cambridge University Press, 1997), 2.

61. George Rochberg, 'Can the Arts Survive Modernism? (A Discussion of the Characteristics, History, and Legacy of Modernism)', *Critical Inquiry* 11, no. 2 (1984): 317–40, 322.

6

Perception[*]

Spahlinger and Perception

Spahlinger's interest in perception is perhaps the most far-reaching of the topics discussed here. Listeners' perception of noise is central to his belief in *musique concrète instrumentale*'s revolutionary power, while the political implications of audible deconstructions of order rely on a listener willing to make the leap from the aesthetic to the political. Finally, open form's exploration of continuity is concerned with challenging traditional modes of teleological listening. That the composer's interest in perception is present in all these areas is not surprising, as music presupposes listeners, whose perception is central to all aspects of musical experience. Yet, an interest in perception is not always regarded as a particularly modernist preoccupation. Many of the critiques of modernism take issue with an alleged disregard for the listener, suggesting that such an interest in this topic from such a composer may be quite unusual.

Spahlinger is chiefly interested in perception because of what he sees as its ability to inform consciousness, creating an intersection here with long-standing debates in German philosophy. These connections will be teased out a little before a more practical examination of his pieces. The composer's essay 'actuality for the consciousness and actuality of the consciousness' delves into somewhat obscure avenues but it is primarily a discussion of what he considers the political potential of music to be.[1] This relates to the distinct ways in which consciousness functions for Spahlinger, which Ruthemeier describes as acting, on the one hand, as a preformed cultural perspective which leads to preconceptions of 'what music as actuality is or should be'; while, on the other, projecting 'sense onto everything

---

[*] Some of the material on *ocean* in this chapter has already appeared as part of Neil Thomas Smith, 'Presenting the Irreconcilable: Protest and Abstraction in Mathias Spahlinger's "Ocean"', *Music&Letters* 99, no. 3 (2018): 427–47.

presented [...] as mere fact', thereby making the 'active work of construction' crucial in musical perception.[2] Consciousness exists, then, both as a precondition of perception – a culturally formed, rather reactive entity – and as an active constructor of meaning. Spahlinger believes that both these sides are dialectically related.

This same dialectic is at play when Spahlinger states that 'forms of thought that maintain the subject-object division [...] never attain reality.' This is because they do not acknowledge that the subject is a 'subjective subject-object', nor do they see the object as an 'objective subject-object'.[3] Ruthemeier provides illumination on these comments by applying them more directly to music, stating that listeners' experience is not a free play of subjectivity but is shaped by previous listening (they are a 'subjective subject-object'); while the music does not exist independently of those who perceive it and is reliant on their constructive capabilities (it is an 'objective subject-object').[4] Such an outlook can be traced to Adorno's conception of the subject–object division, as well as the materialist, Marxian sensitivity to the social context of individuals, upon which Adorno's philosophy is partly based.[5] Spahlinger's distinction provides the context for the exploration of the political elements of music which are tied inextricably to his exploration of perception. The formation and function of consciousness is fundamental to his belief in what music can achieve and impacts directly on the surface of his compositions.

Perception, then, is the foundation of all musical experience. Recognition of this is important, yet rather too general to provide a particularly illuminating insight on the composer's music. There is, however, a more overt way in which Spahlinger approaches this topic in his pieces, one in which the nature of perception directly affects the musical material employed. Such pieces will open the discussion below, beginning with the work for string orchestra *und als wir...*; chamber piece, *gegen unendlich*; and percussion work, *off*. The central portion of the chapter considers an overtly political choral work, *in dem ganzen ocean von empfindungen eine welle absondern, sie anhalten* in detail, providing as it does a particularly good example of how the relationship between 'reality', consciousness, perception and politics functions within the composer's practice. This places him squarely within debates around politically 'committed' music in the twentieth century.[6] It also raises questions of the mode of listening required by these pieces, which will be the topic of the critical commentary. Finally, the perceptual and political thought of Rancière will be employed for a second time to point to the wider aesthetic potential of Spahlinger's approach.

Perception in Spahlinger's Pieces

passage/paysage *and* und als wir …

Numerous examples of this perceptual exploration can be found throughout Spahlinger's oeuvre, even in pieces that do not specifically refer to this agenda. *passage/paysage*, a work that has already been discussed, makes for a good first example. Here, the desire to restructure perception can be found in Spahlinger's interest in drawing listeners' attention to aspects of the music that were previously thought 'inessential'.[7] In the second section of this piece, what is essentially a long, held chord is presented to listeners so that they might begin to notice the pauses for breath and the changes of bow that necessarily take place within it. What seemed at first a smooth edifice of sound is shown to possess small fissures of articulation. These small disturbances were present before in the more dynamic music, but had gone unseen and unheard. Spahlinger seeks to bring them to our attention.

Second, the long Bartók pizzicato passage at the work's close is designed almost as a study in rhythmic perception. At first all strings play in rhythmic unison, before minimal distances are introduced between individual entries. The result is a chord that gradually morphs into a cloud of individual articulations. The purpose is to explore how the listener perceives unison rhythms and deviations therefrom. Even in the chords that should be completely together, there will be tiny deviations: pizzicato chords are notorious for sounding poorly coordinated, a fact likely to have informed Spahlinger's choice of playing technique. By experiencing this rhythmic process, it is intended that listeners come to a better understanding of what unison chords actually are – that is, that no chord is ever exactly together and what is heard as 'together' is as much the work of our own perception as it is the synchronization of entries. The listener should become more sensitive to rhythmic deviations, clearly demonstrating the nature of this perceptual education.

passage/paysage integrates certain perceptual concerns into its musical ideas. Exploration of ideas of reality being, in part at least, the work of perception is, however, at the very core of *und als wir* … for 54 strings (*and when we* …, 1993). This sees the strings arranged in a cross formation with each of its arms comprising its own separate orchestra. This formation is ingenious in that it allows for various lines of communication between the players, as shown in Figure 6.1. It also gives space for the audience to sit between each arm, rather like in Xenakis's circular orchestral arrangement in *Terretektorh* (1966). For Spahlinger, this arrangement is designed to show that there is no centre, no single 'correct' way of listening to the piece: everything is simply relative to everything else. It is intended that spatial hierarchies of listening that exist in the vast majority of performance spaces are eliminated, or at least relativized.

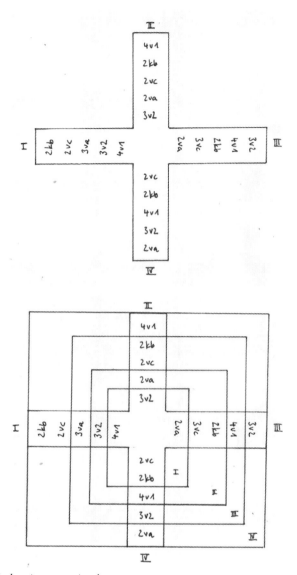

FIGURE 6.1: *und als wir …*, seating layout.

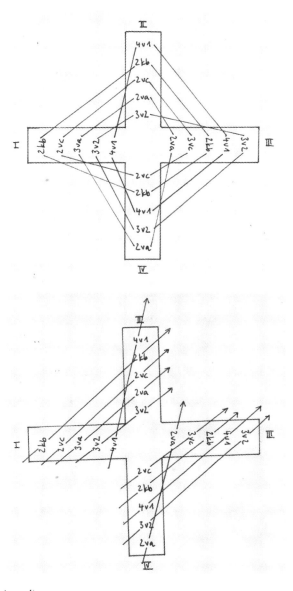

FIGURE 6.1: (continued)

As these diagrams demonstrate, not only is a 'complete' string orchestra of violins, violas, cellos and basses seated in each arm of the cross in different configurations, but also in concentric squares, and in spirals round the space, opening up various possibilities for spatial exploration. These possibilities are designed in part so that events can occur on different sides of the cross – sometimes simultaneously and sometimes slightly apart – to encourage the listener to question their perceptual faculties. Distance should be shown as a vital part of musical perception as it affects what the listener considers loud or soft, together or apart, while the continual reconfiguration of instrumental groups will also problematize listeners' perceptions that are accustomed to the more static arrangement of the concert hall.

The material is also designed to exploit the potential of this arrangement. The first section is heavily based on pizzicato, which, as in *passage/paysage*, is used to provide a very clear attack and, therefore, bring any rhythmic differences to the fore. After a rather fractured opening with scattered plucked pitches, violent rhythmic outbursts and occasional ghostly arco chords, the music builds to some incredibly dense clouds of pizzicati. Suddenly, it changes to ever-shifting chords that move round the space in a manner rather reminiscent of early electronic works due to their crystalline timbre and strong emphasis on high partials. Where one chord begins and the other ends is impossible to tell as they overlap and merge with each other in this mercurial texture. By the end of the piece, these chords have risen to the heights, creating an unstable hissy trilling that sounds remarkably like a rainforest field recording, though this illusion is shattered by the starts and stops that let silence intrude and which signal the end of the piece.

Spahlinger describes in the programme note to the piece how the second section labelled in the score, which is the heavily pizzicato section, attempts a rigorous exploration of the perceptibility of a regular pulse that is 'influenced and irritated' by moving in space, a complex relationship to the main tempo, different sizes of interval and variations in the pulse itself. Sebastian Claren describes how the section is a systematic exploration of the possibilities of combining pitch with pulse in space, with sketches describing such states as 'constant tempi/as many pitches as tempi/as many chords as tempi/tempi according to register'.[8] The spatial setting of the piece is intended to allow a thorough exploration of rhythmic issues, pointing to the fact that there is no absolute vantage point from which to hear any two musical events.

Pitch and Rhythm: gegen unendlich *and* off

Such issues of categorization and hearing difference are also relevant to the chamber piece *gegen unendlich* (*towards infinity*, or, alternatively, *ad infinitum*, 1995), which focuses on the endless possibilities of dividing the pitch and time continuum, that is, that pitch deviations can be infinitely small, while the time between two rhythmic values can also be divided without end. Such metaphoric spaces, whether relating to pitch or time, can always be split into a smaller entity.

Kreidler describes this piece as a 'key work',[9] and it is even mentioned as a positive example of Spahlinger's 'critical composition' by Mahnkopf, albeit in comparison with what he sees as the deficient example of Spahlinger's percussion work *éphémère*.[10] *gegen unendlich* is in two starkly opposed sections – the first concentrating on pitch, the second on rhythm – though ostensibly the piece has one single theme. Such bald formal contrast from a unified theme has been observed in previous chapters, and is also present in *passage/paysage*, which has four discrete sections that all, according to the composer, explore the nature of transition.

The intended effect of such increasingly small divisions of pitch and time is to problematize listeners' instinct to categorize. In the realm of pitch, which is the focus of the first and longer section, this means that what might first have been heard as a semitone becomes a more complex entity in a sea of microtonal intervals. The music here, even though there are ebbs and flows of density and activity, does not have a particularly strong directional pull. Instead, it dwells on the close, raw dissonances, drawing multiphonics from the piano that are all the more fascinating for the close listening that is encouraged. As the title implies, there is little suggestion that the instruments may at some point align to resolve to consonance, rather the feeling is of a constant, probing return to the wound of imperfect intonation that will never be healed.

Figure 6.2 is a short extract in which such differences of intonation are brought to the musical surface, indeed they *are* the musical surface. From the middle of this system, labelled 'only C#' above the top stave, it can be observed how the piano uses different harmonics to create a variety of colours with minimal pitch variations. At the same time the trombone plays a C# consistently 12 cents flat, joined by the clarinet (sounding) C# 25 cents 'too low.' Such deviations are intended to explore the boundary between what listeners consider 'different' and 'the same', showing the difference between categories of perception and actual experience, a theme that also can be traced back to Adorno.[11]

The shorter section that focuses on rhythm is characterized by constant semiquavers that never settle into an obvious metre. At first, the vertiginous leaps of the individual lines create something of a frenzied atmosphere before the music settles onto a single pitch. This focus allows listeners to hear how the pulse is forever malleable depending upon the emphases of the instruments that articulate it. For a time, this single pitch stays within one pulse but to hammer home the composer's desire to explore the 'gaps between' there is also a passage that explores some of the potential that competing pulses can bring.[12] In Figure 6.3, the piano begins to speed up while the others' semiquavers remain constant. While the piano slows down to rejoin the primary pulse, the bass clarinet tempo dips for a short time before it too resumes the main pulse. The audible impression is similar to the slow phasing in the early work of Steve Reich.

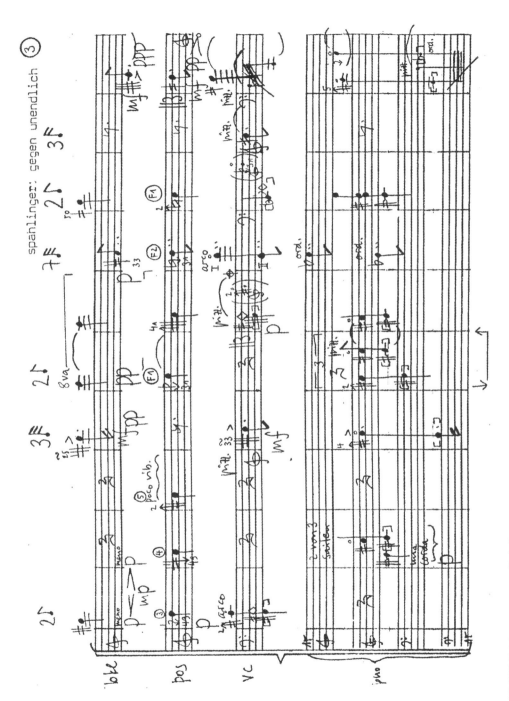

FIGURE 6.2: *gegen unendlich*, bars 51–60.

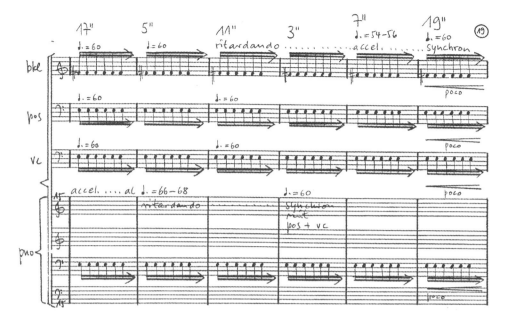

FIGURE 6.3: *gegen unendlich*, page 19, top stave.

As Spahlinger identifies in the programme note to the piece, even when the pitches are notated identically, there is the chance that listeners may hear them differently, especially considering the natural inaccuracies of performance and the different colours, such as mutes and harmonics, the composer employs: 'the experience of boundlessness of quantification is a theme of the piece. in the first half, even identically notated pitches should be able to be heard just as approximations towards infinity.'[13] And, as he states at the opening of this programme note: 'without a tonal system of reference there are infinitely many, therefore no two identical, pitches; without metre, there are an infinite number of points in time, therefore no synchronicity.'[14] Pointing out these problems of perception is, then, the main impulse that spurs Spahlinger's creativity.

Perception of rhythm and pulse is also a vital concern of *off* for six snare drums (1993–2011). This piece includes certain open form elements, with a score that acts 'like a subway map' in that it allows the players to move along predefined lines to create a route through the piece, though such decisions will presumably be made prior to the performance.[15] Rather than attempting to explore divisions of time seen in Figure 6.3, this work is concerned primarily with listeners' understanding of metre and pulse, presenting them with various perceptual problems such as competing stresses that imply two different time signatures, or offbeats that

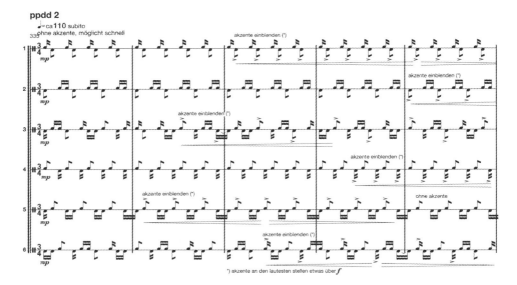

FIGURE 6.4: *off*, bars 335–339.

become stronger than their partnered on-beats. Much of this exploration makes use of accents in order to articulate different metres and, in certain circumstances, no metre at all. The following passage, for example, successively introduces accents on each semiquaver beat, destabilizing any strong sense of the 3/4.

Another significant detail here are the various conflicting groupings between the left and right hands of individual players (indicated by the opposing directions of the stems). The drummers play various figures that are three, four or five semiquavers long, as indicated by the boxes in Figure 6.5. As can be seen here, the figures of equal lengths always appear one semiquaver apart to minimize any feeling of established pulse. For example, the figure of five semiquavers' length played by snare 6 begins on the last semiquaver of the same figure played by snare 3. Both of these figures have the added variation of alternating the hands on each iteration, meaning that ten semiquavers are in fact required for a full repeat. In other figures, such as those of three semiquavers' length, the distribution among the hands remains opposed throughout.

This construction appears to be designed to vitiate any sense of metre, particularly at the opening where there are no accents indicated at all, a state to which the music quickly returns after this extract. There is a certain sense, therefore, of a transition from complete semiquaver equality through lack of accent to a texture of only accents, the latter of which is of course akin to no accents at all. Such non-accented textures occur throughout *off* as a kind of raw state from which metres

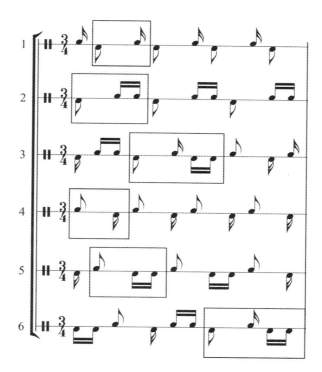

FIGURE 6.5: *off*, rhythmic patterns.

and rhythms can arise. This allows different rhythmic groupings of particular instruments, indicated by accents and hand distribution, to emerge, establishing briefly a dominant sense of metre that is quickly dissolved. Manipulation of the ametric background can be seen when considering the dynamics of this extract, which show how the accents are staggered in their appearance.

Similar issues are at stake in Spahlinger's exploration of the difference between off- and on-beats. The following short passage is a compact example of how this might function. Here, the changes of metre mean that the quavers that are on the beat and off the beat change in the first and final bars of this symmetrical construction. At the same time, the dynamics mean that the syncopated quavers begin (and end) as the loudest. So, at the very moment that the dominant, loud beat is about to appear on the downbeat, the bar changes so that it becomes a syncopation. Spahlinger is playing with metrical hierarchies and, as in the semiquaver passage above, he effects a transition between two similar, in this case effectively identical, states. The interest for him, then, lies in the movement between these, in

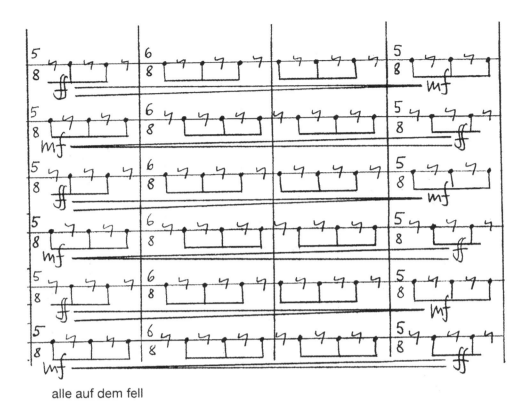

alle auf dem fell

FIGURE 6.6: *off*, bars 253–256.

which the metrical perception of the listener – their categorization of strong and weak beats – is problematized.

und als wir ..., *off* and *gegen unendlich* are some of the clearest examples of how perception is explored on the surface of Spahlinger's music. It is yet to be seen, however, how the composer's implied political agenda is aided by these explorations. For this, it is instructive to consider one of Spahlinger's most openly political pieces to uncover how a less overt perceptual investigation can also take place.

in dem ganzen ocean von empfindungen eine welle absondern, sie anhalten *(1985)*

This work (henceforth *ocean*) is unusual for the composer in its use of electronics, which accompany the choir of 36 singers with what is essentially a tape part (i.e.

a fixed and immutable series of recorded sonic events). As with *und als wir ...,*
the soundworld of the piece is regularly dense, dissonant and at times bewildering: whispers, shouts and cries punctuate the musical surface; spoken text
with factual information is also used extensively to aid the expression of theme of
the piece, which the composer states is world hunger. The 1980s in Europe saw a
huge growth in awareness regarding this issue, leading most famously to LiveAid
in 1985.

Despite the title's length – this piece narrowly beats *vorschläge, konzepte zur
ver(über)flüssigung der funktion des komponisten* (1992) and *Über den frühen
Tod Fräuleins Anna August Marggräfin zu Baden* (1995) to achieve the accolade
of Spahlinger's longest title – it is not immediately apparent how it relates to the
question of world hunger. It is in fact a quotation of part of a passage from Johann
Gottfried Herder's *Treatise on the Origin of Language* (1772), in which he talks
about the conditions for reflexion:

> Man demonstrates reflexion when the force of his soul becomes freely active
> in such a manner that it isolates in the whole ocean of sensations which rush
> through all the senses, a *single* wave, if I may say so, when it arrests this wave,
> directs its attention to and is conscious of its attending to it. He proves his
> reflexion when he gathers himself into a moment of awakening out of the whole
> floating dream of images which passes his senses, if he freely rests on a *single*
> image, takes it into calmer observation and isolates for himself those marks that
> make it this and no other object.[16]

As Schick identifies, it is likely Spahlinger came to this quotation through
Liebrucks.[17] The philosopher takes up this passage to describe what he calls 'first'
and 'second reflection':

> Man can in the ocean of his perception arrest one wave, he can direct his atten-
> tion to the wave and to his attention of it. Here lie two reflections.[18]

A situation in which listeners direct attention to their own perception is precisely
what the composer wishes to achieve in his pieces. Liebrucks's second reflection
is the basis of what the composer calls the self-reflexivity of art.

For Spahlinger, then, this passage is evidence of the potential of art to alter perception in the manner he seeks. He wants to make listeners aware of this wider
realm of perception and to encourage a reflexive attitude in relation to the means
by which the 'reality' of such situations is conveyed. More than this, however, he
appears to want to mark original events as distinct from their reproductions, for
a reflexive attitude, according to Herder, can assess the distinctive details of an

object of experience. Peter Niklas Wilson describes how this reflection relates to two particular aspects: first, the 'the horrifying, familiar and yet politically tolerated fact of world-wide hunger' and, second, the 'way this fact begins to take on an illusory character through its daily presentation in the media'.[19] Spahlinger talks of how media representations of world hunger present a 'dichotomy between the perceived object and its perfect reproduction',[20] one that Wilson states is 'a difference not simply of degree but of kind' for the composer.[21] He puts a social theme at the centre of this piece, but he approaches it through attending to the faculties of his audience.

It is in such explorations of the false 'reality' of the media that art can contribute to this political issue for the composer:

> with the victory march of the objectivist, in reality illusory, media, art must thematize the question how presentation should relate to its object in order to make actuality visible; it must bring to consciousness that the negligible difference between the object and the perception of its perfect reproduction makes the world of difference.[22]

Art can, according to Spahlinger, show the inadequacy of the media's attempts to approach this theme, while also breaking through its claims of purely objective representation. All this suggests a rather abstract engagement with media messages, one that encourages reflexion, yet this approach has very concrete effects on the material employed. Concentration on media message rather than the events themselves is intended as a way of avoiding the anesthetization of suffering that Adorno warns against,[23] yet more effective than this is the fact the 'real world' of objective report and clock time, of suffering and injustice, is not smoothed over in *ocean* but is presented on an even footing with the aesthetic argument.

Playback, Actuality and Reality

Christian Leuschner, the production chief (*Produktionsleiter*) of the South German Radio (SDR) who was responsible for working with the composer to create the playback, gives a pithy description of why the themes Spahlinger wishes to explore are suited to the use of electronic sound as well as live singers. He states that an 'essential element' of the piece is an opposition between pairs such as 'actuality and image' and 'original and reproduction' so that it is 'unsurprising that the work was composed for choir groups and play back'.[24]

Though not known as a composer concerned with technological advances, Spahlinger immediately seeks to engage with the medium in an unusual manner, critiquing the means with which he is working at a time when the general trend was to pursue ever greater technical capabilities. Spahlinger's tape part differs from many in that it must be recorded anew for each choir that performs the piece: his search for as exact a reproduction as possible in the recorded sound – a reproduction that nevertheless does not match listeners' experience of the live singer – means that the tape part must be recorded by the same voices that perform the live material, a feature that greatly increases the effort required to reperform the piece. The tape and the work of the live singers in fact simply run alongside each other, though a good deal of, at times complex, interaction between the two is written into the score. Arguably, this interaction makes both feel 'live' in performance, connecting with an ongoing debate in electronic music as to whether pre-recorded material necessarily inhibits a feeling of 'liveness'.[25] This interaction is also encouraged by the fact that the electronics are made up entirely of vocal material sung by the choir with some light manipulation of the sound, at least by today's standards.

In his writings, Spahlinger prefers to separate what he calls 'actuality' (*wirklichkeit*) from 'reality' (*realität*), a distinction the German language facilitates rather more than the English. This idea has particular relevance for this piece with its critical response to the media's attempts at expressing objective reality. In 'thesen zu "schwindel der wirklichkeit"' (theses on the 'sham of actuality', 2014),[26] much of the content of which he attributes to Liebrucks, Spahlinger explains his conception of reality as that which can never be known as itself – in essence the Kantian 'thing in itself' – while actuality is what we understand, and perceive of, as what exists. Crucially, actuality is both influenced by the societally formed subject and by agreement between different subjects: we are formed by society to see things in certain ways, and we see things differently after discussing them with others. Actuality is the perceptually mediated realm between the subject and reality, whatever the latter might be. It is, then, far from static, as self-reflexion can both change how it is construed and increase knowledge of the work of the subject, or subjects, in constituting what we perceive of as our reality. Just as Adorno warns of the consequences of presuming identity between concept and object, Spahlinger believes that there is a danger in a general belief that our perception of events (actuality) corresponds absolutely to an objective reality. By attempting to disorientate listeners' perceptions he wishes to raise this important distinction, to create a space between perception and any absolute sense of reality. The influence of Adornian dialectics is apparent here in the immanent character of this critique: Spahlinger does not invoke any authority outside of listeners' perceptions but attempts to bring about reflexion from *within*.

Though his interest in this theme manifests itself in the majority of his work, *ocean* engages particularly closely with these ideas of actuality and reality due to the use of technology, which allows Spahlinger to introduce the concept of (sonic) reproduction and original, with the intention that it reflects the relationship between the media's representation of events and the events themselves. This idea is particularly unusual for the composer as, in appearing to suggest a certain primacy of the original over its reproduction, it creates a hierarchy that goes against his usual arguments concerning perception's work in constituting any event, even if the perceiver is party to its original occurrence. The original, it appears, is somehow superior, or even more truthful, than its reproduction, even though both are perceived within actuality. This hierarchy is further emphasized by the fact the opposition between original and reproduction brings to mind Walter Benjamin's concept of aura as discussed in 'Art in the Age of Mechanical Reproduction', one of the arguments of which attempts to explain how an original artwork differs from its, almost perfect, reproduction.[27] Though Spahlinger makes no direct reference to this essay, he does mention it in correspondence,[28] but, by the evidence of this piece, he would not agree with its argument that nonauratic production immediately produces more democratic art.[29]

Forms and Materials

The political message of the piece, and its vital explorations of musical material versus objective information, is not only present in the use of technology. The piece is many-layered in its formal argument and characterization of materials. Its course is, therefore, important to grasp. It begins with a quiet pattering of spoken material that emerges from the noise of the audience, which develops into longer spoken phrases on world hunger and scattered sung pitches.[30]

The texture builds before a loud and complex entry from both live singers and recorded playback. A similar entry returns, much extended, later in the piece (see Figure 6.8 for a form table). Figure 6.7 displays a partial score of this second entry and is typical of the sung material of the piece in its dynamic ebb and flow between the different choirs, the dissonant harmonic material (often semitone clusters that are widely spaced), and the extremes of register so reminiscent of Nono. The text here is not defined, singers being given the choice to sing vowels ad lib.

These are not simple tutti entries, rather they are dramatic moments filled with a great deal of dynamic detail: groups of singers and playback fade in and out as the sound moves round the space to create a sense of living sonic organisms. Schick states that their expressive effects are due to their relationship with 'sound-realities [klanglichen Realien]' with 'breathing, sobbing and shouting' having expressive effect not because of their place within a symbolic system of representation but 'because of their real-life meaning'.[31] The same expressive factors are certainly in play in works such as Lachenmann's Consolations I and II (1967–68) and Berio's

FIGURE 6.7: *ocean*, partial reduction from 6′53″.

A-Ronne (1975) from previous decades. These chords in fact present an important issue of the work in microcosm. The fact that such cries are pitched, albeit with a contour that imitates that of a shout of human suffering, points to a more complex relationship between 'real-world' sounds and musical system than Schick admits.

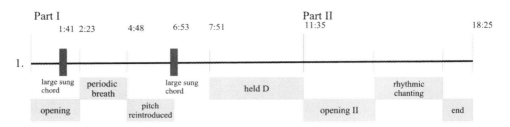

FIGURE 6.8: *ocean*, first layer of material.

These chords have a more contradictory function in that they are simultaneously on both sides of the divide between music and sounds of the external world.

The formal context of these large chords and opening material are shown in Figure 6.8, which describes the proportions and sections of the material once the playback begins. The opening of both parts I and II are very varied in the material they employ, with singing, spoken text and chanting mixed into a diverse surface. Other sections labelled here, such as the long breathing passage and the held D, are far more homogenous musical entities, which provide moments of aural recovery.

What is striking when the most important musical sections are laid out in this manner is that what defines the form is a simple, almost primal, musical profile. After all, the clearest units defined in Figure 6.8 are characterized by periodic breath noises, a single held pitch and rhythmic chanting that emerges from breath sounds: some of the most basic singing materials available. The breathing section and held D also have a more concrete musical relation to each other in their meditative periodicity. The held note swells at 5-second intervals while rocking back and forth between singers and playback, creating a slow cyclic feel not unlike the regular breathing, which is maintained for just short of two and a half minutes in a regular fashion. This regularity also provides a connection, unacknowledged by the composer, with the waves mentioned in the title. The relatively simple nature of some of these materials might be thought unsurprising considering certain technical challenges the piece posed, yet striking contrast between dense eventful music and stasis has been identified as characteristic of Spahlinger's compositional approach.[32]

Alongside the materials displayed in the first form table above, there are two further layers that make up the piece. The second, indicated by Diagram 2 in Figure 6.9 are moments in which the word 'jetzt' ('now') occurs, or in which ascending numbers are spoken by the choir. Both refer to a statistic employed in the piece that 'every two seconds a person dies of hunger', with 'jetzt' drawing attention to single moments in time in which a person is said to die, while the numbers

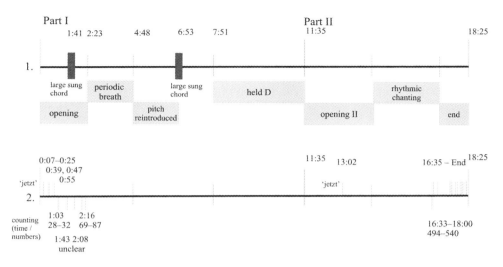

FIGURE 6.9: *ocean*, first and second layers of material.

reflect how many have died during the piece's performance. The fixed time of the playback means the figures can be quoted with some accuracy, though Spahlinger avoids stating numbers at 2-second intervals, which would be the most literal interpretation of the statistic. The closest he comes to such a periodic expression of numbers is at 2′15″, which transitions into the regular sounds of the breathing section.[33] The counting provides an external, quasi-objective thread through the work, one that is not fully integrated into the musical experience: a reminder of the incontrovertible fact at the heart of its message.

The meaning of this layer is only revealed at the conclusion when 'every two seconds a person dies from hunger' is clearly stated for the first time. Listeners, therefore, retrospectively make sense of the numbers and statements of 'jetzt' heard at the opening. It is significant that this material is absent from the middle section, as spoken word gives way to sung material and a succession of more abstract musical ideas. In listening to the piece, however, the regular spoken material that contains other facts about world hunger, and the occasional use of the consonant 't' in various textures, gives the counting and 'jetzt' material more presence throughout the whole piece than Diagram 2 would indicate. Only in the breathing and held D sections does it feel truly distant. The punctuation created by these recurring utterances provides concrete definitions of time in the work, while the sonic qualities of the word itself are taken as musical material for the more abstract musical narrative. Sonic and political characteristics can no longer be divided absolutely.

The, admittedly rather faint, dramatic arc created by the revelation of the counting material is a surprising presence in Spahlinger's work, with a sense of teleological drama not in keeping with his ideas of openness and false conclusions. The comprehensibility of the text is carefully controlled here to encourage this retrospective, and terrible, final realization as to the significance of the numbers and statements of 'jetzt' that have occurred throughout, betraying, as Wilson describes, 'their macabre significance'.[34] As mentioned, part of Spahlinger's particular conception of form in new music is a belief that all endings are only apparent endings without the final feeling of conclusion that tonal pieces achieve with a perfect cadence.[35] Yet, here in *ocean*, the piece ends with a revelation of meaning, bare spoken instances of 'jetzt' and a rare sense of an ending the seeds of which are sown at the opening. Other works by the composer certainly end with dramatic flourishes (e.g. *éphémère*), but the insistent 'jetzt' here speaks of a quiet horror quite unlike his other work.

A final layer can also be identified to accompany the materials indicated in the form table above and the references to this statistic. This is a layer of what Marion Saxer describes as 'medial ruptures [*mediale Brüche*]' that occur throughout the piece and is shown in Diagram 3 in Figure 6.10.[36] These are a series of very different events, the simplest being the opening and closing of the doors of the concert hall. This controls the clarity of the playback from speakers 7 and 8, which are placed in the foyer, and creates a sense of moving between an everyday space and the hermeticism of the concert hall, one that mirrors the movement between abstraction cut off from the outside world and a political statement that invites the world into the concert space. Schick notes that after the first closing of the doors five minutes in, there are no more news-report-like statements, therefore dismissing the 'fragments of reality',[37] though the continuing 'jetzt' layer means there is still an important spoken element.

Perhaps more immediately arresting, however, is at the end of part I when, according to the score, the recording of a 'harsh, shouting crowd (eruption, revolt, protest)' intrudes, followed by the sound of a woman crying: 'TV-sound loud, from neighbouring room with a half-open door'. This first sound is played on the speakers positioned outside the hall, giving both a sense of distance and the feeling that it comes from the 'outside world', though the descriptions given by the composer, and the general theme of the piece, would suggest that he is under no illusion that this is any kind of direct representation. Finally, during part II, the choir place their hands on the shoulder of a member of the audience 'in passing'. The intention here, as described by Saxer, is to break through another barrier, to literally touch the audience in a manner where media representations of such a problem might fail.[38] She describes the 'double line of attack of the piece' as it 'undermines both the hermeticism of the concert hall in which bodily contact never takes place' as well as engaging with 'the distal detachment of electronic media'.[39] To this should be added that these actions serve to interrupt the more abstract musical narrative

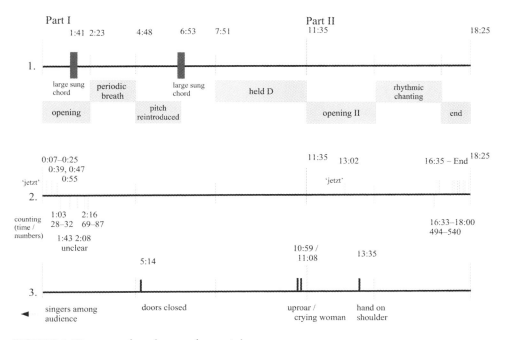

FIGURE 6.10: *ocean*, three layers of material.

implied by the first two formal layers described above, bringing it into contact with the real-world sounds and actions that more overt protest pieces employ.

The three layers identified here show the fissures within the fabric of this work. 'Purely' musical sound is heard alongside material with clear semantic content, both of which are interrupted at times by elements that disrupt the concert situation. The nature of this interaction will be explored further below but it is important to understand at this juncture that all three are fundamental to the effect of the piece: in searching for the essence of this work there must be an openness to it containing contradiction, or at least a central heterogeneity.

1. Modes of Listening in *ocean*

Expressing the Political Message

Thus far, the discussion of *ocean* has focused on how Spahlinger attempts to explore the theme of world hunger in this music using text, sonic events, the contrast between original and reproduction and dramatic elements. The impression may be that the theme of world hunger and its concrete political nature is always at the forefront of the audience's experience. Yet, when listening to the piece, obvious engagement with the theme is far from omnipresent. Of the three main sections identified above – the breath section, the held D and the emerging rhythmic chanting – only the latter contains unambiguous political material, and that relatively fleetingly. The atmosphere differs somewhat from pieces like Giacomo Manzoni's *Ombre* (1968), in which the regular rhythmic chants give the impression of dwelling on the edge of public unrest. The chants in Spahlinger emerge from a texture of rhythmic breath sounds, making the text inaudible for much of the time, thereby encouraging a mode of listening sensitive to the musical, as well as semantic, attributes of spoken text. Breath has an obvious connection to life and death but is, at the same time, appreciated as a part of the sonic argument of the piece and not necessarily as an exploration of the transience of human life.[40] Sung material – usually without any obvious semantic comment – can be understood as contributing to a musical argument and, often, as cries of anguish. All this suggests a complex relationship between abstract musical material and unambiguous political content.

It is in this question of text comprehension that we also come to the most fundamental opposition the piece contains. The politically charged texts employed in the piece in fact shift in and out of focus, with moments of complete clarity at a premium. Text is used for its sonic possibilities as well as to be clearly understood, encouraging a musical understanding of spoken words and an, albeit often frustrated, attempt at semantic understanding of more complex text textures. It is here that we come up against the divide Schick identifies in *verfluchung* between 'unmistakeably clear political statement of the text' and 'differentiated', 'complex music'.[41]

Text, in the same way as screaming chords or breath material, is understood as contributing to the political meaning and to the sonic argument. It acts as both, yet this dual function does not serve to illustrate how Spahlinger has overcome the divide between abstract material and protest music. On the contrary, these moments show that our perception of these is fundamentally, and for politically engaged composers tragically, divided. The piece presents the impossibility of reconciling the desire to present an autonomous musical narrative and make specific political points, just as the duck-rabbit made famous by Ludwig Wittgenstein in his *Philosophical Investigations* is both duck and rabbit to our eyes but never both simultaneously.[42] The different layers of the piece identified above are open to various interpretations but they can never be comfortably whole: the compositional approach is one that starts out from contradiction. This approach is thoroughly Adornian: in the aptly named 'The Dialectical Composer', the philosopher says of Schoenberg that 'the work does not turn the contradiction into harmony but conjures up its image, again and again, looking for duration in its cruelly ravaged traits.'[43] In *ocean*, there is a prolongation of just such a contradiction.

Contrast, an area of great interest to the composer, can then be seen not just as a question of differing musical materials but of colliding aesthetico-political stances. Yet, the piece does not feel like an aesthetic or stylistic collage: one of its most startling achievements is how it creates a continuity of experience: the piece is not defined by a dialogue between two characters but the contradictory existence of presenting an irreconcilable divide within itself. As Adorno states, '[d]ialectics is the consistent sense of non-identity. It does not begin by taking a standpoint. My thought is driven to it by its own inevitable insufficiency, by my guilt of what I am thinking.'[44] Spahlinger's approach also does not take a standpoint, but works against the pre-established positions of 'pure' abstraction and overt protest that have significantly defined thought on political commitment in twentieth-century composition.

The description of Leuschner – that this piece concerns itself with opposition between 'original and reproduction' – is a little misleading in its simplicity, however.[45] Saxer notes that 'to follow and comprehend these relationships [between tape and live material] with the ear may prove very difficult: the connections Spahlinger creates are too complex',[46] while Schick argues that, despite some very detailed imitation present in the score, the tape part primarily contains very similar material as the live singers and presents it simultaneously.[47] The complexity of the interaction between original and reproduction is of a similar degree to the spatial element of the piece, which often gives the listener little time to assess from which direction sound is coming, and rarely offers exact repetitions from different angles to really hammer home its point. The effect in much of the piece is more an overload of sensation, though often one that is musically compelling. In this it can be seen to echo the often uproarious expression of a piece like Nono's *Intolleranza 1960* (1961).

The more serene sections in which these spatial and imitative relationships are more easily discernible may help to make sense of the previous music, yet it is clear that the density of ideas, particularly in the opening of parts I and II, makes this very difficult. This piece is typical in that Spahlinger's regularly stated interest in perception does not result in music that is easily perceivable. Instead, he often oversteps what is possible for a listener to grasp to explore the limitations of listeners' perceptual apparatus. Separating original and reproduction in this piece completely is probably impossible, but identifying more and more of the differences between the two is a challenge for listeners who approach the work with an analytical ear.

The relatively complex level at which the interaction between original and reproduction occurs can, therefore, make it rather difficult for listeners to grasp what Spahlinger describes as a crucial element of the piece: the critique of media representation. This is an example of the reflexive attitude to listening that the composer assumes proving potentially vulnerable. The sonic variety heard here does not necessarily invite the ear to compare and contrast live and recorded sound, though in live performance this may come further to the fore. Perhaps even more significantly, during the moment in which this comparison is truly encouraged – the held D section – one of the chief impressions is how beautifully live and recorded notes dovetail. A message taken from this experience might be quite different from that intended: one of humans living in harmony with technology, for example, or technology as a liberating force, or even the spirit of the departed moving from this life to another.

ocean certainly brings the themes Spahlinger is dealing with into a more visceral and arresting form than an objective news report, while the objectivity of the factual statements begins to lose its moorings in this musical context. There may well be an intention that through the complex material the piece offers, any claim to an objective, complete experience of the music is impossible, just as the truth cannot be transported by any media report. This is certainly what is attempted by *und als wir* .... Ultimately, the complexity of both the spatial elements and the original/reproduction relationship point to the tension between the composer's wish to explore a theme and his preferred musical material. Direct connections between live and recorded sound in *ocean*, for example, would imply a music in which repetition has a much more important place than is usually the case in the composer's work and would, for him, blunt its critical potential.

There is also another, more telling interpretation of this complexity, one the composer himself does not advance but which does make use of his conceptions of reality and actuality discussed above. For, if the material of the live performers, as well as that of the tape, is perceived as contingent within individuals' conceptions of actuality, then this piece does not offer the hierarchies between original and reproduction that appeared to be the consequence of Spahlinger's position. Instead, it shows a relativist emphasis on the inevitability of mediation. In this complex experience, listeners are given a musical object to behold that overreaches any attempts at fully grasping its features.

What saves this from relativistic meaninglessness is the incontrovertible fact, embodied in the statistic that runs through the work, that millions in the world are starving to death. Listeners are confronted with an exploration of both different ways of perceiving the world and a seemingly uninterpretable truth. In a move that gives more freedom to the listener even than his perceptual explorations, the question of how far this uninterpretable truth extends is left open for individual listeners to decide. This is in fact the centre of Spahlinger's dialectical composition: the point at which concrete fact, relativistic perception and abstract musical expression meet. Though in *ocean* there is an acceptance of the necessary work of interpretation the audience does – the impossibility of fully removing the veil of actuality – this constant mediation is nevertheless continually rooted by the insistent tug of the fact that people have died during this piece's performance because of a lack of food. That Spahlinger himself does not point to this is an indication of the somewhat experimental nature of this work, even for an artist who regularly attempts to revisit his compositional foundations. As Paddison notes,[48] the composer attempts what Adorno describes as making 'things in ignorance of what they are'.[49]

2. Critical Commentary

Modes of Listening: und als wir … *and* off

Perception, then, is a vital compositional concern for Spahlinger, one that he considers many of his pieces to explore. Yet, this focus on the listener appears to imply a full understanding of these perceptual exercises on their part: that an exploration of perception must be perceptible. Claren, in his conclusion from his analysis of a single section of *und als wir …*, finds this not necessarily to be the case, stating that 'Spahlinger almost continuously moves on the side of the unknowable'. Claren comes to the conclusion that this means the composer is not concerned with perceptibility, rather the 'transition into the expressive gesture is more important than trials for the psychology of perception' for 'there can be few orchestral pieces in which the impression of unhinged, crazed, wild orchestral forces is so incisively articulated'.[50] The emphasis Spahlinger places on perception in his musical thought would rather contradict Claren's conclusion that this piece is 'not about' perceptibility, in fact it would suggest that it is an absolutely fundamental theme of the piece. His conclusion is certainly valid, however, in that it contributes to an important debate in Spahlinger's music that concerns the analytical mode of listening presumed by the composer.

There may also be unintended consequences regarding the unconventional layout of the piece. The intention that there is no central, hierarchically privileged point from which to listen, with the orchestral arrangement seen to be encouraging a more democratic organization of the concert hall, is idealistic. During a performance I attended of Xenakis's *Terretektorh* in 2011 in Frankfurt, for example (admittedly a piece with quite different aims but with similar practicalities), my ticket permitted me to sit only in seats looking onto the orchestra rather than in the limited number among the players. In certain circumstances, therefore, such arrangements simply displace hierarchies rather than doing away with them altogether.

The composer assumes that the audience will listen in a self-reflexive manner. In encountering difficulty, he expects them to consider the failure of their own perceptual faculties rather than the craft of the composer, in this his work takes risks as it courts aesthetic failure with the aim of finding greater artistic success. Spahlinger also expects the audience to relate their musical experience to the same philosophical and social world he inhabits, one that was discussed in Chapter 2 as quite specifically German. Such careful – and probably repeated – listening is particularly difficult in works such as *und als wir ...* or *ocean*, which require large forces and unusual seating arrangements. Both have suffered from lack of performance, even by Spahlinger's standards. The cross-form seating also means that the key intention of the piece will not transfer appropriately to a live stereo recording. The composer himself will have had few opportunities, then, to hear these perceptual explorations at work.

Claren's suggestion that Spahlinger works on the 'side of the unknowable' does clarify the composer's position in relation to perception: that he is not interested in simply writing what can easily be perceived. Rather, his interest often consists in deliberately overstepping the bounds of the perceivable, in the hope that listeners will be conscious of the points at which their own faculties begin to encounter difficulties. This might be done by a process, such as the increasingly prominent deviations from a pitch or pulse that characterize some of his deconstructions of order. The point at which the deviations are perceived has no quantitative beginning but depends entirely on when listeners hear the deviations as significant. It is at this point they might become aware of the work of their own consciousness and the importance of their own perceptual capabilities in constructing meaning. Schick discusses a 'dialectic of understanding and not-understanding' at work in Spahlinger's music to which this question of perceptibility relates. He states that there is a 'disruptive resistance that defies the will to understand' in the composer's pieces, one that cannot be integrated into listening habits and that can 'encourage a consideration of one's own categories of musical understanding and perception'.[51] There is a sense that the composer is provoking listeners' perceptions rather than schooling them.

Born, in her ethnographic study of IRCAM, describes technologically aided analysis as providing universal and ultimately oppressive aesthetic criteria at the institute,[52] and similarities can be observed here in Spahlinger's approach to 'the consciousness'. His perceptual explorations are manifest in particular materials and processes, and result in distinct aesthetic decisions. Yet, at the same time, they are also an invitation to listeners to identify differences between themselves and other listeners. The composer's approach is one that mixes a generalized and particular picture of perception. Perhaps the most important difference is that Spahlinger's explorations are primarily about challenging and isolating the work of listeners' perceptions, rather than creating particular aesthetic rules that the music must follow.

It is worth noting, too, the similarities that some of this rhythmic and metric exploration, especially in *off*, bears to minimalist music, with Reich a particularly apt forerunner. There are, of course, important differences: the rhythmic shifts of Reich's music tend to occur over a longer timespan while remaining for significant periods within one overarching pulse that is easier for listeners to grasp, a hierarchical relationship that Spahlinger finds unacceptable. Minimalism also tends to use a tonally influenced harmonic language with which the composer disagrees and avoids completely in this unpitched piece. Yet, in this systematic examination of metric perception, it is the minimalists who are his most significant predecessors, though he shows interest in such themes of repetition in the somewhat earlier *verfluchung* (1983–85). The composer's courses at the Freiburg Musikhochschule on different types of 'world music' show that he was interested in the same African drumming that was the starting point for Reich. That Spahlinger fails to recognize any debt to minimalist music in this piece written decades after many of its most famous works, however, appears to be an example of technical musical innovation being dismissed because of genre bias. As noted in the previous chapter, he is a typical modernist in his lack of engagement with, or even disdain for, popular music and culture, and arguably a typical German modernist in his lack of interest in minimalism. One consequence is that his thought does not go to any lengths to break down this genre hierarchy, and, through lack of recognition, might be seen to enforce them. In his defence, there are few musicians who are not raised within one or two particular musical genres or traditions, though in the context of his particular project of self-reflexion it is more necessary than usual to consider these ingrained genre biases. This is particularly worth bearing in mind in the discussions concerning the more universal applications of his aesthetic position.

Rancière's Aesthetic Politics

Spahlinger's exploration of perception provides another example of when his aesthetic project can be usefully understood within the framework of Rancière's philosophy, this time in relation to debates around perception and politics. 'Politics' in the philosopher's lexicon has a more specific meaning than in regular parlance and, therefore, his criteria for deciding when politics occurs are more stringent. He states that '[p]olitics revolves around what is seen and what can be said about it, around who has the ability to see and the talent to speak, around the properties of spaces and the possibilities of time'.[53] In this description of politics, it will have been noted how sense information plays a vital role. The unseen and unheard may as well not exist to society at large, that is, until they demand to be seen and heard by others. Particular configurations of who is understood and listened to denote important social hierarchies. The philosopher states that the 'speech of refusal uttered by people who are made unemployed because of relocation and restructuring is conceived simply as the noise made by a victim. However well-argued, it is always interpreted by the rulers and their experts as the noise of suffering'.[54] Rancière describes any change in these configurations of perception – seeing what was before unseen – as a 'redistribution of the sensible'.

The 'distribution of the sensible' [*partage du sensible*] (sometimes also translated as the 'partition of the sensible') describes the boundary between what society literally *sees*, and does not see; what it *hears* as meaningful sound, and what it believes is meaningless noise. According to Davide Panagia, it 'refers at once to the conditions for sharing [...] (i.e. "*partager*" as sharing)' and the disruption 'of that same order (i.e. "*partager*" as separating)'.[55] Every society at a particular point in history will distribute the sensible in a different way, indeed it is a society's shared notion of the sensible that allows it to function. This is the 'sharing' element described above: communities have a common distribution of the sensible which comprises a 'set of concrete correspondences between knowledge, awareness, sound, sight, and so on'.[56] Particular distributions of the sensible also affect artistic production and reception and are crucial in defining the philosopher's regimes of the arts. In the creation of societal cohesion, however, certain people will be excluded or 'separated'. Battles in historiography that wish to include black and feminist narratives, for example, are prime instances of attempting to right now-dated distributions of the sensible: these people were written out of history because they were not seen, their voices not thought worthy of report. Rancière's understanding of the *partage du sensible* is 'the tension between a specific act of perception and its implicit reliance on preconstituted objects deemed worthy of perception'.[57] What this means is that Rancière is seeking to understand what forces determine not what we think of what we see – not our opinions of peoples and things – but what defines our categories of perception: what we fundamentally *see* in the first place.

The distribution of the sensible defines and is defined by the political and social landscape that we inhabit: rupturing this distribution has the potential to bring about political change. Panagia explains how changing the configuration of who and what is perceptible is for Rancière an act of politics. Emancipation, according to Panagia, is therefore defined on the basis of 'aesthetic part-taking: it is a reconfiguration of the perceptual disposition of sights and sounds by those who are excluded from the fields of the visible and of the sayable'.[58] Politics is aesthetic for Rancière not in the sense that its forms aspire towards a kind of beauty, but in the sense of being based on and changeable through perception.

Politics, in his specific definition, 'is an activity of reconfiguration of that which is given to the sensible'.[59]

Spahlinger and the Role of Perception

Spahlinger believes a crucial element of art's critical potential is its manipulation of perception in order to bring about increased self-awareness, or to put it another way, increased knowledge of perception itself. New music, shown, for example, by the advances of *musique concrète instrumentale*, encourages the listener to listen to sounds in a new manner, accepting them as viable material for musical expression. For Spahlinger, the exploration of perception concerns more than simply widening the sounds permissible in composition. Training, or educating, the listener in the workings of their own perceptual apparatus is a key aspect of his philosophically informed approach. This he describes once again in relation to what he believes is a fundamental question of new music:

> the question 'what is sounding in reality?' is posed by new music, and it implies: only so much can come into consciousness from the object of perception as comes from consciousness itself, from the conditions of our perception and interpretation, be they the biological premises of our perceptive apparatus, or the musico-cultural premises of our society.[60]

As seen in *ocean*, Spahlinger argues that there is no 'reality' of a sound divorced from our perception of it, and Rancière would most likely agree as the 'musico-cultural premises of our society' is a rather pithy description of his distribution of the sensible. Again, it is clear that Spahlinger sees new music's purpose as uncovering or manipulating the premises the listener brings to the piece. This occurs not just through introducing new sounds but by employing musical material that tests the limits of listeners' perception.

Spahlinger's description of tonality as a system that was 'the human reality of perception' is very similar to Rancière's distribution of the sensible in its predefinition of what is considered meaningful sound. New music for Spahlinger creates a redistribution of the sensible so that these other sounds can then be understood as musical. The transformation of such sounds that exist *outside* the system can also be seen as a metaphor for the political subjectivication of Rancière's *le part sans part* (the 'part of no part'), which is a group of the disenfranchised who in raising their voices and demanding to be heard create an act of politics for the philosopher. The claims of non-musical sounds to musical expression and subsequent inclusion within the musical are, therefore, akin to an act of politics as Rancière understands it. Neither philosopher nor composer, however, would state that this translation into the aesthetic sphere *is* an unequivocal political action: both are wary of reductionist approaches to the political potential of art.

Rancière's distribution of the sensible provides a framework for better understanding Spahlinger's perceptual explorations. This is no passing coincidence; rather it is based on a fundamentally similar understanding of the situation of art in the twentieth century, codified in Rancière's aesthetic regime. It is important to note, however, that Spahlinger's *explicit* interest in perception makes him quite different from the authors and filmmakers that Rancière takes as his examples, while the philosopher's particular interest in the changes between regimes means that he only rarely discusses truly contemporary art, despite his interest in modern artistic reception. In his writings, Rancière often decodes the ways in which seemingly technical or expressive changes in art – such as the advent of realism – in fact contribute to a redistribution of the sensible. With Spahlinger, the 'author's' intentions in this direction are quite clear, making him unusual. The application of Rancière's ideas offered here is, therefore, quite unlike what the philosopher himself attempts. Naturally, this need not inhibit the employment of his thought to better understand the intentions and effects of Spahlinger's music, but it does mean that few other examples from the philosopher's writings can be engaged with in a similar manner.

While the confluence of ideas between these two figures gives important context to how Spahlinger's perceptual explorations operate, it is important to record that Rancière's ideas also provide a challenge to the composer's interest in perception. This is unsurprising considering the philosopher is avowedly anti-modernist, with his aesthetic regimes in part designed to undermine a sense of rupture at the beginning of the twentieth century, just when modernists identify their heroic period. Rancière's examples, such as Charlie Chaplin, are regularly consumed by a far larger audience than the still specialist world of new music allows: as he himself states, cinema 'was a popular art reclassified by its consumers, an art that allowed a pretty significant number of people to make their way into the domain of art and aesthetic judgement'.[61] He is keen to stress the interdisciplinary nature of the works he believes bring about a redistribution of the sensible, whereas Spahlinger's take place primarily within the musical sphere. Both of these points lead back to the persistence of modernism in the composer's work, for he is keen to explore the most 'radical' material that has little in common with that of mainstream consumption, and attempts to create new ways of experiencing a specific art form, music, rather than fusing different forms together. In this light, he begins to appear rather like Rancière's negative characterization of Greenbergian modernism.[62] Yet, crucially, Spahlinger's understanding of new music as an open realm of possibility is very different from the teleological viewpoint the philosopher ascribes to Greenberg.

The open field of contingency described in the aesthetic regime has been identified as a vital element of the politics of aesthetics that the philosopher's thought contains, one that has an equally important place in Spahlinger's own aesthetic project.

Spahlinger's Modernist Exploration of Perception

Though Rancière himself holds an avowedly anti-modernist position, the foregoing discussion has in fact shown that the philosopher's thought gives a wider artistic context for Spahlinger's aesthetic stance. Implicit in this concord is in fact a challenge to the composer's belief in the uniqueness of new music in approaching an increased knowledge of consciousness, as Rancière suggests other means by which a redistribution of the sensible might be achieved. Possibly, Spahlinger would not deny the idea that other forms of art also point towards the future in a similar manner as he is, after all, no philosopher attempting a general theory of the arts but a composer trying to understand the innovations in music he believes are important. Yet it is clear the philosopher's thought undermines any exclusive claim on the part of new music to achieve political effect. Rancière's identification of this wider artistic movement can, however, add a breadth to Spahlinger's approach that the composer would understandably never have attempted. It relates to what Johnson and Gulbrandsen describe as the 'long view' of modernism, which identifies modernist moments far further back into the nineteenth, and even eighteenth, centuries, as well as showing how they continue to hold importance today, even outwith the spheres of 'high art'.[63] In turn, Spahlinger's description of new music gives far more depth to an understanding of music as it operates in the aesthetic regime. Music, often demoted in the philosopher's thought, can, in Spahlinger's conception, be seen to provide an exemplary case of Rancière's modern understanding of art: Spahlinger makes the case to put music at the heart of the aesthetic regime rather than keeping it on the periphery.

That this modernist music is a particularly strong example of Rancière's thinking is important considering his regular criticism of his particular version of modernist theory. Far from obscuring or contorting the aesthetic regime, Spahlinger's compositions openly embrace it. This is an observation that identifies Rancière's relationship with modernism as an area of fruitful challenge. This is seen, too, in Spahlinger's focus on the sense-making activities of the listener, which prefigures an area of the philosopher's thought that has only recently received focused attention. In this the composer addresses fundamental questions of how to approach artistic production at a time in which criteria for constituting the art work are far from absolute. That he *consciously* attends to these themes makes him a particularly valuable case in considering the philosopher's thought. In taking perception as his basis, Spahlinger finds a vital source of artistic sustenance, one he would contrast with an uncritical 'postmodern' hodgepodge.

In this discussion of perception and politics, both philosopher and composer are still open to criticism regarding whether the connections they make in these areas are effective and unavoidable. Both rely on a significant degree of reflexion and self-awareness on the part of the audience. In Rancière, there is a tension between the development of individuals' redistributions of the sensible and those of society at large: the philosopher attempts to describe both a personal experience and a societal trend yet, in such an arrangement, the personal will always appear inferior to the large-scale historical and societal forces. These redistributions attempt to be at once social and personal: the description of an individual's subjective experience and the changing perceptions of whole generations. The question remains, however, what room there is for personal experience that does not match that of wider social trends, for redistributions of the sensible that stake out their own path. There is a hierarchy here, as Rancière only considers those changes that are far-reaching, therefore societal, a hierarchy that does not sit well with his passionate interest in equality, while also connecting with the tension already identified in the composer's engagement with 'perception' in general as opposed to the free associations of the aesthetic experience.

Furthermore, a listener to Spahlinger's music – even if they attempt to assume the desired mode of listening – may well miss many of his chief musical aims entirely, whether they be the contingency of our perception or the pliability of formal understanding. The previous chapters have shown, however, that the political intentions of the composer are fundamentally tied to the musical experience, whether it be in the more 'abstract' anti-narrative of *passage/paysage*, or in the presentation of both protest and abstraction heard in *ocean*. That this music requires reflexion and attentive listening is undeniable, yet Rancière's thought helps us to understand Spahlinger's project because it states that the perceptual themes to which the composer attends are not fundamentally separate but are a part of political understanding. It is not, as Schick states, a translation of music into 'forms of thought' which are then projected onto the political: music and politics take place in the same field of perception and experience. Reflection on this experience, on the work of our perception, will lead to a better understanding of the perceptual and societal factors defining, and potentially constraining, our reception of music, and of the sights, sounds and temporalities that define our political experience. Spahlinger's belief that his music shows a fundamental change of consciousness holds, in this light, the very same tensions as Rancière's personal and societal redistributions of the sensible: the contradiction between seeking emancipatory personal experience that is at the same time part of a societally necessary trend.

Crucially, however, in this case, the trend described is not one of restriction but of openness and contingency.

Finally, the historical continuity Rancière identifies in his notion of the aesthetic regime, which provides a challenge to Spahlinger's ideas, is, at the same time, a strong endorsement that important parallels can be found between artistic conditions today and those throughout the twentieth century. Modernist art, as opposed to Rancière's modernist theory, is, therefore, a response to similar questions of contingency and meaning, a point Spahlinger makes in his descriptions of past modernist music. The composer's project identifies long-standing issues of artistic production and reception. In particular, the focus on perception with its potential political applications displays a unique engagement with these issues, one identified by Rancière in his aesthetics only relatively recently. That Spahlinger attempts this within a modernist frame of reference should give modernism's critics, including Rancière himself, pause for thought. Though dismissed by the philosopher as obscuring the nature of the aesthetic regime, Spahlinger's interest in all the issues covered here – artistic contingency, continuity of artistic practice in the twentieth century, and the political potential of perception – strongly suggest this conception of modernism is inadequate and that the relationship between it and the aesthetic regime is far less clear cut. Spahlinger's modernism and Rancière's aesthetics can in fact combine to present a compelling description of the conditions under which the reception and production of art take place today.

NOTES

1. Mathias Spahlinger, 'wirklichkeit des bewußtseins und wirklichkeit für das bewußtsein: politische aspekte der music', *MusikTexte* 39 (1991): 39–41.

2. Dorothea Ruthemeier, *Antagonismus oder Konkurrenz? Zu zentralen Werkgruppen der 1980er Jahre von Wolfgang Rihm und Mathias Spahlinger* (Schliengen: Edition Argus, 2012), 115.

3. Spahlinger, 'wirklichkeit des bewußtseins und wirklichkeit für das bewußtsein', 41.

4. Ruthemeier, *Antagonismus oder Konkurrenz?*, 115.

5. See David Held, *Introduction to Critical Theory* (Cambridge: Polity, 1990), 202–13.

6. See Theodor Adorno, 'Commitment', in *Aesthetics and Politics* (London: Verso Books, 1980), 177–95; Rainer Nonnenmann, *Der Gang durch die Klippen: Helmut Lachenmanns Begegnung mit Luigi Nono anhand ihres Briefwechsels und anderer Quellen 1957–1990* (Wiesbaden: Breitkopf & Härtel, 2013); Mark Carroll, 'Commitment or Abrogation? Avant-Garde Music and Jean-Paul Sartre's Idea of Committed Art', *Music & Letters*, 83 (2002): 590–606.

7. Mathias Spahlinger in Markus Hechtle, *198 Fenster zu einer imaginierten Welt* (Saarbrücken: Pfau-Verlag, 2005), 114.

8. Sebastian Claren, 'Tempo Explosion: Ein Ausschnitt aus Mathias Spahlingers *und als wir für 54 Streicher (1993)*', *Musik-Konzepte* 155: 95–113, 99.

9. Johannes Kreidler, 'Mathias Spahlingers Zumutungen; Gegen Unendlich und gegen Krieg', *Musik-Konzepte* 155 (2012): 23–30, 34.

10. Claus-Steffen Mahnkopf, 'What Does "Critical Composition" Mean?', in *Critical Composition Today*, eds. Claus-Steffen Mahnkopf, Frank Cox and Wolfram Schurig (Hofheim: Wolke Verlag, 2006), 75–87, 83.

11. See Max Paddison, *Adorno's Aeshtetics of Music* (Cambridge: Cambridge University Press, 1997), 177.

12. Jörg Mainka, 'Mind the Gap; Spahlingers Vorliebe für "die Dinge dazwischen"', *Musik-Konzepte* 155 (2012): 75–94.

13. Mathias Spahlinger, programme note to *gegen unendlich*, (1995).

14. Ibid.

15. Mathias Spahlinger, interview with Neil Thomas Smith, 11 August 2014, Groß Glienicke, recording: unarchived.

16. Herder in Dorothea von Mücke, 'Language as the Mark of the Soul: Herder's Narcissistic Subject', *Herder Today: Contributions from the International Herder Conference, November 5–8, 1987, Stanford, California*, ed. Kurt Mueller-Vollmer (Berlin: De Gruyter, 1990), 331–44, 335.

17. Tobias Eduard Schick, *Weltbezüge in der Musik Mathias Spahlingers* (Stuttgart: Franz Steiner Verlag, 2018), 111.

18. Bruno Liebrucks, *Sprache und Bewußtsein*, vol. 1 (Frankfurt am Main: Akademie-Verlag, 1964), 63. The use of 'Man' is rather less forgivable in the twentieth-century than Herder's in the eighteenth, indicating again the gendered nature of this intellectual climate.

19. Mathias Spahlinger in Peter Niklas Wilson, 'Music as a Play of Language and Society', booklet notes to *Mathias Spahlinger*, CD, Wergo (1993), 22–32, 25.

20. Ibid.

21. Ibid.

22. Ibid.

23. See Adorno, 'Commitment', 189; and Theodor Adorno, *Philosophy of Modern Music*, trans. A. G. Mitchell and W. V. Bloomster (London: Seabury Press, 1973), 30.

24. In Marion Saxer, 'Die "anderen Räume" der Medien: Mathias Spahlingers *in dem ganzen ocean von empfindungen eine welle absondern, sie anhalten* für Chorgruppen und Playback (1985)', *Musik-Konzepte* 115 (2012): 114–29, 120.

25. Marco Stroppa, 'Live electronics or … live music? Towards a critique of interaction', *Contemporary Music Review* 18, no. 3 (1999): 41–77.

26. Mathias Spahlinger, 'thesen zur "schwindel der wirklichkeit"', *MusikTexte* 142 (2014): 15–17. This references a programme of events at Berlin's Akademie der Künste on the 'sham of actuality'. The fact Spahlinger is quoting this part of the title means that it is unclear

how this 'wirklichkeit' described by the Akademie sits within Spahlinger's separation of *wirklichkeit* and *realität*.

27. Walter Benjamin, 'Art in the Age of Mechanical Reproduction', in *Illuminations* (London: Pimlico, 1999): 211–14.

28. Mathias Spahlinger, private correspondence with Neil Thomas Smith, 31 August 2016.

29. A different interpretation of this can be found in the present author's article on *ocean*: Smith, '*Presenting the irreconcilable*'.

30. The Wergo CD recording, which is a studio production, begins with the gentle burble of the audience for around 35 seconds before the playback begins, giving an aural impression of the performance situation.

31. Schick, *Weltbezüge in der Musik Mathias Spahlingers*, 127.

32. *passage/paysage*, to name but one piece, operates in a similar manner. See Neil Thomas Smith, 'Mathias Spahlinger's *passage/paysage* and the "Barbarity of Continuity"', *Contemporary Music Review* 24, nos. 2–3 (2015): 176–86.

33. An exact translation of the statistic would also date the piece to a particular time or statistical methodology.

34. Wilson, 'Music as a Play of Language and Society', 28.

35. See Dorothea Ruthemeier nee Schüle, '"…dann wird offenbar, daß alles auf Vereinbarung beruht": Zur Idee der offenen Form in Mathias Spahlingers "verlorener weg" (1999/2000)', *MusikTexte* 95 (2002): 35–49.

36. Saxer, 'Die "anderen Räume" der Medien', 116.

37. Schick, *Weltbezüge in der Musik Mathias Spahlingers*, 120–121.

38. Saxer, 'Die "anderen Räume" der Medien', 117.

39. Ibid.

40. Breath as a theme is also present in Nicolaus A. Huber's *Nocturnes* from just one year before. See John Warnaby, 'The Music of Nicolaus A. Huber', *TEMPO* 57, no. 224 (2003): 22–37, 29.

41. Schick, *Weltbezüge in der Musik Mathias Spahlingers*, 107.

42. I am indebted to an anonymous reviewer for suggesting this analogy. Ludwig Wittgenstein, *Philosophical Investigations* (Oxford: Blackwell, 1958), 165–66.

43. Theodor Adorno, 'The Dialectical Composer', in *Essays on Music*, ed. Richard Leppert (London: University of California Press, 2002), 203–12, 205.

44. Theodor Adorno, *Negative Dialectics*, trans. E. B. Ashton (London: Continuum, 1973), 5.

45. Saxer, 'Die "anderen Räume" der Medien', 120.

46. Ibid., 116.

47. Schick, *Weltbezüge in der Musik Mathias Spahlingers*, 114.

48. Max Paddison, 'Composition as Political Praxis: A Response to Mathias Spahlinger', *Contemporary Music Review* 34, no. 2–3 (2015): 167–75, 173.

49. T. W. Adorno, 'Vers une musique informelle', *Quasi una fantasia*, trans. Rodney Livingstone (London: Verso, 1992), 269–322, 322.

50. Claren, 'Tempo Explosion', 113.

51. Schick, *Weltbezüge in der Musik Mathias Spahlingers*, 279.

52. Georgina Born, *Rationalizing Culture: IRCAM, Boulez, and the Institutionalization of the Musical Avant-Garde* (London: University of California Press, 1995), 319.

53. Jacques Rancière, *The Politics of Aesthetics*, trans. Gabriel Rockhill (London: Continuum, 2004), 13. The political implications of the 'possibilities' of musical time are discussed in relation to Spahlinger's *passage/paysage* in Smith, 'the "Barbarity of Continuity".

54. Jacques Rancière, 'Jacques Rancière and Indisciplinarity', trans. Gregory Elliot, *Art & Research* 2, no. 1 (2008): 3. http://www.artandresearch.org.uk/v2n1/jrinterview.html (accessed 16 September 2018).

55. Davide Panagia, '"Partage du sensible": the distribution of the sensible', in *Jacques Rancière: Key Concepts*, ed. Jean-Philippe Deranty (Durham: Acumen, 2010), 95–103, 95.

56. Ibid., 99.

57. Ibid., 95.

58. Ibid., 102.

59. Davide Panagia and Jacques Rancière, 'Dissenting Words: A Conversation with Jacques Rancière', *Diacritics* 30, no. 2 (2000): 113–26, 115.

60. Mathias Spahlinger, 'this is the time of conceptive ideologues no longer', trans. Philipp Blume, *Contemporary Music Review* 27, no. 6 (2008): 579–94, 581.

61. Rancière, 'Jacques Rancière and Indisciplinarity', 7. Though perhaps the distance to Chaplin is not so great as it seems, with Adorno an admirer of the comedian: see John Mackay, 'Chaplin Times Two', *Yale Journal of Criticism* 9, no. 1 (1996): 57–61.

62. For further information on Rancière's conception of Greenbergian modernism, see Joseph J. Tanke, 'What Is the Aesthetic Regime?', *Parrhesia* 12 (2011): 71–81.

63. Erling E. Gulbrandsen and Julian Johnson, 'Introduction', in *Transformations in Musical Modernism*, ed. Erling E. Gulbrandsen and Julian Johnson (Cambridge: Cambridge University Press, 2015), 1–18, 2.

Conclusion

In attempting to write a critical companion, there is a paradoxical tension at the heart of the enterprise. Spahlinger's concerns must be discussed and explored sympathetically before they are critiqued, while the composer's intentions and philosophical preoccupations must take precedence over other, more adventurous interpretations. The arrangement of themes in Part 2, which employs illustrative examples from his works, means there is a danger of perpetuating what has been a weakness of Spahlinger scholarship hitherto: a lack of consideration of how works function as wholes, and the context of these works, as well as how contradictions arise from the musical relations formed outside of these model passages. Furthermore, such passages are often highlighted by the composer himself to illustrate his ideas, pointing to the significant role he has played in the analysis of his pieces.

Yet, it has been the intention here to point not just to Spahlinger's achievements and the challenge, excitement and importance of his music, but to also show what areas might be critiqued or further developed. The critical commentaries should go some way to avoiding an unreflexive position, but in wishing to give a broad understanding of much of his work succinctly, passages certainly have been selected that are particularly fine illustrations of Spahlinger's ideas. It is my hope that the partial analyses here, and fuller discussions elsewhere, will spur others to engage enthusiastically and critically with these works in the future. There remain, however, some ends to be tied up regarding the debates that have run through the discussions of the composer's primary concerns. Chief among these is the question of modernism and its contemporary relevance, which is at the heart of many commentators' critiques of the composer. This will be picked up first, before a final consideration of Spahlinger's aspirations regarding musical style and politics. Finally, the issue of contemporary relevance will be addressed specifically, pointing to what might be learned from the composer's approach.

Spahlinger's Modernism

Criticisms of modernism often follow particular lines of attack. Modernist works are singled out for their willful difficulty, their belief in an autonomous artistic sphere outside of society, the outmoded hierarchies they embody, and the institutions they form or bolster (such as the academy) in order to rule in an authoritarian manner over artistic practice. From these it is possible to assemble a crude stereotypical image of the modernist composer. Convinced of the unstoppable march of musical progress, he writes for a future public more sympathetic than that of the present; certain of music as an autonomous sphere of activity, he eschews any contact with political or social reality; confident in his own music as superior to that which surrounds him, he disdains popular tastes and musical customs. Spahlinger, in openly stating allegiance to this inheritance, is in danger of courting the same criticisms.

Certainly, he describes new music as being, or reflecting, 'the very revolution of revolutions' in that it negates, or has the potential to negate, all aspects of its previous tradition.[1] Such statements appear to contribute to well-established modernist claims of sole musical legitimacy, that is, that any music not making use of the most recent musical innovations – as decided by modernists – is not worth even considering. Furthermore, he discusses at some length intricate compositional construction and shows a pronounced lack of interest in popular music. Yet, there are areas in which the fit becomes rather more difficult. On many key debates – such as the contested status of musical autonomy, hierarchies both compositional and social, teleological views of musical progress and the mode of listening assumed by modernist composers – Spahlinger's position has been shown to be nuanced, while his works often take these precise debates as their themes. In a number of debates the ideas of the composer and critics of modernism are not so very different. For example, Spahlinger's central exploration of the political nature of music displays a critical understanding of the status of the artwork as a social and political phenomenon, while he also describes a similar suspicion of hierarchies and teleological progress throughout his oeuvre.

This does not mean, however, that Spahlinger is any less a modernist. It has been shown that his stance shows a fundamental continuity with modernist predecessors, both in his conception of music's function and his approaches to composition. His suspicion of mainstream modes of expression, his belief in pursuing 'radical' musical material and his desire to challenge and provoke listeners all point to this fact. Rather, it is a sign that the composer's aesthetic project, in these issues at least, presents a critical modernism that can all too often be ignored by critics. This study, therefore, bears out the assertions made by writers such as Heile who describes modernism as 'an ongoing concern, unfinished business'.[2] Gulbrandsen and Johnson also describe it as 'an attitude of musical practice' that 'remains alive and kicking as a vibrant musical force among musicians, festivals and audiences on all continents of the contemporary world'.[3] Despite sustained criticism, then, modernism persists, while the positions of its most trenchant detractors have themselves come under some scrutiny. Oversimplified and monolithic readings of modernism have been seen to underplay its regenerative critical potential.

There are undoubtedly tensions within Spahlinger's position, however. His belief in the fundamentally unique nature of new music naturally creates the genre hierarchy critics identify, one that is borne out by his complete disregard for popular music, though not jazz. He does not admit the potential for utopian moments in many other musics, even though, according to his own theoretical framework, there is potential for them to be 'political' at the very least: exploring the means of production, for example, does not necessitate the material of modernist music but could be explored in many different ways. In this sense, Spahlinger's personal predilections intervene in the more general, theoretical basis of his work, leaving him open to criticisms of writing for an informed minority *au fait* with modernist musical material.

One of the most significant areas of tension identified by the criticisms of modernism is Spahlinger's strong belief in a mode of listening that involves keen engagement with what is sounding, and intellectual reflection upon it, a position that is in danger of straying into the academic and potentially elitist assumptions about modes of musical experience. He unashamedly believes that music partakes in a field of intellectual enquiry, a stance that has its roots in the figure of the politically active artist-intellectual that was particularly prevalent in Germany after the Second World War. Many of his aspirations for the listener remain unrealistic, however, as few will make the leaps of thought that he encourages without recourse to his own writings, and will make their own interpretations of the sounding events his music presents. The latter is hardly a 'problem', as it is an essential part of the musical experience, while such imaginative reinterpretations will be to the benefit of a continuing Spahlinger scholarship that can increasingly, if desired, assume a critical distance from the composer's intentions. Despite his interest in perception, then, Spahlinger is reluctant to fully accept an emphasis on the unique situated experience of his listeners, a point on which he consistently differs from postmodern deconstructionist thought. Spahlinger's practice is a negotiation between the ideas and experiences he wishes to express and the creative faculties of the audience.

The analyses of Spahlinger's works that have been carried out in this project, however, do bear out the composer's interpretations of his own pieces to a quite remarkable degree. This is, in part, due to the decision to engage fully with Spahlinger's thought and, therefore, his descriptions of his own pieces, one necessitated by a relative lack of other English language literature, and encouraged by the compelling nature of his ideas. Yet, the place of the composer's thought in these analyses is also due to the manner in which his intellectual and political ideas are tied in such a significant way to the experience of his pieces. It is argued here that, rather than intellectual posturing, his is a project characterized by a genuine attempt to engage critically and intellectually through his musical offerings. This can be observed in the manipulation of temporal experience in *passage/paysage*, as well as the simultaneous presentation of abstract musical argument and bold, semantically clear statement in *ocean*. It has been argued through discussions of Rancière that the composer's political messages are essentially tied to the musical experience of the works he creates, while reflection upon these is not a translation but takes part in the same perceptual field as the political. This is not to say that listeners will immediately come to the same conclusions on historical narrative and the role of the media as the composer, but it is crucial in understanding that there is no absolute divide between Spahlinger's musical and political aims. He presents a fundamental challenge to the divides between the 'musical' and the 'extra-musical' in his exploration of the nature of musical autonomy.

The question of modes of listening is an important one. While much room has been given here to discussing the composer's intellectual preoccupations – as well as giving an impression of why such concerns were formed – it is important to stress that awareness of these is not a prerequisite to an appreciation of the music. It would be a positive if more people were given the chance to engage with Spahlinger's pieces *as music* before becoming familiar with his entire theoretical perspective. The richness and challenge of his position, as well as his unconventional ideas around musical continuity, can be gleaned by attending to his works as aesthetic objects. Nevertheless, for many critics, the music and justification are difficult to separate: claims made for his music are pored over and dissected, raising a number of avenues for continuing debate.

Ongoing Debates: Style, Politics and Institutional Critique

It has been argued throughout this study that various of the composer's compositional decisions result in regularly returning features that, despite his insistence on negation of any established order or hierarchy, approach a unique compositional style. This can be seen in his handling of material, which in open form pieces is intentionally limited to a small number of elements to highlight the transitions between them. It is seen, too, in his formal, anti-narrative approach, which often creates stark contrasts both on a local and global level. However, there is still a sense that he is influenced by the styles of other composers. Spahlinger's vocal writing bears close resemblances to his predecessors Nono and Lachenmann in the cries, groans and shouts that he employs, while in his instrumental music, the techniques of *musique concrète instrumentale* are hugely influential, though their attraction decreases over time. It is this that has led to criticisms of elements of Spahlinger's music being at times 'epigonal', that is, a cheap imitation,[4] though important differences between Spahlinger and Lachenmann have been explored in this study. Finally, Spahlinger's almost complete avoidance of tonal material can in itself become a 'positive' musical attribute. Having assessed all these features, there is a strong sense that they contribute to an identifiable and consistent musical surface and structural approach, even if it is often a contradictory 'consistency of being unpredictable', at least within a particular range of new music materials.

This appears to contradict Spahlinger's insistence on fundamentally reevaluating artistic practice in each instantiation. Paddison states that 'it becomes clear that new music is not a style but at best a method, according to Spahlinger, and it is seen as a process that is constantly changing its procedures'.[5] If this were so, would such a sense of style be possible? Enno Poppe suggests that the composer does achieve this goal, stating that 'no two pieces by Spahlinger are the same', which is 'far from easy to accept' for his 'listeners and fans'.[6] Spahlinger attempts more than many composers to radically alter his creative approach, indeed the very fact that he attempts this may set him apart in the first place. Regularly, a recognizable style is seen as a mark of a mature creative voice or even the bearer of genius. Certainly, Spahlinger takes risks in certain pieces, such as the quasi-improvisatory open form works and the brush with technology in *ocean*. Yet, for the reasons already identified, including formal instability and a noisy, unpredictable musical surface, the composer's fingerprint remains.

This raises the question of whether such an assessment sabotages the composer's aesthetic project, which is built upon the undermining of such hardened stylistic attributes. Two points are crucial here: first, as discussed in relation to musical order, the negation that Spahlinger seeks is not abstract, but should always result in something concretely new out of that which already exists. A sense of 'style', therefore, is not an immediate admission of failure. Second, a number of these elements – particularly his attitude to material – allow him to explore hierarchies and instability in far greater depth than would otherwise be the case. This was seen in a brief comparison made in Chapter 5 between *passage/paysage* and *extension*, for example, in which it was argued that the lack of tonal reference in the former allows a more equal sense of material and, therefore, a more successful expression of the thought that any music can transition to any other. There are certainly elements of this stylistic surface that the composer himself overlooks in describing his aesthetic project, yet they do not stop Spahlinger from writing pieces that we, in Paddison's words, 'cannot easily accommodate [...] to existing concepts and categories' and that must be engaged with 'through reflexive experience with the possibility of understanding "something new"'.[7] The question is ultimately subjective as to whether listeners experience a wide variety of challenge and sensation in his works.

A more forceful criticism arose in the holistic view of society that is favoured by much German sociology, which has struggled to highlight injustice along lines of gender and ethnicity. That Spahlinger does not emphasize these issues in his work is hardly unusual for a modernist composer: identification of this blind spot is an important criticism of Marx-inspired German modernism in general, as the prioritizing of class divides has obscured other restrictive societal structures. As Marxist feminism has shown, however, this does not mean that the composer's thought is of no use to those who wish to explore such issues in more depth. Spahlinger's interest in challenging musical hierarchies, both in terms of production and compositional system, might well provide the tools for further musical and institutional critique in areas he himself has left untouched. The similarities of approach with Rancière, whose political project is far more concerned with emancipation of the suppressed and ignored, also point to possible applications for Spahlinger's interest in perception that tackle the plight of the *part de sans-part* more specifically. The criticism sticks here but the tools show further potential.

Finally, there is the sense that, for all his talk of institutional critique, Spahlinger benefits hugely from the institutions that govern and perform contemporary music in his homeland. This relationship is reminiscent of the composer's connection with tradition, which he seems tied to yet attempts to negate. Some might argue that his attempts at institutional critique are hollow gestures as his work is complicit in the very processes against which he is protesting. It is difficult to assess to what extent, if at all, his critical position has limited the opportunities and recognition he has received in his career. Certainly, there are examples of ideas, such as the abandoned opera *suoni reali*, that could not be realized, while certain difficulties in performance – such as those observed in *doppelt bejaht* – are in part signs of the tensions in his attempt to present critique of institutions through the institutions themselves.

Such difficulties show that his desire to explore musical production has consequences, for him and, more directly, for his performers. In this light, the critique is more effective than if it had sought extra-institutional routes, as Spahlinger is able to directly manipulate institutions' practice, yet it also raises questions of performers being subject to a composer's will. The contradictions of this position cannot fully be untangled, arising from the ambiguous position of the composer in society, one that Spahlinger describes in 'this is the time', that relies on institutional funding and performances for the expression of their ideas, even if these are informed by fundamentally critical viewpoints. Such concerns are far from specific to Spahlinger, in attempting to tread a fine line between critiquing institutions and becoming part of them, the composer is navigating a core tension in the modernist project as well as attempts by revolutionary socialists to work within the confines of parliamentary democracy.

Historical Phenomenon or Contemporary Thinker?

Plotting the persistence of modernist ideas in Spahlinger's aesthetic project naturally provides a good deal of ammunition to those who see the composer as a relic of a bygone era, one that can have little to offer the contemporary world. Their assertions and assumptions must be explored to see what Spahlinger has salvaged from his modernist precursors and to assess whether the composer's brand of modernism is a resuscitation of 'obsolete avant-garde thought',[8] or a renewal of vital ideas for our time. Certainly Spahlinger, like any composer, bears the marks of the times through which he has lived and, in his case, a particularly modernist context. This can be observed in the *musique-concrète-instrumentale*-inspired surface of much of his music, and his ongoing avoidance of tonality, the latter a position to which younger composers are less likely to subscribe. He is also now a firmly established voice in contemporary German music: like Lachenmann, he is something of the elder statesman. Spahlinger, therefore, is not developing along the lines of any compositional *Zeitgeist*, while his previous previous 'outsider' position in German contemporary music may suggest he never was. The familiarity of his position, within German contemporary music at least, may lead to the impression that what there is to learn from his aesthetic project has already been obtained.

Criticisms from Mahnkopf and Nonnenmann have already been explored, with the latter seeing in the composer's 'fixation on Hegel' a suspicion of being 'uncritical and historical', while his constant reference to established philosophic authorities is described as more of an 'attempt at intellectual legitimation' rather than an engagement with contemporary issues in music.[9] Both have fundamental doubts about what Spahlinger's music can offer contemporary understanding and, it is tempting to infer, what inspiration he can give to future composers. There is a sense of frustration underlying these criticisms that the composer refuses to engage with more recent developments in music and more contemporary theory. In this criticism, there can be seen the tacit acceptance of his established position in German new music: he is now someone to rage against. As discussed in Chapter 4's brief note on deconstruction, for Mahnkopf at least, there is potentially an overstatement of differences in order to more fully demarcate the 'next generation'. Writers such as Ruthemeier and Brian Kane have also begun a conceptual counteroffensive, linking concerns in Spahlinger's music to more recent critical theory.[10]

In this book, it has been argued that Spahlinger's music does provide new experiences and unique angles from which to view vital ongoing debates within contemporary music. Questions of musical autonomy and of artistic production in a field of open contingency are still fundamental to today's practitioners. The continuity of artistic practice observed both in post-Second World War German art and Rancière's conception of the aesthetic regime underline how Spahlinger's concerns remain relevant. The philosopher's rejection of a modernism/postmodernism divide undermines assertions of a revolutionary change in thought that makes the composer's work incompatible with modern comprehension. Spahlinger's music and thought is of its time certainly, but is a vital and powerful response to questions of artistic creation that remain fundamental. It is also worth noting that these ideas may be old hat to someone in Mahnkopf's position, immersed in the world of German new music, but much of it still remains inaccessible to Anglophone readers.

This means of course that his music does have the potential to offer inspiration for future composers. Direct emulation of the surface of his music is unlikely, however, not least because the types of sound he uses are not his most original contribution, as shown by his, particularly early, reliance on *musique concrète instrumentale*. Rather his approach to structure, his exploration of the means of production, the conceptual edge to his compositional approach and his exceptional exploration of the relationship between politics and music are more likely areas of further work. Spahlinger's musical descendants may, therefore, sound very different from him, while at the same time embracing many of his ideas. This can already be seen in one of his most prominent pupils, concept artist Kreidler.

In describing what Spahlinger might offer contemporary understanding, there is an implicit role for continued scholarship. Certainly, there is an urgent need for further research on the composer, particularly in English. Though this book has covered his primary concerns and many of his most important pieces, there are many facets of his compositional work, and a great many of his compositions, that remain underexplored. It has also been argued that his is a significant contribution to modernist aesthetics that can be brought into contact with a whole host of viewpoints in contemporary theory, with only one particularly apt example, that of Rancière, employed here. If Spahlinger is becoming a historical phenomenon, then it is a process that is going hand in hand with the first realizations of what his aesthetic project entails and the potential it offers. Fundamentally, the question of Spahlinger's influence rests on the open field of possibilities he describes in contemporary artistic practice and his own ingenious ways of coming to terms with this situation. Though in his own music he limits himself in terms of harmonies and materials, there are far fewer boundaries to the applications of his thought. The modernism he describes, that of continual self-reflexion and renewal, will remain a source of artistic sustenance. Spahlinger's work is a particularly compelling, powerful and thoughtful response to this phenomenon, but is by no means the last.

NOTES

1. Mathias Spahlinger, 'this is the time of conceptive ideologues no longer', trans. Philipp Blume, *Contemporary Music Review* 27, no. 6 (2008): 579–94, 580.
2. Björn Heile, 'Introduction', in *The Modernist Legacy* (Farnham: Ashgate, 2009), 1–12, 3.
3. Erling E. Gulbrandsen and Julian Johnson, 'Introduction', in *Transformations in Musical Modernism* (Cambridge: Cambridge University Press, 2015), 1–18, 1.
4. Rainer Nonnenmann, 'A Dead End as a Way Out', in *Critical Composition Today*, eds. Claus-Steffen Mahnkopf, Frank Cox and Wolfram Schurig (Hofheim: Wolke Verlag, 2006), 88–109, 108.
5. Max Paddison, 'Composition as Political Praxis: A Response to Mathias Spahlinger', *Contemporary Music Review* 34, nos. 2–3 (2015): 167–75, 163.
6. Enno Poppe, *'Laudatio an Mathias Spahlinger* anlässlich der Verleihung des Berliner Kunstpreises', in the programme booklet to musica viva Ensemble Modern Orchestra concert, 28 September 2018, 45–50, 47.
7. Paddison, 'Composition as Political Praxis', 164.
8. Dorothea Ruthemeier, *Antagonismus oder Konkurrenz? Zu zentralen Werkgruppen der 1980er Jahre von Wolfgang Rihm und Mathias Spahlinger* (Schliengen: Edition Argus, 2012).
9. Rainer Nonnenmann, 'Bestimmte Negation: Anspruch und Wirklichkeit einer umstrittenen Strategie anhand con Spahlingers "furioso"', *MusikTexte* 95, (2002): 57–69, 61.
10. Dorothea Ruthemeier nee Schüle, 'Concertare Means Reaching an Agreement: On Mathias Spahlinger's "Piano Concerto" inter-mezzo (1986)', *Contemporary Music Review* 27, no. 6 (2008): 611–23; Brian Kane, 'Aspect and Ascription in the Music of Mathias Spahlinger', *Contemporary Music Review* 27, no. 6 (2008): 595–609.

Mathias Spahlinger: List of Works

The following is an edited version of the works list from the composer's own web-site, https://mathiasspahlinger.de/ (Spahlinger 2020).

fünf sätze für zwei klaviere (1969)
(*5 movements for two pianos*); Duration: 7′
Premiere: Darmstadt 1970

drama (1969)
For 12 voices; Duration: 9′30

fürsich (1970)
For one performer; Duration: 12′
Premiere: Darmstadt 1971

szenen für kinder (1970)
Duration: 12′
Premiere: Ludwigsburg 1970

phonophobie (1972)
For wind quintet; Duration: 9′
Premiere: Stuttgart 1972

entlöschend (1974)
(literally 'un-erasing', also 'non-extinguishing') for large tam-tam;
Duration: 15′
Premiere: Stuttgart 1974

sotto voce (1973–74)
For vocalists; Duration: 5′–10′
Premiere: Stuttgart 1974

wozu noch musik ? (1974)
ästhetische theorie in quasi ästhetischer gestalt (collage)
(*why still music? aesthetic theory in a quasi-aesthetical gestalt [collage]*)
Duration: 62'55 (abridged version); 100'40 (original version).
Premiere: Süddeutscher Rundfunk (SDR): 1975

morendo (1975)
For orchestra; Duration: 7'
Studio Production Hessicher Rundfunk (HR): 1979
Premiere: Südwest Rundfunk Orchestra (SWR) Baden-Baden/Freiburg 1996

vier stücke (1975)
(*four pieces*) for voice, clarinet, violin, violoncello and piano; Duration: 4'
Premiere: Stuttgart 1975

störung (1975)
Electronic music; Duration: 2'40
Premiere: Stuttgart 1976

128 erfüllte augenblicke, systematisch geordnet, variabel zu spielen (1976)
(128 fulfilled moments, systematically arranged, to be played variably) for voice,
    clarinet and violoncello; Duration: variable (max. 30')
Premiere: Stuttgart 1976

éphémère (1977)
For percussion, veritable instruments and piano; Duration: 24'
Premiere: Stuttgart 1977

alban berg: sonate für klavier op. 1
transcription for orchestra (1977)

el sonido silencioso, trauermusik für salvador allende (1973–80)
(*the silent sound, funeral music for salvador allende*) for seven female voices;
    Duration: 30'
Premiere: Stuttgart 1980

extension (1979–80)
For violin and piano; Duration: 50'
Premiere: Venice 1983

pablo picasso: wie man wünsche beim schwanz packt (1980)
('pablo picasso: desire caught by the tail') drama in six acts; Duration: 41′
Radioplay

aussageverweigerung/gegendarstellung
zwei kontra-kontexte für doppelquartett (1981)
('refusal to testify/contradictory presentation two contra-contexts for double-
    quartet) for clarinet, baritone saxophone, double bass and piano/bass clarinet,
    tenor saxophone, violoncello and piano; Duration: 12′
Premiere: Boswil 1982

Rou^aGH_iFF (strange?) (1981)

For five jazz-soloists and orchestra; Duration: 47′
Premiere: Mönchengladbach 1981

′πὸ ′′ (*apo do*) (1982)
(*from here*) for string quartet; Duration: 12′
Premiere: Berlin 1983

adieu m'amour: hommage à guillaume dufay (1982–83)
(*farewell, my love: homage to guillaume dufay*) for violin and violoncello; Dur-
    ation: 12′
Premiere: Berlin 1983

signale (1983)
('choral scenes without singing'); Duration: 7′30
Premiere: Berlin 1983

música impura (1983)
(*impure music*) for soprano, guitar and percussion; Duration: 6′
Premiere: Montepulciano 1985

verfluchung (1983–85)
For three vocalists with wooden percussion instruments; Duration: 30′
Premiere: Basel, 1989

in dem ganzen ocean von empfindungen eine welle absondern, sie anhalten (1985)
For three choruses and eight-channel playback; Duration: 20′
Premiere: Stuttgart 1987

inter-mezzo: concertato non concertabile tra pianoforte e orchestra (1986);
    Duration: 30′
Premiere: Frankfurt 1986

passage/paysage (1989–90)
For large orchestra; Duration: 50′
Premiere: Donaueschingen 1990

furioso (1991)
For 14 players with 23 instruments; Duration: 20′
Premiere: Witten 1992

nah, getrennt (1992)
For alto recorder solo; Duration: 25′
Premiere: Cologne 1993

vorschläge: konzepte zur ver(über)flüssigung der funktion des komponisten (1992)
(*suggestions: concepts for making the role of the composer superfluous*);
    Duration: variable
Premiere: Berlin 1993

presentimientos: variationen für streichtrio (1992–93)
('variations for string trio'); Duration: 30′
Premiere: Witten 1993

und als wir … (1993)
For 54 strings; Duration: 15′
Premiere: Donaueschingen 1993

off (1993–2011)
For six snare drums
Version 1993; Duration: 8′
Premiere: Zurich 1993
Version 2011; Duration: 26′
Premiere: Malleray-Bévilard 2011

gegen unendlich (1995)
(*to infinity*) for bass clarinet, trombone, violoncello and piano; Duration: 17′
Premiere: Berlin 1995

Über den frühen Tod Fräuleins Anna Augusta Marggräfin zu Baden (1995)
(*On the Untimely Death of Miss Anna Augusta, Marchioness of Baden*)
For five male voices, five trombones, three female voices, clarinet and trumpet
Duration: 14′30
Premiere: Stuttgart 1995

akt, eine treppe herabsteigend (1998)
(*nude descending a staircase*) for bass clarinet, trombone and orchestra; Duration: 32′
Premiere: Donaueschingen 1998

farben der frühe (2005)
(*colours of dawn*) for seven pianos; Duration: 53′
Premiere: Stuttgart 2005

verlorener weg (1999–2000)
(*lost way*) for ensemble
Version 1; Duration 17′
Version 2; Duration: 19′
Premiere: Cologne 2000

fugitive beauté (2006)
(*fleeting beauty*) for oboe, alto flute and violin, bass clarinet, viola and violoncello; Duration: 17′
Premiere: Witten 2006

lamento, protokoll (2011)
For violoncello and orchestra; Duration: 52′
Premiere: Munich 2013

doppelt bejaht (2009)
(*doubly affirmed*) etudes for orchestra without conductor; Duration: variable
Premiere: Donaueschingen 2009

konzepte und varianten:
(*concepts and variants*)

  1/ ausgang (2010)
  (*exit*) for ensemble; Duration: Variable
  Premiere: Berlin 2010

  2/ rundweg (2010)
  (*looping path*) for recorder, violin and violoncello; Duration: variable
  Premiere: Berlin 2010

  3/ einräumung (2012)
  3 simultaneous solos for violin, viola and violoncello; Duration: at least 1′41
  Premiere: Bremen 2003

  4/ pnw (2003)
  For eight violoncellos and five double basses; Duration 0′34

entfernte ergänzung (2012)
For four (also three or two) guitars; Duration: 17′
Premiere: Stuttgart 2013

ausnahmslos ausnahmen (2013)
For drumset; Duration: approx. 24′
Premiere: Chicago 2015

asamisimasa-zyklus:
(cycle for the asamisimasa ensemble)

  faux faux faux bourdon (2016)
  For bass clarinet solo with accompaniment (percussion, guitar, piano, violon-
    cello); Duration: 12′
  Premiere: Darmstadt 2016

  kuboå (2015)
  For voice, clarinet, percussion, guitar, piano and violoncello; Duration: 4′

  still/moving (2015)
  For clarinet and violoncello; Duration: 8′
  Premiere: Oslo 2015

nachtstück mit sonne (2014)
(*nocturne with sun*) for ten-string guitar solo with accompaniment (clarinet, percussion, piano and violoncello); Duration: 17′
Premiere: Oslo 2015

don't kill me, i am beautiful (2019)
For bass clarinet, snare drum, piano und violoncello; Duration 4′

nahe null (2019)
For clarinet, percussion, guitar, piano und violoncello; Duration 12′

k141 (2018)
For piano; Duration 5′

Discography

entfernte ergänzung (2012), aleph gitarrenquartett
Includes: *entfernte ergänzung* (2012) for four (also three or two) guitars
SWR /Neos 11710

Composer Portrait: mathias spahlinger
furioso (1991–92) for ensemble
gegen unendlich (1995) for bass clarinet, trombone, violoncello and piano
fugitive beauté (2006) for oboe, alto flute and violin/bass clarinet, viola and violoncello
apo do (1982) for string quartet
Ensemble Modern, Hans Zender; Ensemble Recherche; Arditti string quartet
WDR/Kairos 0012692KAI

farben der frühe (2005) **for seven pianos**
Ensemble Surplus
BR/Neos 10710

Composer Portrait: Mathias Spahlinger
Deutscher Musikrat
inter-mezzo (1986), concerto non concertabile tra pianoforte e orchestra
Robert Regös, piano; Sinfonieorchester des Hessischen Rundfunks, Jürg
   Wyttenbach
128 erfüllte augenblicke – systematisch geordnet, variabel zu spielen (1976)
For voice, clarinet and violoncello.
Dietburg Spohr, Walter Seyfarth, Ulrich Heinen.
in dem ganzen ozean von empfindungen eine welle absondern, sie anhalten (1985)
   for choir groups und playback
Südfunkchor Stuttgart, Klaus-Martin Ziegler
HR/SR/SDR/Wergo 286 513-2

Gründungskonzert, Ensemble Modern
Ensemble Modern
Includes: *phonophobie* for wind quintet (1972)
DLF/EM Medien EMCD-025

Composer Portrait: mathias spahlinger
Ensemble Recherche
aussageverweigerung/gegendarstellung (1981), zwei kontra-kontexte für
   doppelquartett
vier stücke (1975) for voice, clarinet, violin, violoncello und piano.
128 erfüllte augenblicke – systematisch geordnet, variabel zu spielen (1975) for
   voice, clarinet and violoncello
fünf sätze für zwei klaviere (1969)
musica impura (1983) for soprano, guitar und percussion
entlöschend (1974) for large tam-tam
presentimientos (1992), variations for string trio
éphémère (1977) for percussion, 'veritable' instruments und piano
adieu m'amour – homage à guillame dufay (1983) for violin and viola
Ensemble Recherche
WDR/ Accord 206222

Mathias Spahlinger: *extension* (1979–80) for violin and piano
Dimitris Polisoidis, Hildegard Kleeb
HR/ Hat Hut Records CD 6131

From Germany
Arditti String Quartet
Includes:
′πò ′′ (apo do) (1982)
(von hier) für streichquartett
walter zimmermann
WDR/ Auvidis Montaigne MO 782036

Donaueschinger Musiktage, 1993
Includes:
und als wir (1993) for 54 streicher
SWF-Sinfonieorchester, Lothar Zagrosek
donaueschinger musiktage, 1993
SWF/Col Legno CD 31875

Donaueschinger Musiktage, 1990
SWF Sinfonieorchester, Michael Gielen
Includes: *passage/paysage* for large orchestra (1989–90)
SWF/Col Legno AU 31819

Ensemble Belcanto, Dietburg Spohr
Includes: *el sonido silencioso, trauermusik für salvador allende* (1973–80)
Aulos schallplatten AUL 66034

Blockflöte Modern I
Johannes Fischer
Includes: *nah, getrennt* for solo alto recorder (1992)
DLF/ Flautando Records FR001

Deutscher Musikrat: Musik in Deutschland 1950–2000
Ensemble Recherche
Includes: *vier stücke* for voice, clarinet, violin, violoncello and piano (1975)
SWR/DLF/WDR/BMG RCA red seal 74321 73627 2

Deutscher Musikrat: Musik in Deutschland 1950–2000
orchesterstücke
Includes:
morendo für orchester (1975)
MDR-sinfonieorchester, johannes kalitzke
MDR/SWR/BR/RBB/
BMG RCA Red Seal 74321 73611 2

Deutscher Musikrat: Musik in Deutschland 1950–2000
angewandte musik
Includes:
individuation 1, schriftlich
frp,: vorschläge (1993)
konzepte zur ver(über)flüssigung der funktion des komponisten
BMG Ariola 74321 73528 2

Deutscher Musikrat: Musik in Deutschland 1950–2000
konzertmusik/vokale kammermusik
Includes:
sotto voce (1973–74)
Schola Cantorum Stuttgart, Clytus Gottwald
Stuttgarter Vocalsolisten, Manfred Schreier
SWR/BMG RCA Red Seal 74321 73538 2

Index

Page numbers in italics refer to figures; page numbers in bold refer to tables.

128 erfüllte augenblicke (*128 fulfilled instants*) (Spahlinger), 37–38, 61, 68, 108, 111–14, *112–13*, 133

A

Accanto (Lachenmann), 71
acousmatic listening, 56
action notation, 57–58, *58*
Adenauer, Konrad, 34–35
Adieu m'amour, adieu mon joye (Dufay), 75–77, *76*
adieu m'amour hommage à guillaume dufay (Spahlinger), 27n52, 31, 75–77, *75*
Adlington, Robert, 27–28n61
Adorno, Theodor W.
    Derrida and, 85
    German sociology and, 44
    on jazz, 23, 33
    on *musique informelle*, 110–11
    on progress, 45
    on Schoenberg, 18, 162
    Spahlinger and, 4, 5, 15, 34, 36, 97–98, 110–11, 129, 142, 147, 155
    on subject–object division, 142
aesthetic contingency, 101–4
'against the postmodern fashion' (Spahlinger), 13, 22, 23, 36, 103
akt, eine treppe herabsteigend (*nude descending a staircase*) (Spahlinger), 41, 83, 86–90, *88–90*

Almén, Byron, 118–20
apo do (Spahlinger), 65, 66–67, 68
Armstrong, Louis, 33
Arnds, Peter, 35
A-Ronne (Berio), 157–58
'Art in the Age of Mechanical Reproduction' (Benjamin), 156
Ashby, Arved, 4–5
Aufhebung (sublation), 106n26
ausnahmslos ausnahmen (*except without exception*) (Spahlinger), 42
autonomy, 14–15, 24

B

Babbitt, Milton, 14
Barlow, Clarence, 135
Bartók, Béla, 30
Baruch, Gerh-Wolfgang, 7n1
Bauhaus, 26n26
Bayrle, Thomas, 36
Beal, Amy C., 25n12
Becker, Günther, 78n14
Beethoven, Ludwig van, 31, 36, 40, 103
Benjamin, Walter, 45, 156
Berg, Alban, 19, 20
Berger, Karol, 4–5
Berio, Luciano, 137n2, 157–58
Biel, Michael von, 56
Blacher, Boris, 49n37

197

Blume, Philipp
   on *128 erfüllte augenblicke* (*128 fulfilled instants*, 1976), 111, 113–14, 133
   on *musique concrète instrumentale*, 20, 55, 73
   on Spahlinger, 7n3, 8n7
   translations by, 2
Böll, Heinrich, 34
Born, Georgina, 23–24, 100, 166
Boulez, Pierre, 20, 109, 133
Bourdieu, Pierre, 25n7
Britten, Benjamin, 122
Brown, Earle, 109
Burdocks (Wolff), 41
Bussotti, Sylvano, 57, 78n21

C
Cage, John
   conductorless pieces of, 42, 130
   Eggebrecht on, 133
   noise and, 62
   Schick on, 98
   Spahlinger and, 17, 19, 20
Cardew, Cornelius, 130
chance procedures, 18, 19–21
Chaplin, Charlie, 170
Claren, Sebastian, 146, 165, 166
Clayton, Alan J., 26n26
Concert for Piano and Orchestra (Cage), 42
Consolation II (Lachenmann), 157–58
Consolation I (Lachenmann), 157–58
critical composition, 70, 72, 147
critical modernism, 5, 178
critical theory, 43–47. *See also* Frankfurt School
Cubism, 86
cymbals, 17, 62

D
Dadaism, 15, 100

Davis, Oliver, 101, 104
The Death of Empedocles (Hölderlin), 15–16
defamiliarization, 56
de Man, Paul, 84
denazification process, 34–35. See also *Vergangenheitsbewältigung* (coming to terms with the past)
Deranty, Jean-Philippe, 103
Derrida, Jacques, 84–85
Dessau, Paul, 49n37
determinate negation, 97–99
'The Dialectical Composer' (Adorno), 162
Dialectic of Enlightenment (Adorno and Horkheimer), 45
Dierstein, Christian, 60
Diesseitigkeit, 15
différance, 85
dodecaphony, 18, 20–21
Domann, Andreas, 98
doppelt bejaht (*doubly affirmed*) (Spahlinger)
   jazz music and, 33
   open form and, 122–25, *123*, *125*–26, 130–31, 133–34
   performance of, 42, 182
   vorschläge and, 41, 120–21
Duchamp, Marcel, 86
Dufay, Guillaume, 27n52, 31, 75–77, 76. *See also adieu m'amour hommage à guillaume dufay* (Spahlinger)

E
Eco, Umberto, 137n2
Eggebrecht, Hans Heinrich, 16, 17–18, 41–42, 83, 133
Engels, Friedrich, 15, 16, 71
entfernte ergänzung (*distant addition or alternatively remote extension*) (Spahlinger), 42

entlöschend (Spahlinger), 17, 59–61, *60*, 63

Enzensberger, Hans Magnus, 26n26, 32, 43, 44, 45

éphémère (Spahlinger), 37–38, 63–65, *64*, 147

Epitaffio per Federico García Lorca (Nono), 68

Ergänzungsleistung (ability to complete), 129

Die Ermittlung (*The Investigation*, Weiss), 49n37

L'escalier du diable (*Devil's Staircase*) (Ligeti), 92

España en el Corazón (*Spain in our Hearts*, Neruda), 68

extension (Spahlinger), 38, 82, 120, 134–35, *136*, 181

F

farben der frühe (*colours of dawn*) (Spahlinger), 41, 83, 87, 90–95, *92–95*

faux faux bourdon (Spahlinger), 42

Fawsetts, R., 76

Feldman, Morton, 98

Fluxus, 41

Fowler, Bridget, 25n7

Frankfurt School
German sociology and, 43–44
Lachenmann and, 55, 72
Spahlinger and, 3, 17–18, 34, 104
See also Adorno, Theodor W.

Fritsch, Johannes, 78n14

fünf sätze für zwei klaviere (Spahlinger), 37

furioso (Spahlinger), 65, 68–70

Futurism, 15, 19, 62, 100

G

gegen unendlich (*towards infinity*) (Spahlinger), 87, 146–49, *148–49*

The German Ideology (Marx and Engels), 15, 16

German sociology, 43–45, 46–47, 182

Germany
1968 in, 1, 30, 34–37
denazification process in, 34–35
Nazi regime in, 30, 34–35
role of intellectuals in, 38–39, 44–45
Vergangenheitsbewältigung in, 35–37, 39–40, 45–46

Geschichte der Musik als Gegenwart (*Music History as a Facet of the Present*) (Spahlinger), 41–42

Goebbels, Heiner, 98–99

Grapefruit (Ono), 41

Grass, Günter, 35

Greenberg, Clement, 170

Grimm, Jacob, 26n26

Großschreibung, 26n26

Gulbrandsen, Erling E., 4–5, 171, 178–79

H

Habermas, Jürgen, 39

Häcker, Carsten, 69–70

Hartmann, Karl Amadeus, 49n37

Hechtle, Markus, 7n1, 38, 116–17

Hegel, Georg Wilhelm Friedrich, 44, 110, 183

Heidegger, Martin, 85

Heile, Björn, 4–5, 28n69, 77n6

Heimat (film series), 35

Henze, Hans Werner, 30, 36, 49n37, 81n74

Herder, Johann Gottfried, 153–54

Hiekel, Jörn Peter, 72

Hillberg, Frank, 56, 78n18, 78n22

Hilsenrath, Edgar, 35

Hindemith, Paul, 30

Historikerstreit, 45–46

Hockings, Elke, 70, 71

Hölderlin, Friedrich, 15–16

Holm, Kerstin, 1

Holocaust, 45–46

Holocaust (TV programme), 35

Honegger, Arthur, 19

Hopkins, Bill, 133

Hoppstock, Werner, 33

Horkheimer, Max, 45

Huber, Klaus, 38

Huber, Nicolaus A., 1, 72, 73–74, 99–100, 135

Hüppe, Eberhard, 70

Huyssen, Andreas, 35, 39

I

Iddon, Martin, 33–34

Incontri musicali (journal), 137n2

in dem ganzen ocean von empfindungen eine welle absondern, sie anhalten (Spahlinger)
  noise in, 62
  perception and, 152–54, 155–65, *157–59, 161,* 169
  political message of, 68, 132–33, 159–60, 161–65, 172, 180
  technology in, 154–56, 181

Institut de Recherche et Coordination Acoustique/ Musique (IRCAM), 23–24

intellectuals, 38–39, 44–45

inter-mezzo (Spahlinger), 38, 62, 83, 95–97

Intolleranza1960 (Nono), 163

Iron Foundry (Mosolov), 62

J

Jarausch, Konrad H., 40

jazz music, 23, 32–33

Johnson, Julian, 4–5, 171, 178–79

Jüdische Chronik (1960), 49n37

K

Kagel, Mauricio, 36, 56, 77n6

Kahlschlagliteratur (clear-cutting literature), 30

Kane, Brian, 63, 183

Karkoschka, Erhard, 37

Kiefer, Anselm, 34, 36, 40

Killmayer, Wilhelm, 36

King, Alasdair, 43

Klang (sound), 59, 61, 70

'Klangtypen der neuen Musik' (Lachenmann), 62

Kleinschreibung, 26n26

Klemperer, Victor, 30

Klüppelholz, Werner, 82

Kreidler, Johannes
  on orchestral musicians, 131
  on Spahlinger, 41, 54, 74, 120, 147
  as Spahlinger's pupil, 38, 137

Kutschke, Beate, 44

L

Lachenmann, Helmut
  international fame of, 1–2
  music philosophy of, 70–73
  musique concrète instrumentale and, 20, 54, 55–56, 57–58, *58,* 73–74
  political stance of, 100
  Spahlinger and, 17–18, 57, 59–62, 66, 67, 180–81, 183
  in Stuttgart, 34

Lachenmann, Helmut: works
  Accanto, 71
  Consolation I, 157–58
  Consolation II, 157–58
  Pression, 55, *58,* 60, 67
  temA, 61

lamento, protokoll (Spahlinger), 42

'The Last Century before Humanity' (Ritsos), 67

Lawrence, Vicki, 35

Lechner, Konrad, 32, 33

Leuschner, Christian, 154, 163

Liebrucks, Bruno, 21, 97, 153, 155

Ligeti, György, 57, 92

Lingua Tertii Imperii (Klemperer), 30

LiveAid (1985), 153

Lyric Suite (Berg), 19

M

MacMillan, James, 3

Mahnkopf, Claus-Steffen, 3, 84, 85, 98–99, 147, 183

Manzoni, Giacomo, 78n21, 162

Marxism, 32, 34, 37

Marx, Karl, 15, 16, 44, 71, 130

Match (Kagel), 77n6

McClary, Susan, 14, 23, 100

mechanical repetition, 18–19, 20–21, 61–65

Meja, Volker, 43, 44

Menke, Johannes, 68, 76

Metzer, David, 4–5

Mikrophonie I (Stockhausen), 59

modernism

criticisms of, 22–24, 178–79

definition(s) of, 3–5

on musical autonomy, 14

musique concrète instrumentale and, 73–77

open form and, 109

order and, 82–83

political stance of, 100, 101

postmodernism and, 39–40

Rancière and, 170–73

Spahlinger and, 1–5, 12, 14, 15, 21, 37, 73–77, 171–73

Modulation I (Fritsch), 78n14

Moeller, Robert G., 35

morendo (Spahlinger), 32, 37, 62–63

Mosolov, Alexander, 62

música impura (Spahlinger), 61, 65, 68

musica negativa, 72

musique concrète, 55–56

musique concrète instrumentale

definition(s) and concept of, 20, 20–21, 54, 55–57

features of, 58

Lachenmann and, 20, 54, 55–56, 57–58, *58*, 73–74

modernism and, 73–77

notation and, 57–58, *58*

perception and, 169

Spahlinger and, 54, 59–70, *60*, 73–77, 91, 180–81, 183, 184

musique informelle, 110–11

N

nachtstück mit sonne (*nocturne with sun*) (Spahlinger), 42

Napoleon, Emperor of the French, 40

narrative repetition, 118–21, *119*

Neruda, Pablo, 68

Newcomb, Anthony, 4–5

New Discipline, 15

noise

musique concrète instrumentale and, 20, 57–58

perception of, 141

Spahlinger and, 54, 61–65

Nonnenmann, Rainer, 33, 63, 69, 98–99, 131, 183

Nono, Luigi

Lachenmann and, 61

modernism and, 15, 44, 100

Spahlinger and, 61, 100, 180–81

Nono, Luigi: works

Epitaffio per Federico García Lorca, 68

Intolleranza1960, 163

Ricorda cosa ti hanno fatto ad Auschwitz, 49n37

Norris, Christopher, 85

notation, 41, 57–58, *58*

Notation in New Music (Karkoschka), 37
Nude Descending a Staircase, No.2
    (Duchamp), 86
Nürnberger Orgie (Bayrle), 36

O
Occupations (Kiefer), 35
ocean. See *in dem ganzen ocean von*
    empfindungen eine welle absondern, sie
    anhalten (Spahlinger)
Oehlschlägel, Reihnhard, 32, 38, 132
Oehring, Helmut, 98–99
off (Spahlinger), 149–52, *150–52*, 167
Ombre (Manzoni), 162
Ono, Yoko, 41
open form
    in *128 erfüllte augenblicke* (*128 fulfilled*
      instants), 108, 111–14, *112–13*, 133
    criticisms of, 133–37
    in *doppelt bejaht* (*doubly affirmed*),
      122–25, *123*, 125–26, 130–31, 133–34
    in *extension* (1979–80), 134–35, *136*
    modernism and, 109
    in *passage/ paysage*, 108, 114–21, *115*,
      117, *119*, 127, 134–35, 137, 181
    political implications of, 130–33
    Spahlinger's conception of, 18, 19, 108,
      109–11, 180
    in *verlorener weg* (*lost way/path*),
      125–29, *128*
    in *vorschläge: konzepte zur ver(über)*
      flüssigung der funktion des
      komponisten, 120–22, 124, 134
order
    aesthetic contingency and, 101–4
    in *akt, eine treppe herabsteigend* (*nude*
      descending a staircase, 1998), 83,
      86–90, *88–90*
    concept and debates on, 38, 82–86
    determinate negation and, 97–99

in *farben der frühe* (*colours of dawn*,
    2005), 83, 90–95, *92–95*
in *inter-mezzo* (1986), 95–97
politics of, 99–101
Orff, Carl, 30
Orning, Tanja, 78n22

P
Pacific231 (Honegger), 19
Paddison, Max, 165, 181–82
Panagia, Davide, 168
passage/ paysage (Spahlinger)
    Beethoven and, 40
    mechanical repetition in, 65
    open form and, 108, 114–21, *115*, **117**,
      119, 127, 134–35, 137, 181
    order and, 87
    perception and, 38, 143, 146, 147
    political message of, 172, 180
Penderecki, Krzysztof, 57
perception
    in *dem ganzen ocean von empfindungen*
      eine welle absondern, sie anhalten and,
      152–54, 155–65, *157–59*, *161*, 169
    gegen unendlich (*towards infinity*) and,
      146–49, *148–49*
    musique concrète instrumentale and, 61
    off and, 149–52, *150–52*, 167
    passage/ paysage and, 38, 143, 146, 147
    playback and, 154–56
    Rancière's philosophy and, 167–73
    Spahlinger's conception of, 24, 38, 43,
      103, 141–42, 169–73
    und als wir… and, 143–46, *144–45*, 153,
      164, 165–67
    verfluchung and, 167
Philosophical Investigations
    (Wittgenstein), 162
piano, 31
playback, 154–56

pop art, 36

Poppe, Enno, 114, 181

postmodernism, 36, 39–40

'Post-Mortem of Order' (Klüppelholz), 82

post-structuralism, 84–85

Pousseur, Henri, 82

Pression (Lachenmann), 55, *58*, 60, 67

Q

'The Question of Order in New Music'
    (Pousseur), 82

R

radical constructivism, 85

Radice, Giles, 30

Rancière, Jacques
    aesthetic contingency and, 101–2
    politics and, 142, 167–73, 180, 182
    Spahlinger and, 3, 83, 85, 102–4, 131,
        180, 182, 184

Ransmayr, Christoph, 35

Reich, Steve, 147

rejection, 70, 71–72

repetition. *See* mechanical repetition;
    narrative repetition

Ricorda cosa ti hanno fatto ad Auschwitz
    (*Remember what they did to you at*
    Auschwitz, Nono), 49n37

Riedl, Josef Anton, 80n68

Rihm, Wolfgang, 98–99

Ritsos, Yannis, 67

RoaiuGHFF (*strange?*) (Spahlinger), 33, *33*

Ruthemeier, Dorothea, 84, 85, 96, 127, 141,
    142, 183

Ryan, Judith, 39–40

Rzewski, Frederic, 49n37

S

Saltzman, Lisa, 36, 40

Saxer, Marion, 160

saxophone, 32–33

Schaeffer, Pierre, 55–56

Schick, Tobias Eduard
    on *in dem ganzen ocean von*
        empfindungen eine welle absondern, sie
        anhalten, 156–57, 163
    on determinate negation, 98
    on *farben der frühe*, 91–92, 93–94
    on Huber, 135
    on music and politics, 172
    on order, 82, 99, 100
    on reflection, 153
    on *verfluchung*, 162

Schlink, Bernhard, 35

Schnebel, Dieter, 80n68

Schneider, Peter, 35, 40

Schoenberg, Arnold, 4, 14, 18, 103, 162

Second Viennese School, 33

self-reflection and self-reflexivity
    German sociology and, 43–44
    Spahlinger and, 17, 21–23, 24,
        153–55, 184–85

Sielecki, Frank, 55, 72

Singer, Peter, 110

Social Theory, 44

Sonderweg ('special path'), 46

el sonido silencioso (Spahlinger), 62

Spahlinger, Mathias
    aesthetic contingency and, 102–4
    compositional style of, 180–83
    contemporary relevance of, 183–85
    on critical composition, 72
    early life and musical education of,
        29–34, 37–38
    German identity and tradition and, 40
    German sociology and, 43–45, 46–47
    Lachenmann and, 17–18, 57, 59–62, 66,
        67, 180–81, 183
    modernism and, 1–5, 12, 14, 15, 21, 37,
        73–77, 178–80

musique concrète instrumentale and, 54,
    59–70, 60, 73–77
political stance of, 1, 32, 99–101, 159–60,
    161–65, 180, 182. See also *in dem
    ganzen ocean von empfindungen
    eine welle absondern, sie anhalten*
    (Spahlinger)
potential criticisms of, 22–24
as professor of composition in
    Freiburg, 38–39
reception and scholarship on, 1–2, 177
student protests of 1968 and, 1, 13, 30
See also open form; order; perception
Spahlinger, Mathias: works
*128 erfüllte augenblicke (128 fulfilled
    instants)*, 37–38, 61, 68, 108, 111–14,
    112–13, 133
*adieu m'amour hommage à guillaume
    dufay*, 27n52, 31, 75–77, *75*
*akt, eine treppe herabsteigend (nude
    descending a staircase)*, 41, 83,
    86–90, *88–90*
apo do, 65, *66–67*, 68
*ausnahmslos ausnahmen (except without
    exception)*, 42
*entfernte ergänzung (distant addition or
    alternatively remote extension)*, 42
entlöschend, 17, 59–61, *60*, 63
éphémère, 37–38, 63–65, *64*, 147
extension, 38, 82, 120, 134–35, *136*,
    181
farben der frühe (colours of dawn), 41, 83,
    87, 90–95, *92–95*
faux faux bourdon, 42
fünf sätze für zwei klaviere, 37
furioso, 65, 68–70
gegen unendlich (towards infinity), 87,
    146–49, *148–49*

*Geschichte der Musik als Gegenwart
    (Music History as a Facet of the
    Present)*, 41–42
inter-mezzo, 38, 62, 83, 95–97
lamento, protokoll, 42
morendo, 32, 37, 62–63
música impura, 61, 65, 68
*nachtstück mit sonne (nocturne with
    sun)*, 42
off, 149–52, *150–52*, 167
'against the postmodern fashion,' 13, 22,
    23, 36, 103
RoaiuGHFF (strange?), 33, *33*
el sonido silencioso, 62
still/ moving, 42
*Über den frühen Tod Fräuleins Anna
    August Marggräfin zu Baden*, 153
und als wir, 143–46, *144–45*, 153,
    164, 165–67
verfluchung, 162, 167
verlorener weg (lost way/path), 41, 87,
    120–21, 125–29, *128*
vier stücke, 61
*vorschläge: konzepte zur ver(über)
    flüssigung der funktion des
    komponisten (suggestions: concepts
    for making the role of the composer
    superfluous)*, 41, 120–22, 124, 134, 153
See also *doppelt bejaht (doubly affirmed)*
    (Spahlinger); *in dem ganzen ocean von
    empfindungen eine welle absondern,
    sie anhalten* (Spahlinger); *passage/
    paysage* (Spahlinger); 'this is the time
    of conceptive ideologues no longer'
    (Spahlinger)
Stäbler, Gerhard, 37
Städtische Akademie für Tonkunst
    (Darmstadt), 33–34
still/ moving (Spahlinger), 42

Stockhausen, Karlheinz, 20, 26n24, 30, 36–37, 59, 109

String Quartet no. 2 (Biel), 56

student protests (1968), 1, 13, 30, 34–37

T

tam-tam, 17, 37, 59

temA (Lachenmann), 61

Terretektorh (Xenakis), 143, 165

Theses on the Philosophy of History (Benjamin), 45

Third Piano Sonata (Boulez), 109

'this is the time of conceptive ideologues no longer' (Spahlinger)
  on chance procedures, 18, 19–21
  on dodecaphony, 18, 20–21
  on mechanical repetition, 18–19, 20–21
  on musical autonomy, 14–15, 24
  on *musique concrète instrumentale*, 20–21
  on open form, 18, 19
  on position of composers in society, 13–14, 16
  on possible progress, 21–22
  potential criticisms of, 22–24
  as social analysis, 46
  title of, 15–16, 104
  on tonality, 16–17
  on traditional listening and reception, 17–18

Tillman, Joakim, 39

tonality, 16–17, 71–72, 82–83, 169–70

Treatise on the Origin of Language (Herder), 153–54

Triumph of Death (Rzewski), 49n37

Trümmerliteratur (rubble literature), 30

Tucholsky, Kurt, 22

Twenty Five Pages (Brown), 109

Twilight of the Intellectuals (*Intellektuellendämmerung*), 39

U

Über den frühen Tod Fräuleins Anna August Marggräfin zu Baden (Spahlinger), 153

und als wir… (Spahlinger), 143–46, *144–45*, 153, 164, 165–67

V

Varèse, Edgard, 62

Vati (Schneider), 40

verfluchung (Spahlinger), 162, 167

Vergangenheitsbewältigung (coming to terms with the past), 35–37, 39–40, 45–46

verlorener weg (*lost way/path*) (Spahlinger), 41, 87, 120–21, 125–29, *128*

vielle (*Fidel*), 30–31

vier stücke (Spahlinger), 61

viola da gamba, 30–31

violoncello, 30–31

Vogt, Jochen, 38

Volans, Kevin, 135

vorschläge: konzepte zur ver(über)flüssigung der funktion des komponisten (*suggestions: concepts for making the role of the composer superfluous*) (Spahlinger), 41, 120–22, 124, 134, 153

W

Wagner Richard, 30

Warhol, Andy, 36

Warnaby, John, 74

Weber, Max, 44

Webern, Anton, 4, 17, 37

Weiss, Peter, 49n37

Weitz, Eric D., 39

'Who Cares If You Listen?' (Babbitt), 14

Williams, Alastair, 77n6

Wilson, Peter Niklas, 62, 82, 85, 138n15, 154

Wirtschaftswunder (Economic
    Miracle), 31–32
Wittgenstein, Ludwig, 162
Wolff, Christian, 41
world hunger, 153–54. See also *in dem
    ganzen ocean von empfindungen
    eine welle absondern, sie anhalten*
    (Spahlinger)
Wüthrich, Hans, 130

X
Xenakis, Iannis, 57, 143, 165

Y
Young Person's Guide to the Orchestra
    (Britten), 122

Z
Zaldua, Alistair, 2, 8n7
Zimmerman, Bernd Alois, 36
Zimmerman, Walter, 135
Zyklus (Stockhausen), 109